Kevin D. Randle

OPERATION
ROSWELL

TOR®

A TOM DOHERTY ASSOCIATES BOOK
NEW YORK

This is a work of fiction. All the characters and events portrayed in this book are fictitious or are used fictitiously.

OPERATION ROSWELL

Copyright © 2002 by Kevin D. Randle

A Tor Book
Published by Tom Doherty Associates, LLC
175 Fifth Avenue
New York, NY 10010

www.tor.com

Tor® is a registered trademark of Tom Doherty Associates, LLC.

ISBN 0-765-34803-9
EAN 978-0765-34803-6
Library of Congress Catalog card Number: 200268485

First edition: September 2002
First mass market edition: August 2004

Printed in the United States of America

0 9 8 7 6 5 4 3 2

"Roswell has long been a point of great interest to me. . . . Butch Blanchard was a very close friend of mine. . . . There is not much we can do about getting the things about Roswell. . . . I tried diligently to get them from General LeMay, and the only cussing out he ever gave me was when I very vociferously asked him for information. . . ."

Senator Barry Goldwater,
Major General, USAFR
July 26, 1994

Written on the flyleaf to *The Truth About the UFO Crash at Roswell*—"Here's the truth and I still haven't told anybody anything!"

Colonel Patrick Saunders,
Adjutant, Roswell Army Air Field, July 1947

"I can't talk about it. I was sworn to secrecy. I told you that."

Colonel Edwin Easley,
Provost Marshal, Roswell Army Air Field, July 1947
Audiotaped interview, January 11, 1990

"It was something that came to Earth, but it wasn't something made on Earth."

Major Jesse Marcel, Sr.
Air Intelligence Officer, Roswell Army Air Field, July 1947
Videotaped interview

AUTHOR'S NOTE

On July 9, 1947, First Lieutenant Walter Haut, a tall, husky man who had served in the Pacific during the Second World War, visited the four media outlets in Roswell, New Mexico. He handed the editors of the two newspapers and the managers of the two radio stations a short press release that announced that the 509th Bomb Group, at the time the only nuclear strike force in the world, had captured a flying saucer on a ranch northwest of Roswell.

The article contained little in the way of description and mentioned that the intelligence officer, Major Jesse Marcel, escorted the material to a higher headquarters, in this case Eighth Air Force in Fort Worth, Texas. Within hours, the Eighth Air Force commanding officer, Brigadier General Roger M. Ramey, a man who had commanded bomber wings in the Pacific, showed reporters the remains of a weather balloon and suggested that a mistake had been made.

These are facts and cannot be disputed. There are documents, photographs, eyewitness testimony, and a host of other evidence to support this. It is the interpretation of all that evidence that begins the dispute. There are plenty of witnesses, who were in Roswell, in Fort Worth, and in Washington, D.C., who have provided information and additional evidence about what fell in 1947.

In 1978, Jesse Marcel, Sr., a retired TV technician who had been in the Pacific during World War II, told researchers that he had been the intelligence officer who picked up pieces of a flying saucer. He told them, as he told others in subsequent interviews, "This was something that came to Earth, but it wasn't something made on Earth."

Research established that Marcel was, in fact, the intelligence officer, and pictures of him, in General Ramey's office, were printed in the newspapers in 1947. He made it clear, based on his firsthand observations, that whatever he had found, it was not part of a balloon.

Other members of Colonel William "Butch" Blanchard's staff confirmed that they had been involved. Major (later Colonel) Edwin Easley told researchers that he had been sworn to secrecy and, although he was careful in what he said, afraid of violating security, said enough to confirm the story of an alien craft and civilians being held on the base. Major (later Colonel) Patrick Saunders didn't want to say much but in copies of the book *The Truth About the UFO Crash at Roswell* wrote, "This is the truth and I never told anybody anything." He meant that the story of an alien spacecraft crash was true, though he might have disagreed with certain of the fine details.

In fact, every member of Blanchard's staff who could be located and who commented, with one exception, suggested that the events were unusual and that they involved the retrieval of an alien spacecraft. Many of the soldiers who were stationed in Roswell in 1947 confirmed that they believed, or had been involved, in the retrieval of the craft.

These, too, are facts, but they can be disputed by others. Several members of the 509th Bomb Group, who were in Roswell at the critical time, claimed they heard nothing about a UFO crash, the recovery of a balloon, or anything else unusual. Some of them believed that if such an event had happened, they would have known about it from friends who were in a position to know. One senior member of Blanchard's staff, who definitely would have known, laughed at the idea of an alien spacecraft and extraterrestrial creatures. According to him, it hadn't happened.

UFO investigators interviewed hundreds of people, gathering as much detail as they could. They published their findings in a series of books that concluded that there had been a crash and a recovery, and that the government had covered up everything, lying about what was found and ordering the participants not to talk about the events. All of this was detailed in a series of video statements and signed affidavits made for the Fund for UFO Research and for the private files of many of the investigators.

In 1994, the Air Force, after denying they investigated UFO sightings, released their final report on the Roswell crash, concluding that what had been found were the remains of a balloon array launched in conjunction with the then-classified Project Mogul. While the purpose of the project was highly classified, the equipment was not. Contrary to what had been suggested, the balloons were standard off-the-shelf weather balloons, and the radar reflectors attached had been used by the military and the weather service to obtain winds aloft data. There was nothing new or unusual about the balloon arrays. They should have been easily recognizable to those who found them in the field.

In 1997, the Air Force released its second final report, this one attempting to explain the bodies described by some of the witnesses. Air Force investigators concluded that anthropomorphic dummies, dropped from high altitude to test ejection systems and parachute escape mechanisms, were responsible for the claims of alien bodies. The problem, one which the Air Force failed to explain, was that the experiments had begun six years after the events in Roswell, and none of the dummies had fallen near Roswell until 1957. Even the normally skeptical news media found the explanation difficult to swallow.

As it stands today, there are two camps: those who believe that some sort of alien ship, complete with extraterrestrial crew, fell outside of Roswell in 1947 and those who believe that Project Mogul, with its long balloon and radar reflector train, is responsible for the debris recovered.

There have been, by now, several books about the crash. For those interested in the pro side, there are *The Roswell Incident* (1980), *The UFO Crash at Roswell* (1991), *Crash at Corona* (1992), *The Truth About the UFO Crash at Roswell*

(1994), and *The Roswell Encyclopedia* (2000). On the other side are *The Real Roswell Crash Cover-up* (1997) and *Roswell: Inconvenient Facts and the Will to Believe* (2001). These books will provide nearly all the known information and include the insights of the various authors and the witnesses they interviewed. Reading all of the books will provide a nearly complete education about the Roswell crash.

As it stands today, the controversy still swirls. For me, the preponderance of the evidence, along with some very persuasive eyewitness testimony, suggests that what happened involved an alien ship and the recovery of the flight crew. This book, a work of fiction, is based on the best evidence and the extrapolation of what happened after the ship was taken from the field. Many of the names used are those of the men who were involved in the case in 1947. I have been to Roswell more than fifty times and have on several occasions, walked the debris field, the impact site where the bodies were found, and the various buildings of the now decaying Roswell Army Air Field.

While I have, quite naturally, taken literary license with some of the events and speculated about others, the basic facts remain the same. In July 1947, a craft built on another world fell to the ground outside of Roswell, New Mexico, and the members of the 509th Bomb Group recovered it. This discovery changed the way the military thought about flying saucers, changed the course of our history as they worked to hide the data, and is one of the greatest events in human history.

CHAPTER 1

It was a strange meeting, held in a conference room in the bowels of one of the inner rings of the Pentagon that had only a single entrance with a vault-like door and no external windows. It was a plush conference room with high-backed leather chairs, a carefully polished table of the finest mahogany that held a shining sterling silver tea service, and carefully created metal nameplates for all the participants.

There was a thick, light blue carpeting on the floor that showed no trace of dirt or wear. The room was paneled in rich, dark wood, and original oil paintings in ornate frames hung on the wall. These were not the mass-produced lithographic prints that graced so many other offices and conference rooms at the Pentagon but authentic, original paintings of military heroes and famous battles.

Although there were chairs for twenty around the table, there were only a half dozen people seated in the room. The door was guarded, on the outside, by an armed, burly MP, his khaki uniform immaculate, and unlike military guards in similar circumstances, his role was not ceremonial. His weapon was fully loaded and he was authorized to use deadly force.

Although the man seated in one of those side chairs, an Army Air Forces major general, thought he should be seated at the head of the table, he was not. Instead, sitting there, wearing a thousand-dollar Saville Row suit, thick glasses with dark frames, and a gleaming white shirt, was a balding man. The hair that remained was salt and pepper. He had a large nose, thin, bloodless lips, and an unhappy look. He toyed with a fountain pen that had a solid gold clip, a gold band around the edge of the cap, and a golden point. In front of him was a thick leather folder. There was no nameplate at his place and even if he revealed his name, none of the others would have recognized it. Dr. Jonathan David Moore was not well known outside his scientific speciality of psychology and was virtually unknown in Washington or the Pentagon. It was the way that he, and his superiors, liked it.

He looked from person to person, as if taking a silent roll, and asked, "Does everyone here know everyone else?"

The Army Air Forces major general, his eyes on Moore, shook his head slowly. He was a stocky man with a thick, unruly clump of black wavy hair and bulldog features. The ribbons denoting his combat and service decorations climbed from the top of the left breast pocket to nearly his shoulder. They were topped by the silver wings of a command pilot. He was leaning back in his chair, eyeing the lone woman at the table as he idly unwrapped a thick cigar. He pointed with his cigar.

"I don't know her."

"Ah. That is Dr. Danni Hackett." Moore glanced at the woman who nodded once, slightly, at the introduction.

She was a young woman, no more than twenty-five or thirty, with light brown hair, blue eyes, and thin features. She sat leaning forward, as if interested in everything that was going on around her. She wore a severe suit of charcoal gray that had wide lapels. There was a small brooch on one of them that looked for all the world like a deformed golden spider with three bright ruby-colored eyes.

The general asked, "Why is she here?"

Moore rocked back in his chair and touched his pen to his lips. "You have a problem with her, General?"

"Is she properly cleared?"

"I would think that you would realize that if she is in this room, at this time, with me sitting here, fully cognizant of each of the others in here and of the reasons for us to be here, that she is properly cleared."

"That means nothing to me. Is she cleared?" There was a hint of annoyance in the general's voice.

"She has a top secret clearance. She has been working at Los Alamos as a biologist. Because of that work, which is of no concern to you, the proper background investigations and appropriate clearances have long ago been completed, granted, and are on file here and with the Army. That makes her position unique and important to us. You may review her clearances later, at your convenience, if you feel that my verbal assurance is somehow inadequate."

The general stared at Moore. There was anger in his eyes, but he kept his voice quiet. Calm. "I'm not sure if that is good enough because I don't know you."

Moore grinned broadly. "Wouldn't you assume that since I am sitting at the head of the table, and we are deep in the Pentagon, that I have both the sufficient clearances and that I can vouch for the others in the room?"

"No, sir, I would not. It simply doesn't work that way."

Moore reached into the inside pocket of his suit and pulled a white envelope from it. He slid it across the table so that it stopped in front of the general.

"Open it."

The general did as told. He pulled out the paper and unfolded it.

The White House
Washington, D.C.

27 June 1947

Dr. Jonathan Moore, special Scientific Advisor to the President, has been directed to investigate scientific questions for the President. United States military forces, as well as all elements of the executive branch of the federal government, will provide such support as he may request.

Dr. Moore has an unrestricted top secret security clearance. All questions concerning his clearances and/or authority should be directed to the Chief of Staff at the White House.

The letter was signed by the President. The general had seen enough documents signed by the President to recognize the signature as authentic.

Moore waited while the general examined the paper and when he glanced up, Moore asked, "Will that be sufficient?"

"Certainly, Doctor." The general shrugged. "You must understand . . ."

"Of course, General. If we may continue?"

Major General Curtis LeMay knew that he had lost the test of will, but cared little. The battle had been meaningless other than establishing his authority for those others in the conference room. They would know that he was important enough that even the president's personal representative had to acknowledge, and respond to, his questions and criticisms. LeMay knew that it was important to establish the lines of authority early on so that questions about who held what power would not develop later. This all provided him with an added edge if he found it necessary to deal with any of these people, individually, at a later date because these people probably didn't know who he was.

To them, LeMay was just another Army general, no more important than the hundreds of others who had fought the Second World War. They wouldn't know that he had survived the reduction in force after the war that saw many generals reduced in grade to captains or majors, and in a few extreme cases, to master sergeants. He was responsible for designing the air campaign against the Japanese that saw the fire bombing of their cities in which tens of thousands of civilians were killed. LeMay's attitude had been one of total war and total destruction. Destroy everything that the Japanese had. Burn their factories, bomb their farms, destroy their capability to manufacture war materiel, obliterate their cities and kill everyone who was part of the Japanese war machine whether they were military men or just civilians who allowed the military to attack. Complete and utter destruction until enough of the country was a smoking waste and enough civilians had been killed that they would surrender unconditionally. He didn't care how it was done, as long as it was done.

This concept of total war was one that he would carry on later, when he was elevated to command of SAC. He would implement rules and regulations that demanded total obedience and keep families apart for so long that they disintegrated. He wouldn't care because his job was to ensure that the American bomber force was ready to take off in fifteen minutes, and that his job would be the total annihilation of the Soviet Union. His attitude was one of complete and total victory or one of complete and total defeat. There were no half measures anywhere and he would do all that was necessary to obtain his goals, no matter what those goals might be, or who might be standing in the way. He knew of only one way to operate and that was full-out, balls to wall.

Sitting next to LeMay was a fairly young man who dressed like a graduate student. A poor graduate student. He was not wearing a suit and tie, but a light green shirt open at that neck. His pocket held a number of pens and pencils. He had long hair that had been heavily greased before it was combed back, dark eyes, and a look that suggested he was half asleep. Jacob Wheeler had been selected from Georgetown University because his father had a high, important role in the Pentagon, and because of that, they believed he, the younger Wheeler, understood the need for government secrecy. His father's background investigations had revealed nothing that would suggest that Wheeler couldn't be trusted. It was a clearance by inheritance. It hadn't hurt that Wheeler, who looked much younger than his actual age, was himself a veteran of the Second World War and had held a low level clearance during the war. The process of checking his background had been rapid, completed in a matter of hours rather than weeks or months.

Next to Hackett, on the other side of the table, was another nondescript man in a gray suit that looked expensive but not as expensive as that of their leader. His name, according to the metal plate in front of him, was Johnson. His red hair was combed and his blue eyes sparkled. He looked as if he was excited by the meeting, but if they had met him in the hall, they would have thought that he was excited by being in the hall. He had never lost his childhood sense of wonder. Everything interested and excited him. Especially that which was new.

LeMay watched as Moore glanced at each of the people in the room, as if to confirm their identity. Without preamble, Moore began the meeting by pointing to the leather folders sitting in front of each of them.

"That is a summary of the flying disk incidents we have collected over the last two years." He waited for a reaction.

Most of the people looked surprised. Johnson, without opening his folder, said, "I thought all this began about a week ago."

Moore ignored the comment. "If you'll turn to page three, you'll see that there have been similar reports made for about the last decade. Our pilots called them foo fighters during the war. Last year, over Sweden and later, over Europe, they were called the ghost rockets. Now they're called flying disks and flying saucers. It all seems to be related in some fashion, which frankly, we don't understand."

"These are real objects?" asked Wheeler. "Not some sort of hallucination or delusion?" He was flipping through the pages of the reports, but he was not reading anything. He just scanned the information.

As Moore opened his mouth, LeMay held up a hand.

"We've gotten some very good reports from our pilots in the last couple of days. I asked the unit commanders, colonels, to interrogate these boys carefully. I wanted to know as much as I could about this so that I could develop some sort of a plan of action."

The general finally opened his folder and flipped through it quickly.

"On page fifty-three is the beginning of a transcript of one of those interrogations. The man was looking at something solid. He couldn't catch it. It was faster than he was. No hallucination because others saw it too including half a dozen officers on the ground."

"Radar?" asked Wheeler.

"We have some radar reports," said LeMay nodding, "but I'm not confident in them."

"That's only because you are not well versed in radar operations," Moore said. "You'll notice that the last tab contains four radar cases. Object seen on the scope, seen by people on the ground, and seen by scrambled aircraft. When we have multiple witnesses with radar confirmation, we can rule out some kind of delusion or hallucination."

LeMay glanced at Moore, the anger evident on his face, but said nothing more about it. LeMay didn't like to be corrected by civilians and he didn't like it implied that he was not fully aware of the technical details of radar, or of anything else for that matter. Moore seemed to be going out of his way to assert his authority over LeMay.

Johnson, unaware of the struggle for power, said, "I'm confused. What are we doing here?"

"I'm confused too," said Hackett. She pointed at the wings on LeMay's uniform. "I can understand why he would be here. I don't know the area of expertise of the others, but I don't understand why I'm here. I know nothing about these . . . flying disks, aviation or the military."

"You have a top clearance. You have a very high clearance. You have a medical degree, and you are a qualified biologist," said Moore, his voice tight.

"That explains nothing," said Hackett, evenly.

Moore leaned forward, elbows on the highly polished table. He cut off the discussion about who had been invited because such a discussion would be counterproductive. Instead, he said:

"We're going to take a look at some gun-camera film taken yesterday in Arizona. So far only twelve people have seen it. The pilot, of course, saw the thing personally, but he has not seen the film. He was told that no image was visible and the film of no value. Photo lab people who developed the film saw it, the base commander saw it, and a few people here, in Washington, have seen it. This is why we are here today."

He looked at each of those at the table. His instructions had been to show them the film cold. Get their gut reactions to the information that was visible on the film. All others, from the pilot of the fighter, to the base commander, to the government officials in Washington, had some idea of what they would see. This would be the first time that a group of citizens, very bright citizens, would see something so extraordinary. Moore was actually looking forward to their reactions. It would be interesting to see how each of them handled information that could be explosive and for which they were unprepared.

Now Moore did something that was unprecedented in Washington and the Pentagon. He stood up, walked to the small projector that was sitting on a table. He glanced at it, crouched at the side so that his eyes were level with it, flipped a switch, and then moved to the right to turn off the lights. Such a menial task was normally reserved for a low ranking enlisted man, not a man who had the ear of the President, who could tell generals what to do, and who was obviously quite rich and important.

The film played through the projector with a vibrating sound. The screen flickered as the markings on the film flashed by. The screen turned a blood red and the words Top Secret appeared. They held there for a solid minute and then a hand-labeled sign appeared. It said simply, "29 June 1947. Tucson Army Air Field, Arizona."

They saw a cloudless blue sky with a pinpoint of light in the distance. It stayed there, as if moving away from the fighter aircraft as fast as the plane was approaching. It grew no larger or brighter, and it took on no shape. The only sign of motion was the dancing of the object in the distance caused by the vibration of the aircraft.

"This is shit," said LeMay, disgusted.

"Just wait."

The aircraft turned to the right, and the object slid from view. They saw a flash of the ground, some dull brown mountains, and then the blue, cloudless sky.

"I don't know what the pilot was thinking at this point," said Moore, speaking over the noise of the projector's electric motor and fan.

The object reappeared in the center of the screen. It was still just a bright, silver light, but it looked a little larger. Now it seemed to have a shape, or rather the illusion of a shape. It no longer seemed to be receding into the distance.

"Pilot claimed that it was a disk," said Moore. "He couldn't see any details at this point."

There was a gasp from both Wheeler and Hackett. The object was suddenly much closer, as if it was challenging for control of the sky. The object was clearly disk shaped with a slight dome on the top of it. There was a thin black streak on one side that showed the object was not rotating. Or rotating so fast it seemed the streak didn't move.

"My God," said Johnson.

The object tilted up on one side and dived to the right. The aircraft followed it and the ground was suddenly visible. They had a good view of a highway and a ranch house. Two people were standing on the ground, watching.

"We have estimated the object at fifty feet in diameter. It is traveling here at only about three hundred miles an hour. But watch."

"Those people?" said Hackett.

Misunderstanding her question, Moore said, "They have been interviewed extensively. They will not talk about what they have seen to anyone other than the proper authorities. We told them it was a matter of national security and they seemed happy to comply with our request that they keep the sighting to themselves."

The object began a gentle climb, as did the aircraft. Now only the sky and a few scattered clouds were visible. The aircraft was getting closer when a series of red spots appeared, bouncing through the sky, moving rapidly toward the flying saucer.

"The dumb son of a bitch fired on it?" asked LeMay.

"He had been on his way to a live fire exercise on one of the target ranges when he was diverted to this intercept."

The machine gun rounds hit the saucer and bounced from it, tumbling away.

"No damage?" asked the General.

"None that we could see."

The firing stopped and it looked as if the plane was catching the saucer when it vanished. It just disappeared.

"What the hell . . ."

Moore turned off the projector, turned on the lights and sat down. "It accelerated. In one frame it was there and in the next it barely registered and in the third it was gone. We estimate that it accelerated from three hundred miles an hour to approximately two thousand miles an hour in a fraction of a second. The gun camera was shooting at eighteen frames a second."

"Well, it's definitely not ours," said LeMay.

"Hell, it's not anyone's," said Wheeler without thinking. "If the Russians had anything like that . . ."

"They wouldn't be flying it over our territory," interrupted LeMay.

"Could we shoot one down?" asked Johnson. He was thinking of the scene in which the bullets bounced off it.

LeMay sat quietly for a moment thinking. This was not unlike a problem presented at the beginning of the war. Both Japan and Germany had developed fighters that were more maneuverable, faster, and more heavily armed than anything the Americans had. Yet, in aerial combat, American pilots had made up for the deficiencies of their aircraft with skill, determination and courage. LeMay wasn't sure that such a combination would work here, but if anyone could knock one down, it would be an American pilot who did it.

Finally, he shook his head. "It would be faster than machine gun bullets. You open fire and it just vanishes. No, we couldn't unless we caught it by surprise and you saw what happened when the rounds struck it. Maybe with something heavier than fifty caliber, like twenty millimeter with explosive heads. Maybe rockets, or heavy anti-aircraft could do it."

Hackett finally spoke up. "I would think the g-forces in those turns and accelerations would crush whoever was piloting that thing."

"Except that you would protect the crew," said Moore. "We could fire people into space in a rocket, but that would surely kill them unless we can develop a way of protecting them from those forces, then . . ."

"There isn't a technology on Earth that could do what we just saw," said Hackett, thinking aloud.

Moore grinned at her as if she was a very bright student. He said, casually, "That's why we don't believe it was built on Earth."

That put, into words, what many were thinking, or beginning to think. There was a stunned silence in the conference room as each tried to grasp the concept. No one moved. They couldn't breathe. They couldn't even think. They had just been shown movie footage that answered the question about life on other planets. Their world had suddenly, radically changed. It had been turned upside down by a short, poorly photographed movie that came from an airbase in Arizona. Their world had been altered by a sudden, new knowledge: they were no longer alone in the universe. Something alien had entered their lives. No one had a clue about their motivations yet. Everything had changed in the space of that—five minute—gun-camera movie.

"But," said LeMay. "But . . ." He couldn't think of the questions he wanted to ask, or the statements he wanted to make. He was so overwhelmed that he didn't realize that the film had been made by an Army Air Forces pilot, but no one had told him it existed. He had seen it for the first time just moments earlier. He wasn't angry about being out of that loop because he hadn't thought of it yet. When he did, there would be hell to pay.

But even as he sat there, stunned, his mind was spinning. He saw this not as a great chance to advance science, that the human race would be able to step to the stars because others had done it, but as a threat. It was an alien presence that had invaded American airspace, played a silly game of cat and mouse with one of the most advanced, modern fighters, and when tired of the game, vanished. These creatures, these beings, were now on his turf and he wasn't sure what he could do about it. All he knew for certain was that he, and the United States Army Air Forces, needed to prove that they were more formidable than this first encounter suggested.

"I know the feeling," Moore said finally. "I've had twelve

hours to digest this. It's unbelievable. We now know that travel in outer space, interstellar flight, is a reality. We now know that there is life, intelligent life, in the universe. It tells us that . . ."

"My God," said Hackett. "The implications . . ." Her voice was filled with awe. Her face was pale and her eyes slightly unfocused. She looked as if she was about to faint.

"We don't know the implications. This is unprecedented," said Moore.

"It's like Columbus discovering the new world," said Johnson but his voice was subdued, and like Hackett his face was pale, drained of blood. He too, looked as if he was about to faint.

"No," said Moore. "It's not like Columbus at all. He found other humans and believed he was in India. He didn't radically alter the way people thought."

"He proved the Earth was round," said Wheeler.

"No he didn't," said Moore. "The educated of the time knew the Earth was round. The ancient Greeks had even calculated the circumference to a reasonable number."

"What I meant," said Johnson, "about Columbus, is to look at it from the view of the Indians. Their world was suddenly altered by the mysterious and strange men from the East. Their societies were not prepared for it, for the hostility, for the change or the implications." But Johnson didn't really care about any of that. He was just trying to find a way of understanding what they had just seen. He was trying to get his mind working again.

Moore sat quietly, enjoying the reactions of those in the room, knowing that they needed time to understand the movie. He had been a part of a similar scene played out when he had first seen the film. It caught everyone flatfooted. The mind reeled as they tried to understand what it meant for them. They saw, with their eyes, the evidence, but the mind couldn't handle it. At least here no one had asked if the film was real. They all seemed to accept its reality and that was a little disturbing in its own right.

"I just can't think," said Wheeler.

"I know what you mean," said Hackett. "Rational thought vanishes. The questions to be asked."

"What is the first question that comes to mind?" asked Moore.

"Are they hostile?" asked LeMay. "That, to me, is the critical question. Nothing else is important until we know if they are hostile or not."

"Where are they from?" asked Wheeler.

"What's this going to mean to our society?" asked Hackett.

Moore pointed at her. "That's the important question. How is the man in the street going to react to this information?"

Hackett said, "Wait a minute. Wait a minute. We had a practical demonstration of that a couple of years ago. What was that radio show? The one about the invasion from Mars?"

Moore nodded as if he was pleased with the answer. "Orson Welles and his 'War of the Worlds' broadcast. People around the country panicked thinking the Martians were here."

"That is all trivia until we make a few determinations about their motives," said LeMay. "You all are beginning to sound like Neville Chamberlain. He thought that he had achieved peace with Hitler and in a year they were in a war. Our first consideration is their mission. What do they want?"

"What we're dealing with here is a somewhat more abstract concept," said Hackett. "That was a radio broadcast that talked of alien invasion with the Martians in the streets killing people. Here we're talking only of strange craft, strange lights, seen in the skies and no indication that they will land or that they are hostile. We really know nothing other than they are here. We shouldn't predicate our actions on what happened because of a radio broadcast of Martian invasion."

"Granted," said LeMay, waving a hand, because he cared nothing for this discussion. It missed the point, but he expected nothing else from civilians. In military matters they always missed the point.

LeMay took out a cigar and studied it carefully, buying himself a little time. The others waited for him. "The second question, after we determine the threat, is whose are they? If the man in the street learns they aren't ours, then they might conclude they belong to the Russians. That's going to cause a big problem. Or as big a problem as Welles caused."

"Are you suggesting that we don't say anything?"

LeMay looked around the room slowly as if attempting to gauge the reactions of the people there. "What we have now, today, are just reports of strange things in the sky. Nobody knows what they are. Maybe they're illusions. Maybe they're aircraft that have been misidentified. Hell, we've got some of those reports already. We don't have any answers, but we don't have to say that."

"You saw the gun camera footage. Those tracers bouncing off the object made it look real enough," said Johnson.

"Optical illusion."

"Hell, General, you don't believe that."

"No, but we can say it and who would know differently?" He looked at Moore. "You said very few people have seen this footage?"

"Correct."

LeMay smiled broadly. He was beginning to feel he was in control of the situation. "Then we don't have to explain it at all because no one knows it exists. If no one knows it exists, then, in point of fact, it doesn't exist."

Moore rocked back in his chair and tapped a front tooth with the tip of his pen again. "You know, we're not obligated to answer this question." He grinned. "We're not obligated to tell anyone anything."

LeMay understood even if the others did not. "The people are out there demanding some kind of response, but all we have to say is that it, they, whatever they are, don't belong to us. We are not responsible. We're investigating. And we throw out a couple of explanations, maybe interview a scientist or two to talk of optical illusion."

Now Johnson chimed in. "We say that we have fulfilled our requirements under the law. We have investigated and we simply are not responsible for the sightings. It is a scientific problem, not one of defense or for the military."

Moore nodded slowly, grinning. "Let the newspapers run wild and we maintain a level of calm reserve. There is no evidence. We have seen nothing to suggest that anything is going on. It's all a big mistake. Mass hysteria. Let the press out there fill in the blanks for us."

"Don't we have an obligation to answer the questions?" asked Hackett.

"Answer what questions?" snapped LeMay. "There are no questions. There are some sightings by people . . ." He stopped talking for a moment and his face went blank as if he had suddenly been rendered stupid. Then his eyes brightened and he grinned broadly. "It's not our fault if people who have been drinking see things in the sky. It has been happening for centuries."

For a moment there was a silence at the table. Moore looked at the faces that seemed to have relaxed, grinned and said:

"Yes. You never know what those drunks are likely to see."

"But that doesn't answer the question," protested Hackett.

"No, it doesn't. But it gives us a position to use as we study the question. The population does not have to know everything we're doing. There is a national security requirement here. This provides us with some breathing room so that we can make our inquiries without worrying about the panic that you suggested might follow."

"So we do nothing," said Hackett.

"No, we continue to do our research, but not in a public arena. We do our work quietly and quickly so that we can determine what is happening and if it does pose a threat to the national security."

LeMay added, "We gather our data but we don't tell anyone that we're gathering it."

"There seems to be something wrong with this," said Hackett.

Moore interrupted. "I'll advise the President about our conclusions here. Does anyone have anything else that he or she wants to say?"

When no one said a word, he stood up. "All right then. That's it. No one talks about this with anyone not cleared to hear it and, at this point, you must assume that no one outside of this room has been cleared. I anticipate another meeting in about five days unless there is a radical change in the situation." Without waiting for a response, he picked up his folder and exited.

CHAPTER 2

Captain Jack Reed, former Eighth Air Force hotshot fighter pilot, and now a squadron intelligence officer, sat in his first floor, oven-hot office, and stared out the open window, hoping for a breeze. He was a fairly young man, promoted quickly during the war but then downgraded to captain in the reduction in force that came with the Japanese surrender. He was tall and slender with a narrow face but wide set eyes of bright blue. He had dark brown hair chopped short because of military regulations and the heat of southeastern New Mexico. Sometimes he entertained the idea of a mustache like that of General Ramey, commander of the Eighth Air Force, but decided against it. It would be just one more thing that had to meet military standards and one more thing that would offend the brass hats.

He wore a khaki uniform that had been freshly starched in the morning but that was now wilted. He wore none of the medals to which he was entitled, but in keeping with Army Air Forces tradition, had pinned his silver wings above his left breast pocket. He had propped his feet, in his highly polished brown shoes, up on the windowsill. It was as comfortable as he expected to be, given his current situation.

His current situation was the heat. During the fourteen months he had been assigned to the 509th Bomb Group, he had not gotten used to the dry heat of the New Mexican desert in summer. Sure, it was a dry heat and, according to many people he knew, would have been worse had there been any humidity. Reed, however, knew better. It couldn't possibly be worse, just different. The inside of an oven was dry heat but it roasted the meat and baked the potato just fine.

Reed turned away from the window and glanced at the papers piled on his battered, wooden desk but there was nothing of importance among them. That was what happened when a fighter pilot found himself in a non-flying position such as base intelligence officer. He had been placed where it was felt he could make a contribution, even if his training had not prepared him for that position. He had what they considered to be on-the-job training, which meant he had listened to intelligence briefings, had been debriefed after missions in Europe, and had read, with very little enthusiasm, the manuals that gave the capabilities of the enemy's weapons systems. Now, according to his local bosses, his superior officers throughout the chain of command, and the leaders of the military, with a mere stroke of the pen, he was the expert in Soviet antiaircraft capabilities, as well as their military doctrine and organization. It was a subject that didn't particularly interest him and he was worried that his work reflected that lack of enthusiasm. Worse, he was afraid that those appointed over him as his supervisor and commander were aware of his shortcomings. Promotion to major would be in the far distant future even if there was a slot that called for a major into which they could push him.

He turned his attention back to the window. Nothing was stirring outside because of the heat. It was so hot that the concrete softened the tires of the cars sitting in the parking lot and made the metal of those cars so hot that it could blister a hand faster than the top of a stove. It was so hot that no one wanted to do anything outside including just walking from one building to the next. It was so hot that they all wanted to stay inside where the fans could circulate the heavy air and pretend that it wasn't as bad as it was or to find an excuse to visit one of the few air conditioned buildings on the post.

Reed sat still with the fan blowing directly on him drying the sweat on his face and his shirt, and stared out the window at the brown expanse that had been, during the heavy spring

rains, a bright green parade ground. The heat was rising from
it in waves so thick that the buildings on the other side seemed
to shimmer and dance. He let his mind wander toward the
mountains and snow and even the green grass as it appeared
in the cool of a spring evening.

A corporal tapped at the door frame and announced, "Major
would like to see you, sir."

Reed wiped the sweat from his face and the back of his
neck with his handkerchief. He wanted to ask if it ever cooled
off in New Mexico but he already knew the answer. It didn't
and wouldn't until late in the fall. Then, to his surprise, it
would get cold. Sometimes there would be snow which was
hard to believe especially now with the temperature lingering
in the triple digits until long after the sun had set.

"He tell you what he wants?"

The corporal, a very young man who had entered the service
at the end of the war, and who had missed the fighting by
only a couple of weeks, grinned broadly showing white, un-
even teeth.

"No sir, but I suspect you'll be taking a little trip. He said
it was urgent."

"Everything is urgent." Reed put his hands on the arms of
the chair and pushed, forcing himself to stand. "It's just too
hot for anything to be urgent."

"Yes sir."

Reed squeezed past the corporal, walked down the green
linoleum hall, turned to the right, passed the posters left over
from the war that told him "Loose Lips Sink Ships," and that
"The Enemy is Everywhere," and walked slowly to the green
door of the major's office. He knocked and then without waiting for a response, opened it.

"Ah, Jack, come on in."

The major, Philip Ryan, a thin man with jet black hair and
very white skin, was sitting behind a desk that had been old
during the First World War. Ryan was a man who burned
easily so he stayed out of the bright New Mexican sun as much
as possible. With brown eyes, a thin nose and lips, he looked
more like a mannequin than a human. He wore sweat-stained

and wrinkled khakis, a single row of brightly colored ribbons above his open pocket that suggested he hadn't seen much action, and above them, the silver wings of a pilot.

He waved at a chair. "Sit down. Hot enough for you?"

Reed dropped into the leather chair, looked at the open window that had much the same view as his own and then at the fan that was roaring away in the corner. "Yeah. It's hot enough."

"Like a trip to White Sands?"

Reed thought about the road that wound through the Capitan Mountains and Ruidoso where it was probably thirty degrees cooler. He thought about the forests filled with green trees, light breezes and mountains that somehow still had snow on them, even in early July.

"Yes, sir. I'd love a trip to White Sands."

"But you can't stop in Ruidoso," Ryan said, grinning broadly. "Or rather, you can't stop there for very long."

"Why would I stop there?" asked Reed innocently.

The major waved a hand as if wiping a slate. Changing the subject, he asked, "You've heard of these flying disks?"

"Yes, sir. Read something about it in the paper." He grinned. "Listened to some of the talk in the club. Laughed with the rest of them."

"The disks have some of the boys in Washington scratching their heads. No one seems to know what's going on, or even if anything *is* going on. But they're concerned about it. Real concerned."

Reed wasn't sure what to say. He nodded slowly and then said, simply, "Yes, sir."

"Well, something's been going on around here, too. Radar has picked it up. Flies around for a while and then disappears off the scopes at fantastic speed. Radar boys say that it is solid but if, and this is a big if, they are right, it flies faster than anything we've got. Got some visual reports to go with those radar sightings, but always of something very high or very far away. Just a light in the sky or a flash of metal in the distance. No way to identify it."

"Yes, sir," said Reed, thinking, suddenly, of the light he had seen over Germany during the last days of the war.

"I want you to drive over to White Sands and take a look at what they've got on their radar. Talk to the people who have seen the thing. Watch it on their radar and see if they're picking up what we are."

"But sir, I'm not trained in radar operations."

"They are there. Just see what's happening. Ask some questions. See what they say and report back to me. I can compare it with what our boys say here. Maybe we can figure something out. If nothing else, I can file a report with Washington which will make the brass hats there happy."

Reed rubbed a hand through his short-cropped hair. He thought for a moment and then said, simply, "Yes sir. When did you want me to leave?"

"You have anything pressing on your plate? Nothing that can't wait a couple of days?"

Reed thought about the hour he had spent staring out the window worrying about the heat and thinking about the war. He thought of the folders of routine paperwork stacked on his desk and the manuals that demanded he read them. He thought about the recognition materials he should study, and the latest information about the Marshall Plan that had come in the form of classified message traffic. It all bored him. He said, "No, sir."

Ryan rose, as if to signal the end to the meeting. "Then you can leave right now. Draw a car and driver from the motor pool if you like and head over to White Sands. I've already coordinated with their people so they'll be expecting you. Call back here when you arrive and let me know what's happening."

"How long will I be gone?"

"Thirty-six hours at the most, I would think. You should see everything you need to see within that time frame."

Reed, on his feet, nodded and then saluted. "Yes sir." When the salute was returned, he stepped to the door. He thought about saying something else, but nothing came to mind. All he could say was that he wasn't happy with the assignment.

It was too hot for it. Too hot for anything, except the base swimming pool, or the main officer's club where there was some air conditioning. And the major wouldn't be interested in that.

CHAPTER 3

I t took no time to get a car and driver from the motor pool, sign both out for White Sands, and get started. They drove out the main gate, north along the highway to the center of Roswell, where they turned west on Highway 70 and headed toward the mountains visible in the distance. The terrain, for the first ten or twenty miles, was as flat and brown as the parade ground on the base. Within thirty minutes, the highway dropped away, began to twist, and then to climb slowly. There were closed fruit stands on either side of the road. Later in the year they would be stocked with apples, cherries, ciders, and peppers. Now they sat boarded up and deserted, somehow looking forlorn. But the air was becoming cooler with each passing mile.

To the left the land became green and there was a river in the distance often lost to view because of the hills. They slowed, rolling up behind a large truck that was grinding its way along with black smoke pouring from twin stacks behind the cab. It didn't look as if it had the power to climb into the mountains.

They passed it, caught another and passed it too. They caught up with a line of cars, but the drivers pulled to the shoulder to let them by. That surprised Reed each time it happened, but someone had told him that the drivers thought an Army car would be on official business. They didn't want to hold up an officer on the way to an important meeting. Instead, they pulled over to allow the Army car to pass.

They finally reached Ruidoso and slowed again. It was much cooler now. Reed wanted to stop and relax for a few minutes. He knew they would continue to climb, once they had driven beyond Ruidoso, eventually reaching an altitude of about 7500 feet. The road then descended on the far side of the pass as they drove through the Mescalero Apache reservation. They would drive out of the mountains near Tularosa where they would remain on flat ground, until they arrived at Alamogordo where it would again be hot and dry and unpleasant, just as it was in Roswell. The only real difference was that Alamogordo was not as pleasant a town as Roswell.

On the west side of Ruidoso, the road began a rapid ascent. A sign told them that the fire danger in the forest was high. No rain for a number of days. Hell, no rain for a number of weeks and there hadn't been much when it did rain. The ground was so hard, almost like concrete, that what rain fell it rolled off, forming arroyos, as it rushed toward the river where it disappeared.

They finally reached the top of the mountain and began the descent. They rolled back onto the desert, drove through Alamogordo on a highway that was lined with cafés, restaurants, service stations, motels, and a huge park that had a miniature train. They drove past the entrance to the White Sands National Monument where the sand was as white as snow and drifted in huge hills. They found the small sign that told them that the Proving Grounds were to the south and that they needed to exit before they began the climb into the Organ Mountains. There was also a sign that told them all photography in the area was prohibited.

At the gate they were stopped, their AGO ID cards checked, and then an MP climbed into the back of the car. He said, "Follow the main road to the third intersection and turn right." He provided directions until they pulled up in front of a single story building that was painted white with only a few windows and those few were covered with aluminum foil.

As they stopped a man in civilian clothes left the shade of a large tree and walked toward them. He said nothing as he pulled open the door and nodded at the interior. The MP exited without a word, happy that Reed hadn't been a spy and that his escort was waiting as he had been told. Still saying nothing, the MP began to walk back toward the front gate.

To the driver, Reed said, "You wait right here. I'll let you know what to do in a few minutes. As soon as I figure it out or someone gives me some instructions."

"Yes, sir."

Without another word, Reed climbed out of the car. When the civilian turned, Reed followed him into the building unaware that what he would see would inside would alter his life radically.

CHAPTER 4

July 3, 1947
The White House
Washington, D.C.

Major General Curtis LeMay, in command of the Army Air
Forces' research and development program, sat in the plush
chair that was set off to one side in the White House Oval
Office. Seated opposite him, in a matching chair, and across
the low, highly polished coffee table, was the President of the
United States. Harry S Truman, wearing his standard bow tie
and round glasses, didn't look all that well at the moment. His
face was pale and his hands were shaking. LeMay knew he
was responsible for the President's discomfort, but there was
nothing he could do about it.

But it also made him question the President's courage. True,
Truman had commanded an artillery battery in the First World
War, but such a command was of finite experience. A battery
commander had to report to a superior officer who was never
that far away. A battery commander certainly didn't have the
autonomy that a president did. Truman had always been in a
position, no matter how high he had climbed, where there was
someone close at hand to make the decisions. Even at the end
of the war, when Truman took over the presidency, the decision to drop the bomb hadn't been that difficult. The wheels
were in motion and Truman agreed with his top military commanders that they had to use the bomb. It ended the war almost
immediately, though there were now some who questioned the
wisdom.

LeMay didn't particularly like Truman, but then, he didn't
particularly like civilian authority, especially when it clashed

with military thought. Civilians, even those with some military experience, didn't understand the concept of war. That was something that professional officers understood. LeMay knew that the purpose of the military was to kill people, destroy industry and to beat the enemy into the ground as quickly and completely as possible. Civilians were often crippled by compassion. That was something that he would not let happen to him. LeMay would do what had to be done.

"Are you sure about this, General?" asked Truman as he removed his glasses and carefully set them on the table.

LeMay glanced down at the top secret folder that he held in his lap. It contained the latest data on the flying disks that had been reported all over the country. Included were still photographs taken from fighter gun cameras that he had seen a couple of days earlier, photographs taken from radar scopes, several transcripts from interrogations of military officers who had encountered the craft but had not had fully loaded gun cameras, or guns, and an assessment about the flying disks from scientific leaders assigned to LeMay's research and development organization. It was a long, impressive document that, if it fell into the hands of a journalist, congressman, or the average citizen, would cause a great uproar.

"Yes, Mr. President."

Truman leaned back in his chair, closed his eyes for a moment, and then said, "They're not Soviet. You're sure?"

"No, Mr. President, if for no other reason than the Soviets would not fly such a craft over our territory for fear of a mechanical failure that would drop it into our hands. But the capabilities are far beyond our current state of technology. If anyone could do this, it would be us and I know for a fact that it's not us."

"How does this tie into the ghost rockets?"

LeMay took a moment before answering. He thought about the ghost rockets which were strange craft seen first in the skies over Scandinavia and then Europe during the summer of 1946. An intelligence team, headed by Lieutenant General Jimmy Doolittle, had been sent to investigate. Doolittle had not been able to solve the riddle of the ghost rockets but had provided a top secret report about them, suggesting, among other possibilities, that some of the ghost rockets represented technology superior to that found on Earth.

LeMay said, "I would think that General Doolittle would be better qualified to answer that than I."

"What do you think, General?" asked Truman, his voice indicating that he expected an answer and not an evasion.

LeMay patted one of the pockets of his uniform jacket, felt the thick cigar hidden there and wished that he could light it. But even LeMay knew that no one smoked in the presence of the president unless the president granted permission. In a tug of war for power in the White House, even one in a room with only two people, LeMay would lose. The president had the power and a word in the right place could easily ruin a major general.

Instead of taking out his cigar, LeMay said, "General Doolittle reported on a number of instances in which the ghost rockets fell to the ground. Nothing was recovered that would suggest a Soviet advancement on our technology or that they may have captured from the Nazis. There was nothing there that would suggest these ghost rockets were of Soviet invention or manufacture."

"But those items you have there change your opinion?"

"Mr. President, we have here some solid evidence in the forms of motion picture footage and radar tracks that suggest something solid in the sky. We now control the data and have a much clearer picture of what has been happening."

"It provides no clues as to origin."

"No, sir, it does not. However, there are no indications from any of the various, shall we say, investigative agencies . . ."

"If you mean spies, then damn well say spies."

"Yes, sir. I was thinking more in the terms of intelligence capabilities. However, not to put too fine a point on it, there are no indications that these things could be of Soviet design, or of German design. If they are artificially manufactured craft, they do not originate on this planet."

"Shit."

"Yes, sir. Exactly."

"Are you sure? Are we actually talking of some kind of Martian here?"

"Without one to examine, and without a representative of the crew, we can't be completely sure." LeMay looked down at his folder as if to take strength from it. He continued, "The reported capabilities, as well as the structure, all suggest that this is an advancement on our technology, but so far advanced that it is virtually inconceivable that these are the result of an Earth-based industry or science."

"Can we bring one down?"

"Yes, sir, I think we can," said LeMay, not at all sure they could. So far the few attempts that had been made, none of which had been coordinated, had been unsuccessful. But those attempts had been pilots firing without any real authorization and only by fighters that were not equipped with the latest or the best weapons. All of that could change the equation, at least in LeMay's mind.

He said, "They have displayed speed and maneuverability that outperforms our best, but in the right circumstances, with the right combination of weapons, we should be able to shoot one out of the sky."

"Do we know where they are seen most often?"

"Figures show most reports coming from the northwest, but there are quite a few sightings in west Texas, New Mexico and Arizona."

"Will it cause any sort of reaction if we put the west coast on alert? I want someone to get me something concrete. I need some hard answers here."

LeMay rubbed his forehead, thinking. "That question should really be posed to the commanding general of the Army Air Forces."

"General Spaatz isn't here, General. I want an answer from you."

"If we are low key in the alert. Individually call the various bases and speak to the commanders. If we don't put out any sort of general alert, then it might look like some sort of exercise. If the press doesn't get a hold of it, then we shouldn't have to answer any tough questions."

"How difficult would be it be do something like that, General?"

"That would be easily accomplished, Mr. President."

LeMay watched as Truman stood up and walked to the windows so that he could look out over the lawns and gardens. Beyond the President, he could see people walking along the sidewalks in the distance. Tourists with the cameras pointing at the White House, the gardens surrounding it, and the fountain set in the middle of the lawn.

Without turning around, Truman said, "You know what this means, don't you General?"

LeMay didn't answer. He stood up, near his chair, the folders and photographs in his hand. He said nothing, but he knew the answer because he had been in that briefing a couple of days earlier. He'd had time to think about the implications, but he also knew that the President did not want him to answer, so he stood silently, waiting.

"Life as we know it is about to change. This is the second time since I became president that this has happened. Two very different events, I grant you, and one of them created on this planet, but shattering nonetheless." He took a deep breath and turned to face the General. "It's not any easier this time."

"No, sir, I wouldn't imagine it would be."

Truman stayed near the windows so that he was backlit, nearly impossible to see other than a shadow caught in the brightness. "I really don't want to hear much more about this, General. I think that you and your superiors should be able to handle this situation. Find out what these things are, and find out if they pose a threat to our nation. That's all that concerns me at the moment. Our national security."

"Yes, sir."

For a moment, LeMay was confused by Truman's request and then he understood. Truman was giving him a free rein to deal with the problem of the Martians. He would be allowed to decide the best way to handle it and that his job was the security of the nation. Truman had just told him that the priority was the national security and that was his only concern. LeMay, and the other generals in the chain of command, would make the decisions. Truman had made it a military problem. If LeMay made a mistake and there was a public outcry, Truman could say that he had been kept in the dark by the military. Plausible deniability. His ass was covered and LeMay's was hanging out, flapping in the breeze.

But he also understood that Truman was not attempting to duck the responsibility for the orders. Truman was maneuvering as a politician, thinking of the consequences that could be encountered in the future. If his men were successful in bringing down one of the alien ships, the President could say that he knew nothing about it.

But, more importantly, if there were ramifications from another planet, if the creatures landed on Earth telling the world that an act of war had been committed, Truman had his scapegoats. If the aliens landed and demanded an accounting, if LeMay was successful in shooting down one of their ships, then Truman could, with a clear conscience, say that he knew nothing about it. No one would know the role of the civilian authorities.

In the European theater, and later in the Pacific, control of the skies was a key to winning the conflict. If the aliens decided they were angry about the loss of their ship, if they thought of it as an act of interplanetary war, there was little that LeMay and the Army Air Forces could do. The aliens could stay in space, holding, in essence, the high ground and push big rocks at Earth. Meteorites could do a great deal of damage and there would be no defense against them.

LeMay knew that Truman understood this. If there came a time when negotiations opened, Truman could say, with a straight face, that someone from the military had initiated the hostile action. That would leave the President in a position to conduct the negotiations.

LeMay was the man out in front, and he understood that. That was what he was paid for, and if things worked out, the rewards would be enormous. If they didn't, then LeMay knew that he would be forced into retirement and he could only hope he was not court-martialed. Being a major general was much better than being a colonel.

Truman then said, as if to make it clearer, "You understand me, General? This is a military, and an intelligence problem, at the moment. It is nothing that needs to concern the President."

"Yes, Mr. President," said LeMay, nodding. "I understand completely."

CHAPTER 5

D anni Hackett and Jacob Wheeler sat at the rear of the small coffee shop hidden away in the bowels of the Pentagon. Most of the tables were tall, so that standing people could rest an elbow on them while they sipped coffee or ate a hurried lunch. Without seats, the tall tables discouraged long conversations and kept the people circulating in and out of the coffee shop which made the proprietor happy because he made more money, and made the various supervisors throughout the Pentagon happy because their subordinates weren't inclined to sit around in the coffee shop evading work.

There were a couple of booths, along one wall and off to one side so that those who had a little longer to drink their coffee or eat their lunch could find a place to sit and relax. The table top was scarred and the red leather seats were well worn, stained and torn, but it was out of the way and it was deep inside the Pentagon.

Dr. Danni Hackett sat with her hands around her Coke glass as if she were afraid that someone was going to steal it. She was staring down at the ice cubes, watching as the carbonation fizzed through her drink and lifted her straw up, to the top of the glass. She hadn't spoken since Wheeler had set it down in front of her, other than to thank him for the Coke.

Wheeler had taken a great deal of time to stir sugar from a glass container into his coffee and then wiped the spoon on a paper napkin. He set it down carefully, to one side, picked up his cup, sipped, and then put it back. He glanced around the room and saw that they were virtually alone, the only other occupants being the proprietor behind the luncheon room–like counter and a lieutenant general who looked as if he was in a very bad mood. The general sat on one of the four stools in front of the short counter and periodically slammed his fist on the Formica top before mumbling something.

Wheeler leaned closer to Hackett and said quietly, almost in a whisper, "I figured it all out. This has to be some kind of test."

Hackett looked up at him, smiled weakly, and asked, "Why?"

"They want to get our reactions to this."

"Why?"

"Because, when there is"—he lowered his voice and leaned closer—"real contact, they'll know how people will react. They'll know how to deal with the situation."

"Nope," she said, her eyes still on the Coke.

"Why not?"

"What would inspire this sort of an experiment? What would inspire it now?"

"Orson Welles," he said, looking around again. He tried to lean closer. "The war got in the way of the experiment. Now with atomic bombs and all, talk of rockets and trips to the moon, they're thinking along these lines again. They want to build some sort of file on this."

"Nope."

"Those ghost rockets put it back in their minds. They found something out. They're testing us."

"We, you and me, don't make good test subjects for something like this." Hackett pushed her drink to one side, out of the way. "You need average people, with high school diplomas who are working to feed a family, not us. There was a general officer at the meeting. The sample is not large enough or general enough to draw any sort of rational conclusion. It was skewed toward the educated and the powerful. This is not a good test. They won't be able to draw any useful conclusions."

"Come on," he said loudly, incredulously, sitting back, as

if to put distance between them. "You can't possibly believe what they said."

"Lower your voice. Besides, you saw the film."

"Hollywood."

"That looked awful real to me."

"Of course it did," said Wheeler. "What'd you expect? Something that we could pick apart easily? Something that looks like crummy special effects so that we aren't fooled? They have to make it look good or we'd never buy it."

Now Hackett sat back, leaning against the comfort of the leather of the booth. She picked up her drink and swirled it, letting the ice cube clink against the glass. She said, "For the first time in my life I wish that I smoked. I think I need a cigarette."

Finally, as if thinking out loud, she said, "You're telling me that you think they set all this up just to see how we would react to it?"

"Of course. You don't really think that there are little . . ." he stopped talking, realizing that he was about to blurt out the secret. To cover it, he said, quietly, "You don't think it's true, do you?"

She thought about that. She glanced around the snack bar. Another officer had entered and sat down next to the general. They began a hurried, quiet conversation, oblivious to anyone else around them.

Lowering her voice so that it was barely audible, she said, "This information was staggering, yet I can think of no reason to reject it. We know the universe is huge and there is no reason that life, intelligent life, life as we know it, couldn't develop on other planets. People had talked of seeing signals on Mars for the last hundred years and science is still debating the canals that Percival Lowell said he saw and mapped through his telescope in Arizona. There was no reason to reject, out of hand, what they saw, just because it's difficult for us to believe. Scientists sometimes were too skeptical, and I can think of no good reason for the government to lie to us. If it is an experiment, they would have used soldiers, in the field, and used enough of them that they could reach some valid scientific conclusions. They wouldn't have limited the sample to half a dozen people in positions of relative power."

"You think it's true," repeated Wheeler, his voice filled with sarcasm. Clearly Hackett had not been persuaded by his arguments against an alien presence.

Finally she nodded slowly and said, "Yes, I do. I think it is all very real."

Wheeler raised his eyebrows, looking as if he couldn't believe that she was so gullible. "Well, it can't be."

"How do you know?"

"Because stuff like this just doesn't happen. It's the stuff of, what do they call it now? Science fiction. That's what it is. Science fiction plain and simple."

But in that moment he knew that it wasn't science fiction. He knew that it wasn't some kind of an experiment or joke or elaborate hoax designed to test their, or the public reactions, to life on other planets. He knew it because he had read science fiction, and he understood how such psychological tests were conducted. What they had seen in that room was real. Life as he knew it in June and had understood it in June had changed forever. Everything else was about to change because the film was real, and the alien creatures were real, and the time for speculation about it was over.

CHAPTER 6

Captain Jack Reed stood in the heat of the late afternoon, outside the radar shack at the White Sands Proving Ground, and looked up toward the Organ Mountains. It was blazing hot, the sky a perfect, deep blue, unbroken by any clouds. He shaded his eyes and stared up, away from the base. He could see nothing in the air. There were no airplanes, rockets, jets, or birds. There wasn't a sound or a breeze.

"Jack," said one of the men with him.

"Yeah." Reed looked at Thomas Williams, a short, stocky man with intense eyes, little hair, and a permanent smile. He had been trained as a radar interpretation officer and had been in the Pacific at the close of the war. Now he was one of the radar experts used at White Sands for tracking of the rockets and missiles launched there. He had no real experience with intelligence and was confused by the sudden appearance of intelligence officers cleared to know everything.

"What did the general say?" asked Williams.

Reed thought about that, and the secured line telephone call he'd had with the intelligence general named Thomas in southern California. Reed had met the general only a few times, often in dark rooms where everyone spoke in a hushed voice. The general was a presence in the dark who listened to everything but said very little. He evaluated and then acted. Reed was a little surprised that Williams knew about the general, given that Williams was outside the intelligence loop, but then this was a special circumstance. Some of the red tape had to be avoided and he believed that the general would have called Williams to impress on him the importance of security.

Reed said, "He said for me to look at the radar. That's all he said. Just like the major said. Look at the radar."

"Christ," repeated Williams.

Reed turned and looked back, into the radar shack. They had erected a mirror near the radar scope so that the operator could signal them with a flashlight if anything happened. Reed could easily see the mirror through the window in the door.

"How much longer are you going to have to stay here?" asked Williams.

"If you mean outside, you can go back in. If you mean here, at White Sands, then I don't know," said Reed. He turned so that he could scan the sky to the north.

"This is just unbelievable," said Davis.

Reed thought about that for a moment. He didn't know what to say about it. He felt they were standing on the edge of the abyss and it wouldn't take much to shove them over, into it. He didn't want to think about what it would mean if they spotted the object overhead, or if they found some kind of physical evidence from it. He wasn't sure what they were looking at, or for, and he didn't want to deal with it. He hoped that he would be sent back to Roswell and that the thing, whatever it was, would just go away. That would make him happy and his life easier. If they found out something, Reed didn't want to have to try to explain it to anyone or make the middle of the night telephone call to the general to explain why he didn't have more information. For Reed, the best scenario would be for the thing to vanish completely, totally, and forever. That would return his life to its easy existence.

"There," said Williams, pointing, his voice an octave higher than normal.

Reed turned, thinking that he had spotted something in the deep blue sky. Instead Williams was pointing at the mirror inside the radar room. The light was flashing on it.

Without a word, Reed tossed his cigarette to the ground, stepped on it to crush the fire, and then pulled open the door.

He allowed Davis and Williams to enter first and then followed them.

The radar man, a staff sergeant with several years of experience, was sitting with his back straight. He was staring down at the pale green line that was sweeping around the face of the scope. Out of the corner of his eye, he saw the men enter and pointed. "There."

The object, the blip, was near the center of the scope, indicating that it wasn't far from the antenna. It was a bright, strong blip.

"That's not weather," said the radar man. "Looks like a solid, manufactured object."

"How fast is it moving?" asked Reed.

"Appeared at about a thousand miles an hour, slowed to seventy miles, turned, and is accelerating again."

"We've nothing in our inventory that will do that," said Williams, unnecessarily.

"Maybe you're getting multiple targets so that it seems like just one moving that fast," said Reed.

"I don't think so," said the sergeant. "This is about the tenth time it's done this. I see nothing to suggest that we've acquired a variety of targets and are making a mistake on the acquisition. That is a single target doing stuff that can't be done."

Reed said, "I remember reading about an object over London during the war that seemed to rise from the ground, rise into the air and then slowly disintegrate. Investigation showed that it was birds taking off in the morning."

"Yes, sir. I read about that too. But that was seven, eight years ago. Radar has improved and we've improved. We've got a real object that can go from a thousand miles an hour to under a hundred in a matter of seconds." He tapped a finger on the screen. "It's right here, big as snot."

"I don't mean to question your competence," said Reed.

"I know, sir," said the operator, interrupting. "I've been here for two years, and I have tracked missile firings. I was in Europe during the war and have been working on radar for a long time. I know what is going on here. I know what I'm doing and I'm as confused as you are."

Reed watched as the blip seemed to fade from the screen but reappear a moment later.

"Crossed over the top of the antenna."

"Where is that?"

"To the north."

Reed whirled and ran to the door, threw it open, and jumped down the steps. He looked to the north but saw nothing. Clouds were beginning to build and seemed to glow a bright white in the late afternoon sun. He scanned from horizon to horizon, unsure of what he was looking for, or exactly where to look. After several minutes, he returned to the radar room.

The sergeant tapped the glass. "It's right there. You see anything?"

"No," said Reed. "How big is it?"

"Don't know. The radar signature shows me a solid object. Could be as small as fifteen, twenty feet across, depending on its angle from us and if it is solid metal."

"I would suspect it's metal," said Williams.

Reed was about to agree and then realized that they didn't know. They didn't know anything other than it was very fast, flew at high altitude, and was rarely seen.

"There it goes," said the operator.

The blip seemed to fade away again. It had been a solid, bright blip, then a dimmer, smaller blip in the same place, and then it was gone, off the scope.

The radar operator leaned back in his chair and laced his fingers behind his head. He kept his eyes on the scope. "That's it. If it follows its pattern, it won't be back for several hours."

"Where'd it go?" asked Reed.

"Well, it was near the edge of our range. I'd guess that it disappeared to the north, northwest or northeast. Maybe up toward Albuquerque, or over toward Roswell." He turned and looked up at Reed. "Mountains limit our coverage here. If it's low enough, it doesn't have to get too far from here to disappear. Drops below the terrain and we can't see it."

Reed had a thought. "Could that account for its apparent speed?"

"Nah. It could account for it seeming to disappear. It just drops below our coverage area."

Reed ran a hand though his hair. He glanced down at the scope and then toward the window in the door. It was beginning to darken outside. "I don't like this," he said. "I don't know what I'm supposed to tell the general." He hadn't given a thought to the major over at Roswell who was probably talking to the general anyway.

Williams said, "Just tell him what we've seen here."

Reed shrugged. "What have we seen? Some strange light on the radar scope. Nothing outside. Nothing to show that what we've seen is anything other than a problem with the radar."

"Set has been checked . . ."

Reed held up a hand. "I know, I know. I'm just saying that from one point of view, we have no visual confirmation that anything was in the sky here."

A sergeant entered, looked at Reed and said, "There's a general on the phone for you."

"Is it a secure line?"

"Yes, sir. If you'll follow me."

They walked down a lighted hallway, past pictures of rockets, missiles and airplanes, and past a few shots of the mountains and the sand dunes and even the creatures that lived in the desert around White Sands. They turned into a darkened office with a single desk.

The sergeant said, "Commo is through that door. Corporal in there will show you what you need."

"Thank you, sergeant."

He entered the room and was pointed to a chair. He sat down in it and the corporal gave him the handset for a telephone. He said, "You know how to work this, sir?"

"No."

"Squeeze the button when you want to talk and let it up when you want to listen. This is a secure line. I'll leave you alone in here and when you're done, tell the sergeant."

Reed grinned up at the man, thinking that leaving him alone in the room was a violation of security in one sense. Then he noticed that there wasn't anything in the room except the chair, a desk with nothing on it, and a wastebasket. It was a ten by ten room that could have been a storage closet at one time.

"Thanks," he said. He squeezed the handset and said, "Reed, here, General."

"You recognize my voice?"

"Yes, sir, I do."

"Tell me what you've seen."

In his mind, Reed could see General LeMay sitting in his huge office, the dark curtains pulled to block out the late afternoon sun, leaving him in shadows. He would be sitting in a high-backed, leather chair, facing a huge bookcase filled with volumes on science, history, the Civil War, World War I, and the classics from the ancient Greeks to the modern works of Hemingway and Fitzgerald. There would be a cold drink near his left hand, as well as a smoking cigar. He would puff on it only frequently enough to keep it burning. He would look like a rich man in his library discussing business. Instead of a suit, he would be wearing a uniform with the general's stars glistening on the shoulders and brightly colored ribbons above the left breast pocket. As he smoked, he would be staring up, at the ceiling, as if something fascinating had just appeared there.

Closing his eyes to focus his thoughts, Reed said, "I haven't seen anything. I have watched the radar, seen the blips, but those have been interpreted by the radar operator. If he has accurately related what we have witnessed, then we were looking at some kind of metallic craft that outperforms anything we have." He let go of the button.

"You said metallic."

"Yes, sir, that I did. It was the interpretation of the radar man that the radar return was caused by some kind of manufactured, and therefore, metallic craft."

"You don't agree?"

"Yes, sir, I do agree. I'm merely pointing out that we have no visual confirmation of the craft from this facility or by personnel who are assigned here that proves the object is metallic. It is an assumption based solely on the strength of the radar return and the radar man's claimed expertise."

"What are you telling me, Jack?"

Reed took a deep breath, exhaled, and then squeezed the button on the phone. "I have a couple of dozen sightings around southern New Mexico by credible observers. They are describing a disk-shaped object that they believe to be metal. I have the radar tracings here that suggest the same thing. I would just be more comfortable if while the object is on the screen here, someone outside was watching it with binoculars while someone else was taking pictures of it for study later. Motion pictures would be best."

"What's your feeling on this?"

Reed knew what he was being asked. He said, "I think that we could stay here for another six months and never get what we want. I think I should go back to Roswell."

"You got a honey waiting there?"

"No, sir. But I can't see where sitting here is going to do any good. Hell, you've got others here who know more about this than I do and we've got radar at Roswell."

"That Ground Approach stuff isn't up and operating yet."

"Actually, sir, the scopes are operating. We've got a couple of the other mobile sets too."

"You don't think you need to stay there?"

"General," said Reed, "I'm not a radar man. I'm standing around here, watching bright little blips jump around the scope and I don't know what I'm seeing. Somebody has to tell me what it is and then I tell you. The guys here, Williams and Davis, can tell you as much as I can. They're probably more qualified."

"But you are seeing something?"

"Yes, General, I'm seeing something and I'm relying on the radar operator to tell me what I'm seeing."

There was quiet at the other end for a moment and Reed wondered if the general had picked up the cigar for a puff or two. Finally the general said, "Go ahead and secure there."

"I can stay here, General."

"No, Jack, you're right. I'll get a radar guy from Tucson. You verified that something is going on, so it won't be a waste of time. You going back tonight?"

"I can stay on here."

"Ruidoso has got to be nice at this time of year."

Now Reed grinned. He said, "Well, it's very cool in the mountains."

"Jack, seriously, hang on there until the morning. You don't have to sit in the radar shack, but have someone there to call you if something appears. Have a nice dinner in the officer's club, get some sleep and head back to Roswell tomorrow morning."

"Yes, General."

Again there was a moment of silence, and when the general came back on, Reed could hear the clink of ice cubes in the background. He said, "If something happens, let me know."

"Yes, sir."

The line went dead and Reed placed the handset on the cradle. He stood up and walked to the door. He told the sergeant that he was through. He walked back to the radar room, and stepped outside for a cigarette. He noticed that it was very dark but the sky was filled with stars. The splash of the Milky Way seemed to be quite bright. He didn't allow his mind to wander. Instead he just smoked his cigarette, tossed the butt down and ground it into the dirt. Then, feeling as if he was about to step into the frying pan, opened the door to the radar room and entered.

CHAPTER 7

Reed was already on his way back to Roswell when the object reappeared on the radar screens over White Sands. It maneuvered as it had done the day before but no one saw a thing from the ground and no one managed to photograph it. After thirty minutes it vanished from the radar scopes and nothing new was learned and there was no new evidence obtained. Everyone was as confused as before.

After the drive through the mountains, with a stop in Ruidoso so that Reed could enjoy, briefly, the cool weather, they reached the base. Reed walked across the blazing hot parking lot, entered his office, looked at the messages stacked on his desk and then shoved them to the side. There was nothing that had to be acted on immediately and nothing that caught his interest. Instead it was the routine work that gave people something to do, used up trees and paper, and provided information to be archived somewhere at some time for those in the future who would find such things to be of interest.

He sat down and looked out the window at the brown grass that had been the parade field, and realized that nothing had changed while he was gone. He wasn't sure what he had expected to change because he had been gone about twenty-four hours, but still, something should have been different. It seemed to him as if more time had passed and that more should have changed. Instead, it was as if he had walked down the hall, gotten a drink of tepid water from the cooler and returned a few minutes later rather than a day later.

He supposed that he should see if the major was around so that he could tell him that nothing had been seen in White Sands. The object, whatever it was, had stayed up in the sky, where no one could get a very good look at it.

The phone rang and he picked it. "Reed."

"Is that the way you were taught to answer a military telephone?" asked the voice at the far end.

Reed searched his memory for a moment and then recognized the voice of an old friend, Jacob Wheeler. "No," he said, "But you're lucky that I answered it at all."

"What in the hell is your problem?" asked Wheeler, laughing.

Reed looked at the stack of messages again, at the stained blotter that had been on his desk for months, at the two pens in the holder, neither of which worked, and the fan that he needed to turn on to help cool the place. It was as if he was being told that his military career was at an end, stagnating in New Mexico even though he was assigned to the only atomic strike force in the world. But that was the point. He was in New Mexico, away from everything of any importance while Wheeler was in Washington where everything was happening or if it hadn't happened, it was about to. Even worse, if it hadn't happened, they were about to cause it to.

"I think it's too hot."

"Hot or not, what can you tell me about these flying saucers?" asked Wheeler.

Now Reed laughed. "You believe there are flying saucers, little boy?"

"It doesn't matter what I believe, or don't believe. What do you know?"

"I don't know anything. What would make you think that I know anything?"

"A conversation I had with a certain general," said Wheeler carefully.

"You are aware that this is an unsecured line."

There was a hesitation and then Wheeler said, "So there is something to the flying saucers."

Reed felt his stomach turn over. He was suddenly frightened, though he couldn't have told anyone why he was afraid. Maybe it was the nature of the inquiry from Washington. Maybe it was the use of an unsecured line for such a telephone call. Maybe it was the tone in Wheeler's voice, or the mere fact they were having the conversation at all.

"I don't know that there is. I haven't seen anything to convince me, one way or the other, that they are something other than misidentifications."

"So the general was wrong," said Wheeler carefully.

Reed was now puzzled. He couldn't figure out why Wheeler had called, why he kept referring to the private call between Reed and the general, or what he hoped to learn. More importantly, Wheeler was ignoring his warning about the telephone line being unsecured. He was pressing hard for information. Reed said, "I don't know which general you're talking about. There are so many of them in Washington."

Wheeler laughed. "Well, I just called to tell you that I was coming out your way for a short visit. Actually, I'm on my way to Santa Ana, but thought I'd drop in on you and make you buy me lunch at that fancy officer's club of yours."

With that Reed relaxed. Now that he knew what was happening, he felt better about it. "How long can you stay?"

"Day or so. Maybe run down to Carlsbad to look at the cave if you can get away."

"Why? That's just a big hole in the ground."

"Well, it's something to see."

"When will you be here?"

"Next couple of days or so, depending on the arrangements. Might be traveling with a woman."

Reed smiled to himself. "She someone important?"

"Not to me. We're just working together."

"Well, you know where I am," said Reed.

"That I do, old man. That I do. I'll give you a shout when I arrive in New Mexico. Got to run."

"See you in a couple of days, then."

"Right."

The line went dead. Reed hung up and then spun around so that he was again looking out the window. The last time he

had seen Wheeler was when they carried him out of the rear
of the battered B-17 in the last days of the war. It had supposed to have been a milk run with most of the Luftwaffe
swept from the sky and Germany open to repeated and deadly
allied bombings. Its cities were in ruin, the industry destroyed
and the military forces retreating on all fronts. Collapse was
only days away and it was getting tough to find targets worth
the effort. Reed, as a fighter pilot, had been escorting the B-
17s on the mission and had landed behind the badly damaged
aircraft that Wheeler had flown.

CHAPTER 8

April 15, 1945
European Theater of
Operations
Wenbelly Air Field, England

Jacob Wheeler, like so many of the pilots in the Eighth Air Force, was a very young man, who had dark hair and dark eyes and who believed that he was invincible. He had dropped out of college with a single semester remaining because he had been assured a slot in flight school so that he could become an Army Air Forces pilot and because he was convinced that the war would be over if he waited for graduation. He had survived flight school and had eventually been trained as a bomber pilot though he, and almost everyone else, had hoped to be trained as a fighter pilot. The glory went to the fighter pilots with the tiny swastikas painted under their canopies showing victories over the Nazis, but the job of winning the war went to the bomber pilot, who would destroy Hitler's capability to wage war.

While he had been somewhat disappointed with the assignment, he had not been overly so. What he actually hoped was that he would not get killed in the war. He had read the newspapers and seen the newsreels regularly so that he knew what the situation was, even as the final collapse of Germany began.

When he arrived in England, he had been assigned to a crew and began the routine, if flying bombing missions against the enemy's homeland could ever be called routine. A number of the missions had been scrubbed simply because the planning could not be completed before ground forces had overrun the target areas. The Russians were nearly to Berlin and Georgie Patton's Third Army seemed to be racing them for that prize.

But that didn't mean that the bombing campaign was going to end. There were still concentrations of German troops, equipment, and supplies that had to be neutralized. If they could be destroyed, they could not be used against the rapidly advancing friendly armies and it could save thousands of American, and Allied, lives.

Wheeler had flown a dozen missions as a copilot, which meant he had little or no responsibility, other than tuning the radios and being prepared to take over the controls if the pilot was killed or wounded. They had been jumped by fighters once and they had been shot at by ground units on every mission. A few planes had sustained damage and Wheeler had watched as two B-17s had fallen out of the formation, one of them in flames. Both had crashed on the allied side of the battle line and only one man had been killed.

Wheeler's last mission had been the rough one. The air mission commander had said afterwards that it rivaled some of the worst in the middle of the war when no one knew for sure who would win and the Germans held all of Europe in their hands. The flack had been so thick that it looked like a single black cloud over the target, and the fighters had been nipping at them almost from the moment they had crossed the battle line. The fighters left only as the flack began to hammer at them.

The sky had been clear as far as he could see. The formation was flying at twenty-five thousand feet where the air was freezing cold and the vapor trails from the four engines of the bombers stretched out behind them, almost like an arrow pointing to the armada. They had crossed the European coast and looked down to see a line of Allied tanks moving toward the east. They had been nearly invisible, the column needle thin.

The fighter escort joined them and fell in with them, like bees surrounding them. Wheeler was always happy to see them because it meant that the enemy fighters would have to deal with them before they could attack the bombers. And each bomber had a number of machine guns for additional protection. The bombers had enough of a sting that the enemy fighters had to respect them.

Wheeler had leaned back in the seat, the chill of the air circulating through the aircraft making his joints ache. He hated the cold. Hated how it infected everything. The electric suits, the heated boots, and the fur-lined flight jackets failed to keep the cold out and him warm. The damp weather in England didn't help either.

But he was enjoying the sight of the pale blue sky with the bright white trails drawn across it. He studied the other aircraft in the tight formation, marveling at how all the pilots could maintain their positions so precisely. It was almost as if they were all connected by wires or beams or metal tubes. Each plane reacting with the others around it in an intricate dance choreographed by the lead bomber's command pilot.

They were going to hit an industrial area that was now little more than rubble, but intelligence had said that twenty or thirty percent of the manufacturing capability remained. That hadn't meant that anything was being built there, only that the Germans had the ability to do so if they wanted to and that couldn't be allowed. Not now anyway.

Over the radios, Wheeler heard some comments by other pilots. Radio discipline had slipped a little because the German air force had been eliminated. Fatso Goering had said no bomb would fall on Germany, but now they were raining out of the sky and Goering wasn't nearly as arrogant as he had been.

Wheeler was busy, figuring how many more missions he would have to fly before he could rotate home and how many hours of flight time that would be if the missions were not all to Germany. He was averaging the length of the missions, the number of missions flown per week and then trying to estimate how many more weeks that would be before he had reached the required number for rotation.

When he finished, he touched the switch for the intercom and said, "Boys, I believe that I have about seven weeks left here, if the missions continue at the same pace as they have and no one changes the rules on us again."

"And then we all go home?" asked the right waist gunner,

a young man from Ohio. He was not the brightest of the men on the crew.

"Well, if not home," said Wheeler, "then we'll stand down and not have to fly. At least no more trips to Germany."

"None whatsoever?"

Wheeler grinned behind the hard rubber of the oxygen mask. It was the easiest way to start a conversation. Just suggest the rotation would come soon and each crewman felt an obligation to make a comment about it.

It was then that the German fighters dived out of the sun seeming to catch everyone by surprise. They burned through the formation, their machine guns blazing, the tracers striking the aircraft around Wheeler.

He jerked upright and said, "Jesus." His first instinct was to grab the controls, but the pilot had his hands on the wheel and the throttles. He was sitting there as calmly has he had been a moment before, seeming to ignore everything that was swirling around the aircraft.

"You want it?" the pilot asked, meaning did Wheeler want to take the controls.

Wheeler shook his head and said, "You keep it." He turned to look to his left and watched as one of the B-17s began to spin away from the formation, two of its engines on fire. Parachutes began to blossom as the crew bailed out one at a time. Wheeler counted them until all ten had gotten out of the burning plane.

The escort fighters broke off, chasing the Germans, firing at them with streaks of red as the tracers cut through the sky. One of the enemy exploded. Another slowly broke apart and Wheeler watched as the pilot jettisoned the canopy, stepped out onto the wing and then jumped away. A few seconds later the plane exploded and the flaming debris seemed to envelop the parachute canopy, setting it ablaze. It ripped and flared and disappeared as the man plunged toward the ground.

"Where are they coming from?" asked Wheeler. His eyes were wide. He was suddenly very scared.

"Got another coming in on the left," said one of the gunners. Then, "I got him. *I got him.* Look at that son of a bitch burn."

And in that instant, all the enemy fighters disappeared. Wheeler knew that meant the flak would be coming up at them. Early in the war the clouds of flak had been so thick they seemed to blot out the sun. But so many German guns had been destroyed by the air force, or peeled away to protect the remnants of the German army trying to defend Berlin, that little flak was now seen. But today, again, the sky was filled. One aircraft exploded as flak ringed it. Another lost part of a wing, but held tight in the formation for the protection it offered. A third caught fire and turned back away from the target.

The formation continued on, reaching the IP and turning in toward the industrial area. They settled down, flying straight and level, letting the bombardier take over who trimmed out the aircraft, kept his eye focused through the bombsight, and then mashed the button that released the bombs. As they fell away, Wheeler grabbed at the controls as the B-17 began to soar with the sudden loss of weight from the dropping bombs.

"I've got it," said the pilot so that Wheeler and the bombardier would know that he was now, again, flying the plane. Wheeler jerked his hands away from the wheel so the pilot would know that Wheeler understood who had physical possession of the controls. He then put his hands back, following through on the movements in case the pilot was wounded or killed.

They turned away from the target and it seemed as if the flak was suddenly behind them. The pilot tested the controls, but they felt fine, smooth, and he knew that his aircraft had not been critically hit.

But more flak exploded in front of them. Wheeler felt the aircraft buffeted by the shock waves of the detonations. There was a rattling, like rain on a tin roof as shrapnel peppered the skin of the B-17. Over the intercom, the pilot asked, "Everyone okay?"

"Fine back here," said one of the waist gunners.

There was another explosion, this one closer, and part of a cockpit window disintegrated.

"That was close," said the pilot as he glanced to the right.

Wheeler slumped in his seat and looked at his gloves. They were stained bright red with his blood, though he hadn't felt anything and felt no pain now. There was just the blood on his clothes that he didn't understand.

"Co-pilot's hit," the pilot said over the intercom, his voice high and tight. "Help him."

One man appeared and reached around to unfasten Wheeler's seatbelt and harness. He pulled at him and tried to work him out of the seat while Wheeler, thoroughly confused, tried to figure out what had happened to him.

Over the roar from the engines, and the icy wind now whipping through the cockpit, the pilot shouted, "Is he alive?"

The man leaned close to the pilot and said, "Alive. Doesn't look too bad. Lots of blood, but I don't think anything vital was hit." Wheeler grinned because he had clearly heard every word.

Outside the flak was still popping, but it was now only thin, occasional puffs of black smoke that seemed to belong in another place and another time and was no longer a threat to them. They had run through the flak corridor and were out, away from it now. Wheeler, still unconcerned about his wounds and still feeling no pain, expected the German fighters to return now, but they didn't.

As they flew away from the target, the flak, and the enemy fighters, Wheeler began to relax. Sweat and blood had dripped down his sides and his underarms were clammy, but he was relaxed. He suddenly realized that his calculations had been in error. It wouldn't be seven weeks, but maybe seven days. The wounds had changed the equation.

He heard the pilot take a deep breath, and then call over his shoulder, "How's Wheeler."

The Ohio gunner yelled back. "He'll be okay. Little shrapnel in his side, and a cut on his forehead."

"Okay," said the pilot. "Get him warm."

As they headed back to England, and they reached the coast, they dropped down, into warmer, calmer air. In minutes, they were near the airfield and were making the landing run. As they did, one of the men fired two flares from the rear, telling those on the ground that there were wounded on board. Before they rolled to a stop, an ambulance was with them, trailing them, waiting to care for the injured.

Wheeler was lifted from the rear of the craft, and stretched out on the grass next to the runway so that medics could take a quick look at the wounds. Wheeler shaded his eyes from the bright sunlight and studied the damage to the bomber. It was superficial. Sheet metal would fix the outer skin in a couple of hours. The cockpit windows would be repaired before sunup the next day. The plane wasn't badly damaged and Wheeler knew he hadn't been badly hurt.

Wheeler later learned that there had been only a couple more missions, but the German resistance disintegrated and the new German government quickly surrendered. Wheeler had survived the war, but only because he had gotten into it so late in the game, or so he believed.

But because of the war, because of the treatment offered, and because there were so many Americans stationed in England, he hadn't had the chance to see much of Europe, except from the air and then he had been so busy that he hadn't gotten a very good look.

CHAPTER 9

Danni Hackett stood in the center of her apartment, a pool of light from a lamp on an end table to the left and the overhead light in her bedroom showing through the door providing the only illumination. She glanced down at the newspaper on the coffee table, over at the radio playing softly, and then back to Jacob Wheeler who sat in an old fashioned, wooden rocking chair. She was dressed in shorts and a blouse to combat the heavy, muggy air of Washington, D.C. in July, and still she felt hot and miserable. She wished Wheeler would go away and leave her alone so that she could take a cool bath and then go to bed.

To Wheeler she said, "I don't understand why we have to go to New Mexico tonight."

Wheeler, dressed for travel on a military aircraft, was wearing dark trousers and a short-sleeve shirt. He reached for the newspaper on the coffee table. He was away from the light so that his facial expressions were lost in the shadows.

"We have to go to New Mexico because they're getting the best of the flying saucer sightings there. They're getting radar and visual stuff."

"Why isn't the military doing this?" she asked. "It seems to be a military problem."

Wheeler grinned broadly, knowing that she would only see his teeth, and said, "I am military."

"You know what I mean."

"General Spaatz is in the northwest with his people. Another team is in east Texas to look at the stuff there. We lucked out and drew New Mexico."

Still agitated, she sat down on the couch opposite Wheeler's chair and looked out the open window. There didn't seen to be a breath of air coming from the outside, just the sound of traffic and the occasional chirp of an insect. The humidity hung in the room like wet laundry. She crossed her legs slowly and said, in a somewhat whiny voice, "I don't want to go to New Mexico. I don't like New Mexico. They have snakes."

"If you're real nice," he said, laughing, "I might take you to Carlsbad Caverns."

She pushed her damp hair away from her face and then tugged at her blouse so that she could blow down the front of it. She looked up at Wheeler, suddenly extremely irritated. She didn't like people telling her what she had to do, when she had to do it, and believing that she would do it because they said so. Orders made her feel like a little girl, and it had been a long time since she had not been in control of her life. She had decided which college to attend, made all the arrangements without telling anyone where she planned to go, and with only a small assist from her parents had paid for it herself. They hadn't liked her choice of majors, nor that she planned on a career rather than a husband, but she had made her own decisions about that. Now there was this. A group of military men, in the world's ugliest office building, had decided that she had to go to New Mexico. Tonight.

She said again, but more forcefully, "But I don't want to go to New Mexico."

"Oh, just pack a couple of things and let's get going. It's only for a couple of days." He waved a hand and then added, "Besides, you don't have a choice."

That really angered her. "I don't have a choice."

"You want to keep your job?"

She smiled evilly at him. "I can find another one tomorrow if you keep annoying me."

Wheeler set the newspaper back on the table and rubbed his face with both hands. "I would think, at this point, with what

you now know, they would much rather have you in jail than
let you quit."

"What in the hell are you talking about?"

"Danni, this is serious. They don't play games at this level.
Too many people can be too easily hurt if things get out of
hand. They have the power to put you into a, shall we say,
'home'? Anyway, you would be held there until the threat had
ended, whenever that might be. They would determine the
threat and when it ended and there would be no appeal. Sometimes you just have to play the game."

"Oh, come on, this isn't the war."

Wheeler was suddenly serious. "You have a unique background, which is why you are here. You are privy to information that would make the Manhattan Project look like a low
level secret. Right now they don't know what they have or
what is happening. There are some frightened people at the
Pentagon. Very frightened."

"Frightened?"

Wheeler took a deep breath. "Yeah. Frightened. I'm not sure
what they are worried about, but I can see it in the eyes. I
think it has to do with the war. Remember, after Pearl Harbor
there were months when it looked as if the war had been lost
already. Our Pacific fleet was in ruins, the Japanese were running loose in the Pacific, the Germans had taken over most of
Europe and were pushing the Soviets toward Moscow. No one
knew if we had the time, or the resources, to turn it around.
There were some badly frightened people. Now, I see the same
thing here. Maybe for the same reasons. They don't know if
we have the time or the resources to combat this."

She stared at him, now slightly frightened herself. "But you
said it was all a test of some kind."

"Yes, I did say that. Wishful thinking on my part. I've
talked to a few of the people. I found out that the leader of
the meeting, Dr. Moore, is a top psychologist but his speciality
is not research. He's an expert in human reaction under stress.
He was brought in to control things because someone realized
how stressful this, what? Invasion? Contact? Whatever you
want to call it, could be."

"Jesus," she said. "I hadn't thought this through." She sat back in the chair, and looked at the darkened street outside her window. She had been intrigued by the possibility of intelligent life on other worlds, and the possibility that they had gotten here. But even with the gun camera film she had seen, it was still an abstract idea. It was just pictures, movies. She had seen a lot of things in the movies that were impossible. There had always been the thought that this was as impossible and as unreal as the horror movies she had watched as a kid. Now she was seeing that the adults, meaning the men in power in the government and at the Pentagon, were treating these events, these sightings, not as a game, or an exercise, or an experiment, but were treating it all as a threat to the United States. It was suddenly more serious than she had believed.

Looking at Wheeler, she said, "Deep down, while I wanted this to be true, I believed it to be a joke. I believed it to be a test of people under stress given impossible information."

"Yeah," said Wheeler, "I know. But it isn't a test. It's real."

Without thinking further, and without realizing that her attitude had suddenly changed, she said, "I don't know what to take. What's the weather like there?"

"Hot and dry. Very hot and usually very dry. Sometimes there are thunderstorms that cool the evenings momentarily. But mostly it's just hot and dry."

"Great."

"We've got a plane standing by at Andrews to take us out there. We should be in New Mexico about four or five in the morning."

Staring at him, she said, "Speaking of morning, why can't we just fly out in the morning?"

"Because we need to get there to see what is happening. And the plane has already been scheduled and I don't have the power to change that schedule."

"I don't know what to wear." But that was just a stalling tactic. She was trying to buy a few minutes to think.

"Wear what you have on. You'll be a big hit with the aircrew."

"I'm not going to New Mexico dressed like this," she said. "How long do we have?"

"The plane is sitting on the tarmac and the crew is sitting in the cockpit waiting for us. We are the only passengers so they're not going any place without us."

"Do I have time for a shower?"

"A quick one. We really shouldn't keep the air crew waiting too long. It's not polite. They have lives outside of the military."

Hackett stood up and walked toward the rear of the apartment. She turned, looked back through the door and said, "I thought I had a life outside of this."

Wheeler turned serious again. "You might not, after we get to New Mexico."

Hackett felt a sudden chill but to Wheeler said, "That's this afternoon's paper if you're interested in it."

"Mind if I turn up the radio?"

"Go ahead. I'll be about twenty minutes or so."

"Thanks."

She walked into the bedroom and closed the door. She looked at her closet, the unmade bed, the pile of books, memos, papers, and documents stacked on the floor and then stepped to the vanity. She glanced at herself in the mirror, staring at her sweat-damp hair and then at the beads of sweat at her hair line and along her upper lip. She wanted to sit down for a minute and think but no longer had the time. She wanted a chance to review what Wheeler had said, to decompress as the combat pilots had called it. Instead, she stripped, grabbed her robe off the bed where she had thrown it earlier in the day, and then headed for the bathroom.

CHAPTER | 10

President Harry S Truman found it difficult to sleep. His world was changing, or rather the whole world was changing, and he was responsible for it. He was the one who cut the military loose, to do what they believed was best for the country.

He threw the covers aside and sat up, but didn't want to turn on the light, afraid that he would awaken Bess.

"Harry, what is it?"

"Nothing. Go back to sleep. I'm just going to walk around for a few minutes."

He left the bedroom and stepped into a sitting room. He closed the door and walked to the couch, but didn't turn on the light. The instant he did, someone would appear to assist him even though all he wanted was to be left alone. He would have to explain that he wanted nothing and he needed no one. He just wanted to relax for a moment, taking a break from the role of President, away from everything pressing in on him.

This late night prowl was LeMay's fault. LeMay wanted to bring down an alien craft so that he, and his scientists in Research and Development, could study it. He wanted it because he saw it as a perfect weapons system, one that would be so far superior to what the Soviets could build that American domination would be unchallenged. There would not be another Pearl Harbor because the Soviets would know that the Americans could destroy them whenever they wanted. We had the atomic bomb and they didn't. Now we would have the delivery system that could outmaneuver and outfly anything they could put in the sky.

But LeMay might not have seen the bigger picture. It was one that confused him because he didn't understand it either. These alien creatures, probably not the Martians of the science fiction books, had traveled an incredible distance to get to Earth. They might have come in peace, or as the advance party for an invasion. No one knew. All that Truman knew was that they were from out there, trillions of miles from Earth.

They needed answers because they had to prepare. LeMay wanted to bring one down, but that was an act of interplanetary war, a war that might have already been started. Truman understood the overall logistics of the situation. They'd had enough trouble fighting a war in Europe and one in the Pacific, trying to move men, supplies and materiel thousands of miles to the front.

It couldn't be any easier for these creatures because there was no evidence they had a base hidden in the Solar System. It meant their lines of communication would be incredibly long so that a war on Earth would be difficult for them to fight. Of course, if they were the beginning of the invasion, then the war was already lost. They held the high ground and could operate so far outside the envelope of anything the United States had it would be like sending the Crusaders against the Marines. The Crusaders wouldn't stand a chance.

But, if they could bring one down, understand it, then the United States had a chance. And, these creatures had to be of superior intellect. It was also possible to convince them that a terrible accident had taken place.

Truman leaned back and closed his eyes momentarily. He didn't feel good about passing the responsibility to LeMay, but then LeMay wanted it. Truman believed that the people might not understand the necessity of bringing one down, and if the activity could be hidden, there would be no Earth-based consequence. If not, LeMay was willing to take the heat, and the fall, because it would give him an aircraft that would outfly the Soviets.

This was the right course of action because the consequences were negligible and the rewards were significant. Suddenly, he wasn't nearly as worried as he had been. Now he felt tired and thought he could sleep. Now he could go back to bed.

CHAPTER 11

Jack Reed gave up for the day and walked from his office to the Officer's Club. It wasn't much of a walk, and although it was late in the afternoon, with the sun sinking toward the mountains west of the base, it was still blazing hot. He wondered about the wisdom of walking, but then he was at the entrance to the club. As he opened the door, he felt the welcome cool of the recently installed air conditioning. Reed thought that he might just take up residence in the club just to beat the heat.

Inside, he popped into the bar to search for a familiar face. Sitting at a table, a beer in front of him, was Thomas Brady. He was a young officer, one of those trained at the very end of the war, who had missed the action in both the European Theater and the Pacific, but who had been sent to Japan after the surrender as part of the occupation force. He had participated in Operation Crossroads, the atomic tests at Bikini in 1946, but then, so had most of those on the base.

"Hi Tom. Need some company?"

Brady looked up and grinned. "Have a seat Jack. What are you drinking?"

"I think a martini tonight. I'm not in a beer mood. After all, it is the Fourth of July."

Brady lifted a hand to catch the attention of the waitress. To Reed he said, "What have they got you doing on a holiday?"

Reed grinned and lowered his voice conspiratorially. "Chasing flying saucers."

The waitress arrived, took the order and disappeared again. As she walked away, Brady said, "There anything to that?"

"You know, you're the second person to ask me that very question in about the last hour or so."

"And?"

"I don't know. Seems that there is something real out there. Seems that we've got them flying over us, but I just don't know. Doesn't seem that it's only drunks who see them, contrary to the emerging belief."

"They Russian?" asked Brady.

The waitress returned, put the drink in front of Reed and then waited until Brady gave her a dollar bill. When he said, "Keep it," she grinned and fled before he could change his mind.

Reed took a long drink and then pulled the olives clear. He ate one and then said, "I wouldn't think so. If you've got the capability to do this, the last thing you're going to do is fly it over enemy territory. If one crashes, then we can do it too. You keep it under wraps, flying it over Siberia until the balloon goes up."

"Propaganda," said Brady. "You fly it over your enemy and scare the shit out of him."

Reed nodded, took a drink and then said, "Nah. You keep it hidden until you need some sort of leverage. If the Russians were trying to take over the rest of Europe, maybe they'd fly it around where we might see it, but at the moment they're happy with what they have. No need to reveal the big secret."

"They got to be worried about us coming back to liberate Eastern Europe."

Reed thought about that and said, "No, I don't think so. We've stripped our armies in Europe and we're demobilizing here and they know it. Hell, we got a sergeant here who was a general during the war."

"What the hell is he doing here as a sergeant?" asked Brady.

"He's got something like a year to retirement. He finishes

out his year and then retires as a general. Wouldn't you do it?"

Brady grinned, thinking of the possibilities. "He's someone you wouldn't want to irritate."

Reed laughed. "Probably making a list of the people he wants to see when he retires." Reed finished the martini.

"Want another?"

"Yes," said Reed, "but I better eat some dinner first."

"Mind if I join you?" asked Brady.

"No, I would enjoy the company."

They stood up and a sergeant pushed through the crowd to them. He leaned close to Reed and said, "We've got a call. Things are popping over at White Sands."

"So?"

"You need to get back to the office, sir."

"Now? I was just going to eat. Besides, it's a holiday."

"Now, sir," the sergeant insisted.

Reed looked toward Brady. "Sorry, Tom. I've got to go back to work."

"You want me to wait?"

Reed glanced to the sergeant and raised an eyebrow. "I don't know, sir. I was just sent to find you and tell you about the call at the office."

"Give me thirty minutes," said Reed, "and if I'm not back, then go ahead."

When Reed walked into the office, he was surprised to see the overhead lights on and two men in civilian clothes sitting there waiting for him. He recognized neither of them but suspected they were CIC, Counter Intelligence Corps, because of their cheap suits. Both were small, thin men, one of them balding and the other with a full head of thick, jet black hair. Reed glanced back at the sergeant who shook his head and shrugged. Reed then said, "Can I help you?"

The man with the black hair, who had a narrow face with a big chin, pulled a wallet from his pocket and held it up so that Reed could see it. The photo ID identified him as John Douglass, and confirmed him as a member of the Army's

Counter Intelligence Corps, but gave no hint as to his rank. He hitchhiked a thumb at the other man. "He's with me."

"Un-huh," said Reed, unimpressed.

"We're here to help you."

"Yeah. And the check is in the mail."

Douglass looked back at his partner and said, "A real comedian."

The phone sitting on the corner of Reed's desk began to ring at that moment. The sergeant reached for it, answered it in a military fashion, and then held the receiver out to Reed. "It's the general, again."

Reed took it, stared into Douglass's eyes and said, "If you'll excuse me."

"We're cleared," said Douglass.

"I don't know that."

"You can take my word for it."

"Actually," said Reed, a hand cupped over the mouthpiece of the telephone, "I can't."

"I have my orders."

"Which I'll be delighted to read when I have the chance. Now, if you'll excuse me."

At first neither Douglass nor the man with him moved. Finally Douglass stood and said, "We'll wait in the hallway."

"That would be fine." As they closed the door, Reed put the phone to his ear and said, "Reed."

"Do you recognize my voice."

"Yes, sir."

"Object is down."

"General?"

"Radar indicated that the object is down, somewhere north of town. We've got to find it before anyone else, meaning civilians, the sheriff, the police, get there."

"North of town. That doesn't mean much of anything. There's a lot of empty space north of town."

"In the next few minutes there will be two Counter Intelligence agents in your office. They'll have the latest information."

Reed had to grin. He'd just thrown them out. To the general, he said, "Names?"

"John Douglass and George Campbell."

"To do this right," said Reed, "I should have some sort of photographic identification."

"They'll hand it to you."

"General, I should have had it yesterday. You've got to understand that."

"Of course I do. That identification is on its way to you by courier. For the moment, you'll have to take the identification they provide and assume that they are who they say they are on verbal authorization from me."

"Yes, sir. A verbal description of them from you would be nice."

The general provided it and then said, "They'll have the information you need to get out there. To the site."

"Yes, sir. And just what am I supposed to be doing."

"Secure the area. Survey the area. Do what needs to be done to preserve it."

"You're telling me that the object, whatever it might be, has crashed."

"Our assumption, based on the data we have at hand, including a reconnaissance flight made about an hour ago, suggests that the object has crashed."

"And if someone has survived?" asked Reed.

"Security is the most important aspect of this. Survival of the injured is secondary to that security. If medical aid can be rendered without compromising security on the scene, then such aid will be provided."

"This is a hell of a thing, general," said Reed. He stood there, looking out the window, but almost unable to think. "A hell of a thing. I think maybe I should point out that I'm just an intelligence officer here with no real authority."

"I know, Jack. I'll make some arrangements with Colonel Blanchard. In the meantime, treat this as if you've, that is the 509th, has lost a bomb." He hesitated, and then added, "You know what I mean. That should give you some guidelines."

Reed walked around his desk and dropped into his chair. It

screeched in protest. He looked at the papers on his desk, but didn't really see them. "I guess that will work."

"This is a special circumstance, Jack. You're going to have to play it by ear. But you've got to get rolling. Start thinking."

"Yes, sir."

"There'll be support coming in shortly. They too will be cleared. Expect them."

"Yes, sir."

"I have faith in you." The line went dead.

Reed sat for a moment and then carefully hung up the telephone. He stood, walked to the door and spotted the two men, standing near a butt can, smoking. One of them, Douglass, was reading the messages posted on the bulletin board, some of which had been there since the end of the Second World War. The other one, Campbell, was staring at the floor as if there was something extremely interesting on it.

Douglass saw him and said, "General clue you in?"

Reed decided that he didn't like the man. Didn't like his attitude. He didn't like his civilian clothes, his brand of cigarettes, his face, or the fact he was standing in the hall asking sarcastic questions. There was an arrogant attitude about him that made him seem self-important.

"Yeah," he said. "He also mentioned that you had other identification and additional information."

"That we do, pal. That we do."

"Well, come on in. I think we've got a lot to do."

Both men threw their cigarettes into the butt cans and started to the office. Once inside, Douglass shut the door and then dropped into one of the two chairs set close to Reed's desk. He pulled an envelope from the inside pocket of his suit jacket and handed it to Reed.

Reed opened it slowly, found photographs of both men and copies of their orders, including the confirmation that both were cleared for top secret information including that relating to atomic weapons, the so-called "Q" clearance. He walked around his desk and sat down, studying the documents that he had been handed. "Okay," he said, "The general said that further identification would be hand carried to me by courier some time in the very near future."

If he had hoped for some reaction, he was disappointed. Neither man seemed to care. Of course, had they been enemy agents, they would have been trained well enough to conceal their reactions to such a transparent attempt to frighten them.

"What is our first order of business?" asked Reed.

Douglass half stood and dragged his chair closer to the desk. He pulled a map from his side pocket and unfolded it carefully, spreading it out. He pointed to a line that had been drawn by a black, broad-tipped marker.

"What we know," said Douglass, "is that the object is down somewhere along this line. Aerial reconnaissance has suggested that it is in this area, here."

"And we're supposed . . . ?"

Douglass looked up from the map. "We need security people, medical people, intel, the whole ball of wax."

"Provost marshal for security," said Reed. "We've got a full hospital . . ."

Douglass said, "I know what you're thinking, but we've got to get into the field. We don't want some civilian stumbling over this in the meantime."

"The general said to treat this as if we had lost an atomic bomb. I suppose that we call the provost marshal . . ." And then Reed had another, more immediate thought. "We've got to coordinate this through Colonel Blanchard's office."

"Why don't you call him," said Douglass. "I'm sure that you'll find that he's already been briefed by higher headquarters and is coordinating things from his end."

"Then why are you here? In my office?"

"Because this is bigger than just this base," said Douglass.

In less than an hour Reed found himself sitting in a jeep. With the map in his lap, a flashlight with a red lens on it in his hand, he was attempting to find a way to head to the west off the main north-south highway. There had been some tracks to the left, but they could hardly be called roads. They led off into the high desert to the west, but Reed had no idea where they went, or even how far they went. They could dead-end a hundred yards from the highway or they could reach fifty miles to the highway from Corona to Tularosa.

They pulled the side of the road and Douglass pointed toward the Capitan Mountains. "What's over there?"

"Nothing," said Reed. "We've got a bombing range. There are scattered ranch houses, but nothing else."

"Well, I see something," said Douglass. He shifted into neutral and set the brake. He stepped out of the jeep and put both hands up, around his eyes.

Campbell hopped out of the back and handed Douglass a scarred leather case that held binoculars. "Use these, sir." It was the first time that he had spoken, or indicated that he was able to speak.

Douglass took them out of the case and handed that back and then put the binoculars up to his eyes. He scanned the horizon. He finally passed the binoculars to Reed who had joined them. "Over there," he said pointing.

"I don't see anything other than a blue glow."

"Yeah. What is that?"

"Don't know. There's nothing over there that should be causing that light." Reed gave the binoculars back to Douglass.

As Douglass handed the binoculars to Campbell, he turned, and climbed behind the wheel. "Well, let's go check it out."

They drove north a mile or so and then found a track to the west. They turned down it, and bounced along. A jack rabbit ran through the headlights. Far to the west, lightning flashed and several seconds later there was the low, quiet rumble of distant thunder.

The road faded and then ended, but Douglass kept driving to the west, swerving to avoid the yucca plants and Joshua trees. Finally they came to a fence line and rolled to a stop.

Douglass looked over his shoulder at Campbell. "See if you can knock down one of those posts."

Campbell climbed out of the jeep again, walked to one of the posts, put his foot against it, shoving. There was a crack like a pistol shot as the post broke away from its base, but the fence still stood.

Douglass pulled forward and stopped when the nose of the jeep was against the barb wire. He waited until Campbell was back in the jeep. Then he rolled forward slowly, letting the pressure build. One wire snapped as did a second and then the third. The fence post that had been hanging fell to the ground.

Douglass stopped for a moment and then shifted again, starting off. They drove across the desert, bounced around a small hill and then topped a rise.

"Christ," said Douglass.

"That's got to be it," said Campbell but his voice was quiet. He spoke in a whisper.

Without thinking about it, Douglass turned off the engine and slowly got out. He stood, staring into the distance, unaware of the wind that had come up.

Reed and Campbell joined him, and Douglass handed Reed the binoculars. Reed looked down at the center of the blue glow as Douglass said, "That's definitely not one of ours."

"I thought we were talking about some experimental aircraft," said Reed. "I really thought that it would be one of ours. I didn't expect anything like this."

"Neither did I," said Douglass.

"We better get on the radio," said Campbell. "We're going to need some help."

"We're going to need a lot of it," said Reed.

CHAPTER 12

July 4, 1947
Andrews Army Air Field
Washington, D.C.

Danni Hackett stood at the picture window in the operations building at Andrews Army Air Field, looking out at the four-engine airplane standing on the tarmac. Men were climbing on it and around it, and one of the engine cowlings was open. Bright lights on long poles stood near that engine as one man seemed to be hammering at it with a huge wrench.

"They say it will be at least another thirty minutes," said Wheeler.

Without looking at him, she said, "This does not inspire me with great confidence."

"It should," said Wheeler. "They caught the problem and are attempting to fix it. Better here and better now than once we've taken off."

A sergeant wearing a wrinkled khaki uniform that showed no ribbons or wings or combat badges approached and said, "Mr. Wheeler, there's a telephone call for you."

Wheeler raised his eyebrows. "Telephone?"

"If you'll follow me."

Hackett watched them disappear through a somewhat battered door, into an office. She looked at the coffee pot that sat on a small table that had dirty brown paper towels for a cloth but didn't want a cup. She looked at the stained couch pushed against one darkly paneled wall but didn't want to sit. She knew that she would be sitting for the next several hours with nowhere to go but another part of the airplane. What she wanted deeply was to be home, in her own apartment, with

her own fan blowing down on her as she lay in bed waiting
to go to sleep. That would be the ideal situation and much
better that standing around in a hot, poorly ventilated building,
at an Army base waiting to board an Army airplane to take
her to another Army base somewhere in southern New Mexico.

Wheeler approached her then, with his eyes wide and bright.
His face was nearly pure white. He waited until the sergeant
had returned to his desk and out of earshot before he leaned
close to her.

"We got one," he said, his voice high with excitement. He
glanced toward the sergeant, making sure that he wasn't close
enough to listen.

"Got one what?"

He looked around carefully and leaned closer. "One of them
crashed," he said.

For a moment she didn't understand what he was saying.
And then, in a sudden flash she knew. She felt her head spin
and the blood drain from her face. She reached out and put a
hand on his arm to steady herself. "Are you sure?"

"Something is down in New Mexico. Ground team hasn't
gone in yet."

She looked at the couch and Wheeler seemed to understand.
He guided her toward it and she sat down.

"You want something to drink?"

"No. I'm fine." She closed her eyes for a moment and then
said, "Quite a coincidence that we're on our way to New Mexico right now."

Wheeler sat down beside her. Then he stood again. One
hand shook as if he was nervous. He walked to the coffee pot,
picked up a cup, put it down and walked back to her. He sat
on the arm of the couch, suddenly trembling with nervous
energy. He leaned close to her. "We are only one team that
was going out. Others will be following us."

"I thought we were the only one going to New Mexico."

Wheeler shrugged. "We were, until this happened. I don't
know all the details. But we were going to check that radar

blip seen in southern New Mexico. Now it seems to be down. Coincidence."

"I'm not ready for this," she said.

Wheeler laughed but not with humor. "I'm not either but I want to get going." He looked as if he wanted to run out the door and to the airplane. It was almost impossible for him to sit still. He stood up and walked to the window to look at the airplane. The men still worked on it, though one of the lights had been pulled back and there were fewer men near the engine. He walked back to where Hackett sat.

"No really," she said, nervously. "I don't know anything that will help. This is all a mistake. This is all way beyond me. I'm a biologist. There is nothing out there that will require my expertise. I told you that. Told them that."

"Take it easy. We don't know what we're going to find out there. All we can do is look. If we're in over our heads, then we can call for help. We're the advance team sent in to assess the situation. They'll get someone else out there."

Hackett shook her head. She wanted to scream, to run, to stand or move. She looked at him somewhat confused and said, "There is nothing on which to draw for information. I can't research the literature to see how others have handled similar problems. I can't pull books from the library. I can't talk to other researchers because nothing like this has ever happened. I have to go into this cold."

"Science fiction," said Wheeler. "That's the only place where this problem has been discussed. John Campbell wrote about it ten, twelve years ago."

"Great," she snapped. "We're talking about doing scientific research in a science fiction library."

"Lower your voice," said Wheeler. "And no, I'm not suggesting any such a thing. I'm only saying that it is about the only place the question has been explored."

The door opened and a man looked at Wheeler and Hackett. "You two waiting for the ride to New Mexico?"

"Yeah," said Wheeler.

"If you're manifested through properly, then come on. We're about ready to go."

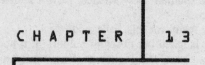

CHAPTER 13

July 4, 1947
North of Roswell,
New Mexico

It was the dull blue glow barely visible against the backdrop of a lightning filled sky. A dull blue glow that looked to be unearthly and unnatural and somewhat frightening to those riding in the lead vehicles. A dull blue glow that marked the broken, rock strewn hills.

There was no road into the desert from the main highway. There had been a dirt track that petered out a quarter mile from the concrete and nothing beyond it except a fairly flat bit of desert that gently rose in the distance. The support team assembled at the base didn't stop for the barbed wire fences that blocked their route. They punched through them with the noses of their military vehicles, ripping great chunks from the fence line, just as Reed and the others had as they first searched the area.

The support team drove down into a muddy arroyo that, during heavy rains could fill with water, washing away everything in its path. They climbed the other side and followed the contour of the hill upward, always pointed at the blue glow. That was the beacon that Reed had told them to follow.

"Seems to be brighter," said one man sitting in the rear of a car. "We're getting closer." Richard Kincaid reached down to finger the holster holding his .45 caliber pistol. At the moment the magazine for it was in his pocket but he thought about loading the weapon before they traveled much farther.

Kincaid was a fairly young man who had been trained in intelligence during the war and who had, somehow, remained with an intelligence agency after the war, as everyone was being demobilized for civilian work. He had studied mathematics in college and had thought that his talents would be used for code breaking duties, but that hadn't happened. Instead, he had displayed a talent for taking random bits of information and combining them into a complex and complete picture. His mind worked on a strange level, a sort of sixth sense, that allowed him to see connections and relations that others sometimes missed. That gave him an advantage in intelligence work, one that some envied, and others failed to notice.

During the war, he had spent his time in Washington and then London and had not heard a shot fired in anger. That had bothered him because he knew the combat veterans were going to get the prime jobs and prime promotions, but here he was, sitting in the back of an Army staff car, giving orders in what could become the biggest event of the twentieth century.

"Let's slow it down a might," said the officer sitting in the front seat, as he leaned forward, his face close to the glass of the windshield. Major Edwin Easley was the base provost marshal. He would be responsible for security on the crash site. Kincaid had only met him briefly, but Easley seemed like a competent fellow who would not hesitate to execute his orders. Just the sort of man who belonged on this.

The driver down-shifted and the engine growled. They were traveling at five miles an hour.

They reached the top of the ridge where a jeep and three men waited for them. Spread out below them was a huge, bowl-shaped canyon that faded into the darkness. Bright lightning revealed a steel water tank a mile or so distant. To the right, at the base of a far cliff, was the source of the blue glow. Trees, scrub brush, and cactus obscured the shape but they were outlined in the eerie light.

"That it?" asked the driver.

"Shit, I don't know," said Kincaid. "Wait here."

He opened the door into the brisk wind. He could smell the rain that was falling somewhere else. He stepped forward into the brightness of the headlights and walked forward, toward the downslope, seeming to ignore the jeep not far from him.

Someone came up behind him. "What you got?"

"I think we can make it. Ground's rough, but the angle isn't too steep. Should be able to drive on down there. Where's Captain Reed?"

"Standing next to his jeep behind you," said Easley.

"Maybe we should get him out here."

"Can't you handle it, Kincaid?"

"I don't like this. I don't like this at all, Major."

Easley walked forward a half dozen steps. He stared into the distance. There was nothing more to see. He turned, looking back at Kincaid, the car, and the small convoy behind it.

"Be light in an hour or two."

"We're not waiting an hour or two. Let's get moving."

Before they could move, they were joined by Reed. He walked up slowly, as if he wanted them to see him approach and recognize him first. As he got close to them, he pointed down into the canyon and said, "Nothing's changed in the last hour or so."

Kincaid looked at him and then back down at the blue glow. "What in the hell is that thing?"

Reed shrugged, not wanting to venture a guess in front of these people. He knew them by sight and by last name, but he didn't know them as friends. "Guess we'll find out."

Easley said, "I think we'd better get this show on the road. We're wasting time here."

"Ground looks a little shaky. Not the best for transport," said Kincaid.

"The ground is fine. We've got our orders." Easley turned and walked back to his jeep.

Reed watched him go and then looked at Kincaid. He was little more than a dark shape against the blue glow from the canyon. "What the hell is his problem?"

"I don't know. Maybe he's worried about the general."

Reed raised an eyebrow in question but knew that Kincaid couldn't see it. "What general?"

"Thomas."

Reed shook his head but said nothing.

Without another word, Kincaid climbed into the car, pulling the door shut. He watched Reed walk back to the jeep and crawl into the driver's seat. He could see him working the gear shift, heard the jeep backfire once and then watched as it rolled forward, down the incline. When it was clear that the jeep would make it, Kincaid said, "Let's go. Slow."

"Yes sir."

He felt the car roll forward and heard the ground crunching under the tires. It looked as if they were about to drive off into space. The hood fell and they began to roll down the hill, picking up speed.

"Careful," said Kincaid, his attention focused on the terrain directly in front of him.

They reached the bottom. The ground was flat again, almost like a table top. They drove forward, avoiding the chula cactus, boulders, and bushes. They rolled ahead, toward the blue glow, until they were a hundred yards from the cliff and then stopped. Now there were bushes and boulders blocking their path.

"Can't get much closer," said the driver.

Kincaid opened the door and got out again. He glanced at the blue glow, now much brighter, and then turned. The other vehicles had spread out on line looking as if they were going to charge forward. Military police hopped out of the rear of the truck, and fanned out but didn't move toward the cliff.

As Easley got out, Kincaid said, "I think this is about as close as we can get."

Now another man, taller, thinner, and wearing a khaki uniform walked up. "I want everyone to wait right here while we check this out."

"You think there's radiation?" asked Kincaid.

"Let's just hang loose back here."

Reed, accompanied by Douglass and Campbell, joined the small knot of men. Reed said nothing to them, listening to what they were saying. The job of security at the site was now in the hands of Major Easley. Overall authority was now Kincaid's, at least for the moment.

One man walked around from the back of a truck. He was

wearing a silver-colored protective suit complete with helmet. In his gloved hand he held a Geiger counter. He stopped when he reached the men.

"I'll go in now, Major."

"You have fifteen minutes. Check it out carefully, and then come back here."

"Yes sir."

"You get high readings, you come back here."

"Yes sir."

"Good luck."

The man started to walk toward the blue glow. He disappeared for a moment, then emerged from behind a bush. He walked down, into an arroyo at the base of the cliff.

Kincaid pulled a pack of cigarettes from his pocket, shook one out, and then offered the pack to the major. When Easley handed it back, Kincaid used his lighter, first on his own and then on the major's. He snapped the top closed, then, thinking about it, Kincaid offered Reed a cigarette, but Reed shook his head.

"Wish I could see what is happening," said Kincaid, finally.

Easley took a drag, blew out the smoke and then looked at Kincaid. "You'll see soon enough."

"You have any idea what it is?"

"Radar track looked like one of the new jet jobs. Fast. Maneuverable," volunteered Reed, knowing that whatever had crashed was not a jet.

"That's not what it is," said Kincaid. He took a pull at the cigarette, the tip glowing brightly.

"No. That's not what it is," agreed Reed.

They were joined by another man. A lieutenant who had been assigned to the base a week earlier. They didn't know much about him other than he had been a POW in Germany when the war had ended. He hadn't been back in the States more than a couple of months. Kincaid thought his name was Hart.

"It seems to be taking a long time," he said impatiently.

"It takes as long as it takes." But Easley looked at his watch noticing that little more than five minutes had passed.

The man in the protective suit suddenly reappeared walking slowly toward them. The blue glow could be seen reflecting in the silver.

The Easley threw down his cigarette, stepped on it, and walked to meet the man. Kincaid and Reed joined him. Behind them, MPs spread out in a semi-circle as if to guard the men or prevent an escape.

The man in the protective suit reached up and pulled off his helmet, letting it drop to the ground. He sat down on a boulder, dropped his gloves on the helmet, and ran a hand through his thick, sweat-damp hair.

"Well?" asked Easley.

"Damnest thing I've ever seen. Damnest thing."

"Radiation?"

"No, sir. No radiation."

Kincaid looked up, past the man, at the glow. "What is that?"

CHAPTER 14

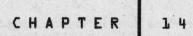

July 4/5, 1947
Washington, D.C.

Major General Curtis LeMay sometimes found it hard to sleep at night. The war in the Pacific had done that to him. He had often stayed up all night, planning and preparing for missions that would be launched late in the afternoon so that they would be over their targets at night. Once the aircraft were launched, he had little to do, so he slept, until early evening when the routine started again. Sometimes he slipped back into that routine, napping in the afternoon and then staying awake all night.

People thought that his periodic insomnia was caused by the war itself, that he felt guilt because he had ordered his bombers to saturate the Japanese homeland, burning their cities to the ground, but that wasn't the reason. He felt nothing for the Japanese. They had started the war at Pearl Harbor. If they had been afraid of getting a bloody nose, they shouldn't have taken the first swing. They hadn't understood the concept of total war. They hadn't understood that their homeland, at one time isolated and difficult to attack, was open for a military force that had long-range bombers.

LeMay had believed that the way to defeat an enemy, especially one who fought to the bitter end on various Pacific islands as the United States worked its way toward Japan, was to utterly crush him. You destroyed his soldiers when you fought them. You destroyed his fleet when you found it. You swept his airplanes from the sky so that you controlled that too. And you took the war to his manufacturing centers so that his war materiel could not be replaced. You destroyed his cities, because the people there could be recruited to continue the fight. You killed him as quickly as you could, and you destroyed his ability to wage war, and finally you destroyed his will to wage war. Total war demanded the total destruction of everything that the enemy owned, made, loved, built or used.

So, there were people who knew that LeMay didn't sleep well at night, but they didn't really understand the reason. They didn't understand him. They couldn't understand a warrior who lived for the war and waged it as effectively and as brilliantly as LeMay had.

Of course LeMay rarely thought about any of this because his mind was always racing toward the next war. He wanted to understand it so that he would be prepared to fight it. He assumed that the enemy would be the Soviets because it was clear that their governmental goals were world domination. To achieve that, there would be armed conflict between the United States and the Soviet Union. LeMay believed that, and he believed that it would come within a decade. If the United States was not prepared, then the United States would cease to exist, and the Soviet Union would have won.

When his aide tapped on his door, LeMay was not annoyed at being awakened because he was already awake, thinking about that next war and how to prepare for it with only a side thought that the war might be interplanetary rather than intercontinental. He was happy to learn that someone else was awake. He was happy that there would be some diversion because, even in Washington, people tended to sleep at night which meant that LeMay was often alone with his thoughts.

"Come in," he said.

The aide entered, stopped, and looked at LeMay who was still dressed, even at the late hour. He held a folder with bright red Top Secret stamps on it.

"What do you have there?"

"Just came through the comm center, General. Special coded message from New Mexico. Operational Immediate."

LeMay took the folder and turned on the lamp next to him.

He opened the file, pulled the cover sheet out of the way, and began reading. Once he glanced up at his aide but said nothing to him. When he finished reading, he asked, simply, "Have you looked at this?"

"No, General."

LeMay rubbed his chin and realized that he needed to shave. He rubbed at his eyes, realizing that suddenly he was tired and found that odd. The message should have revitalized him, not made him tired. He set the file down and asked, "Where is Doctor Moore?"

The aide grinned, but only because he had anticipated the question. He said, "Doctor Moore is in Washington state with General Spaatz."

"And Johnson?"

"East Texas."

"Who have we got going into New Mexico?"

"That would be Wheeler and Hackett. They should have left Andrews about four hours ago. It'll be a couple of hours before they're on the ground in Roswell."

"Not exactly the first team," said LeMay. "Have General Spaatz and Doctor Moore been alerted?"

"Messages have gone out, General, but I don't know if they have received them at the other end, meaning that the messages are there, but I don't know if they have been delivered. As of an hour ago, there had been no confirmation."

"Okay, get my car around here. I'm going to have to go into the office to stay on top of this. I'll want thirty minutes for a shower and a shave. I'll want coffee at the office with some breakfast rolls, not donuts or that other sweet crap, and I'll want the car ready when I am."

"Yes, sir. The message?" said the aide, meaning that he wanted it back so that it could be locked in the vault.

LeMay looked at the file folder again. He was surprised at the magnitude of things that had been handed to him in similar file folders. Information that changed the world around him. In the Pacific, it affected the men in his bomber command and the course of the war. It affected the Japanese homeland and indirectly, the war in Europe. But this, it affected the entire world. It would alter the face of the planet, and there the information sat, in a manila file folder that looked no different from the hundreds of others he had seen.

"Put that in the safe, and then get the car."

"Yes, sir."

CHAPTER 15

Jack Reed stood quietly, suddenly aware that there was virtually no sound on the desert. There were no insect noises, no nocturnal birds hunting, not even the quiet talking of the soldiers dragged out in the middle of the night. It was almost as quiet as a grave and that was a little frightening.

Kincaid looked at Reed and asked, "You have any idea of how to proceed?"

"We need to get security out."

"That's being done by Major Easley."

Reed wiped a hand over the side of his face and took a deep breath. "Then I suppose that we go take a look."

Kincaid grinned, the expression barely visible in the darkness and blue glow. "Why so hesitant?"

Reed pointed. "We don't know what it is."

"Then let's go find out."

Reed headed toward his jeep and then waved at Douglass and Campbell. Douglass threw his cigarette to the ground and crushed it.

Slowly they all walked forward as if afraid that something was going to jump out at them. As they approached, the shape of the craft became evident. It had a fat, low fuselage with a stubby delta-wing shape. It didn't look as if the wings were big enough to support the craft as it flew. The nose was crushed and bent. There was a rip in the left side of the fuselage, exposing the interior. There seemed to be a windshield on the front of the craft that had been laid in so that it was molded into the body and it looked to have been made of aluminum. There were inwardly slanted twin tails in the rear.

Although the nose had been damaged in the crash, it was clear that it had been rounded, as had the wings, giving the craft an almost circular shape. Seen from the ground, flying at high speed at twenty-five or thirty thousand feet, it would look like a disk because the edges had been blunted.

As they approached, the damage became clearer. Although the nose had been smashed, the windshield, if that was an accurate description, was unbroken. The right side was undamaged and there was a tear, or rip, in the left side, starting two or three feet behind the windshield and extending for ten feet, ending in front of one of those twin tails.

Reed stopped about ten or twelve feet away from it and looked at the rip in the side. Through it little could be seen. There was part of a wall or bulkhead, what might have been a hatch, and a single, small, chair.

"Oh my God," said one of the men, his voice quiet, but high and tight.

Reed turned and looked. At the base of the cliff, near a boulder, sat a human-looking creature. The head looked swollen and the eyes looked large, but they were closed. The creature was very thin, almost emaciated and about the size of a ten-year-old child. The arms were rail thin and the hands small, almost delicate with fingers that were long and thin.

Reed stood flatfooted, unable to move. It was clear to him that the being was not human. It was a creature from another world who looked as if it had crawled from its damaged ship and sat down to sleep. There was no sign of any injury and no sign of blood.

One man took a single step forward, toward the creature, and then froze. He was breathing heavily, sounding as if he had run in from the base rather than just walked the last fifty yards.

"What . . . ?"

Reed understood the confusion. He didn't know what to do either. The plan, to treat this as if a plane with an atomic bomb had crashed did not cover what to do about the crew. They had thought about a craft and what it might be carrying in the way of a cargo, but not much about a crew.

Reed wiped a hand over his face and rubbed his leg. He stared at the little man. At least he thought it was a man. It was bald and had no breasts. It looked as if it was a man, but then he realized that he had no way of knowing. This was an alien being and the terms, male and female, might mean nothing.

"We need to move forward," said Douglass, but his voice was strained, and if he meant the statement to be an order, no one moved.

"The craft," said someone. "It's not ours."

"No shit."

Reed still stared at the little creature, his mind blank. He couldn't think. He knew that he should be doing something. He knew that he should be gathering data and preserving the scene before it was disturbed and ruined by the others blundering around, but he just could not move. He was paralyzed. Not by fear but by sensory overload. It was too much to comprehend.

There was a flash to his right and he turned to look. A small, thin man, wearing a wrinkled khaki uniform, held a camera up, close to his face. He was photographing the alien body. He popped the flashbulb from his camera, letting it fall to the desert floor, and inserted a new bulb. He took a second photograph and then moved around so that he could get another shot from another angle for later comparison. Reed didn't recognize him.

"Yeah," said Kincaid, nodding. "Let's fall back and get pictures of everything first before we track up the landscape. Then we'll take a better look at this thing."

Reed didn't move. He stood rooted firmly to the ground, fascinated by the serene look of the alien creature. It seemed so peaceful. It seemed so non-threatening. It was just some small non-hostile alien being sleeping on the New Mexican desert that might awaken in the morning.

"Come on," said Kincaid, reaching out to grab Reed's sleeve. "Let's give the photographer a chance to do his work."

Reed took a step backward, and then turned. He walked down into an arroyo and up the far side of it. He found a large rock and sat down on it where he could still see the body of the alien creature.

"Looks as if it's asleep," he said to no one.

"Nothing could have survived that crash," said Douglass.

"How do you know?" asked Reed.

"Well . . ." he started and then fell silent. He didn't know.

The photographer and his assistant, a bigger man who carried a bag filled with film plates, made notes on a clip board. Together the men moved around the crash site documenting what they had found. They photographed the craft, the lone body, and then concentrated on the tear in the fuselage of the alien ship. The photographer climbed up where he could look down into it and took pictures of the interior.

Reed envied the man. He didn't have to think. He had a job to do. A clear, routine job. Photograph the crash scene so that investigators, looking back on this and attempting to learn what had happened, could study those pictures. He was doing a job he had been trained to do even if the circumstances were unique to human history.

The photographer dropped back to the ground and waved at the rest of the men. "I'm done here."

And still no one moved. The hot wind was whipping down the arroyo, rattling the leaves on the trees and bushes that had grown up there, smelling of the rain falling fifty or a hundred miles away. The air was hot, even that late at night, or rather early in the morning, but there was no humidity to make it oppressive.

Reed finally stood up and slowly worked his way back to the craft. He tore his eyes from the body and tried to concentrate on the ship. Here was a vessel that could travel interplanetary distances. It could operate in space. It had been built on another planet.

For some reason Reed reached out and touched the edge of the wing, noting that it was nearly razor sharp. He pushed and felt the craft shift slightly. He realized then that it was incredibly light. He would have thought that he had no more chance of moving the craft manually than he would have had pushing a Sherman tank across a parking lot.

He climbed up on the wing and looked into the rip into the side. He noticed that the edge of the metal that bent back looked more like a bee's honeycomb than solid metal. A piece of it was flapping in the breeze.

He looked down at the deck about three feet from him and wondered if he should climb in. Here was a craft built on another world and he could be the first human to step into it.

Without thinking further, he dropped down to the deck with a quiet, almost imperceptible thump and was inside. He looked through a hexagonally-shaped hatch in a solid gray bulkhead toward the front of the craft. Through the windshield that looked more like a movie screen than a windshield, he could see the cliff face. It looked as if it was high noon outside. It was brightly lighted, though it had a reddish tint to it.

It was then that he noticed the chairs near the windshield facing toward it, almost like seats in a theater except they were high-backed with wide panels on the sides. They were staggered in two rows so that each had a unobstructed view of the windshield and each seemed to be on a pedestal so that it could swivel. The bulkhead opposite of him held some sort of small, dark windows that might have been gauges, except there were no needles or markings on them. They seemed to be set in an a series of arcs.

Reed crawled through the hatch. It was narrow, built for the smaller dimensions of the beings. He knelt on the deck which was soft, almost like padded concrete but smooth and dark with no sign of debris or dirt, other than that he had tracked in. Reed thought about the cockpits of the aircraft he had flown, and how dirty and worn everything became. Everything here looked fresh and new, as if it had just been manufactured. His attention was drawn to the windshield and he put a hand on the arms of one of the chairs. It shifted and he realized that each chair was occupied. There were creatures inside the craft.

"What do you see?" Douglass called down through the rip.

Reed turned and looked up through the hatch and through the tear in the side of the craft, at the man. "More of them in here. The windshield seems to lighten the land."

"What?"

"There are more of them in here."

"Dead?"

"I guess. I don't know."

"Go take a look."

But Reed didn't move. He sat back on his heels, looking at the forward section of the cockpit of the alien craft. He saw nothing that he recognized as controls or instruments. Under the windshield was a short shelf that looked something like the dashboard of a car, but there was nothing on it or in it. At least nothing that Reed recognized. There were three dark windows spread across the dashboard and Reed suspected that information could be displayed on them, but he saw no way to activate them.

Kneeling there on the floor or deck he realized that it was much cooler inside, even with the hole in the side of the craft the air conditioning, or the environment of the craft, seemed to have maintained its integrity. The air was quite breathable, though it was icy and felt heavy in some fashion. Reed didn't understand that.

Three creatures were sitting in the cockpit and a fourth lying face down on the floor hidden from easy view by the chairs. All the creatures looked to be dead through only one showed any sign of trauma and there was no blood on it, just its arm bent at a strange angle. Looking at the beings, Reed realized that he didn't know if the arm had been broken or not. Maybe the creatures could normally bend the arm into that strange position.

"You see anything?" Now it was Campbell. He had apparently displaced Douglass.

"I've got four more in here," he repeated. "I think they're all dead."

"Are you sure?"

"Fuck no," snapped Reed. "I don't know. They might be unconscious, asleep, or in a coma. They're just here, sitting in the cockpit."

He spun one of the chairs so that he was staring into the

face of the alien. Its eyes were closed and it looked relaxed. It wasn't breathing, or wasn't breathing as Reed understood it. He touched the wrist. It was dry, papery, and felt like the warm top of a freshly baked cake. Reed didn't know if that meant the creature was alive and unconscious, or dead and the body had yet to cool.

Reed then realized that he was on alien turf. He was in their ship. If they were merely unconscious, then they could awaken at any moment and he would be the one who was surprised. He wasn't sure what they could do. They looked fragile, as if they could be broken easily. There were no signs of weapons, or anything that could be used as a weapon.

For an instant, he was frightened, and then realized there was no point in it. These creatures, these aliens, were from a civilization that was technologically advanced. They had created this lightweight ship that had come from deep space. Their first reaction, if they awoke, would not be to attack. They would probably be curious. They might be frightened because they had crashed on a foreign planet. But Reed knew, just knew, that he had nothing to fear from them at that moment. Now was the time to learn as much as they could.

He was going to have to get out and let someone else in, someone trained in medicine, or an engineer, or someone who might be able to understand the ship, but turned to look out the windshield one last time. He saw two men on top of the cliff over him. They looked strange in the red filtering of the windshield but he could see them easily, as if the sun had risen early and was high over head. He watched as one of the men moved close to the edge of the cliff and looked down at him. The soldier squatted, picked up a rock, and for a moment it looked as if he was going to toss it at the ship. He then dropped the rock to the ground and turned, moving back until he disappeared from sight.

"You okay in there?"

Reed turned and looked at the hatch. "I'm fine. I'm coming out now."

When he reached the hole in the side of the ship, he looked up at Campbell crouched there, surprised that it was still dark.

The windshield had gotten him used to the idea that it was daylight outside.

He reached up, grabbed the side of the ship, and hauled himself out. The heat wrapped him immediately, but it wasn't as bad as it had been. There was a hint of a breeze and a taste of rain somewhere nearby.

"Well?" asked Campbell.

"Four, just like that one. None were moving. I think they are dead."

"Controls? Books? Charts? Any clue where this came from?"

Reed stared blankly. None of those things had come to his mind. He had seen no controls but he hadn't thought about navigation charts or books or any other documentation. He hadn't seen anything that would suggest they held charts. It was a clean room that looked as if it had been made from molded metal with the five chairs stuck in the center of it and a few silver-colored disks scattered on the floor.

"No," said Reed. "I didn't see anything like that."

"Living quarters? Radio?"

"Nothing," said Reed. "Just the room, cockpit, with the four bodies sitting in it."

Douglass moved closer to the ship from his point near the tail and looked up. He said, "Move aside. I'm going to look at it myself."

Reed slipped along the fuselage and dropped to the ground. His eyes fell on the creature sitting by the cliff. No one had moved forward or touched it. No one wanted to touch it.

The look on its face still disturbed him. It looked as if it had no cares and it certainly didn't look as if it had died in the trauma of an aircraft accident on a strange planet circling a far-off star.

Finally two men approached carrying a stretcher. Neither was a big man, and both wore armbands with red crosses on them. They set their stretcher down and then knelt on either side of the alien creature. One of them used a small light, flicking it at the eyes as a doctor might do. He leaned in close, then shined the light directly into one of its eyes. They were large, dark eyes with a very clear white in them. The pupils were large and dark, maybe brown or black. There was no reaction from it.

Reed moved closer and crouched at its feet. He noticed that it wore boots of some kind that looked as if they had a hard, distinctive sole to them. He looked at the ground but could see no evidence of footprints but the earth was hard and packed and might not take prints and besides, it was still dark and hard to see.

One of the men reached out and gently touched the throat of the alien. He moved his fingers around and then shook his head. "I don't feel a pulse."

"If it would have one there," said the other.

"We're way out of our depth here," said Reed. "We've don't have a clue."

Campbell walked over and announced, "Kincaid radioed the base."

"That's not going to help." Reed stood up and waved a hand to indicate the craft near them. "We're not dealing with anything Earthly here."

"What do you suggest?"

"I think we ought to secure this location and then back off. Let the brass get some experts in here. Someone who can make a few guesses about this."

All four of the men moved away from the body. They stood looking at it as if they expected it to move. As if they expected it to attack them in some fashion, as if they believed that it was still alive.

Reed noticed that everyone was beginning to move away from the craft and the body almost as if a verbal order had been given. They were filtering through the arroyo so that they stood opposite of the crash site or sat on the large boulders, studying it as they had before anyone had moved in. They looked like the crowd in a museum, seeing some kind of interesting, maybe a somewhat frightening, display. They didn't want to look at it but had to.

Kincaid drifted over to where Reed stood and asked, "What do you think?"

"We're completely out of our depth here."

"There are some people coming in from Washington. Should be here in a couple of hours," said Kincaid.

"They going to know what to do?"

"I don't really know," said Kincaid. He pulled a pack of cigarettes from his pocket, shook one out and then offered the pack to Reed.

"No, thanks."

"Damnedest thing," said Kincaid, quietly without looking at Reed. "Damnedest thing."

Reed nodded but knew the words did not cover the situation. There was nothing he could think of to say that would cover the situation. It was a stunning, mind-boggling, brain-shattering event.

"I think we better wait for someone to figure this out for us," said Reed.

"We're on the scene. It's our job," said Kincaid. "We've got to figure it out."

"No," said Reed, shaking his head. "Our job is to secure the site, prevent further damage to the craft. Our job is to keep civilians away from this place. That's our job at the moment."

And in that moment, the job changed. One of the men peeked a head out of the craft and shouted in awe, "I think one of them is alive."

CHAPTER 16

July 5, 1947
US Army Air Forces Aircraft
Somewhere over southern
Missouri

D anni Hackett was nearly asleep. The roaring of the engines and the discomfort of what were laughingly called seats had given way to the long hours she had been awake and the boredom of the darkened interior of the droning aircraft. Even with the discomfort, and the noise, and the odors, she couldn't stay awake. She had tried to read the file folder that Wheeler had given her, but it was filled with statistics and dry verbiage that failed to excite her even when talking about the possibility of life on other planets. Someone had taken great pains to teach the author of the report how not to write.

The three photographs weren't much better. Two showed spots of brightness in an otherwise dark background and the last was of a smudge of gray in the daylight sky. These were the very best of the flying saucer pictures that had been taken by civilians over the last couple of days. Hackett didn't care. She'd seen the gun camera footage that had been spectacular.

Hackett closed the folder and closed her eyes. It was strange that she was actually in the aircraft, now flying over the Midwest. She hadn't started out to be a scientist. Like so many other girls, she had always been taught that females just didn't worry about careers because they would grow up to be married. Her mother was of the generation who believed that the purpose of a university education for a woman was to put her into a position to find a well-educated and soon to be prosperous husband.

But Hackett had been different. As a child she was more

interested in science than in tea parties. She had been fascinated with the night sky and had read all the books she could
find on astronomy until she could spot the planets and name
the constellations. She spent hours with her cheap telescope
looking at the distant nebulae and galaxies and once or twice
dim little smudges that were comets.

She had planned, in college, to study astronomy, but the
United States entered the war and she thought about changing
her major. She also thought about joining one of the women's
military auxiliaries, but wondered if she would be of great use
as a typist. She had a good understanding of math, was interested in biology, and even could speak fairly good Spanish.
Had she been fluent in Japanese or Chinese, then her language
skill might have been useful, but the United States was not at
war with any country in which Spanish was the official language or in which Spanish would be of any sort of advantage.

Math was useful in cryptanalysis. She was also learning a
little Japanese when Donald Menzel approached her. He was
setting up a team to study the Japanese codes to make sure
that the United States could keep reading much of the en-
crypted Japanese radio traffic. Through espionage, code breaking, and a few inspired inventions, the United States had the
ability to read some, but not all, of the Japanese codes. It
would be the biggest secret of the war, eclipsing even the
development of the atomic bomb. As long as the analysts
could read the Japanese messages, plans could be drawn to
thwart Japanese attempts to develop the Greater Asian Co-
Prosperity Sphere.

Menzel sat with her one autumn day when the air was crisp
but the sun was warm and explained that her abilities were
important to the war effort. She could make a real contribution.

"But I have nearly completed all my graduate studies," she
said.

"Yes, but given the contribution you could make, the university has approved a plan in which you could complete those
studies while I become your faculty advisor. You finish your
studies and give some of your time to me. You get valuable

on-the-job training and you get your degree on time."

She sat there quietly for a moment, watching the students cross the campus, hurrying to the next class, with little thought about the war. Millions were fighting and the world was in flames, but there wasn't much of a sign of it on campus. If she looked hard she could see, in the distance, a billboard asking for help with the purchase of war bonds.

"I don't know," she said. "I want to do what I can, but I want the contribution to be valuable."

Menzel nodded and grinned. "When the history of the war is finally written, in the 1960s or 1970s or in a hundred years, our contribution will be fully recognized. You have no idea, and the world has no idea, what we can do for the war."

Hackett didn't like buying a pig in a poke, but that was what she was being asked. Menzel would tell her nothing of what she would be doing without her agreeing to work for him. He would tell her nothing about the job other than her skill as a mathematician was the valuable asset at the moment.

She rubbed her eyes, and then shivered as an icy wind whipped down, out of the trees, touched her and then faded. "I don't know," she repeated.

Menzel shrugged. "I have a dozen others to talk to. I'll find who I need. You're at the top of the list, but . . ."

She held up a hand and said, "I didn't say I wouldn't do it. I just wish that I knew more."

"I can't tell you more. Security. I can tell you that it is important and you will be well compensated for your assistance by the university here and by certain governmental organizations." Menzel fell silent.

"I'll be able to get into medical school?" she asked.

"As long as you are otherwise qualified, you will be guaranteed a slot at one of the better medical schools as a partial payment for your contribution to the war effort. No, you will not get special treatment once in school, but your name will be at the top of the list so that you will suffer no penalty for your momentary unavailability."

Hackett made up her mind and nodded. "Okay, then, as long

as I can continue my studies, and I won't be penalized for time lost in those studies."

Menzel stood up and said, "There will be someone to help get the paperwork finished and we'll begin the in-processing."

Hackett was afraid that she had made a career decision without understanding exactly what she was doing. But the war was on and it was nearly impossible to listen to the radio, go to a movie, read a magazine, without the war intruding. Now she wouldn't be a bystander, afraid of what might happen and unable to do anything at all. Now she would be someone who could contribute to winning the war.

She realized that what was happening to her now, with the war over, was an outgrowth of that snap decision made years earlier. As she thought about that, wondering if it had been the right decision, Wheeler dropped into the seat next to her, leaned very close, and over the roar of the engines, said, "They're saying that one of them was alive."

She was startled by that, frightened and not sure what she had heard. "What's wrong?"

"Nothing's wrong," said Wheeler. "Got a radio message from New Mexico. One of them is supposed to be alive."

She thought quickly, trying to shake the cobwebs from her mind. "You mean that a flying . . . you mean that one of the . . ." She couldn't finish the statement.

"That's exactly what I mean but I don't want to say much about it now. Fuck," he said, unaware that he had said it. "I just don't know what any of this means."

She looked at the deserted rear of the aircraft. The flight engineer, wearing a gray flying suit, was twenty feet away and seemed to be fascinated by the coffee pot. He was paying no attention to them as he attempted to pour himself a cup.

Hackett pointed and said, "You got a radio message."

"Cryptic message," said Wheeler, "that I took to mean that one of the . . . creatures . . . survived when their ship hit the ground. I don't know anything more than that and I didn't want to infer anything from it."

"Quite a coincidence," she said, unsure of why she had said

that. If the flying saucers were real, then it made sense that there would be crew members in them.

Wheeler leaned back and closed his eyes. "We'd better try to get some rest now because things are going to really pop when we land."

She looked at him and said, "I was trying to sleep when you woke me up."

"Thought that you would want to know." He kept his eyes closed and didn't look as if he had anything else to say.

But now she was wide awake and didn't feel like sleeping and knew that with the information she had been given, she wouldn't be able to sleep. It was getting late, or early, depending on the point of view. And he had said that one was alive in New Mexico. It could be a garbled report, and probably was, but what if it was not, then the questions they had would be answered so much easier. The answer had dropped, literally, right into their laps.

Her mind ran wild as she thought about it. A craft from another world piloted by a crew born on another world. Something that had been created by minds and intelligence on another planet. They would be so different. They would be unlike anything that had ever set foot on the planet Earth.

All throughout human history, as one group came into contact with the next group, they had always started with the same base of understanding. They had always been human. The culture of the Aztecs might be radically different from the culture of the Spanish, but the bottom line was that they were all human. There was that basis for creating a dialogue and a basis for understanding.

But that basis didn't exist any more. The craft had a crew, and if it was a craft built on another world, there was no basis for understanding. They were not human. They had never experienced anything that was human. They had not evolved the way humans had, they might not have fought all the wars humans had, they had not climbed from the primordial soup the way humans had, the result of billions of years of human evolution. They, whatever they were, simply were not human.

The only possible basis for understanding was intelligence.

They had developed a technological society which was obvious because their technology had brought them here. And scientists and philosophers had developed a technological society that stood on the brink of some of the greatest steps that the human race could make.

So the two societies, one clearly more technologically advanced than the other, were about to come together. Or already had come together, depending on what was waiting for them in New Mexico. That was, of course, if the flight crew really was alien and that the craft was not something developed in secret on Earth.

But this was going to be an alien civilization and the small basis they held for understanding one another, that they both represented sentient beings, simply might not be enough. Or maybe the alien creatures, thought of as more enlightened, might be no more enlightened than the Spanish had been upon the discovery of the New World. Technology didn't equate with morality. There was nothing in human history to suggest that technology provided any sort of morality. These alien creatures, who had traveled so far to get here, might be the vanguard of the alien invasion force.

There was really no way to tell. Maybe they had been part of a reconnaissance force and had been killed attempting to complete their mission. That meant, of course, that other craft, from the same place, would soon be flying over New Mexico and the southwestern United States.

That led her in another direction. The home world of the aliens might not know that an accident had brought down their ship. They might believe that the American military had somehow shot their ship out of the sky. If they believed that, if there had been no sort of distress call made, the aliens, who were merely studying the Earth, might return to extract retribution from Earth-based civilization.

Hackett suddenly grew cold because she knew, from the little that she had seen and heard, that the American Army could not defeat an enemy from space. During the war, control of the sky had been important and those at the higher altitude held the advantage. The aliens could launch their attack from space and there was nothing in the inventory that could touch it. If they were invaders, then their invasion would succeed. She couldn't see anyway for it to fail unless H.G. Wells's germs assisted again.

She didn't like the direction of those thoughts. She stood up and walked over to one of the small windows in the aircraft. The stars were shining brightly. She could see the big dipper and the north star. They seemed to be closer somehow. It was almost as if she reach out to touch them.

She tried a different track. A society out there, in space, would have to be more civilized than the one on Earth. They would have been around longer, probably faced many of the problems facing the human race, and had overcome them. On Earth, technological advancement threatened all human life. For the first time humans possessed the power to destroy themselves. Atomic weapons were so destructive that they could, if employed by enough countries engaged in a war, destroy the environment that supported the human race. Life, as she knew it, would cease to exist.

But Hackett believed that humans had learned how to control their weapons. All sides during the Second World War had possessed poison gas. Many of the nations had used it during the first war, but even as the Germans and the Japanese were being overrun and their countries destroyed, as they fought the last desperate days of the war, they refrained from using the gas.

That filled her with hope. As did the craft, whatever it was, down in New Mexico. The alien beings would have faced the challenges, beaten them, and could offer those solutions to the human race. They could provide an enlightened way of dealing with technology and the problems that it brought. They were not alien invaders but guides for the human race.

She knew that she was engaging in wishful thinking, but it was better than waiting for the invaders. The real point was that they knew almost nothing, other than would they could deduce from the scattered clues they had. Maybe there would be more information in New Mexico. Maybe there would be something that would tell her if the aliens would benefit or destroy the human race.

She peeked over at Wheeler who had somehow fallen asleep. She glanced at the flight engineer who was sitting by himself, a tiny light shining on the magazine he held. From the front of the aircraft was the red glow of the instrument panel and the shapes of the pilots who sat at the controls, flying them to New Mexico.

She moved back to her seat, looked at the manila folder that held so little important information. She picked it up and then sat down again. She wasn't going to read now. She didn't feel like reading it now because she knew that it was hopelessly out of date. She would sit quietly as the miles slipped under them, wishing that they were already there so that she would finally have a couple of answers.

It seemed that all the lights were on in the White House and that everyone was wide awake though it was only about four in the morning. Major General Curtis LeMay, wearing a class A uniform, complete with all his awards, decorations and badges, and sitting in the rear of the black Cadillac limousine, held a locked brief case that contained only the somewhat confusing TWX from the Roswell Army Air Field. To LeMay it was the most important piece of paper that he had ever seen or held and he had no idea how the President of the United States would react to it, especially since the President had suggested that he wanted to know as little about this as necessary. Plausible deniability, he called it.

The limousine stopped at the iron gate and one of the guards from the small white guard hut to the right, walked forward. He waited until the driver had rolled down the window and then shined a light into the backseat. He smiled at LeMay and said, "Good to see you, General. The President is waiting." He stepped back, and opened the gate.

They drove to the lighted, covered entrance where a Marine sergeant rushed to open the rear door for LeMay. The sergeant stepped back and saluted crisply. LeMay returned it without a word. Normally he would have said something to the sergeant but it was just too early in the morning and the information he carried was a little too shocking. Instead, he ducked his head like a man pushing his way through heavy rain and high winds. He saw nothing but his destination up the steps.

Just inside the door he was met by Colonel David Stockwell, who would, in about a year, be promoted to brigadier general before suddenly retiring. Stockwell, a tall, heavyset man with thick black hair and the beginning of a five o'clock shadow even though he had shaved an hour earlier, was also dressed in a class A uniform. He had fewer awards than LeMay but they were topped by the command pilot wings. He looked neither happy nor wide awake. He said, "I hope this really is important, General."

LeMay lifted his briefcase slightly, as if to show it, and said, "This could be the most important thing that has happened in the last thousand years."

"Yes, sir."

They walked down a long hall in which only the occasional lamp burned creating pools of light and pockets of darkness. They reached and then stopped in front of a closed double door with a guard sitting to one side. The guard paid no attention to either Stockwell or LeMay.

Stockwell said, "I'm not going in with you, General. I'll wait out here if you need anything."

That surprised LeMay. He asked, "Do you know exactly what is going on?"

"I have a general idea, but I am not going to listen to this tonight."

LeMay was going to knock on the door when it was opened by an Army master sergeant holding a stenographer's notebook and four yellow pencils. His uniform was fresh, he was recently shaved, and looked as if it was nine o'clock in the morning rather than just after five. He was prepared to take dictation, record the meeting, or provide any other secretarial service necessary. He looked up at LeMay and said, "I was just coming to look for you."

"I was just coming to look for you, General," repeated LeMay, letting the master sergeant know that he had violated military protocol and that LeMay didn't care if he worked for the President or not. Military customs and courtesies would be obeyed.

"Yes, General. Sorry."

LeMay walked through the doorway and saw President Truman rising to meet him. LeMay said, "I'm sorry to bother you so late, Mr. President."

Harry S Truman, dressed in pajamas and a bathrobe and holding a cup of coffee in one hand and a saucer in the other, grinned and said, "Or that you caused me to rise so early."

"Yes, Mr. President."

Truman set the cup and saucer down, stood, and walked toward LeMay. He asked, "Is it really that important?"

LeMay didn't speak for a moment but turned his attention to the master sergeant who held nearly every security clearance it was possible to hold because of his proximity to the President. He was cleared to hear things and knew things that LeMay didn't know. He knew things about the government that members of either political party would love to know about the other, but he would never say anything to either of them. As a source to the press, he could almost name any price and there were those who would cheerfully pay it. The thought of selling the information hadn't crossed his mind, but the tale that LeMay brought the President would be worth more than a million dollars. LeMay didn't want to chase the man out, really couldn't, so he wanted the President to make a conscious decision about the sergeant remaining to hear the briefing. If the sergeant's clearances were good enough for the President, they were good enough for him.

Truman seemed to understand LeMay's hesitation and said, "That will be all, sergeant. Thank you."

As the sergeant closed the doors as he exited, Truman said, "Do you want something to drink? Maybe something a little stronger than coffee?"

"No, sir."

"Then let's get at it." He pointed to a couple of chairs set near a fireplace. There was a single glass that held three ice cubes and a brown liquid that could have been Scotch or bourbon but was, in reality, iced tea sitting on a small table near one of the chairs.

LeMay sat down, put the briefcase on his knees and fingered the locks until he had dialed in the combinations. He took out the single sheet of paper that had a bright red cardboard cover with the words Top Secret in huge letters on it and handed it over to the President without a word.

Truman pushed the cover sheet out of the way and looked at the short message printed there.

TOP SECRET

050215Z JUL 47
FM   HEADQUARTERS,   509TH   BOMB   GROUP (HEAVY)
ROSWELL ARMY AIR FIELD
ROSWELL, NEW MEXICO

TO HEADQUARTERS, STRATEGIC AIR COMMAND WASHINGTON, D.C.

SUBJECT: FLYING DISKS
DUPLICATION FORBIDDEN

THIS MSG IN TWO PARTS.

PART 1.

   AT 0832Z THIS MORNING THE 509TH BOMB GROUP (HEAVY) OBTAINED POSSESSION OF A FLYING DISK. CRAFT WAS MANUFACTURED, ME-TALLIC AND OF UNKNOWN ORIGIN.

PART 2.

   CREW OF CRAFT WAS RECOVERED AT THE SCENE. RACIAL IDENTIFICATION AND NATIONAL ORIGIN ARE UNKNOWN AT THIS TIME. ONE (1) OF THE FIVE (5) CREW MEMBERS SURVIVED THE CRASH.

EASLEY, EDWIN M., MAJOR, USA
PROVOST MARSHAL

FOR
BLANCHARD, WILLIAM, COL, USA
COMMANDING

TOP SECRET

LeMay watched the President as he read the short message. The color drained from his face and he reached automatically for his coffee, tasted it, and then was annoyed that it wasn't something stronger. He looked up at LeMay. "This . . ."

"I know, Mr. President. I've had that message for about an hour. I still don't know what to think."

"We've got to get some people out there."

"I have a team on its way. Two of the people who were in on the June 30 briefing, Jacob Wheeler and Danni Hackett, are en route."

"They're kids," said Truman.

"Wheeler was a bomber pilot during the war. Hackett is young, but she is a trained biologist and mathematician. She, and Wheeler, had already been cleared for this. She worked with Menzel during the war."

"I want some senior people sent in," said the President. "This is too important to be detailed to a couple of kids, no matter what their background."

LeMay nodded but said, "If I may, Mr. President. We must be careful with our reaction. We don't want to draw attention to this. We send in people with too much rank or too high in the government and someone is bound to notice."

The President, the color coming back to his face said, "One of them is alive?"

"I know nothing more, sir. I had, frankly, a hundred questions, but I didn't want to communicate them to Roswell."

"You're afraid of compromise," asked the President, meaning, simply, was LeMay worried about someone intercepting the messages or seeing a sudden increase in the radio traffic directed toward New Mexico.

"Again, I didn't want to do something that might call attention to this. As you may know, Mr. President, Roswell is out there by itself, in the middle of nowhere. We can contain the situation simply because of the distances. We have been fortunate that this happened there and not near Washington or New York or some other large city."

The President stood up and walked to a wooden cabinet that had been used by Thomas Jefferson and Abraham Lincoln. He opened it, grabbed a bottle of bourbon and splashed it into a glass. Without benefit of ice, he tossed it back. He poured another, but left it sitting on the cabinet.

"This is worse than learning of the bomb." He turned and looked at LeMay. "I knew about that, General. I had an inkling about that. You couldn't be the Vice President and not know something, so that when they came to me to tell about the weapon and that they wanted to use it, I wasn't completely surprised. But this . . . two weeks ago, we weren't thinking about these things. We were worried about the Russians and rebuilding Europe, not about something from space."

LeMay said, simply, "Yes, Mr. President."

"I want some senior people sent in. I want someone on the scene who can make some decisions without having to call me or you every ten minutes. We have to contain this before too many people learn about it."

LeMay nodded but said nothing. He understood what was happening. He understood that the information had to be contained because of the potential value of it. They had been handed a gift, literally, from the gods. If they could figure how the craft worked, if they could develop similar craft, then the Russians presented little danger. The Army would have a craft that outperformed everything, was strong enough to withstand some of the air-to-air weaponry, and that could fly across the Soviet Union in an hour or two. The balance of power in the world would shift and the Soviets wouldn't even see it coming. They would have no way of understanding what the United States had.

All it really came down to was protection of the information. Convince people that nothing had crashed at Roswell, or that something fairly mundane had fallen, and the attempts by Soviet spies to learn the truth would end. They wouldn't be spying on something that didn't exist. They wouldn't consider risking their assets on something like that.

In that moment, he understood what the President was attempting to do. Remove himself from the loop, let this be contained at a lower level and he could tell the truth about it. He wouldn't know all the details. Create a team to exploit this, but keep it outside the mainstream.

LeMay watched as Truman picked up the bourbon, idly sniffed at it, and then took a sip. He looked at LeMay and held up the glass, as if asking LeMay if he wanted a drink.

LeMay shook his head. There was another story here as well. The president was drinking at four in the morning. The fact that he was drinking because some kind of alien ship had crashed in New Mexico might not strike some reporters as the important point.

Truman finished the bourbon and then repeated, "We must contain this."

"Of course."

"Do you have some recommendations?"

"Yes, Mr. President. I took the liberty of writing them out for you." He handed the document to the President.

CHAPTER | 18

There was a stunned silence. Reed felt his knees go weak and then his head begin to spin. He reached back, felt the rough texture of one of the rocks and sat down quickly, thinking that it was just one more blow to the midsection. In the last twelve hours there had been a parade of such shocks.

Kincaid was thinking faster. He ran forward toward the craft and then stopped. He shouted, "Are you sure?"

"Yeah. It moved."

Kincaid turned, cupped a hand to his mouth and yelled, "We need a medical team up here."

But they hadn't brought a medical team. No one had really thought in terms of a crew, alive or dead. They had thought in terms of a craft, maybe piloted by remote control, but certainly not in terms of a living, breathing flight crew. And if anyone did think of a crew, they had thought in terms of a dead crew that would be well beyond any help that could be offered.

Reed pointed at one of the enlisted men. "Get on the radio and tell them we need a medical specialist here. Now."

"Yes, sir."

Now that he was thinking, Reed rushed back across the arroyo, to the trailing edge of one of the craft wings. He stood by Kincaid. "Should we go in?"

"You have any medical training?"

"Pretty standard first aid stuff. Some college biology, but I don't think any of it's going to be much help."

"Couldn't hurt."

Reed climbed up on the stubby wing and then dropped through the rip in the side again.

The man who had been in there crawled through the hatch and then pressed himself up against a bulkhead. Fortunately he was a small man whose face was now pale and who looked to be no older than twenty. His fatigue uniform was wrinkled and there were sweat stains under the arms. His boots might once have been highly polished, but now they were scratched and dirty. He said, "It's the one in the far seat."

"You sure it wasn't some kind of postmortem spasm?"

"I'm not sure of anything, sir. All I know is that I saw it move."

"Okay, why don't you get out of here."

"Yes, sir."

Reed hesitated at the hatch, looking once again into the cockpit. He stepped through and crouched, staring into the face of the creature that had moved. Like its fellow outside, it looked at peace with itself and the universe around it. And like its companion, it was small, thin, almost fragile, with a large head and large eyes. The ears were set low on the head and there was no hair or eyebrows.

There were no signs of injury on this creature. There was no blood, or anything that could be blood, staining its clothes. It sat upright, belted into its seat, almost as if it expected the flight to continue momentarily.

Slowly Reed reached out and touched the hand that rested on the arm of the chair. This one felt cool to the touch, but he knew that meant nothing. He had no idea what the skin of the creature was supposed to feel like or what the normal body temperature would be.

He reached up and opened one of its eyes. The bright blue pupil stared back at him. It didn't seem to react to the light in the cockpit.

Finally, he unbuckled the seat belt and shoulder harness that looked for all the world exactly like its earthly counterparts. It had a buckle that might have been metal, though Reed didn't recognize it as such. It was lighter and, for some reason, he thought, stronger.

When the creature was free, he lifted it and placed it on the deck, flat on its back. He was surprised at how light the being was. It was no heavier than a child of seven or eight. It was taller than that, but much thinner.

Suddenly he felt sweat dripping and realized that he was tense. He was waiting for the thing to jump at him, or grab him, or to attack him. He'd watched one too many of the horror movies with Dracula seeming to be harmless, only to kill quickly and efficiently after jumping out of the dark corner.

Now he examined the creature carefully, looking for any sign of life.

"What's going on in there."

The voice, at the hatch, startled him and he jumped back. "Christ. You scared me."

Kincaid nodded at the creature. "Well?"

"I don't know. I don't see any signs of life."

"We've got the medics on the way."

"Well, there's nothing that I can do. I don't see anything wrong. I could stop the bleeding but I don't see any bleeding. I could clear the airway, but I don't see any sign that it can't breathe or that it was choking or that the airway was blocked."

"Then why don't we get it out of there?"

"We're not supposed to move the victim until a proper medical examination has been performed. Besides, why rush? It's probably better off in here than outside."

Kincaid sat quietly for a moment and then shrugged. "I guess there is no hurry. It's not like we're going to take it into the base hospital."

Reed sat back, away from the creature, leaning against the bulkhead. He looked up, through the windshield, at the red tinted world outside.

"Christ," he said.

Kincaid nodded. "I know what you mean."

"This changes it all, you know."

"Yeah." Kincaid didn't say anything for a while and then added, "At least we know it's not Russian."

"It might be better if this was Russian. Think about what it means to the world."

"I'm not interested in what it means to the world. I'm only interested in what it means to us. To the United States."

There was a noise from outside and the ship shifted as if someone had climbed up on the wing. The motion reminded Reed of a small boat on a lake and then he wondered why he hadn't felt the craft shift as others climbed on.

Douglass peered through the rip and said, "We've got a doctor here."

"Come on in doc," said Kincaid.

Reed watched a pair of boots appear and then a man dropped onto the deck. He wore civilian clothes and looked pale and sick. His dark hair was in disarray, and he hadn't shaved. He looked as if he had been suddenly awakened, grabbed the first thing he saw and then dressed in the dark. His appearance did not inspire confidence.

He sat back quickly, leaning against the bulkhead, and put his head between his legs. "Too much club time."

"Come on, doc," said Kincaid. "Your patient is in the cockpit."

Reed reached out, through the hatch and said, "Give me a hand, Doctor." Reed recognized him as one of the flight surgeons, Major David Dillon.

Dillon looked at Reed, surprised to see him. "What can you tell me?"

"Very little."

Dillon crawled forward and looked into the cockpit. "How many are there?"

"Four in here." Reed pointed. "That one, according to one of the men, moved."

"I don't see any signs of life."

Reed shrugged. "Neither did I. I moved it from the seat to the deck. It didn't react at all."

"I'm completely out of my depth here. This is a . . . an alien life form." He stopped, as if thinking about it. "I mean, it developed elsewhere. We have no baseline. We know nothing about it, its habits, its body, its life cycle."

Reed grinned and said, "We're all overwhelmed here. We don't know what we have."

Dillon stepped through the hatch. He stared at each of the bodies in turn, and then looked up at the windshield. Finally, he crouched near the creature lying on the deck and set his bag down, next to the body, but didn't bother to open it.

"I really don't know," he said quietly, as if thinking to himself. He touched the throat, where the pulse would be in a human, then reached down for the wrist. He lifted it and then set it down, carefully. "Might be broken," he said.

Reed moved backward to give Dillon more room. "Maybe if we moved it."

Dillon didn't answer. Instead he opened his bag and touched the instruments and medicines in it as if they gave him power or reassurance. He needed to feel and see something that was familiar. Finally he took out his stethoscope and listened to the chest of the being.

"I don't hear anything. No heartbeat or respiration. Nothing."

"Then it's dead," said Reed.

"I don't know. Maybe it doesn't breathe. Maybe it has no heart to pump the blood. Hell, maybe it doesn't have a circulatory system as we know it. I can't tell much of anything here. It's not like we've had a body to examine."

"Then what do we do?" asked Reed.

Dillon put his equipment away. "We get them out of here and back to the base hospital. That way we'll have all the equipment we need and I'll have a chance to talk to a colleague or two."

CHAPTER | 19

Just after the plane landed at the Roswell Army Air Field and taxied to a stop near the operations building, Wheeler and Hackett were told to remain in their seats. Someone was coming on board to brief them momentarily.

Hackett felt slightly sick. She hadn't sleep well, it was early in the morning, and the air blowing into the plane was hot and dry. Her eyes burned and she felt as if she had licked the floor. She wanted to get a shower, or something to eat, or a cup of coffee or, at the very least, to brush her teeth. Anything to make her feel slightly human again.

She sat in the seat, her eyes closed, listing to the sounds around her, wishing the wind would stop blowing and the vibrations would stop rippling through the fuselage and that they would let her get out of the airplane. Eventually, the engines had wound down and then had been shut down, and now were popping and clicking quietly as they cooled, but at least the vibrating had ended.

A man entered, framed momentarily in the sun-bright hatch. He was a portly man who had a long torso and short, stocky legs. His face was long and narrow with wide set eyes. He had a thin nose and short cropped hair and was one of the ugliest men that Hackett had ever seen. But he had a wide smile and his eyes seemed to dance with pleasure. He was friendly, quiet, and tired.

He walked down the short aisle and then sat down opposite of both Wheeler and Hackett. He said, "My name is Captain

Martin. I'm one of the intelligence officers here."

Hackett took a deep breath. She turned her attention from the hatch, back to Martin. His khaki uniform was wrinkled, dirty and sweat-stained. His shoes were scuffed and it looked as if there were cockleburs caught in his socks and one stuck to his trousers near his knee. He was unshaven.

He sat there for a moment, as if unsure what to do, and then said, "I suppose you both have orders."

Wheeler reached over to his briefcase and took out a sheet of paper. "I think you'll find that in order."

As Martin scanned the document, Hackett leaned close to Wheeler and said, "We have orders?"

"Properly signed, dated and drawn," said Wheeler. "I have some copies for you."

Martin handed the documents back to Wheeler. "You have identification?"

Wheeler said, "You have seen my orders."

"I've seen orders for Wheeler and Hackett but I don't know if you are they."

Wheeler laughed. He handed over his Department of War identification card. "This do?"

Martin inspected it and handed it back. "And her?"

"She's Hackett."

"I need to see documentation," said Martin.

Wheeler asked, "What the hell is going on here? You meet us on the aircraft that came from Washington. You know that we are who we say we are, otherwise we wouldn't be on this aircraft. You've seen our orders and you've seen my identification. I can think of nothing so highly classified that these procedures wouldn't be sufficient."

Martin didn't move. He locked his eyes on Wheeler and said, "I need to see some identification."

"Oh hell," said Hackett, and produced her own identification card that was so new that she worried that the ink might not be dry on it.

When Martin handed it back to Hackett, Wheeler asked, "Satisfied now?"

Martin said smiling, "I have to be very careful. There are Russian spies in New Mexico."

"I have read the preliminary reports," said Wheeler, ignoring the comment about the Russian spies. "We know that something is down near here." He didn't explain about the coded message they had received several hours earlier. Martin had no need to know that the code existed, or that messages were being exchanged using it.

Martin rocked back in his seat and said, "The situation has changed. What I'm about to say does not get repeated to anyone at anytime. Do you both understand?"

Wheeler said, "Yes," and Hackett nodded. Wheeler then said, "But I don't understand what is going on here."

Martin leaned closer and lowered his voice. He glanced around the aircraft quickly, as if looking for those Russian spies, or aircrew with big ears. He said, quietly, almost in a whisper, "We have found the craft, downed in the desert north of here. I have seen it myself. I have to tell you that I don't know what it is. I don't know who built it. It is like nothing that I have ever seen before even in the drawings of what jets are supposed to look like in 1980. It is incredible."

"We're aware of that," said Wheeler. "We have been briefed on this." What he didn't say was that Martin was the first eyewitness to talk to them. Everything else had been in reports and photographs, all second hand at best. Nor did he tell him that their information, for the most part, was days old. All they knew that was fresh was that something was down.

"Yeah, well, what you don't know is that one of them apparently survived," said Martin, watching to see their reaction.

Wheeler said nothing. He just nodded.

Martin raised his eyebrows, surprised by the lack of reaction, and then said, "Then I guess there isn't much that you don't already know." His voice was exasperated, as if he had been rushed to meet the airplane for no good reason.

"Specifics," said Wheeler. "We don't have any specifics about anything."

Hackett spoke up. "I would like to know a few things about the anatomy of the beings."

Martin shook his head. "I don't know anything about that. I was just told to tell you what we know now and get you ready to go to the crash site. I was to let you know that we had something that was not of this Earth."

Wheeler stood up, stretched, and said, "Then let's get going."

CHAPTER 20

Dr. Danni Hackett had hoped for a BOQ (Bachelor Officer's Quarters) room with a soft bed, clean sheets, and fan to keep her cool so that she could catch a few hours of rest before they started to work. She had hoped for something to eat, preferably eggs or a sandwich, and a chance to decompress. She thought that she needed a chance to digest the information they had been given and a chance to relax after the long, late flight from Washington. Unfortunately, the schedule had accelerated because there had been a flight crew and one of them had survived the crash. There was no time to think, just time to react, and she didn't like the pressure being applied to supply answers that she simply didn't have because she hadn't even seen much of anything other than cryptic reports and vague, nearly useless statistics.

She stood in a corridor of the base hospital which was composed of a number of single story, white buildings spread over a couple of acres. Each building had a different function and there seemed to be no real pattern to it. The highest ranking officer got the best location with the others fighting for their specialties and facilities in a descending order of importance. That importance was judged solely on the basis of rank and not experience or medical speciality. The operating area, the morgue, and the recovery rooms were set back, away from the streets where there would be little in the way of distractions for either doctors or patients and the noise level could be reduced.

She leaned against the wall and felt her head spin because of the odors in the building. She recognized ether and formaldehyde which reminded her of college biology and late night labs. She was thinking about biology classes because it kept her mind away from what she had glimpsed inside the operating room. She knew that it was not born on Earth, that it was an alien being that was, in some respects, amazingly human, and something that could announce the beginning of the end of the human race. She was depressed by the sight of the dead creature, though she couldn't explain why it should be depressing.

A doctor she had never seen before appeared in the corridor. He was dressed in a white lab coat but she saw he was wearing regulation pants. From somewhere she had heard that he had been flown in from El Paso, though she didn't know if he had been stationed there or if it had been one of the stops on a flight that originated somewhere else. He had been dragged to Roswell in the same fashion as she, and she figured he was as annoyed about it as she was.

"You about ready, Doctor?" he asked.

She shook her head no, but said, "I suppose."

He swiped at his forehead with the sleeve of his coat. "This is all preliminary, you understand. We can't draw any positive conclusions."

"I know."

"I've got us set up in a small conference room in this building. It's not very fancy but it will do. Give us a chance to talk to one another before we begin."

Together they walked down the green tiled hallway. There were doors on either side, also painted green, though a slightly darker color. Each was labeled with a small, white sign, giving them a clue as to the function. They came to the one marked "Conference Room," and the doctor leaned forward, turned the knob and pushed it open for Hackett.

"After you."

She entered a room that was no more than twelve by twelve. Opposite the door was a large window that looked out over a grassy field that might have been green in the spring but was now a light brown. There were several trees shading some of the buildings, keeping the sun off them.

Inside there was a small table with six chairs around it, one each at the head and foot and two on either side. There were file folders stacked near the head and one man sat there, but was turned so that he could look out the window. He was wearing a white lab coat. When he turned around, Hackett saw that he had a thin, black mustache on a face that looked lumpy, almost as if he had been beaten sometime recently. One eye was half closed but the other was wide open.

He waved a hand and said, "Come in, Doctor Hackett."

She entered and took the chair at the foot of the table where she could look out the window if she wanted. She reached forward, toward the files sitting on the table, but then decided to leave them where they were.

The man sitting at the head of the table, smiled at her and said, "Well, we know you and maybe you'd like to know us. I'm Colonel Walter Miller. I've flown in from . . ." He stopped and grinned again. "Well, I guess that's not important."

The other man slipped into a chair. He said, "I'm Lieutenant Colonel Russell Warren."

Miller turned his full attention to the table in front of him. "We have some preliminary observations here, based on a quick examination of one of the bodies. I think before we begin our work, that we need to discuss this situation."

Hackett understood that. They had three other samples, not to mention the living creature. They had to take a few risks with this one so they could understand a little about the internal structure of the aliens in case they needed to treat the living sample. She caught herself, thinking of it as a living sample. It was an intelligent, rational creature with as much right to live as she had. It was not an animal, nor was it a dummy designed to teach students about human anatomy and body structure. She had to keep reminding herself that this was not an exercise. That this was real.

Miller said, "My thinking is that before we begin to cut, we X-ray everything carefully so that we have some feel for the internal structures."

Hackett grinned and said, "I have two reactions to that. One is that an X-ray might destroy any disease, but it is more likely to destroy delicate tissue. I'm not sure that we want to use X-rays at this point."

"We've got three others," said Miller. "Four really."

"Only three, at least for the moment. We're not likely to get any more in the very near future," said Hackett.

Miller nodded and made a note. He then said, "We need photographs of everything in color. Motion picture footage. All this before we even begin to think about cutting."

"We have the photographers laid on," said Warren. "I can coordinate that if you'd like."

"You know what to get?"

"We have sample number one, in essence, here. The base sample. We start from scratch."

Hackett shook her head. "Do they have a proper lab here?"

"They have the equipment," said Miller. "Hell, any hospital will have the equipment."

"This isn't as if we'd found a new species of pig or ape. We can't assume anything about it."

Miller rubbed a hand over his face. "I know that."

"It would seem to me," said Hackett, "that we need all the photographs completed, of the external structure, before we even begin to cut. I would want to be there to direct the photographer because he's not going to know what we, as scientists, are going to need. We've got to make sure that every photograph has a scale, that the distance from the body to the camera lens remains constant, and that we do nothing until pictures are taken of everything."

Warren nodded, but said, "We know nothing about these beings and the breakdown of their tissues after death. If we delay, we could lose valuable data. We need to make the preliminary examination as quickly as possible."

"Doctor Hackett," said Miller.

"I think we could make a judgement about that easily. External examination of the orbital area and optic nerve might provide a clue as to the degeneration of these soft tissues. That would provide some clues."

She hesitated and Miller nodded. "What is it?"

"I'm just not sure that we should be cutting into anything here. This is not a properly designed research lab, it is a working hospital. We need an environment in which we can control the contamination and we just don't have that here. I did take a quick look into the operating theater and while I'm sure that it is adequate for the work they normally do, it simply is not adequate for what we need to do. We'd have trouble just collecting and cataloging the samples, making sure that they weren't contaminated, and getting any sort of lab work done in a timely manner."

"No," said Warren, slapping a hand on the table. "I'm not going to let a civilian come in here and stop me from beginning work on what could be the most important dissection in human history."

Miller raised an eyebrow. "A civilian isn't coming in here to do anything," he said. "We're attempting to explore the options that we have."

Hackett was taken aback by the sudden outburst. She didn't believe that she had said anything that should offend Warren. She glanced at him and said, "I was only suggesting that we need to proceed carefully."

"Yeah, like I have to be told that by some kid."

"All right, Colonel," said Miller. "That will be enough of that."

"The hell. We have a unique biological sample. Those who dissect it will find their names spread throughout the medical and biological literature. We'll be right up there with Pasteur. But now I have to listen to some . . . some kid, tell me that we have to proceed carefully." He turned on Hackett. There was anger in his eyes. "You think I need to be told that?"

"That will be all, Russ," snapped Miller.

Warren took a deep breath, let it out slowly and then said, "I do not want to lose this opportunity."

Hackett started to speak, but Miller held up a hand to silence her. He said, "We are dealing with an event that is unique in human history. We don't need to think in terms of credit or history but in how not to screw this up. We need to think

ahead of the game and if that means that we suspend the preliminary work here until we have a better idea of what to do,
or we can arrange for our sample to be transferred to a better,
meaning different, facility, then that is what we are going to
do."

"No, sir," said Warren. "I've got my orders and you've got
yours. We are to begin the preliminary work here and now
and I plan on doing that. If you try to get into the way, I'll
go over your head."

Hackett sat back and watched with fascination. She knew
that Miller outranked Warren, but they had been talking to one
another almost as if they were equals. Now Warren was trying
to usurp Miller's authority and although Miller was willing to
let some of it slide, there was a point where he would stop it.

"This is becoming counterproductive," said Miller. "You
will not make any telephone calls to anyone about this."

"You can't . . ."

"I certainly can and I will. This is something that we need
to work out here and I'm not going to let your desire for fame
get in the way of the job. If you continue to follow this line,
I will have you arrested by the counterintelligence people here.
Is that understood?"

When Warren didn't respond, Miller said, "I asked you if
that was understood."

"Yes, sir. I understood."

Miller grinned broadly, but Hackett could see that he was
still angry. He turned toward Hackett and said, "You were
saying?"

But Hackett didn't remember exactly what she had been
saying. She sat quietly for a moment, aware that time was
ticking, and finally said, "I think it would be better for the
preliminary work to be done in a facility geared for research
rather than at a military hospital."

"Reasons for that?" asked Miller.

Hackett knew that he was just trying to give Warren a
chance to cool off. She said, "I think that we need to examine
the being carefully before we do anything else. I just don't

have enough information about it to develop an intelligent plan for study."

"Then you believe that we should study it?" said Warren, sarcastically.

"Of course we need to study it, but we don't need to rush into this. We don't want to screw up the sample."

Miller pulled a file folder toward him. There was a "Top Secret" cover sheet on it. He opened it so that the first page of the document was visible.

"This," he said, "tells me what I am supposed to learn during the preliminary autopsy. I have looked at it carefully and believe it to be inadequate for the task."

"What's wrong with it?"

"I think they assumed that we would have a better facility and they based it on earth norms."

"So, call higher headquarters," said Warren, almost in triumph. "Get some additional instruction."

Now Miller had to laugh. "Unfortunately, I think that is exactly what I need to do."

CHAPTER 21

There was a quiet tap at the door and the President nodded so that one of the others in the office would open it. A brigadier general followed by two full colonels entered. The general, a tall, thin man with dark gray hair, bright blue eyes that were nearly outlined by crow's feet, and wearing a perfectly tailored uniform, walked across the expanse of light blue carpet and stopped near the President's desk.

"General Robert Thomas, reporting with a detachment of two, Mr. President."

Harry S Truman grinned and pointed at a couch pushed against the wall and said, "Have a seat, gentlemen."

Thomas grinned back and said, "No one me told the protocol for reporting to the President. I didn't know if I was supposed to salute, stand at attention, or just let you know, with the proper respect, of course, that we had arrived."

Truman raised his eyebrows and then said, "I would have thought that you would have been briefed about the protocol before you entered the White House."

Major General Curtis LeMay, who had been sitting off to the side, out of Thomas' line of sight, said quickly, "Normally, before a military officer who is unfamiliar with the Washington protocol is allowed to visit the White House, he is told precisely what is expected of him. General Thomas and his staff were summoned on short notice because of the situation and I guess that briefing was overlooked."

The President turned his attention to the new men. "Would you care for a beverage? Coffee? Lemonade?"

"Lemonade would be very nice, Mr. President," said Thomas. The colonels nodded in agreement, but neither of them spoke.

Truman moved from his desk to a chair opposite the couch, sat down and then glanced at LeMay. "How much do each of these men know?"

LeMay opened a folder, handed it to Thomas and sat back so Thomas could review the latest from New Mexico. LeMay said that the craft was not an experimental airplane or rocket that belonged to the United States because, as the chief of research and development, he knew everything that was being done. He also knew that it did not belong to the Soviets because, although the story given to the press was that the Soviets had captured the majority of the German scientists at the conclusion of the Second World War, the fact was, the American Army had captured most of them. Operation Paperclip, a clandestine mission, had brought the top scientists to the United States and many of them were in New Mexico, at the White Sands Proving Ground, where they were attempting to get captured German V-2 rockets to work so that the United States could take the first steps into space. These scientists, according to the top secret communication LeMay had received only two hours earlier, said that nothing they had worked on for the Nazis, or for the United States, resembled the object reported in New Mexico. Given what they knew, they were sure it wasn't of Russian origin.

One of the colonels asked, "Are we sure?"

"Gentleman, think this through. If we thought that it was Soviet, if we thought it was from one of the other countries on this planet, if we didn't have the craft in our possession, and if we hadn't examined the bodies of the deceased, then you could ask that question. Yes, we are sure," said LeMay.

"Jesus H. Christ," said Thomas, more for show than because he was astonished.

"General Thomas," said LeMay. "What we need is a low profile officer who can take charge in New Mexico, accomplish what needs to be done, and get out of there without alerting the press. The very last thing that we need at this point is some sort of discussion by reporters about these flying disks. Not until we have a little more information."

Truman rose, looked at his desk where the little plaque claimed "The Buck Stops Here," and passed the buck. He said, "I have a meeting with General Marshall about the European situation that can't be postponed without creating questions I would rather not answer. General LeMay speaks with my authority here. If I finish before you leave, I'll drop back in here. If not, it was a pleasure meeting you gentlemen."

Truman walked across the carpeted expanse, shook hands with Thomas, the two colonels and stepped to the door. It was opened from the outside and Truman disappeared into another part of the White House.

With the President gone, LeMay said, "Questions."

"Any indication that they are hostile?" asked Thomas.

LeMay nodded approval. "That is one of the things that we need to find out as quickly as possible. Just among us here, they hold all the high cards."

Thomas, still looking down at the folder LeMay had given him, said, "I'm not sure what my first move would be."

"Of course you do, General," said LeMay. "Security is the first move. Get the craft and the bodies out of the desert, into a secure location, and then worry about getting them out of New Mexico. Obvious."

Thomas nodded. "Yes, sir. I would imagine that there is security on the scene?"

"Provided by the base personnel there. Make sure that it remains secure and use those people if you have to. They are already privy to the secret, but let's not expand this any farther than we have to," said LeMay.

"When do we leave?"

"As soon as we're finished here. You'll have a briefing package to take with you but you cannot show it to anyone else. It should be destroyed as soon as you've finished with it and have the proper facility to ensure its destruction."

There was a quiet tap at the door. Thomas closed the folder

so that the contents were concealed. LeMay leaned back in his chair and clamped the cigar between his teeth. When all evidence of the discussion was hidden, a secret service man opened the door. The orderly, carrying a silver tray filled with glasses of lemonade, appeared and asked, "Are you gentlemen ready?"

LeMay, the look of annoyance obvious, nodded and said, tersely, "Yes."

When the lemonade was set out, and the orderly had withdrawn, LeMay looked at the secret service agent. They were part of the furniture. LeMay had been unaware that he had been in the room until he opened the door. LeMay said, "You can go too."

The secret service man, who if anyone asked would have been described as average in height, weight and with brown hair and brown eyes, and dressed in a gray suit, blended into the background. He said, "I'm supposed to be here."

"No, you're not," said LeMay. "Get out."

"Sir, my orders are . . ."

"To get out," said LeMay nastily. "And you heard nothing that went on in here."

For a moment the man hesitated and then nodded. He said, "Yes, sir." He opened the door and disappeared through it.

LeMay waited and then turned his attention back to Thomas and the two colonels. He said, "There are a couple of things that are not in that briefing folder."

Thomas leaned forward, picked up the lemonade, drank, and set the glass back. He looked over at LeMay and waited.

LeMay took his cigar from his mouth, and then said, "Gentlemen, would you excuse General Thomas and me for a few minutes. Take your lemonade and wait outside."

When the two colonels were gone, LeMay said, "What I tell you is not to leave this room. You do not discuss it with anyone else, ever, not even the two men you brought here this morning. I want that completely understood."

Thomas nodded.

LeMay put the cigar in his mouth, puffed for a moment, until there was a blue cloud around his head and said, "There are things that the president doesn't know and he doesn't want to know. He has given this baby to me and told me to do what I think is necessary."

"Yes, General."

"Two days ago I issued an order through fighter command that we were to search the southwest for one of these flying disks, and if we found one, with no civilian witnesses around, we were to bring it down. Shoot it down."

Thomas sat unmoving, staring at LeMay, but he felt his head spin. It seemed to be fairly short-sighted to try to shoot down a craft from another world. If nothing else, it suggested how hostile the people of Earth were. No one had to worry about the aliens, they had to worry about the United States Army. Thomas could think of no good reply, let alone a good reason for the action.

LeMay seemed to understand this because he said, "Think of the technological leap we could make if we could capture one."

"Yes, General."

"More importantly, we are no longer at their complete mercy. They control the high ground. They control the sky. We can only watch as their craft dance around the heavens, and if they decide to attack, our response would be feeble. There is not much we could do against them, even if every country on the Earth cooperated."

Thomas understood this and nodded.

"Last night we were apparently successful. A fighter over west Texas and eastern New Mexico, in that broad expanse of nothing, found one of these saucers, played with it, and finally fired on it. A missile hit it, there was an explosion, and the craft fell out of the sky."

"Good Christ, general, was that smart?" said Thomas without thinking about it.

LeMay had to grin. "Probably not, but now we've got one, on the ground. I want to make sure that we keep it. I think that we're going to need it."

Thomas took another drink of the lemonade, wished that it was something stronger, and waited.

"Anyway," said LeMay, "smart or not, we now have one. I'm telling you this, so that you understand that the need for secrecy goes beyond the fact that we have one. We can't let anyone know that we shot it out of the sky."

"General," said Thomas.

LeMay, paying no attention to Thomas, actually laughed. "I didn't think it would work, given what we had seen. Their acceleration is fantastic. They can outrun bullets, and I figured they could outrun the missiles as well. We just caught them off guard and the missile did what it was supposed to do. Damaged it and knocked it down."

"Well," said Thomas, "that explains how we knew where to find it."

LeMay laughed again. "Told the men on the scene that it was radar and reconnaissance that found it." He waved a hand. "The point, Robert, is that we have to keep this under wraps. We don't want anyone finding out why the thing crashed, or, for that matter, that we have it."

"Yes, General."

"There are probably a couple of other points that need to be made, in case you haven't figured them out."

Thomas raised an eyebrow and said, "Yes, sir?"

"Have you wondered why these things are being seen in the southwest?"

"No, General, but in all honesty, I've just been brought into this thing. I've reviewed the materials that we had, and looked at the situation boards where these things have been posted. I noticed that there was a heavy concentration over the southwest, but I also noticed a concentration in the northwest, around the Seattle, Washington, area."

"Think about it this way. The first atomic bomb was dropped on New Mexico, and, we are firing rockets into space from New Mexico. Much of our atomic research is being conducted in New Mexico. Seems to me, that if I were a space traveling race, I would want to know what sort of threat this newly discovered civilization would be to me. So, I check out their capabilities and the most advanced research on the planet is being conducted anywhere. That explains why there have been so many sightings here. They're making a recon of our facilities and capabilities."

"And Washington state?" asked Thomas.

"More atomic research going on there. I don't know what sort of instrumentation these creatures might have, but if they are looking for signs of atomic research, then the northwest would draw their attention."

LeMay held up his hand to stop a comment and added, "Yes, we can test that by seeing if there are large number of sightings around Oak Ridge. There have been some, but not in the numbers that we have seen elsewhere."

"Yes, sir," said Thomas, confused. He had no real need to know this and suspected that it was speculation by LeMay, or one of his staff. He had learned, long ago, that when a superior begins to speculate, or in this case, ramble, the best course was to nod and agree with him.

"Given that," said LeMay, "we put a few airplanes into the sky in the locations most likely for a sighting."

"Yes, sir."

"General, I can't stress the importance of this. Think about Pearl Harbor and how unprepared we were for the war. We knew it was coming but when the war started, we still had biplanes in the inventory. Think of how long a World War One fighter would last against a Mustang. Seconds. That's where we are here. The capabilities that we have observed put us in the fighter and them into jets. We are outclassed, can be outmaneuvered, and are probably outgunned."

"A position we found ourselves in frequently in the last war," said Thomas.

"But that is no way to fight a war. Now we have an advantage. We have, you might say, stolen the plans for the enemy's fighter."

"We don't know they're an enemy," said Thomas.

There was anger in LeMay's eyes, but it faded rapidly. "No, General, you're right. We don't know they're an enemy. But, for our own safety, and until we learn differently, I think that we have to assume the worst."

"Yes, General."

LeMay stopped talking, looked down at the folder and then back at Thomas. He said, "You see how important this is. How soon can you leave?"

"I'm ready now."

LeMay stood, as did Thomas. They shook hands. "I know that you'll keep this thing contained."

"Yes, sir."

CHAPTER | 22

Captain Jack Reed stood at the top of a ridge and looked down at the scrub brush, dried grass, cactus, and rock. There was a flat-bed truck, a crane, a half dozen jeeps and seven or eight big trucks known as six by sixes. A hundred men were working to remove the craft from the arroyo and get it up onto the flatbed for transport to the base. No one had bothered to worry about the route they would take once they had left the desert. At the moment they merely wanted to get the craft loaded and covered so that it would be out of sight.

On the ridge with him were another twenty or twenty-five solders. Each was armed with an M-1 carbine. They all wore fatigues, helmets, and pistol belts. Their job was to make sure that no one, meaning no civilian, was able to reach the top of the ridge where he or she would be able to see down to the craft that clearly was not an airplane.

The bodies, and the one survivor, had been removed from the scene as the sun had come up. The survivor had been carried in one of the ambulances, a box-like vehicle that had huge red crosses on the sides and tiny windows in the rear. It had been accompanied by the two men who had helped Reed lift it from the damaged ship. They had come out on the ambulance.

The bodies of the other crew members, covered and then wrapped in canvas, had been taken out in the rear of a big truck. It rolled out about fifteen minutes after the sun had come up. Reed had watched the soldiers load it, and then watched as it had driven away, following the path that had been carved out by the first vehicles in. Now, all that was left was to get the ship itself out of the valley and under cover before any one learned that it had crashed.

Douglass climbed the rocky hill, stood up and walked to where Reed waited. He hitchhiked a thumb over his shoulder and said, "I think it'll take another fifteen minutes. It'll fit easily on the truck. That thing can't weight more than a thousand pounds."

"Once it's out of here," said Reed, "I think we should bring in some experts on camouflage to clean up. And to hide the tire tracks of our trucks."

"Not until we sweep this area with mine detectors and then a police call on hands and knees. We've got to make sure we pick up every little scrap."

"And then?" asked Reed.

"It's out of our hands. It'll be someone else's problem."

There was a flash of sunlight as one of the stubby delta wings caught and reflected the sun. Reed watched as the ship was lifted ten feet in the air. The engine on the crane belched black smoke, and the cab and arm with the cables around the ship swung around and deposited it on the flat bed. A dozen men scrambled over it, releasing the cables, and then jumped clear.

"We're going to have to cover it," said Reed. "Hide the shape some way."

"Easily done," said Douglass. "Put some two by fours up and drape canvas over it. People will think it's a rocket for White Sands or something like that."

Reed crouched down and picked up a handful of stones. He tossed them away one at a time. "We're about through here. There's really nothing else for us to do."

"But plenty on the base," said Douglass. "I'm going to want a roster of everyone who was out here. I want each of them briefed on the penalty for revealing classified information to those not authorized to have it. I want to make sure that no one talks out of turn."

Reed look up at him. "Is that really necessary?"

"In this case, I think the generals are going to demand it. They're going to want to make sure that no one says anything about what this is until they're ready to release the information."

Reed dusted his hands off and stood up. The men below were attempting to pull canvas over the ship so that no one would see it. They had stuck poles in the side of the flatbed to hold the canvas up, off the ship. They were tying down the ends and slowly the ship was beginning to disappear.

CHAPTER 23

Brigadier General Robert Thomas, who had arrived an hour earlier and who had immediately requested the use of Colonel William Blanchard's conference room, stood at the head of the table. The khaki uniform he wore was rumpled from the long flight across the country and was decorated only with the stars of a brigadier general. He wore none of the ribbons for the medals he had won, none of the qualification badges he was authorized to wear, and no name tag that would have told those who didn't know him what his name was. He was, as President Truman had requested, and General LeMay had underscored, the anonymous officer who could take charge of the situation in New Mexico and handle it. Thomas was a man with enough rank to be responsible, but not so high in the table of organization that reporters, senators, or other military officers would miss him while he was in New Mexico taking care of the situation.

At the table were the two colonels who had accompanied him, neither of whom wore their ribbons, their name tags, and in their cases, not even the silver eagles that would identify them as colonels. They were even more anonymous than their boss.

The authority for what they were doing came from the single copy of the orders that Thomas carried, and from Colonel Blanchard who had, when Thomas and his team arrived, communicated with Brigadier General Roger Ramey at Eighth Air Force Headquarters in Fort Worth, Texas, who had, in turn, communicated with General George Kenny at Strategic Command Headquarters in Washington, D.C., who had then called the Chief of Staff of the Army, General Dwight D. Eisenhower. Word had filtered back, rapidly, that Thomas was exactly who he said he was and that everything he wanted to do had been approved at the highest levels. No further discussion of the situation was encouraged or desired.

So Thomas, holding a glass of water in his hand, stood at the head of the table in Colonel Blanchard's conference and looked at the assembled men and the single woman. They were seated around the battered oak conference table, sitting in oak chairs that looked as if they had been on the ark with Noah, each with a pad and pencil in front of him or her. There was a glass water pitcher on a platter, with a half dozen glasses, sitting in the middle of the table. The few pictures on the walls showed scenes of the Army in action but included nothing of Army Air Forces. Unlike the rest of the building, the conference room was air conditioned, with the unit installed in a window, quietly throwing out the cold air.

Thomas looked down at the table, where his notes had been laid, and at the file folder, open to the picture of the alien creature sitting against the rock wall of a cliff north of town. All the material in his folder was classified as top secret and would have commanded a top price had Thomas wanted to sell it.

"I want a full briefing of the current situation," said Thomas. "I want it from the beginning and I want it in complete detail."

Jack Reed, whose khaki uniform was now dirty, torn in two places, and sweat-stained, said, without preamble, "I believe that I began this on July 1."

Reed, because he had been formally introduced to Thomas, but who pretended that he hadn't for security reasons, then told the general everything that had happened since July first that he believed Thomas didn't already know. He mentioned the appearance of the two CIC, Counter Intelligence Agents, who had gone out to the crash site with him the night before.

"Are they in this room?" asked Thomas.

"No, sir."

Thomas turned to one of his colonels and said, "Find them and get them in here."

"Yes, sir." The colonel left the room.

"Continue," said Thomas.

Reed told of the arrival, though he had not been part of that, of medical personnel, he believed from Washington, D.C., though he didn't know that, of two civilians from Washington, D.C., but didn't mention that he knew one of the civilians which was why he knew they were from Washington.

"Are they in this room."

"The medical doctors are not," said Reed, "but the other two are."

Thomas looked at Danni Hackett. He said, "And you are?"

Hackett said nothing but pointed at Wheeler who took a copy of his orders from his pocket and slid them across the table so that Thomas would be able to read them. Thomas reached out, spun them around and then pushed them back toward Wheeler.

"Okay," he said.

There was a quiet knock, a hesitation, and then the door opened and the colonel returned with the two Army Counter Intelligence Agents. Douglass looked at Thomas and without waiting for Thomas to say a word, said, "General, I am not in your chain of command and I am not responsible to you."

Thomas stared at Douglass for what seemed to be a full minute, though it was much shorter, attempting to intimidate him with his gaze. When that failed, Thomas said, "You are a member of the United States Army?"

"Yes, sir."

"And, if you are not a general officer, we may assume, safely, that I outrank you?"

"Yes, sir."

"Then never tell me that you are outside my chain of command," he said, furiously. "If you ever say that again to me, you will find yourself unemployed. Do you understand me?"

Douglass stood quietly for a moment, thinking it over. Realizing that a general officer could, indeed, make trouble, he said, "I apologize, General. I believe we have a simple mis-understanding that can be clarified in private."

That had not been what Thomas expected. "When I ask you if you understand, I want to hear either yes sir or no sir but no long-winded explanation of the facts from your point of view. Do you understand that?"

Douglass nodded and said, "Yes, sir."

"Sit down. And be advised that my authority comes from the Commander in Chief, meaning the President and from the Chief of Staff of the Army, and this bullshit about CIC being separate from the rest of the Army is not going to be tolerated in this situation. The sooner you understand that, the better it is going to be for you."

"Yes, sir."

"Then sit down and shut up. I'll come back to you." Thomas turned his attention back to Reed. "Have you finished your report, Captain?"

"I just wanted to mention that we got the bodies off the site at first light. They were transported here, meaning the hospital on the base. They craft has also been transported. I don't know what happened to the bodies or the craft."

Thomas glanced at the roster he had set on the table. "Doctor Hackett?"

"Yes, sir," she said. Without waiting for further instruction, she said, "We did a little preliminary work, which means that we weighed and measured the bodies, photographed them, and looked for external signs of trauma. We have not cut into them yet, fearing contamination at the facility here. We wanted another environment where contamination, both from us and from them, could be contained. The operating rooms here, as well as the morgue facility, did not provide adequate safe-guards."

"Why not?"

"Simply because, when constructing an operating theater and a morgue, it is not necessary to isolate it to the degree that I think necessary in this case. You have to admit that this is a unique situation."

"So you don't know what we have here," said Thomas.

"You haven't thoroughly examined the samples."

Hackett took a moment before answering. She said, somewhat formally, "We know enough to suggest that the bodies are not indigenous to this planet. They are of no known racial or ethnic background, nor do they seem to be an evolutionary diversion that has remained in isolation on the Earth."

Thomas rocked back in his chair, tented his fingers under his chin and said, "I would have thought that made more sense than beings from another world."

"Where would you suggest they developed their technology? Where would they be hidden?" asked Hackett. "The inner Earth? Haven't we explored this planet well enough that if there was any sort of a pocket of a technologically advanced race we would have found it, or more to the point, they would have found us and stopped us before we started the war and then developed atomic weapons. Is there much of this planet that wasn't photographed by air for mapping prior to the war, and certainly during it, by us, our allies, or our enemies to reveal such a race?"

"Point taken, Doctor," said Thomas.

"They are certainly humanoid," said Hackett, not giving any ground, "and surprisingly human, though there are some obvious differences. The skull is about twenty percent larger, the eyes are twenty percent larger, and the pupils are almost fifty percent larger. There are no finger or toenails, the joints are much more flexible on the fingers, and the fingers themselves are about thirty percent longer. That gives their fingers a look that is somewhat reminiscent of a tentacle."

She glanced down at her notes and then back up at Thomas who remained silent. She continued. "There were no obvious sexual organs, either primary or secondary, that we recognized. The body was surprisingly thin and the bones seemed to be very lightweight. I hesitate to say anything here, but it seems they are more like bird bones. They may be brittle. It could suggest an evolutionary process that lead to intelligence from a bird-like species rather than that of the apes as happened on this planet."

She waved a hand and said, "But this is all speculative. We

need to perform a detailed autopsy to get the answers to some of these questions."

"How long would that take," asked Thomas.

"Properly done? Ten days at a minimum."

"Could you do it here?"

"It could be done here, but I would think that a more controlled environment would be better," said Hackett. "Something where we have positive air pressure, air locks, and something that is more isolated than Roswell. We should concern ourselves with contamination, that in both directions, meaning we should worry about contamination from them and to them. We don't want to find Earth bacteria in them."

"Isn't it a bit late for that?" asked Thomas.

Hackett shrugged and said, "Why? If there has been contamination of the samples, at this point, it is minor. There is no reason not to begin those procedures, which would be to perform the autopsy in isolation."

One of the colonels said, "I though this was isolated."

Hackett misunderstood the joke and said, "No, you've got a town and about fifteen thousand people here. We need something far away from a population center."

Thomas said, "Like the Antarctic."

"That would be perfect," said Hackett. "The cold would inhibit the growth of any bacteria, either ours or theirs. It is isolated so that there is no problem with either contaminating people or the bacteria escaping into the outside environment. And it would discourage idle curiosity."

Thomas pointed at one of the colonels and said, "Find out what we have in the Antarctic."

"I suspect," said the colonel, "that the proper facilities will have to be built there."

"Find out," repeated Thomas, an edge to his voice.

"Yes, sir."

"Is that it?"

Hackett nodded and said, "That's all we have right now. There wasn't much we could do without contaminating the specimen and without cutting into it."

"Okay," he said. "I'll want to take a look at one of them

when we finish up here. Now, what about the craft?"

One of the officers pulled a rolled up paper from his brief-case and then set a file folder next to it. He said, "We have photographs of the ship itself, of course, both inside and out-side. And we have a drawing, rough, of it in three exploded views."

Thomas indicated he wanted the folder, thumbed through the photographs, and then returned them to the file folder. The ship was triangular-shaped, with a couple of slanted tail fins. Everything was rounded and molded together. He could see, from the man standing next to it, that it was no larger than one of the smaller fighters being used by the Army. It didn't look radically different from an airplane though there seemed to be something alien about the design.

Thomas listened as the officer explained that the ship was extremely light and that four or five men could lift it. They hadn't needed a crane to lift it onto the truck, though they had used one, and if they could have securely tied it to the back of a pick up truck, the truck could have hauled it to the base. The craft was a lightweight ship that was strong enough for flight in outer space.

When the officer finished, Thomas asked, "Anything else?"

Another officer, who looked as if he was a college profes-sor, but whose uniform held combat decorations including the Distinguished Service Cross, the second highest award for valor the country had to offer, stood. Though his hair was thinning, it was dark and he had bright eyes.

He took a small piece of material that could have been metal, or it could have been wood, and set it on the conference table. To Thomas, he said, "My name is Rafferty, General, and I have been looking at the composition of the skin of this thing. Small pieces of it were broken off and I confess I don't understand the dynamics here. This metal, wood, whatever, has resisted our efforts to cut it, drill into it, or melt it. It's stronger than hell, seems to be some kind of a composite metal alloy with a honeycomb weave in it, but I don't really know."

"The ship is made of that?"

"As far as I can tell," said Rafferty. "I studied a little metallurgy in college, and have worked with our metal people here, and I've never seen anything like this. I don't know how they broke up on impact. It should have held together, or the forces to rip it apart should have been strong enough to shred the bodies."

"Meaning?" asked Thomas.

Rafferty looked at Hackett and she said, "An impact of sufficient force to cause damage to the ship should have been great enough to destroy the rather weak, thin-skinned, crew. They should have been little more than smears on the deck or the bulkheads, not the intact bodies we found."

"Do you have an explanation for that?"

Hackett took a moment, and then said, "No, sir, I don't unless there is some sort of a force field that surrounded the crew compartment, meaning, I suppose, that the forces that damaged the ship had been dissipated on the outside. Something absorbed the energy and dispersed it throughout the hull."

"I'll need some kind of analysis of that, Rafferty," said Thomas.

"Yes, sir."

"News release?" asked another officer, when he was sure that the discussion of the metal had ended.

"No. Not at this time. We'll talk about that later."

Thomas waited for a moment and then said, "If there is nothing else, let's get back to work. Doctor Hackett, Captain Reed, and Mister Douglass, I'd like to you remain. You too, Mister Wheeler."

When the others had left the room and the door was again closed, Thomas said, "Move on up closer. I don't want to have to shout across the table."

When they had complied, and everyone was crowded at the one end of the table, Thomas said, "Each of you, in some capacity, has been involved in this from the very beginning, or nearly the beginning. We're going to need a special team, and I don't want to tell any more people about this crash than I have to. That means we form the team from those who are already directly involved and who have complete knowledge of the situation, which, of course, means you."

"There are quite a few people who know more about this than I do," said Reed.

Thomas held out his hand and one of the colonels put a file folder with a red Top Secret stamped top and bottom in it. Thomas opened it, read for a moment and then said, "You were dispatched to White Sands."

"Yes, sir, but that doesn't qualify me to report on what was observed and the functioning of the radars there."

"I see that you were consulted by Mister Wheeler, here."

Reed glanced at Wheeler and then said, "Not consulted, per se. I knew him in Europe. He called to tell me he was coming to the base, but said nothing about his involvement with these flying disks."

"And you were first to enter the ship."

"General," said Reed, "all this is true. But I have no real expertise in aerodynamics, biology, space flight, rockets. I'm a simple intelligence officer who was trained on the job and who would much rather be assigned to flying status."

"And your are the only person in the country who can say that he was involved from the very beginning." Thomas grinned broadly. "Besides, you are a trained intelligence officer, even if it was on the job, so you know how to evaluate and analyze data. That is a talent that should come in handy as we proceed with this." Thomas closed the folder signaling the end to the debate.

"Lady, and gentlemen, what I see here is the core of the team. You all have an expertise that will be useful to us in planning a way to exploit this . . . what should we call it? Happening? Situation? Well, whatever. We need to begin to think of what we want to do and how we want to do it."

Douglass said, "I'm not assigned here. I'm assigned to the CIC."

Thomas grinned at him, but it was a more evil grin, and one that held no humor. "Mister Douglass, or should I say, 'Captain'? As a member of the CIC you will have the responsibility for those assigned to our project after we get to our new location. Don't worry. Your assignment has been cleared with your command structure."

"General," said Douglass, "I don't want this assignment."

"Well, gee," said Thomas sarcastically, "I don't believe anyone asked you for your opinion. You have your assignment and it won't be altered at this time." When Douglass didn't say anything, Thomas added, "When given your instructions, you say, 'Yes, sir,' enthusiastically."

"Yes, sir." There was no enthusiasm in Douglass' voice.

"And I don't want to have to remind you of this again," said Thomas.

"Yes, sir."

"I have only the preliminaries worked out here," said Thomas. "As we get more information, it will be provided. I would suggest that each of you begin the preparations for a transfer from this facility."

Hackett spoke for the first time. "I live in Washington, D.C."

"Yes, you do," said Thomas. "As does Mister Wheeler. We will either close your apartment, or keep it open for you for the duration of this assignment."

"How long will that be?" asked Hackett.

Thomas grinned once again. "Well, that is a question that I can't answer at this time. I'm just putting together the teams. You'll have to play it by ear."

"That's not much help."

Thomas stood up and said, "If there are no questions, we have work to do. I'll expect to be kept informed of where each of you will be. Plan on another get together in ten or twelve hours. By that time we should have a better handle on things."

"General," said Reed.

"I'll talk to each of you in turn before that meeting. Now, please, I have a lot of work to do." Thomas moved toward the door. One of the colonels opened it and he disappeared through it, holding it open. Thomas and the other colonel walked through, and the three of them disappeared down the hall.

Douglass waited for just a moment and then said, "Bullshit."

CHAPTER 24

July 5, 1947
The Pentagon
Arlington, Virginia

Major General Curtis LeMay sat behind his highly polished desk, a cigar clenched between his teeth, and waited impatiently. Before him sat a leather folder that contained several highly classified documents, including a list of names of scientists who could be trusted and military officers who understood the workings of atomic weapons, and who had been with him during the firebombings of Japan at the close of the war.

There was a quiet tapping on the door, it opened slightly, and LeMay's aide stuck his head in. "Colonel Lloyd and Doctor Smith are here."

LeMay raised his hand and gestured, telling his aide to have the men come in.

Lloyd walked briskly into the room, stopped short of LeMay and saluted sharply. "Colonel Lloyd reporting, General."

Lloyd was a tall, very thin officer who had little hair on top of his head. He had a very round face with features spread across it so that his head looked almost too large for his body. His uniform was well-tailored, and had been freshly cleaned.

LeMay removed the cigar from his mouth, returned the salute, and said, "Have a seat, Lloyd. You too, Doctor."

Smith was a smaller man in a well-fitted suit, but one that was neither expensive nor fashionable. Though his tie was conservative, his shirt was a nearly brilliant white. He had light-colored hair that made it look as if he was balding, but close inspection proved his hair thick. His eyes were dark, but intelligent. He had avoided combat by being an essential em-

ployee in one of the engineering fields that dealt with the new
science of nuclear physics.

Smith dropped onto the blue couch and looked at the spread
of magazines on the coffee table in from of him. They were
not light reading, but technical journals that covered a range
of aeronautical subjects. He leaned back, looked at the paintings on the opposite wall.

LeMay got up from behind his desk and walked around it
to sit in the chair opposite Smith and next to Lloyd. He left
his cigar in the ashtray at his desk so that the cloud of blue
smoke was rising from it. He sat for a moment, looking at
Smith and thought that Smith didn't fit his view of a scientist.

"Gentlemen," said LeMay. "We have a problem." He
stopped talking, but neither man filled the silence. LeMay
leaned back in his chair and stared up, at the ceiling, as if
thinking about what he wanted to say.

"Colonel," said LeMay, "you have some expertise in working with our atomic weapons."

"Yes, General," said Lloyd.

"Doctor . . ."

Smith grinned. "General, why not come right out with it?"

LeMay laughed and said, "Sometimes these things are hard
to begin. I'm not at liberty to provide you with a great deal
of information here, and the information I do have is highly
classified. We won't be discussing it outside these walls."

"I understand," said Smith.

Carefully, LeMay said, "There have been, in the last few
days, a set of circumstances developed that might be considered unique in human history."

"You mean like the development of the atomic bombs, the
air war in Europe and the Pacific or the use of rockets to kill
people hundreds of miles away?"

"Doctor, if you have a problem with our decisions made in
the heat of a world war, maybe this is not the place for you.
Maybe a nice, quiet job in academia, where you could convince your students that we were somehow the aggressors in
the war and that our mission was colonialism."

"I'm sorry, General, but you misunderstand. I was suggesting that we have been faced with many such events in the last few years. No one in the last century could have imagined what would happen."

"Yes," said LeMay. He repeated, "Unique." He thought for a moment and then added, "We have a classified research facility hidden in the deserts of Nevada. It was created during the war and it had a number of functions, one of which was to provide a secure location where certain sorts of experiments could be accomplished without having to worry about problems with either the civilian community or the press."

Smith grinned and said, "You mean biological warfare."

LeMay half smiled and said, "Of course. We feared that the enemy would develop and use biological weapons."

"But they didn't," said Smith, accusingly.

"Actually, Doctor," said LeMay, "the Japanese tried. You might have heard of the balloon bombs. Japanese scientists discovered a current of air, high above the ground, that rushed from west to east at a hundred knots or more. They believed that if they could put balloons into that current, those balloons would be pushed to the United States. They tested the theory with fragmentation and incendiary weapons. They managed to start some forest fires and they killed six people."

"But that isn't a biological weapon. That is an extension of the sort of aerial warfare we conducted."

LeMay felt the anger rise. This was typical of civilians. They didn't understand warfare and thought of it as something soldiers and sailors did, but high-minded and educated civilians did not.

He said, controlling his voice, "Their plan, had they believed that any of their balloons had reached us, was to use anthrax as a biological agent. They tested their weapons on American prisoners of war."

Lloyd spoke for the first time in several minutes. He said, "What does that have to do with us, General."

LeMay shot him a glance, almost surprised by the statement, and then said, "I was simply providing some background about the research facility and why it had been located where it was."

"Yes, sir."

"I have been giving all this a lot of thought, considering the unique circumstances in which we find ourselves."

"That is the second time you brought that up, General," said Smith. "Just what are these unique circumstances."

LeMay said, "The Soviets are building an arsenal of biological weapons."

"Which doesn't mean we are required to follow their lead," said Smith.

"The reason, I believe, that chemical weapons were not introduced in the war was that everyone had them and everyone knew what they could do. Everyone knew that if one side used them, then the other side would use them. We prevented the use by having our own arsenal. Do you suggest that we fail to follow the Soviet lead because of some higher, moralistic reasoning?"

Smith was quiet for a moment and then shook his head. "No, General. I just find the idea of employing biological weapons to be abhorrent."

"Doctor . . ."

"No, General, let me finish. We're not talking about a weapon that has a limited destructive power, or a weapon that's effect will be restricted to a small area. We're not talking about a weapon that can even be seen, but one that can kill without being seen. You mentioned anthrax. Do you know anything about it?"

"I know enough, Doctor."

"Well, let me tell you a little more. The first danger is that it will infect livestock, killing them. If a person eats beef from an infected animal, he can contract intestinal anthrax. Though rare, it is fatal. But more dangerous is the strain known as woolsorters' disease. It attacks the lungs because it is breathed into the body. A suffocating bronchitis develops that is usually fatal. I stress that. It is fatal."

"Localized outbreaks of the disease can be controlled," said LeMay.

"Yes, but at what costs. They can drop the spores, allowing the wind to take them over large areas and suddenly there are thousands dead. That windblown spore might have been dropped hundreds of miles from the outbreak. It would be difficult to stop and it would result in a mass panic, not to mention the deaths."

"I understand that," said LeMay.

"But let's say that there are only a few human deaths. That the anthrax infects only the herbivores. The animals either die from ingesting the spore, which is looking for a damp, warm place, or they are destroyed by the government to halt the outbreak. Millions of cattle are killed and the impact is in the natural products that would be lost, not to mention shutting down one section of the food supply, would be catastrophic. That could create shortages in many areas, leading to hunger, riots, and more killing."

"Yes," said LeMay.

"Now, let's postulate a use of a more easily vectored disease, such as smallpox. We have seen what it can do to a population that is unprepared for it."

LeMay was becoming bored with the lecture. "Smallpox is a thing of the past."

"The point, General, is that if the enemy can introduce, to a population, a disease similar to smallpox, that is airborne, and can be transmitted from individual to individual, and that has an incubation period of days to weeks, the infection can be spread throughout that population before anyone is aware that the disease has erupted."

"We seem to have lost our focus here," said LeMay. "To return to that . . ."

"If I may, General. We are talking about a weapon system and the means of employment."

"And all I have suggested, to this point, is that we have a facility that is being used to conduct research."

"Abhorrent research."

"Doctor," snapped LeMay, "if you find this abhorrent, then you may go. Now."

Smith looked as if he was going to stand up and leave, looked as if he was going to erupt into anger, and then visibly calmed. He said, "I'm sorry that you have misunderstood me,

General. I was merely indicating some of the problems with any attempt to use biological weapons."

"I appreciate your candor, Doctor, but if you are not going to be a happy member of the team, now is the time to say so."

Smith nodded and said, "I think my presence on this team will be of benefit to everyone."

"I agree," said LeMay.

He waited to see if Smith had anything else to say and then said, "As you can see, we have a problem with the facility and that is the possibility of contamination." LeMay looked at Smith and asked, "What is the best way to eliminate the contamination?"

"Heat will destroy any bacterium."

"How hot?" asked LeMay.

"Boiling kills them. That's two-twelve at sea level. Most are dead by a hundred sixty. Anything over that will kill them."

"How long?"

"How long?" repeated Smith. "I don't understand."

"How long must it stay at that temperature to destroy the bacteria."

"Fifteen minutes. Thirty," said Smith.

"What we need," said LeMay, "is a way of insuring that we have no contamination from our facility into the general population. We have done everything that we can think of, as this facility was constructed, to isolate it."

"Blow it up," said Lloyd.

"Problem with that," said Smith, "is that the explosion might not produce sufficient heat over a wide enough area to ensure that all the bacterium have been incinerated. The explosion just might scatter the bacterium over a wider area more quickly than it would be done in just a general, non-catastrophic release."

"There seems to be but one way to do this," said LeMay.

Smith looked directly at LeMay, stared at him, and then nodded as if he understood it completely.

"I have an atomic weapon at my disposal, that could be

placed and that can be remotely detonated," said LeMay.

"What in the hell for?" asked Lloyd.

Smith, who seemed quite comfortable with the idea, asked, "Are the people assigned to that facility aware of this?"

LeMay shook his head. "No."

Lloyd sat there, shaking his head, as if unable to believe what he was being told. Smith, who had been in government service for over two decades, and had heard some very strange requests during the war, was not shocked. Instead, he asked, pragmatically, "You don't expect either one of us to remain on the scene to detonate the weapon do you?"

LeMay wished that he hadn't left his cigar on his desk. He said, "I want you to transport the device, install it, and then get out."

Lloyd said, "But General, you can't just install this thing and not tell those in the facility that it's there."

"That decision, Colonel, has been made."

"But . . ."

"No further discussion on that point is desired," said LeMay, coldly.

"When would we leave?" asked Smith.

"I'm working to get the various components collected and available in Nevada inside of thirty-six or forty-eight hours. You'll have time to pack and arrange your schedules before you need to get out to Andrews for the flight."

LeMay looked at Lloyd. The colonel's color was bad, and he was sweating heavily, even in the air-conditioned coolness of the office. Lloyd was a technician, a man who held expertise in a field where there were few experts. He held his rank, not because he had been a combat officer, not because he was a natural leader, but because of his technical knowledge in very specific fields. He had never sent men out to their deaths, nor had he ordered fire raids that burned whole cities to the ground. He had not ordered those raids knowing that tens of thousands, possibly hundreds of thousands, would die. Even though he had been through the war, he lived in a different world than combat officers.

"I understand, General," said Smith.

"General," said Lloyd, shaking his head as if in disbelief. "We haven't been properly briefed on this."

LeMay nodded and said, "There'll be an officer on the plane with the material you need. He'll be able to answer your questions." LeMay hesitated, ran a hand through his thick, black hair, and added, "I can't tell you the importance of this. Maybe nothing will happen, but if it does, we must be prepared. We thought of the war as a challenge to civilization and the world, but this ... thing ... area of research and experimentation could literally destroy life on this planet as we know it."

Lloyd said, simply, "Yes, General."

CHAPTER | 25

July 8, 1947
Roswell Army Air Field
Roswell, New Mexico

The headline in the newspaper said it all. "RAAF Captures Flying Saucer On Ranch In Roswell Region." Although the story itself was vague, giving few details and mentioning only a few names of local residents or base personnel, it was the leak that Thomas had feared from the moment he had set foot in New Mexico hours earlier. And even though the story had only been out for an hour or so, it was generating telephone inquiries from around the country and around the world. The base switchboard was swamped with incoming telephone calls, making it nearly impossible to get an outside line.

Thomas sat in the office that had been provided for him. It was small, containing a battered desk, a telephone hooked to the base switchboard but no access to the civilian telephone system except through the switchboard, an extraordinarily bright light on the edge of the desk, a single typewriter, and a chair with a wheel that refused to turn. To make it worse, the window had been nailed shut and it was furnace hot inside and out.

Thomas looked up when he heard a noise at the door. The man held the headline. Thomas read it and said, "Bring the damn thing here."

He read the newspaper quickly and said, "I'll need to talk to the public information officer."

"The one here?"

"Yes. He didn't do this on his own. And I want to talk to

our specialist. I want to know how badly this is going to hurt us."

"Yes, sir. May I say that I believe that it is hotter in here than it is outside."

Thomas laughed. "They didn't exactly give us the best accommodations, did they?"

"If I might be so bold. Maybe you should pull a few strings. A call to Washington . . ."

"When I get too uncomfortable I will move over to the officer's club where there is air conditioning, find a table, a drink, and continue to work. Besides, Blanchard understands the situation and he understands that as a general I can fuck him up royally. If I ask, he'd vacate his office."

"Yes sir."

"Get the PIO for me."

A moment later another man tapped on the door. He was a short, thin man who was balding. He seemed to be nervous and his light colored eyes were darting back and forth. He wore a sweat-stained khaki uniform that had wilted in the heat. The silver bars of a captain were pinned to his collar, and there were aircrewman wings above his left breast pocket. He was not a pilot.

When Thomas looked up, he walked in, stopped near the desk and saluted. "Captain Davis reporting as ordered, sir."

"At ease, Davis." Thomas spun the newspaper around so that he could read it. "What can you tell me about this?"

"Colonel Blanchard ordered it. I walked it over to the newspapers and the radio stations, sir."

"What was Colonel Blanchard thinking?"

"The colonel rarely takes me into his confidence."

"You're beginning to annoy me, Davis. I want an answer."

Davis stood there for a moment and it looked as if he was not going to answer. Then he glanced at the newspaper and said, "I think Colonel Blanchard wanted to explain what was going on."

"Fine," said Thomas. "Why call it a flying saucer?"

"I think," said Davis, "because no one knows what they are, the flying saucers I mean, Colonel Blanchard thought it best to suggest that we were on top of the situation."

"I see," said Thomas and then said, "Okay. Thank you."

The man came to attention, looked as if he was going to salute, and then turned, leaving the office.

Thomas thought for a moment about that as he stared out at the parking lot. Heat shimmered on it, telling him how hot it still was outside.

Finally Thomas turned and picked up the telephone. He said, "I need an autovon line." An instant later he heard a dial tone that told him the Army long distance system, the autovon, had been activated. He dialed a five digit number and then waited.

When the phone was answered, Thomas asked for the general, and a moment later he heard, "General LeMay."

"We have a problem," said Thomas.

"This is not a secure line," said LeMay.

"I understand that, General. I wanted you to know that the afternoon edition of the local newspaper has a story about the flying saucer."

"Shit. I sent you out there to avoid this sort of a problem," said LeMay, angrily.

"Yes, sir. This was in the pipeline before we arrived. The local commander authorized it."

"He in your office there? He handy? I'd like to talk to his ass."

"No, sir. He's not handy. General, I've been with my staff about this, and I believe that we have a solution."

There was a momentary silence and then LeMay, seeming to be calmer, said, "Go ahead."

"It's relatively simple, sir. We have the General substitute debris from a balloon and or some wreckage from an airplane or rocket. Claim that is what has been found."

"Nobody is going to believe that," said LeMay.

"Actually," said Thomas, "I think they will. We'll have Marcel there, the man named in the original article, with the material. General Ramey will call it all a simple error and there won't be anybody to say otherwise. The sheriff won't talk if we ask him not to and we can bring the rancher in here. We have it all in the bag. There'll be no place for the reporters to go."

LeMay was quiet, as if thinking about it. He said, "If you're sure. What about the people there?"

Thomas knew what LeMay wanted to know, but he also remembered that the line was unsecured.

"I believe most of them can be released. I'll have a couple of days of clean up here and then I'll be coming home. I'll debrief the local commander and his staff before I leave. I think we have the information contained."

"Okay." LeMay asked, "Is there anything else you need from me?"

"No, General."

"Please keep me advised about the situation there."

"Yes, sir."

The line went dead.

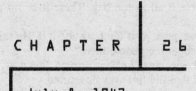

CHAPTER | 26

July 8, 1947
Los Alamos
New Mexico

Dr. Christian Smith sat looking out the window at the tall peaks of the Rocky Mountains, surprised to see some snow still on them. Of course, north of Albuquerque and Santa Fe, and surrounded by the Santa Fe National Forest, and up at the higher elevations, Los Alamos wasn't the same as the hot, dry environment of the deserts around Roswell. There was bright sun playing down on the dark greens of the pine and spruce trees and the blues and blacks of the ground. It was lovely country and it had been used to create harsh ugliness. Smith could think of the atomic bomb as nothing but ugly. It was, of course, just a tool, used to end a much larger ugliness, but that had been during the war.

In front of him were the documents that identified him for the administrator of Los Alamos, though no such identification had been necessary. They had known each other during the war. And, there was another document, one that he had been told to destroy when his mission was completed, that gave him access to everything he would need. It was signed by Major General Curtis LeMay, Secretary of War Kenneth C. Royall, and by the chief of staff for President Truman. It authorized Smith to acquire practically anything he needed for his unspecified mission, and to give orders to anyone in any branch of the United States Armed Forces or in government employ. It was a powerful document, that if found in the wrong hands, could create great trouble.

If all that wasn't enough authority, there was a telephone

number to call that would insure compliance with Smith's instructions by anyone who questioned his orders. At the moment, Smith was one of the most powerful men in the world because he had access to, and permission to deploy, an atomic bomb, which meant that he could take the bomb somewhere and prepare it for detonation. He didn't have the necessary permission to detonate it yet, but then only one man had that much authority and that man was the President. Given the right set of circumstances, and Smith could even get permission to fire the weapon, though he hoped those circumstances would never exist.

He took a deep breath, picked up the cigarette and took a long drag on it. The glowing ember burned down, close to the filter, and Smith crushed in the ashtray. He blew out the smoke but was reluctant to stand up. The air was cool, crisp and clear. The weather was perfect, and he was just a little tired from the long flight, and then the uncomfortable ride, that had finally brought him from the airport near Albuquerque to Los Alamos.

The door to the small office opened and David Lang stepped in. Lang was an older man, nearly sixty, with dark, but graying hair, thin features, and wearing a suit that was old fashioned five years earlier. Smith was a scientist who now looked more like a millionaire businessman or a senator than he did a scientist. Lang was a scientist who looked as if he had selected his wardrobe based on his opinion of what a scientist would wear.

Lang dropped into the closest chair, saw the remnants of the cigarette smoke and waved at the pack on the desk. "You got another one of those?"

Smith indicated the pack. "Help yourself."

Lang shook a cigarette free, lit it, and then blew out the smoke. "I've quit, you know."

"Quit buying?"

"No, smoking. Just once in a while, I need a drag or two." He nodded at Smith. "Your letter and instructions could make anyone want to start smoking."

Smith said nothing in return.

Lang set the cigarette in the ashtray and leaned forward, lowering his voice. "I'm not thrilled with this. The, ah, equipment, is being prepared for a remote-controlled detonation. The trigger assembly will have to be attached once the device is in place. You'll need a technician for that."

"I can't do it?"

"I wouldn't want to if I were you," said Lang. "We've two Naval officers who are experienced at this sort of thing. And, to your benefit, they are both well aware of security requirements. They won't be inclined to speak out of school."

"Good. When do we leave?"

"Given what you said, we'll be ready by seven this evening. You can leave under the cover of darkness. Where will you go from here?"

"Do you need to know that?"

"If you want the trigger, I do."

"Actually," said Smith grinning, "you don't. You put me in touch with the authorities and I'll arrange for the trigger to be delivered."

Lang reached over for his cigarette, took a deep puff and crushed it out. "We're not supposed to work that way . . ." He held up a hand to stop the protest. "I know, I know. These are extreme times and extreme measures are called for here and you have that damned letter. I'll put you in touch with the right people and let you make your own damn arrangements."

"Thanks, Dave," said Smith. "What are you going to do about dinner?"

"Thought I would have some."

"Join me at the club and I'll buy it."

"Of course."

"And you know that I was never here and we never had any of these conversations."

Lang grinned broadly. "I haven't seen you for what, eighteen months? Two years?"

"Exactly."

CHAPTER 27

July 10, 1947
Over the Rainbow
North of Las Vegas, Nevada

The building looked as if it had been deserted since before the beginning of the Second World War. The paint was flaking from the walls, several of the windows were broken and others were cracked. Shingles were peeling from the roof and piles of them lay on the ground around the perimeter of the building. At one time there might have been a trimmed lawn but that area was now overgrown and choked with weeds.

Dr. Danni Hackett, wearing a business suit that was out of place in the Nevada desert, pulled up next to a line of cars parked outside the hangar. It was the only way that she knew that there were others inside and that she had finally found the right place. The drive from the motel, some fifty miles to the southeast, had been long and boring, and she had believed from the beginning of the trip that she was lost. She wished that she had been allowed to stay with Wheeler, rather than flying out here on her own. She wished she understood what was happening, but no one had told her a thing, except that she was expected at a base in Nevada that was so secret they wouldn't even tell her the name of it. They had just told her that it was somewhere over the rainbow and gave her instructions on how to find it. They cautioned her not to ask for directions from the locals because they didn't know the base was there or how to find it.

On the drive, she had almost decided to turn around so that she could get better and more detailed instructions from Washington. They had given her a telephone number just in case she needed help. But then she saw the hand-lettered sign stuck onto a fencepost that looked as if it had been made a hundred years earlier. Had she blinked at the wrong time, she would have missed it and would have eventually found herself in Montana or Idaho or even Canada.

The dirt road showed some recent traffic, but the wind and rain had eroded parts of it making the journey bumpy and nearly impossible for a passenger car. Hackett slowed to twenty miles an hour and kept her attention focused on the road about fifty feet in front of her, looking for rocks, bumps and potholes or snakes, jackrabbits and even tarantulas. She saw two rabbits run across the track in front of her, saw a single snake that she couldn't identify, and was convinced that large spiders were watching her from some hidden web. The guard shack set in the middle of the road popped up suddenly, surprising her, and she jammed on the brakes, sliding to a stop in a cloud of dust. When an MP, armed with a pistol appeared, she gave her name, showing her ID card. He consulted a list and then waved her through, assuming that she knew where to go.

None of the other buildings on the base, all looking dejected and abandoned, had cars parked near them. Hackett assumed she had found the right place, pulled in, and then stopped.

As she got out of the car, snagging her stocking on the thorns of a weed that had pushed its way through the cracked asphalt, she wondered about the wisdom of her clothing selection. She had wanted to appear professional and competent which had dictated the business suit, but she had also expected an active base, not something hidden in the middle of a desert with no signs of life, other than the abandoned buildings, a high flying bird soaring on the thermals, and the rundown, sad-looking guard shack.

She turned, pulled the seat forward and leaned in, grabbing an attache case and a tube that held rolled-up drawings. She straightened, slammed the car door and stood staring at the building wondering if she should enter. To the right was a door that looked as if it hadn't been used in a long time, and she was sure that there were other doors around elsewhere. She just didn't know which one to use.

She walked to the closest entrance, stuck the tube under her arm and pulled on the handle, opening the door. She entered the building that smelled as if it had been closed for a very long time. It was oven-hot inside and she felt the perspiration bead on her forehead and along her upper lip. She also noticed that no one was visible anywhere in the long hallway to the right, through the doors that opened into a hangar opposite her, or in the huge office to the left. There was a single desk and a broken chair. Dust coated everything and it looked as if no one had set foot in there for years but she could hear the hum of a compressor, suggesting that there was air conditioned comfort somewhere close. It suggested there was life in the building, somewhere, if she could just find it.

"Hey, Danni, glad you made it."

Jacob Wheeler had appeared in a doorway across the hangar and was holding his hand up as if waving to her, trying to catch her attention.

"What is this place?" she called to him. She tried not to show how happy she was to see him. Of course, she would have been happy to see any human, as long as that person could answer a couple of questions.

"Our new home, at least for a while," said Wheeler walking quickly across the floor. "No one knows that we're here."

"What is this place?" she repeated.

Wheeler met her as she walked through the door, reached out and took the attaché case from her hand. He waved the other around, indicating the hangar and the base beyond its walls. "Airfield built during the war. When the size of the military was reduced, the base was abandoned. At least on the surface."

They began to walk across the hangar floor, the only sound now the tapping of her high heels. The compressor had wound down so that it was deadly silent.

They entered a small office that had once belonged to a maintenance supervisor. There was a broken down desk shoved against one wall, papers on the floor, piles of dirt and even bits of broken glass here and there. The windows were nearly opaque with the accumulated grime. On the far side was a door that Hackett believed would lead her back to the outside world. Wheeler walked to it.

"This is where things get interesting," he said. He tapped on the door, waited for a moment and then turned the knob. Gesturing, he said, "After you."

Hackett stepped, not outside as expected, but into a small clean room that held a panel by the door that looked for all the world like the controls of an elevator. The operator, a tall, thin, and very young man dressed in fatigues and wearing a holstered pistol, studied her very carefully.

To Wheeler, he said, "I will assume, on your assurance, sir, that she has the proper clearances."

"You may so assume."

The door closed and the soldier manipulated the controls. Hackett felt the floor drop away with a jerk and then the motion smoothed out.

"We're going down about fifty feet into, what . . . a command post. This place was designed, I guess, as an underground fortress to be used in the event of a nuclear attack by our competitors. An underground command and control facility that the Soviets shouldn't know exists."

"What in the hell are you talking about?" asked Hackett.

"We have appropriated the facility that would be used if Washington, D.C. and a few key bases were eliminated by the Soviets at the beginning of the next war."

Hackett took a deep breath and asked, again, "What in the hell are you talking about?"

"We have, below us, a fully functioning military base, complete with a small hospital, cafeteria, base exchange, housing for nearly three hundred, and a huge communications net. It is a small, underground city."

"When did they build it?" asked Hackett.

Before Wheeler could answer, the elevator stopped and the door opened. Hackett looked out on a wide, brightly lighted corridor. Across from her was a door that looked as if it belonged in a bank vault, a windowed room in which she could see two armed guards, and a desk where another man sat. She didn't know if the guards were ceremonial, or if their weapons were loaded.

Wheeler stepped out into the coolness of the underground base. He waited for Hackett and then walked to the window, pulling a small leather wallet from his pocket. He held it up so that one of the men could inspect it and then stepped back, toward the vault door.

"We'll get you your own proper identification in the next couple of hours."

"We're going to be staying down here?"

"Yes, of course."

"I have nothing to wear. I've got to call my parents. Nobody said anything about having to stay here for any length of time. I thought it was for some kind of classified conference for the weekend or something. How long will we be here?" She felt confused and betrayed. She had been told that they would be in Nevada for a short time, but now it seemed as if the stay could expand into weeks or months.

There was a quiet buzz and the guard at the desk stood, spun the wheel on the vault door and pulled it open. He stood back, out of their way.

Wheeler again gestured and said, "After you."

Hackett leaned to the right so that she could look through the door. She saw another woman, dressed in a uniform walking briskly close to a pale green wall. She wore flat, dark shoes and looked as if she had just finished high school. In other words, she was very young.

"Jake, I really don't think I want to do this."

"This is a temporary situation," said Wheeler. "We're in a secure facility so we don't have to worry about spies or reporters or congressional interest. All we have to do is figure this thing out quickly. And, more importantly, it is air-conditioned."

All around them people were hurrying from one place to another. It looked as if all of them had a high purpose and were too busy to stop to talk. Hackett wondered if the activity had been this frantic just prior to the invasion of Europe. No one seemed to have the time to stop and chat, find a cold drink, or to think. They just kept moving, carrying files, documents, reports and photographs, all with grim determination as they moved from one door or office to another.

"We're going to the conference room first," said Wheeler. "I know that you were in on the preliminary examination of the dead creatures."

"Creatures?" echoed Hackett.

"The beings. The aliens. Whatever they should be called." He stopped in front of a door, waited for a moment, and then opened it for Hackett. For an instant she thought that she had been transported back to the Pentagon where all this had started just a few days earlier. She stopped for a moment and thought about that. It had only been days and yet she would have sworn that weeks, or even months, had passed. Too much was happening too fast for it all to register.

"Doctor Hackett," said the man at the head of the table. Doctor Jonathan David Moore, the nattily dressed man who had started her on her journey only days earlier from the conference in the Pentagon, waved to a vacant seat and added, "We were about to begin."

Wheeler set her attaché case on the floor and then pulled out a chair. Hackett dropped into it, somewhat overwhelmed by the situation. She reached down to touch the attaché case, as if to reassure herself that it was really there.

"Gentlemen, and Doctor Hackett, now that we have finally reassembled, let's catch up on where we are. I think we can stop speculating about the nature of the flying disks and get down to the business of figuring out exactly what we have here."

CHAPTER 28

July 11, 1947
Roswell Army Air Field
Roswell, New Mexico

Captain Jack Reed stood outside the collection of rambling buildings that made up the post hospital and looked at the boxy, enclosed ambulance that had big red crosses painted on the sides and back. It was polished and clean but it was probably five or six years old. He would be hot and uncomfortable inside it, especially as they drove through the high deserts of New Mexico, Arizona and Nevada.

His instructions were simple on one level and overly complex on another. All he had to do was transport a single, living alien creature from the base in Roswell to another, secret base hidden in Nevada. The living creature was not supposed to be observed by anyone either on the base, in New Mexico, or anywhere along the route to Nevada. The enclosed, nearly windowless rear of the ambulance would fulfill the requirement of keeping the curious and the unauthorized from seeing something inside they should not.

All of that seemed of little consequence. It was the heat that worried him. The dark green paint would absorb the desert sun and that could make the back of the ambulance unbearably hot and possibly deadly. The ambulance was not designed to make long distance runs through the heat of the day. It was designed to make short runs, from the battlefield to a hospital where the wounded could get quick help, have their wounds quickly bandaged, and once stabilized, they would be transported to the rear areas where proper medical care could be provided.

Reed shook his head and said, "I'm just not sure if this is going to work out."

"It's about the only thing that I have that meets your requirements, Captain." The man was the senior noncommissioned officer in the motor pool. He was in charge of assigning the vehicles, based on need, priority and rank. He ruled his shop with an iron hand and would not budge once he had made a decision for anyone, regardless of rank, with the exception of Colonel Blanchard, who could get anything he wanted at any time.

The NCO was dressed in fresh fatigues, highly polished boots, and had a hat that showed no sign of having been worn until that day. He was a man who had been in the service before the beginning of the war, and he would be around for another ten or fifteen years. It was his career. He looked as if he had been born in the Army.

Reed opened the rear door and looked inside. It was a fully equipped ambulance. He would have to replace some of the equipment so that his unique passenger would have all that it needed. He shook his head and wished again that he could fly. Seven or eight hours in an airplane and he could be at the base. But the brass had said no to the idea. They were worried about a crash that would kill the passenger. No one worried about the pilots or other passengers getting killed, only the special one. And no one seemed to grasp the fact that the flight would be quicker and safer, with fewer opportunities for the curious and the unauthorized to compromise security. Besides, ambulances sometimes crashed.

"How hot does it get back there?"

"You got your side vents, and if you open the windows in the cab, and the communication window between the front and the rear, you got good ventilation. Doesn't get that hot in the back as long as you're moving down the highway at a good clip."

Reed walked around the ambulance, opened the door of the driver's side and climbed up into it. He studied the dashboard carefully, put his feet on the gas pedal and brake and his hands on the steering wheel at ten and two. For all the world he looked like a man trying to decide if he really wanted, or needed, to buy a new car.

"What's the range of this thing?"

The motor pool sergeant, accustomed to dealing with officers who didn't seem to know what they wanted, or what questions to ask, scratched his head and said, "About five hundred miles without a fill up."

"Not enough."

"Christ, Captain, the tanks only hold so much gas. Nothing I can do about that."

Reed didn't respond. He was thinking of five gallon jerry cans that could hold extra gas to extend the range so they wouldn't be required to use either the facilities at another military base or civilian gas stations. He could get to Nevada without having to stop for fuel. Of course, the drivers would have to stop for food and calls of nature and to fill the tanks from the jerry cans. And the extra gas would be dangerous to transport unless he got another vehicle and the last thing he wanted was a convoy.

Reed shook his head, thinking again that the whole idea was ridiculous. They should just use an airplane and get the problem settled in a matter of hours instead of a matter of days, driving across the deserts.

"Okay. Have one of these ready to leave at 1700 tonight. I need two drivers. Someone will be over inside the hour to check the equipment in the back."

"I can't do that, Captain, without I get orders from the motor officer."

"You just get started preparing the vehicle, and you find two reliable drivers with top secret clearances, and I'll take care of the motor officer."

"Yes, sir."

Reed grinned. On almost any other base, it would have been impossible to find drivers, that is privates or corporals, who had top secret clearances. But at the home of the only nuclear strike force in the world, many people, because of the 509th's mission, had top secret clearances. It made it easy to find drivers with the necessary clearances.

He walked from there, into the main administration building of the base hospital, surprised to find that it was cool on the inside. Not overly cool, as the officer's club would have been, but certainly cooler than it was outside and cooler than it had been walking around in the motor pool.

He wasn't sure what he was going to do in the hospital. He had little reason to be there before 1700 hours now that he had found a vehicle. He thought that he should talk to the administrator and walked down the green-tiled corridor until he came to a suite of offices that looked as if they were standard issue. He opened the door to find the single desk of the receptionist, two chairs against one wall, a short bookcase that held loose leaf notebooks containing the appropriate regulations, and an Army issue lithograph of the cavalry fighting Indians in Montana.

He entered and looked at the secretary sitting behind the desk. She wore a pair of the ugliest glasses he had ever seen and found that he was staring at them.

"How can I help you, Captain?" she asked.

Her voice was pleasant and her dark hair was glossy. The glasses distracted him. He stepped to her desk and said, "I believe I would like to talk to the administrator."

"Do you have an appointment?"

"No," said Reed. He thought for a moment and then said, "But I need to talk to him about the special project."

"Please have a seat," she said. She stood up, turned and walked to the closed door behind her.

Reed looked at her, studying her carefully. Now he found his eyes drawn to her hair. She was a woman of contrasts that seemed to focus attention on various clothing items and parts of her body. He wondered if it was intentional and then decided it wasn't. No one would pick such ugly glasses if it was intentional.

She turned and said, "Colonel O'Neill will see you now."

Reed stood up, stepped past her, and entered the office. It wasn't a big room but it was dominated by a big desk flanked by two windows, that seemed squeezed into a corner. There was a single chair in front of it, and a table off to one side littered with medical journals. There was a four drawer file cabinet set in one corner.

O'Neill, a balding, greying, stocky man, sat behind the desk. He glanced up as Reed stopped about three feet from the edge of the desk and saluted. "Captain Reed to speak to the hospital administrator."

O'Neill returned the salute by touching his forehead near his right eye and said, "Please have a seat."

Reed dropped into the chair. "Thank you, sir."

"Now, Captain, what can I do for you?"

Reed was suddenly stuck. He didn't know what he wanted to know or how to proceed. He scratched his chin and began, "I have the responsibility for transporting . . . our guest to a new facility."

"And that affects me how?"

"Well," said Reed, "I guess I don't know what the health requirements would be. What do we know about him?"

O'Neill leaned back in his chair, laced his fingers behind his head and then said, "I have very little useful information. We just haven't had much of a chance to learn anything. We've been proceeding with caution."

"My requirement," said Reed, "is to move from here to another facility several hundred miles away. I have been thinking of using one of the ambulances."

"Heat won't be a problem," said O'Neill. "He seems to thrive in a hotter environment than that we enjoy."

Reed raised his eyebrows in surprise. He hadn't thought about that. He had assumed, for no good reason, that a comfortable Earth environment would be comfortable for the being from another world. Then he remembered that humans were acclimated to various zones on the Earth. There was no reason to assume that what Reed found comfortable would be the same for a man from Africa or from the Arctic and certainly no reason to assume that a being from another world would enjoy the same climate range that he did.

"The oxygen level seems excessive," said O'Neill, "judging from his simple reactions, though I don't have good figures for that." Seeing the look on Reed's face, he added, "I mean that he seems to find the level of oxygen in our atmosphere excessively high."

"Food and water?"

"We have seen him ingest nothing. We have supplied a variety of foods, both animal and vegetable, but he ignores them, possibly not understanding what they are for or understanding but repelled by the thought."

"I would think that he would need the water sometime," said Reed idly.

"Well, you would, wouldn't you," said O'Neill. "My training in biology suggested that all living things need water. Life couldn't exist without water, but he has taken none since he arrived here. Of course there are many animals who can go a long time without water. They store it in their bodies. And what I know applies simply to life here on Earth. Maybe a species developing on another world would not have the same requirement for water that we have. I just don't know enough to make any intelligent observations."

"I guess that someone has been in the room with him since he arrived?"

"Not right in the room all the time," said O'Neill. "But certainly just outside the door."

"Will he survive an automobile trip? Ambulance trip? How is his health?"

"I have no idea," said O'Neill. He held up a hand to stop Reed from asking another question and added, "We have no baseline. We don't know what the normal readings for internal body temperature, heart rate, respiration, blood pressure would be. We don't know what, or how, a healthy individual from his world would react to the various stimuli here. All we know is that he is resting, in the darkened room, and seems to be in good health. He seems to preferred the reduced light levels and elevated temperatures."

Reed took a deep breath and looked down, at the floor, lost in thought. Finally he said, "I'm responsible for moving him across the country."

"I have another thought for you, Captain. How are you going to explain this to him?"

"What do you mean?"

"Think about this. You're stranded on a foreign world. You cannot communicate with the natives. There are millions of them and only one of you. Your ship is wrecked and in their hands. Your friends, colleagues, crewmates are dead. You are unable to communicate with your home and ask for assistance. Now, you are taken from the hospital, which, by the way, you probably don't recognize as a hospital, put into an ambulance and taken hundreds of miles from the only location that would be known to your fellows if they came to search because it is where your ship crashed. How would you feel if the situation was reversed and you were the one who was alone?"

"I have my orders," said Reed.

"I'm not questioning your orders, Captain. I'm merely pointing out a couple of things that might have been missed by those issuing your orders."

"How do I explain it to him?" asked Reed.

"I don't know. We have no common ground here. He is an alien creature that is obviously intelligent. He has fallen into our hands. He knows that we are intelligent. We just can't communicate."

Reed wondered what to say and could think of no appropriate comment about the situation. Reed was the man in the middle, ordered by those in Washington to make certain moves. They had no more information than he, and probably less. They were making decisions based on security and scientific requirements without thought to practicality. Reed could do nothing but execute the orders as best he could, advising those making the decisions of facts as they developed, if those facts seemed to impact on the mission.

Finally, he just said, "I'll be here about 1730 tonight to pick up our visitor. If there are any special needs, or problems, I guess now would be the time to tell me."

O'Neill leaned forward, his elbows on his desk. He said, "I don't envy you this mission, Captain. I don't know what to tell you because we just don't know anything."

Reed got to his feet. "Thanks anyway."

"If I could be of some assistance, please let me know." O'Neill held out his hand.

CHAPTER 29

July 11, 1947
The Pentagon
Arlington, Virginia

Major General Curtis LeMay sat in his office, a single light burning on the end table by the couch, and stared through the gloom at the painting of Eighth Air Force bombers on their way to Germany. He sat with a cigar in one hand, a glass of bourbon setting near the other, and felt as if the world had collapsed around him. He had seen the pictures from New Mexico, flown to Washington, D.C. by a special courier, he knew that an alien flight crew had been found in the wreckage, and he knew that one of the beings might have survived the crash.

He knew all that, knew that it was true, and it scared him badly. He had not been as frightened during the first dark days of the Second World War when it seemed that only the Germans and the Japanese could win battles. He had not been frightened because he knew the oceans protected the United States from both the Germans and the Japanese, and that any invasion would be a monstrous, logistical nightmare, and it was likely that those problems would defeat the Germans or the Japanese just as surely as the Russian winter had beaten Napoleon.

All that was now gone. The protection of the oceans had been eroded by long range bombers and huge, fast moving fleets. Any society that could cross the vast distances of space was not going to be slowed by the few thousand miles of ocean that protected the United States from Europe and Asia. Only LeMay understood these implications. No one else got it. They sat around and talked of a crashed ship that proved the aliens weren't perfect, and the dead bodies which proved they weren't invulnerable. They talked of interceptions and hot new jet fighters, but they didn't understand the larger implications. They didn't understand what the crashed ship meant to the United States and the rest of the world, especially since the crash was not an accident, but the result of hostile action. American hostile action.

That was the key here. He had ordered the ship fired on and had expected nothing. He thought it would demonstrate to these creatures that the United States would not be beaten easily. The results had surprised and frightened him.

Setting in his locked safe was the report from the pilot of a fighter that had chased the flying saucer over the New Mexico landscape. The pilot had taken off from the base in Tucson, had found the saucer, and had engaged it, all on orders that had been issued by LeMay. Orders that he had originated and orders that he might not have had the authority to originate.

LeMay picked up his bourbon, swirled it around in the glass and then took a drink. The liquor burned his throat and pooled warmly in his stomach. He rocked back in his chair and closed his eyes, trying to imagine the scene over New Mexico.

The pilot told the debriefing officer that he had spotted the glow, off to his two o'clock and turned toward it. He had pushed the throttle to full military power, picking up speed as he burned through the fuel like it was pouring through a fire hose.

But the tactic worked because the pilot, a major named Joseph B. Miller, had closed on the light and seen a shape behind it that indicated a manufactured object. Miller had used his gun camera to photograph the object, and then he lined up to attack it, as were his orders. Miller would later say that he didn't fully understand the necessity of attacking the object, but he did understand that his orders were his orders.

The object, whatever it was, didn't respond to Miller's presence. It flew along, slowly, at about seven thousand feet, reminding Miller of Sunday pilots who were examining the ground below them, doing little more than sightseeing, and sometimes forgetting that they were piloting an aircraft and not driving a car on the highway.

LeMay set his glass on his desk and then leaned over. The 16mm color film had already been threaded into a projector by his aide. LeMay dimmed the light on his desk and flipped the switch, letting the film run once again.

Now he could watch the encounter from Miller's perspective. He saw that Miller approached to within two or three hundred yards of the object, which was flat, almost triangular in shape, the two slanted tail fins and the slightly rounded rear. There was no sign of a propulsion system. There was no sign of the crew, if there was one, and no real sign of intelligent control.

LeMay watched as Miller dropped back, lined up behind the object, which still took no notice of him and fired several rockets. They leaped from the rails, flashed through the dark sky. Two of them streaked past the object, the twin balls of fire disappearing in the distance. Two others struck the craft on the left side, about halfway back on the fuselage. There was a fiery blast of bright yellow orange and the craft dipped to the right, down, away from Miller. He followed it, and fired his machine guns at it. He watched the tracer stream, bright, glowing, red balls, converge on the left side of the craft. There was a sudden, brilliant flash of light and the object plunged toward the ground.

Miller pulled up and away, turning sharply, seeing the craft seem to right itself, strike the ground, or flash over it only a few feet high, and begin to regain some altitude. Miller rolled out, again behind the object, lining up for another shot, but the craft suddenly pitched forward, dived at the ground and crashed. It slid along and impacted against a cliff. As soon as the object impacted, the film ended with a white leader and a flash of red numbers. The screen filled with a bright red warning that the film was classified top secret.

LeMay turned off the projector and picked up his bourbon again. He took a deep pull at it, breathed out slowly, and tried to relax. This film was dynamite. It proved that the flying saucers were some kind of manufactured craft, but more importantly, it proved that the United States Army had destroyed one of them.

Miller, once the object was downed, and once he had reported his actions over the radio, pulled up, circled and waited for a few minutes. He saw no movement below him, saw no sign of fire on the prairie, and saw no evidence that the alien craft would take off again.

Miller returned to his base, reporting that he had been successful. He gave the coordinates of the downed craft, told, in detail, how he had brought it down, and then was held in isolation for twenty-four hours.

The report had contained everything that LeMay had wanted to know about the incident. He had grinned when he read it, wondering if the intelligence officer who prepared it had read his mind. LeMay was told that the rockets had been effective, but that the machine guns had not, something that he already knew.

He was told what the pilot had done, what he had thought, and what he had seen. The pilot's reactions to the situation had been provided. Then, with the gun-camera film, he had been able to watch the scene unfold, almost as if he had been in the cockpit with him. The films were absolutely stunning and had taken LeMay's breath away the first time he had watched them.

With the films, and with the intelligence officer's report, LeMay could think of nothing else he needed to know about the engagement. He had a letter prepared to place in the officer's file, commending him for his fine work but that did nothing to explain what that work might have been, only that it had come to the attention of a major general in the Army.

There was a tap at his door, and LeMay looked up from the tip of his cigar and the rim of his glass of bourbon, and said, "Come on in."

The officer who entered was not a member of the Army Air Forces. The branch insignia on the lapels of his uniform were the crossed rifles of the Infantry. The ribbons above his pocket indicated that he had been in combat, under fire, and that he was a brave man. He wore the Distinguished Service Cross, the Silver Star with two oak leaf clusters, several lesser awards for valor, and the Combat Infantryman's Badge. On his shoulder was the tab of a trained ranger, and the patch on his right sleeve indicated combat service with them. A brave and trained man who was now a lieutenant colonel and LeMay would see that he made full colonel in the next couple of days.

The officer walked across the darkened carpet, stopped near the desk and looked at LeMay's face, which was lost in the gloom and shadows. He saluted LeMay, and said, quietly, as if he knew the need for secrecy, "Lieutenant Colonel Joseph P. Cavanaugh, reporting as ordered, General."

LeMay returned the salute smartly and then waved at one of the two chairs close to his desk. "Have a seat, Colonel. You want a drink?"

Cavanaugh had been in the Army long enough to know that if a general offered a drink, he expected you to take it, but more to the point, he expected you to need it. It meant, quite simply, that the coming information would not be welcome.

"Whatever you're having, General."

LeMay pointed into a darken corner and said, "The booze is over there, but the ice has melted. I would suggest that you get yourself a stiff drink."

Cavanaugh stood up, walked to the bar. He could not read any of the bottle labels, but he recognized the bourbon. He poured himself four fingers, splashed some of the cold water that had been ice into the glass. He held the bottle up, asking if LeMay wanted another, but LeMay shook his head. Cavanaugh returned to the chair. LeMay's offer of a drink had not calmed him.

Without preamble, LeMay asked, "What do you know about our research facility in Nevada?

"I didn't know that we had a facility in Nevada. Doesn't surprise me."

"Why not?"

Cavanaugh shrugged unconsciously and said, "Because there is so much Nevada out there. You could lose an aircraft carrier out there and we'd be hard pressed to find it."

LeMay picked up his own glass, drained the bourbon, and

slammed the glass to his desk. "For some reason, we have been given the task of protecting it."

That wasn't, of course, the truth. LeMay knew exactly why he needed to protect it. He wanted no one who was unauthorized to approach the facility. He didn't care if they were military, government, press, lost civilians or Russian spies. He wanted the base isolated to stop the curious and the nefarious.

"Yes, sir," said Cavanaugh, but now he was confused. He didn't want LeMay to think that he was unprepared, or that he was uninformed, so he attempted to cover his confusion by taking a drink of his bourbon. He gulped at it, taking a healthy slug to mask his muddled thinking.

LeMay picked up his cigar, puffed, and then said, "Do you have any questions, so far?"

"I guess that if I had to ask a question it would be how am I involved in this."

LeMay said, "There is a consideration here that I don't think anyone else has thought about. I'm smart enough to understand world politics. The Soviets believe that they are destined to rule the world. The perfect world, to them, is a communist world with the Soviets at the top of the heap while the rest of us are populating the planet to serve them. We know from past history that they will operate in their own self-interest, and if an opportunity arises, they'll exploit it."

LeMay leaned back in his chair, puffed on his cigar and looked up, toward the ceiling, as if organizing his thoughts. Finally he looked back at Cavanaugh. "In other words, if the Soviets acquire this technology, this germ warfare technology, before we do, they will use it against us. World War Two would pale in comparison by the destruction that can be brought against us. They would have the capability to attack us without fear of retribution."

"Yes, General."

"None of this must fall into Soviet hands."

Cavanaugh raised his glass to his lips, but it was still empty. He said, "I understand."

"No, you don't," said LeMay. "But you will. And, there is another consideration that I don't believe our scientists have thought about." He grinned and added, "Did you know that there are no snakes in Hawaii?"

"No, sir."

"Now, what about zoos? Should the curators of the zoos be allowed to bring snakes to Hawaii for exhibition in the zoo? Should scientists be allowed to import snakes for research?"

Cavanaugh didn't answer the question. He just sat there wondering if LeMay had lost his mind.

"And if the snakes escape, then Hawaii suddenly has to worry about snakes. There would be no predators to hold the snake population in check. They would do a great deal of damage to the animal populations and would probably kill people. The obvious solution is to require those who wish to do research on snakes to visit the mainland and those who wish to see snakes, see them in zoos on the mainland."

"Yes, sir."

"I find myself in with a similar problem. We are beginning to deal with a bacteriological situation that is similar. We are developing strains of disease for which there is no natural immunity. If those germs escaped the labs, the damage to the American population could be extraordinary."

"Yes, sir."

"The solution is simple enough. We have isolated the base to inhibit the escape of those germs but there is always the possibility they can escape. Therefore, I want you to form a small force. A reaction team, almost, that will be responsible for keeping this technology away from the Soviets and to keep it confined to the base in Nevada."

Cavanaugh nodded, but said, "That would seem to be more of a counterintelligence role than something for me."

"No," said LeMay. "What I'm looking for is someone who could contain the damage and destroy bacteria, if necessary."

"General?" said Cavanaugh, now more confused than ever. "You want me to destroy the bacteria?"

"Not now, of course," said LeMay. "Maybe not ever. I'm just trying to cover the bases. Anticipate the problems and provide solutions for them in advance. If it appears that there is a breach in the base, and that the bacteria might be released into the surrounding environment, then yes, you must destroy it."

"How?"

LeMay grinned, but it was lost in the shadows. "Fire, of course."

CHAPTER | 30

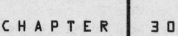

When the meeting ended, Jacob Wheeler took Danni Hackett's elbow, steered her away from the crowd and asked, "Would you care for a tour of the rest of the facility?"

"What I'd really rather do is return to town and get my clothes and call my parents before I drop off the face of the Earth," she said.

"Tell you what," said Wheeler, grinning evilly, "I'll take you on the tour and then we'll go to town to get you checked out of the motel. I'll even buy you dinner there because once we get back and to work we're not going to have much time and access to and from the base is going to be restricted."

"If you insist," she said. She didn't really want to walk around the base because she was tired and she knew that her stocking had run. She felt it as the snag had spread, running up the inside of her thigh. She wanted to get rid of the stockings, the shoes, and into more appropriate clothing now that she was here and knew what was expected of her.

More importantly, she just wasn't ready to begin the work. She wanted a day or two to get oriented. She did not want to have to begin thinking right away. She wanted some time to adjust to the new situation, but she saw she wasn't going to get it. Everything had come flying at her too fast, first in Washington, then in New Mexico, and now here. Just too fast to deal with it. She wanted some time to herself without having to leap into work almost as she set foot on the base.

Wheeler, on the other hand, hadn't realized that because he

was ready to work the moment he stepped off the airplane. He had been anxious to get to work and believed that everyone thought the way he did. He wanted to see the facility, to understand the working environment, so he assumed that Hackett was the same way. That she thought the same way. He suddenly turned into the professional tour guide.

He said, "Think of a giant tire from an automobile. Not the whole wheel, but the tire." He guided her down a corridor that was brightly lighted, painted in a soft, rather pleasing shade of green, and carpeted rather than tiled.

"Now," he said, "on the inside of the tire, that is to say, the inside of the outside . . ." He laughed. "What I mean is that we're now standing on what would be the interior of the tire and if you turned right, you would reach the outside except in here, you find individual rooms that were originally designed as offices but that are now used as private apartments. The higher the rank of the occupant, the closer to the elevator and the larger the apartment. You have been assigned quarters that are appropriate to your current rank."

"And that would be?" asked Hackett, idly, but not really caring.

"I think you are a simulated lieutenant colonel, but I will have to check."

"Great," she said. "A simulated lieutenant colonel."

Wheeler resumed the lecture as they continued to walk. "Toward the interior of the wheel, we find the various labs, offices, and other special accommodations. There is a fully equipped operating room, a six-bed hospital ward, and a smaller emergency room. We have a fully functioning PX although the selection of goods is somewhat limited. There is a cafeteria rather than a dining room, the conference room which you have seen, offices and other meeting rooms. Beyond that, the entire center on this level is open. That would be, I suppose, the hub, if you think of all this as a wheel. It can be used as a large gymnasium, a theater or lecture hall, depending on the configuration."

They continued to walk. The curve of the corridor was subtle enough that it was nearly invisible. It looked as if the corridor ended in the distance, but the perspective never changed. There were doors spaced more or less equally distant on either side. There were a few windows that opened into the interior rooms or offices on the inside of the ring showing that the rooms were, as Wheeler had said, offices. Inside some of them, Hackett could see men and women working. To her, it seemed that they were merely shuffling paper from one desk to the next until it ended in a basket near the door. It looked like busy work because the people had to have something to do and the more frantic the pace, and the more papers they shuffled, the more important they felt.

Eventually they returned to the point where they had started, that is, near the conference room. They had walked past a short corridor which lead back to the elevators and which, in turn, led up to the ground level or deeper into the facility. But the approach was through the vault door arrangement that was concealed on this side so that the exit was not obvious. Wheeler confessed he didn't understand the psychology behind it, but that was how things had been designed.

Wheeler said, "I'm not supposed to know this, so you're not supposed to know this either, but there are four identical levels directly below us. The level above is designed more along the lines of an office building rather than a wheel."

"What's the purpose of this?"

"I think that we have seen how the other half will live in the event of an atomic war."

Hackett thought about that and realized that no one in the world had atomic weapons except the United States. It meant that someone was anticipating a situation in which other countries not only developed such weapons but developed a delivery system for them that could be either long range bombers or rockets. And it meant that someone here believed that someone there would use those weapons. It was a prospect that she didn't want to think about at the moment. And then she realized that such considerations might not matter any more, given what they now knew.

She also realized something else that was implied in the creation of the facility. Someone was thinking in terms of survival for key governmental officials. The population might be irradiated in the atomic blast, incinerated in the fireball, but the government would keep functioning. It suggested a mind that was capable of thinking in terms of huge population losses, but that was more concerned with the survival of the United States. Hackett wasn't sure if such a mind was to be admired for its devotion to the United States, or feared because of its cold-blooded rationalization of the deaths of millions.

Wheeler apparently didn't understand the implications because he continued the lecture. He wasn't sure if Hackett understood that the facility was circular, buried deeply in the ground, and was filled with offices, apartments, labs, workshops, and all the other structures needed in a small city.

Hackett grinned at him as he searched for words and said, "I get it, Jake. It's a big wheel with us in the center."

"That's the tour, then," said Wheeler. "Now we retreat to the outside. I don't suppose I need to tell you that you are not to mention this to anyone. In fact, there are very few people who even know this facility exists."

"No, you don't need to tell me I'm not supposed to talk about this," she said, only a hint of annoyance in her voice.

They walked down the short corridor and opened the door that led to the exit. The man at the desk checked his clipboard and then nodded to them as if giving them permission to leave.

Wheeler explained, "Only a few of us have permission to come and go on our own authority. When we get you properly in-processed, you'll, of course, be on that very short list."

"This is more like the military than the Pentagon."

"Exactly."

They reached the elevators and Wheeler touched the button to call for it. "If the area is compromised, the elevators are shut down, of course."

"What do you mean compromised?"

"I mean if tourists stumbled across it, or some nosey reporter bursts into the hangar, the elevators would not work. They, whoever they are, would be stuck there."

"Oh."

They entered the elevator and rode to the surface. Wheeler

opened the door and stepped out as if checking to make sure that it was safe. Hackett followed, surprised at the darkness in the hangar and the heat of the desert. The contrast between what she had seen below ground in its ultra-modern glory had been eclipsed by the run-down and ancient look of the hangar.

They walked across the dirty, rubble-strewn floor, reached the doors and exited. Wheeler directed her to his car. "Why not let me drive?"

"Sure," she said. She climbed into the passenger's seat and looked out through the windshield. Other than the cars in the parking lot, there was nothing to indicate that there was anyone else on the base. She thought about that for a moment, and then realized that all the high-level security was being compromised by the cars.

To Wheeler, she said, "Shouldn't the cars be hidden?"

"Tomorrow one of the other hangars will be opened and swept. Cars will be parked in there."

"Great," she said, but she didn't know why she had said it.

Wheeler said, "But it shows you're thinking about security."

She closed her eyes, leaned her head back and said, "I'll nap while you drive."

"Fine," said Wheeler and he started the car.

CHAPTER 31

July 11, 1947
Roswell Army Air Field
New Mexico

Reed walked around the front of the ambulance, looked at the two drivers, both staff sergeants, who were sitting up front, and then walked around to the back. He opened the doors and saw that the gurney had been removed and the chairs that he had requested had been bolted to the floor. He climbed in, checked on the supplies and then jumped back out.

One of the sergeants appeared in front of him and saluted. "How may I help you, sir?"

"Take this around to the rear and then back it up to the door next to the ramp."

"Sir?"

"You heard me."

"Yes, sir."

He then walked into the front door of the hospital administration building. Sitting in the lobby were Douglass and Campbell looking as if they were waiting for a doctor. Both were reading magazines that were months out of date.

Douglass spotted him and stood up. Without preamble he asked, "Where do you think you're going?"

Reed stopped but said nothing.

"You are not authorized to remove the patient from this facility," said Douglass.

Reed stared at him for a long time and then asked, "How do you know what my plans are?"

"Irrelevant."

"I have my orders." Reed looked around, saw that no one was paying attention to them and said, quietly, "The ship is gone. Now the passenger is going to be moved. To the same place."

"We're concerned about overall security," said Douglass.

"I don't have time for this," said Reed, exasperated. "My orders come from the highest levels of the Pentagon. You are not in my chain of command and I will not take orders from you."

Douglass shrugged. "I'm not giving orders but I might make suggestions. I thought we might tag along to make sure that security is not compromised."

Reed stared at the man and said, "I'm not sure that you're authorized to do that."

"You may assume, since we are here and since we know of the plan, that we are authorized."

Reed felt the rage burn through him. The arrogance of the man, because he wore civilian clothing, was unbelievable. He said, "You'll excuse me if I don't take that as the gospel."

He turned and walked to the desk. He grabbed the phone, spun it around, and dialed three zero one quickly. When it was answered he said, "Is the colonel in?"

As he waited, he looked back at Douglass and Campbell. Both were seated, quietly watching him. Douglass was staring at him, but Campbell was sitting quietly, paging through an old magazine. He looked as if he was a senior NCO who didn't want to get caught in the flack between two officers.

When Reed heard Blanchard come on the line, he said, louder than necessary, "Colonel, I have two counterintelligence agents here."

Blanchard said, "Where is here?"

"Hospital."

"Who are they?"

Reed grinned as he said, "Douglass and Campbell."

Blanchard was silent for a moment, and then, the anger obvious in his voice, said, "I am sorry about this, but those two men have been cleared for everything. Your trip is still on, as authorized by the Eighth Air Force commander, but

Douglass and Campbell have the authorization to accompany you if they want. The decision is left to them."

Reed took a deep breath and said, "Yes, sir."

"I'm damned sorry about this, Jack," said Blanchard, "but the orders have filtered down to me."

"I don't suppose you could speak to General Ramey about it?"

"Captain, it was General Ramey who passed the word to me. It is a dead issue at this point. Further discussion, according to Ramey, is not desired."

"Yes, sir," said Reed. "Thank you, sir." He cradled the phone and turned to Douglass, "I had hoped to keep this low key so that we don't attract unnecessary attention. A convoy would do that."

Douglass tried to make peace. He said, "I was thinking of a single car to follow the ambulance. An unmarked, civilian car, to hang back half a mile or so."

"Since I have no choice," said Reed, "I guess that will have to do."

Campbell, who still held a magazine in his hands said, "I would have thought that you would want armed guards."

Reed looked at the man as if he was stupid. "Why would I want that? It would only draw attention to us."

"Protection."

"From whom? It's an ambulance, not an armored car. There's no pile of money in it. Just us on a routine mission. A mission that came up today so there could be no leak."

Campbell shrugged, laid his magazine on the table, and said, "Protection for the creature."

"I had planned to ride in the ambulance with the being," said Reed. "I doubt it will try to escape. There's no place for it to go. It knows nothing about our society. It couldn't survive without our care and assistance. Just one man in the ambulance, except for the drivers."

Campbell asked, "Is that a good idea?"

"I don't know. I just thought, if someone was there, with him, it would not be quite as frightening." Reed hadn't realized that he shifted from calling the creature it to him and back again. Had he noticed, he wouldn't have been able to explain why he did it. The whole process was unconscious.

Campbell shrugged as if it didn't matter to him. He had been ordered to the assignment and would carry it out.

That seemed to settle the matter. Reed waited for a moment and then pushed past the two counterintelligence agents. He walked down the brightly lighted corridor toward the room where the alien was being held. He stopped near the nurse's station to think for a moment. The events seemed to be running ahead of him without giving him a chance to think. He seemed to be reacting to the situation rather than thinking it through and planning out an intelligent course of action.

Now, suddenly, he was responsible for moving the creature, which he hadn't seen since they had pulled it out of the ship. He was being treated as if he was an expert on alien life forms and he had never seen the being conscious. Now he was thinking it would be better if he rode in the back with it to provide it with some comfort, though he had consulted with no one. If the situation was reversed, Reed wasn't sure that he would find the presence of an alien creature, no matter how benign, no matter how friendly, comforting. Maybe his sitting in the back of the ambulance would make the situation worse.

And he wondered if Douglass might not be right. An armed escort might be a good idea. And then he realized that it was unnecessary. The drivers could be armed with pistols, he could carry a pistol, and surely both the counterintelligence agents had weapons. He would be safe from the creature, which, as far as he knew, had made no hostile move toward anyone at any time since it had arrived on Earth. And no one from the outside would try anything because they wouldn't realize the importance of the ambulance. They could just drive straight through and in twenty hours or so, the ordeal would be over.

Satisfied that he understood the situation, he started forward again, and reached the guarded door. He put a hand in his pocket and removed his ID for the military policeman.

"Captain," said the guard, as he examined the card. "Doctor Hendricks wanted to be notified when you got here."

"I have no problem with that, Sergeant."

"Yes, sir."

Now Reed hesitated. He wasn't sure what to expect and he hadn't thought about this moment. His thoughts, and planning, had been designed to get from Roswell to the new base with as little aggravation as possible. Get the alien into a vehicle, and get the hell out of town with the creature. He had arranged the logistics of the move. Now it was time to confront the alien.

Talking a deep breath, he turned the knob, opened the door and entered, slowly, cautiously. The alien was sitting in a hospital bed, its back propped against a couple of pillows. It turned its attention to Reed and looked at him with intelligent eyes, and a look, if human, that was incredibly sad. It raised a hand as if to shade its eyes from the light bleeding into the room from the hallway, but that was the only movement it made.

Now that it was conscious, Reed could see the facial muscles working. The head was large, looking more like a grey, hairless light bulb with huge, black, almond-shaped eyes set up high. There was no real nose, just a slight bump with two holes that might have been nostrils. There were no lips, just a slit where the mouth would be, and then a very pointed chin. It was a strangely pleasant face, that seemed, even in the alien environment of a military hospital, to be at peace.

The body, while certainly humanoid, was not human. The trunk was straight with no hint of a waist. The arms were thin, looking as if they could be easily broken. The hands were long, looking almost graceful, but the fingers were thin and flexible giving Reed the impression of tentacles rather than fingers.

Reed stopped near the bed and said, quietly, gently, "We have to move you to a new location. A better location." He waited for a response and then asked, "Do you understand?"

The creature made no move. It didn't nod or wink or reply. It sat quietly, watching him warily, awaiting its fate.

Reed took a final step forward but there was no reaction from the being. He reached out, touching the blanket. "We have to go to a better place. Equipped to deal with this." He found himself fumbling for words.

Still the creature didn't move. Reed, for some reason, believed that the alien understood him on some level but refused to react, as if that would be giving away a secret. Finally the creature looked to the left, toward the single window and the blinds that had been drawn blocking the view of the outside world. There was a brightness at the window caused by the sun in the low western sky.

As Reed wondered what to do, there was a sound at the door behind him and Reed turned. A short, thin man stood there, centered in the frame. He had a very round face, small eyes and a small nose, but large, heavy lips. He was dressed in a white lab coat and there were captain's bars pinned to the lapel and a black name tag near his pocket that said, "Hendricks." Reed knew that it was unauthorized for the captain's bars to be pinned to the lapel, but it also told him the rank and status of the man.

"You've come to take the patient?" he asked in a voice that seemed to be deeper than it should have been.

"Yes, Doctor."

"I'm not sure that he is in any condition to travel."

"What makes you say that?" asked Reed.

Hendricks walked into the room slowly and then up to the side of the bed. The alien turned and looked at him, its large eyes unblinking. Reed noticed that it seemed to relax as if the familiar human face was its single friend on the planet. At that moment Reed thought that he understood how to make the trip more comfortable for the alien. Rather than riding in the ambulance with it, Hendricks could do that. He would keep the two of them together for the trip.

Hendricks reached out and turned the alien's head slightly so that he could stare into its eyes. Without looking at Reed, he said, "I believe that we have a slight concussion here but I can't be sure. I'm concerned that there might be internal bleeding of some nature. And I'm concerned because he has not taken any food or water and there has been no elimination of waste since he was brought here."

"That could be a normal condition," said Reed.

"Or it could be indicative of greater trauma than we have discovered."

"Without any evidence of that trauma," said Reed, "we are going to have to move the patient."

"My medical advice is to wait." He dropped his hands and turned to face Reed.

"I can't wait," said Reed. "We're going. You will be coming along with us."

"I'm afraid that is impossible. I'm not going anywhere, especially on your authority."

"I can have Colonel Blanchard call your boss. I can have the orders cut. And you won't be able to delay the situation for more than thirty minutes."

Hendricks considered that and then shrugged. He asked, "What arrangements have you made?"

Reed told him.

"I can't think of anything I would do differently, except use a car rather than an ambulance. You can't see out of the ambulance."

"And no one can see in," countered Reed.

"How long will we be gone?"

"You could be back late next day, maybe the day after. We won't be back for a while."

"Let me get a bag and some clean clothes."

"Hurry."

"Certainly."

When Hendricks was gone, Reed walked to the single chair in the room and sat down. He watched the creature that was now ignoring him. He wondered what it was thinking. He couldn't imagine the terror, or the sadness, that had to fill it. It had to know that it was stranded on this planet with no hope of getting home. It had to know there was absolutely no hope of rescue.

Reed knew that they, meaning other soldiers at Roswell, had been watching the skies north of town, but there had been no sign of a rescue ship or any kind of a search. He also knew that the sightings in New Mexico had dropped off dramatically after the crash, though they hadn't ended. He began to understand that many of those sightings were not of an alien ship, but of balloons, airplanes, and even strange looking clouds that had been misinterpreted. There might have been only a single alien ship and it was now in the hands of the Army.

If there had been a single ship, then the creature in front of him knew that. It would end its life on an alien world, surrounded by alien creatures who didn't understand a thing about it. That made Reed sad. He understood the loneliness the being had to feel. It was completely isolated from everything it knew and there was no way for it to return to its home. It had to understand that even if they, meaning the Army, wanted to send it home, they simply didn't have the capability to do so.

The creature wasn't repulsive. It seemed small and almost helpless and Reed wished there was something he could do for it, but knew there wasn't. He couldn't even tell it he was sorry for its predicament.

Douglass appeared at the door, stood for a moment looking at the alien and then turned his attention to Reed. He asked, "You about ready?"

"The doctor is coming with us. He seems to have established . . . a rapport with the being."

"This is getting out of hand," said Douglass. "Too many people in on it."

Reed laughed. "The doctor already knows. And if he can keep the creature calm while we move it, then isn't that a benefit for us?"

Without another word, Douglass turned and retreated down the hallway. Reed glanced at the alien being. It seemed to have remained calm during all the activity and visitation. Reed wasn't sure what his reactions would be under similar circumstances, but he was sure that calm wouldn't be among them. And then he took that thought a step further and realized that this wouldn't necessarily be unique to the alien. Surely they would have explored other worlds and just as surely there would have been problems at some point during those explorations of those other worlds. Just as the Army seemed to have a plan to cover nearly all alternatives in a disaster, a space-faring alien race would know how to respond to a crash on a foreign planet. If there were intelligent creatures on that planet, then the being might just remain calm until it had a chance to . . .

That line of thinking began to bother Reed. No one had thought about what the creature might do. To everyone's thinking it was stranded on Earth just as the old Spanish sailors had sometimes been stranded in the New World. They would know that there would be no rescue. Of course, they were lost among humans, even if those humans were nearly as alien to the sailors as this creature was to them.

Hendricks arrived, interrupting Reed's thoughts. Hendricks was carrying a small bag. He set it on the floor and again stepped to the bed. In a quiet, low voice, he said, "We're going for a ride. There is nothing to worry about."

Over his shoulder, he said to Reed, "You carry my bag."

As Reed picked it up, Hendricks pulled the sheet and blanket away from the creature and draped it over the end of the bed. To Reed's surprise, the alien was wearing a standard issue hospital pajama bottoms that looked to be a couple of sizes too large.

With Hendricks' help, the being swung bony knees and strange, narrow feet from the bed. It hopped off, not unlike a kid jumping into a cold pool, and then stood swaying back and forth. It looked as if the creature was about to pass out.

"I think he comes from a world where the gravity is not as heavy as here on Earth. Heavier gravity would suggest it would need a thicker, heavier bone structure to counteract the weight of the gravitational pull."

"Thank you, Doctor," said Reed, "but that is really more information than I need right now."

When it seemed that the creature had recovered, they all stepped slowly into the corridor, and the armed guard moved back, out of the way. He fingered the trigger of his rifle, as if he was thinking about shooting the creature, or was ready for it should it spring at him.

Reed followed the doctor and the creature down the darkened hallway. They looked, to Reed's mind, almost like a father his small, thin son. Together, their pace was slow, and the being seemed to be having trouble staying on its feet. It seemed to be extremely weak with little in the way of energy.

"Could be a result of not having eaten in several days," said Hendricks, looking back at Reed.

Before they reached the rear of the building where the ambulance waited, they stopped. Hendricks pulled a large pair of comical looking sunglasses from his pocket. The lenses were very dark, and the bows had been bent to accommodate the larger cranium of the alien.

To Reed, as if in a lecture hall, Hendricks said, "We have noticed that the bright sunlight bothers his eyes. To me, that suggests that they come from a world where their sun is dimmer than ours."

"Or maybe just that they're nocturnal," said Reed without really thinking about it.

Hendricks put the glasses on the alien and then guided him toward the door. He reached around and opened it, and the two of them exited. Reed followed and watched as one of the sergeants opened the rear door of the ambulance and then stepped back, out of the way. It almost seemed that the sergeant was trying to hide behind the ambulance door.

Hendricks half lifted and half pushed the creature into the rear of the ambulance. He guided it to one of the chairs and then sat in the other without a word.

Now Reed moved forward and said, "I'll shut the door. The ambulance will drive around to the front where a car is waiting. I'll ride in the car."

"That will be fine," said Hendricks.

Reed was about to the close the door and then stopped. He looked at Hendricks and asked, "Can you communicate with it at all?"

Hendricks shrugged. "What's communication? He seems to understand what I want and that I'm not going to harm him. He seems to understand what the food and water is, but refuses to take any. He made it known that the sunlight hurt his eyes. That, I would guess, is a form of communication."

"Has it made any sounds?"

"He. Has he made any sounds? Just a sort of grunt when we first exposed him to the bright lights."

"Okay," said Reed. "Just so you know, we plan to drive through the night. With luck, we'll reach our destination before the sun is very high in the sky."

"Thank you," said Hendricks.

As Reed closed the door, he decided that it had been a strange thing for Hendricks to say. He hadn't done anything other than to set it up so that, at the last minute, Hendricks had to accompany them into the Nevada desert.

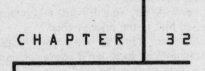

CHAPTER 32

Lieutenant Colonel Joseph P. Cavanaugh stood on the raised stage of the post theater and looked down at the two dozen men assembled in the front row. All wore fatigues, all looked as if they had just "broken starch" on fresh uniforms, and not one of them was under the rank of sergeant first class. They were all top officers and NCOs who had seen combat in various theaters during the war, had been trained as Rangers at some point, and were cleared for top secret material. They were the cream of the troops available to him.

Cavanaugh nodded his approval as he walked from the right side of the stage to the center. He stopped there, looked at the rear where another sergeant stood and waited. The sergeant called out, "The doors are locked, Colonel, and the guards are posted. No one will be coming in."

"Thank you," said Cavanaugh. "Please step outside."

"Yes, sir."

Cavanaugh said to the men assembled in the front row of seats, "I know that I don't have to tell you that this meeting is classified as top secret. You will not discuss it outside this building, you will not discuss it with anyone who is not in this building, and you will not mention this meeting to anyone at any time. If you are not selected for the follow up activities, you will forget that this meeting ever took place. Are these instructions understood?"

Had these not been professional soldiers, and had it not been a mix of high ranking NCOs and officers, Cavanaugh would have expected them to all shout the answer to him. There were a couple of mumbled answers, some nodding heads, and Cavanaugh took that to mean that all of them had understood what he wanted. Had they not understood, they would have asked questions. Had they not understood, he would have had them escorted from the meeting because it meant they weren't as bright as he had been led to believe they were.

"Gentlemen," he said, "We are about to undertake a very important assignment. We'll be redeploying to the deserts of Nevada, somewhere north of the Las Vegas area, but south of Reno, for training purposes."

Cavanaugh had been proud of that little deception. He was suggesting to the men that the real assignment would come after training in the desert, but the real assignment was for them to be on hand, in Nevada, if needed. The logistics to move them into place, if needed, would be much less noticeable, if they were already, more or less, on hand.

Cavanaugh pointed toward the projection booth, and the captain there turned on the slide projector, showing the bare desert north of Las Vegas, Nevada. Cavanaugh stepped out of the way, toward the lectern that was placed to the side, snapped on the small lamp and turned to the first page of his prepared briefing.

"Sometime in the next day or so, we will board transport aircraft to be flown out to Nellis Army Air Field. We will then be trucked from there to the site of an abandoned airfield where we will set up camp. At that point we will began to acclimatize ourselves to the desert weather, and run a series of training missions and patrols into the desert."

Cavanaugh spoke for about twenty minutes, running through the slides that had been provided by LeMay's aide. He detailed the types of training they would undergo, who would be in charge of what elements of that training, and that the training would last for about a month. When he was finished, he asked for questions, answered them, and then thanked the men for their attention. Everyone was prepared for the airlift at dawn, the next day. It was short notice, but they were supposed to be able to deploy on short notice. That had been part of the original training, given to them during the war.

With that, Cavanaugh, turned off the light on his lectern. Someone yelled, "Attention," and the men climbed to their feet. Cavanaugh left the theater.

CHAPTER 33

Curtis LeMay sat at the head of the long, wide, and highly polished conference table, looking at a young lieutenant colonel named Kennedy who looked as if he had traveled all night, whose dark hair was mussed, who needed a shave, and he was pale, as if the things he had seen had shocked him. He stood holding a file folder stamped top and bottom with large red letters. The report he was reading had been labeled as top secret. It was the latest of the news from New Mexico, and it told a story that LeMay, who had been involved from the beginning, found to be as shocking as anything he had seen. He knew it was all true because he had seen the color photographs flown in for him, he had talked to some of the people involved in the recovery and yet, it was nearly unbelievable.

The lieutenant colonel, who had personally escorted the color film from New Mexico, who had stood on the small section of desert where the ship crashed, who had inspected the bodies before they had been flown out of New Mexico, and who, therefore, also knew all the stories were true, found it difficult to relate what he had seen to real life. The sights, the sounds, the knowledge had overwhelmed him. He hadn't been as confused, excited, concerned or uncomfortable since the Germans had surrendered and he had received orders to join the fight in the South Pacific. He was moving from the comfortable world that he knew, even it if was dangerous, into unknown territory, which was always more frightening.

"General," he said, "we now evolve to the world of speculation. These are observations made by the officers in Roswell, and made by some of the experts that have been flown in." He waited for LeMay to comment.

"Continue, Colonel, but please keep the speculation in the realm of reality. I don't want to hear anything that isn't partially supported by the facts." Even as he said it, LeMay realized that it would be an impossible task. A week ago, he wouldn't have listened to anyone who suggested there was life on other planets. Now, he was being briefed on the form that life took, and their ability to travel from one planet to another, and their arrival on Earth.

"Certainly, General. Our preliminary examination of the ship itself suggests a technology that is decades ahead of us. Four men, without strain, were able to lift the craft from the ground. It is made of a lightweight material that resembles plastic but that is much stronger than that and has a much better high temperature property. We have been unable to cut it at this point, even using a torch."

He flipped a page and said, "What we do know is that it is giving off some form of electromagnetic radiation. The field is not strong, however, and we don't know if it has only to do with electronics inside the cockpit, or the ship, if it has a communications function, or if it is somehow related to the power plant."

"I'll get the full details from the engineers," said LeMay. "What can you tell me about the crew?"

He flipped to another page and said, "Four of the crew were dead. One seems to have survived, but we have been unable to establish communication with it . . ."

"It?" asked LeMay.

The colonel shrugged slightly. "Yes, General. We assume that it is male, but we have no way of knowing that. There were no, ah, outward indications. We don't even know if male or female apply. It is, after all, an alien species."

"Continue."

"General, this is all very preliminary. The creature has not been seen to ingest any food or water. There is no outward sign of trauma or bleeding. We don't know why it survived and its fellows perished. Autopsies will be performed by a number of teams and the results will be consolidated, but all we have is some of the preliminary work now." Kennedy grinned, not because he found anything amusing in what he was saying, but the discussion had taken such an impossible turn. He was telling a major general in the Army what they had learned about alien creatures, or had failed to learn. The point was, they were talking about creatures that were not from Earth and the situation was so unexpected that Kennedy's mind was almost numb.

LeMay waved a hand, as if to signal for attention. He said, "What I want to know, what I need to know, as quickly as possible, is where do they originate and are they hostile."

"We assume, General, that they come from outside our solar system."

"Why?"

"This isn't my field of expertise, but from what I have been told, were they from inside the Solar System, we would have seen evidence of them before now. A technological civilization on Mars or Venus would have been discovered by our observations of those planets and certainly they would have traveled here long ago."

"I thought Venus was hidden behind clouds."

"Yes, General, but we would have detected the electromagnetic radiation generated by an advanced civilization. We would be hearing their radio communications just as they would be hearing ours. There would be other signs. With Mars, quite obviously, we would have seen something before now. We have made good observations of the surface and a civilization would have left signs that would be visible on that surface. The other planets, Jupiter and beyond, are either too large, or too far from the sun. That would exclude them."

"Outside the Solar System," said LeMay. "Think of the technical achievement." And then, as his mind whirled, "Think of the economic impact. Think of the cost to the world that launched them."

"Yes, sir," said Kennedy. "I hadn't really considered the economics."

LeMay closed his eyes and remained silent. He opened his eyes and asked, "Do you have anything else?"

"Well, General, again, just the preliminaries, and the orders moving the operation into Nevada have been transmitted. The operation is moving smoothly."

LeMay nodded. "Okay. If that's all, let's move on to other topics."

Kennedy sat down and closed his folder.

CHAPTER | 3 4

When the ambulance moved, Hendricks saw no reaction by the being sitting in the other chair. There was no change in the muscles of the face, no narrowing, or widening of the eyes, no instinctive clasp of the arms of the chair. It sat calmly, unmoving, as if waiting for its fate without thought or fear, almost as if it knew what to expect.

It sat, its feet dangling as if it was a child sitting in an adult chair. Its hands were in its lap, the fingers intertwined in a very unhuman fashion. Its head was resting against the back of the chair, not unlike a human pilot who expected a sudden acceleration.

Hendricks felt he had to say something, even if the being couldn't understand any of the words. Quietly, he said, "We're going to move to a different base, one that will have better, more up to date facilities. One where I think we can get some help for you."

The ambulance slowed and stopped. Hendricks stood and looked out of one of the small, square windows in the rear doors. He saw Reed climb behind the wheel of a civilian passenger car, and that a couple of other men were already inside. That would be their escort out of New Mexico. There was nothing on the car to suggest that it was military, other than the fact that the driver was in uniform. As he watched, Reed stripped his tie and then pulled the brass from his collar. Suddenly it appeared that three civilians were sitting in the car, though one of the men wore a khaki shirt of obvious military origin. In New Mexico, that wouldn't mean much because of the number of veterans of the war who had taken up residence in the state.

Hendricks sat back down before the ambulance moved and faced the alien. They started rolling again and he felt them cross the railroad tracks that marked the northern boundary of the base, and knew that they were on the way. Ten, fifteen minutes later, they slowed as they drove through Roswell and then out the northern edge of town where they again picked up speed. Hendricks knew that it would be a couple of hours before they hit any large towns, through they would pass through a number of very small ones, one or two of which looked deserted.

He looked at the creature again. It had removed the sunglasses and was holding them by the stems in a very human way. It sat with its knees together. It looked artificial, stiff and uncomfortable, but it didn't move. It could have been a child sitting still under the watchful eye of an adult or it could have been a big, ugly doll.

Hendricks said, quietly, "We'll probably be driving for a couple of hours before we need to stop. It should be fully dark by then. Easier for you to see. Easier on your eyes." He touched the side of his head.

Hendricks thought about the night sky and the blaze of stars that were visible in the clear New Mexican air after sunset. He wondered if the alien would be able to identify its home world among the stars and if it could, would it tell him around which star it circled. He decided that there would be no way to communicate the question except, if they were standing outside, to point into the sky and shrug. But, of course, the alien might not, probably would not know what the shrug meant. Communication still had no common basis.

He thought about that for a moment and wondered what he would do in an alien environment, maybe one that was tropical, with tall trees with huge leaves that blocked the sun, a soft, spongy layer of dead and rotting vegetation that smelled, and insects that could kill and gigantic snakes that thought of you as food. An environment that was completely alien to anything he had experienced in his life.

What would he do if he was surrounded with alien beings that were as different from him as he was from a mouse. Yes, he and the aliens were sentient, but that was all they had in common. Maybe they ate food that looked like gruel but smelled like a sewer. How would he tell them that he needed something else. That their food wasn't his food.

Then, to compound the problem, he was all alone. Not like the Spanish sailors who washed up in the New World, but a single creature that had no hope of telling its colleagues where he was, or to tell them that he was alive hoping for rescue. He was caught, for the rest of his life, on a strange world, among strange creatures, and the best he could hope for was that someday he would be able to learn their language.

Hendricks couldn't imagine the loneliness the creature had to feel. Its fellow crewmen were dead. He had to know that. So he was unique. There was nothing like him anywhere else on the world. His only hope was rescue, but what were the odds.

A hundred years ago, a ship could disappear without a trace. If anyone survived, found himself on a deserted island, he might feel the same loneliness. He would have no way to tell his fellows that he had survived and he had no way to call for help. He was there for the rest of his life.

He just couldn't get his mind around the concept of being the only one of its kind on some distant planet with no hope. The concept was as alien as the creature sitting across from him.

He glanced at it and felt himself growing tired, sleepy. That wasn't unusual. He had been awakened before the sun rose, had worked all day, and now was riding in the back of the ambulance. The gentle rocking and the hypnotic whine of the tires on the concrete made him feel tired. He wanted to relax and to sleep and since he couldn't talk to the alien, there was no reason for him to stay awake.

Some time later he awoke with a start. It was dark in the rear of the ambulance and the sky beyond the square windows was black. They were still moving steadily across New Mexico.

Hendricks sat up and felt a sharp pain on his arm, not unlike that from a needle. He tugged at his sleeve and looked at his arm but could see nothing there. He figured that he had bruised himself at some point and hadn't noticed it until now.

There was a sudden pop and the ambulance swayed to one side and then the other. It rocked on its springs as it fishtailed slightly. There was a squeal from the brakes and they slid to a stop. From the front, one of the sergeants yelled, "Got us a flat tire."

Hendricks looked toward the alien creature but in the darkness could see almost nothing. It was a vague outline until the headlights of the car following them pulled onto the shoulder of the road behind him. Then he could see the alien sitting in the same position that it had taken when it had entered the ambulance. The loss of the tire, the swaying and jolting inside the ambulance, the sudden squealing noise, didn't seem to have bothered it. It was almost as if it understood that the problem was minor, easily remedied and probably not fatal.

Hendricks waited until he heard voices outside of the ambulance and then stood. To the alien he said, "Please wait here." With that, he threw open the rear door and climbed out. Without thinking about it, he shut the door behind him. He turned and watched as Douglass and Campbell got out of the car.

As he approached, he heard the ambulance driver, Sergeant Schaffer, say, "Take us about thirty minutes to change this tire. It's a bitch to change them fuckers on the road."

"I would have thought that you would have inspected the tires before we began the trip," said Douglass.

Schaffer said, "Inspected by me and the motor sergeant. Can't tell about the wear on the other side of the tire, or if there is a soft spot on the tube inside. Only can look at it on the outside, inspect the tread and make sure that everything visible is in good shape. These things happen."

Reed appeared, setting his hat on his head, even though, with his insignia removed from his shirt, he wasn't required to wear it and probably shouldn't. He squatted to look at the tire and then up at Hendricks. "The passenger?"

"Undisturbed by the blow out."

Without thinking about it, Reed stood and walked around to the rear of the ambulance. He opened the door and then stepped back, surprised. The alien was standing there, as if it had been looking out the little window, watching what was happening outside. Neither he, nor Reed, moved.

Hendricks said, "Hey, now," and reached up, as if to take its hand.

The creature was looking up into the night sky, its head moving back and forth, as if it was searching for something. It stood still, finally focused on a section of the sky to the south. It stared at the stars there and didn't move.

Douglass saw that and asked, "It see something?"

"No," said Hendricks, but he wasn't sure. He couldn't see anything other than the stars, but he didn't know how good the alien's eyes were, or how good its sense of celestial navigation might be. The alien might be able to see much better than any of the humans.

Campbell, for some reason, had pulled his pistol. He stood at the side of the road, looking toward the south, afraid that something was coming. He held the pistol along the seam of his trousers, where it wouldn't be visible from any car that might pass them. He said, "I don't see anything."

"You want us to fix this tire," said Schaffer, "you're going to have to move out of the way." Then, as an afterthought, he added, "Sirs."

"Hendricks," said Reed, "Why don't you see if you can get our passenger to sit down again. In the back."

When Hendricks didn't move, Reed added, "Before someone comes along and sees something he shouldn't."

"Maybe it made the tire go flat," said Campbell.

"Just how would it have done that?" asked Reed.

"Well, maybe it has friends out there who did. Maybe they plan to rescue it."

"Wouldn't that have been easier at the base where we weren't moving around?"

"But we were surrounded by what, six, seven thousand armed troops. Here we're all alone. Maybe they were waiting until we got out here all alone."

"Shit," said Schaffer. "You guys finished? You want us to get this thing going again or what? Sirs?"

Reed nodded and then, aware that they wouldn't see that in the dark, said, "Yes. We'll get back out of the way."

Hendricks climbed up into the rear of the ambulance and gently moved the alien back, out of the door and into the darkness where the chairs were set. He nudged the creature and it sat down.

Reed closed one of the doors, and then set the other one so that it was open slightly. No one on the road would be able to see into the rear of the ambulance and glimpse the creature.

The two sergeants had gotten out the tools and a spare wheel. They were working on the lug nuts, loosening them before they began to jack up the rear of the ambulance. Hendricks dropped out of the back of the ambulance, and stood watching them as they worked. Douglass sent Campbell around to the front of the ambulance, almost as if he was putting out a sentry. He then walked back and leaned on the rear fender of the car and folded his arms as if he was annoyed at the flat tire.

In the distance, the headlights of another car appeared. They grew quickly, but the driver didn't slow very much as he reached the ambulance. Once he was past it, he began to pick up speed, uninterested in what was happening.

The next car slowed and then pulled off the road. The driver got out, waved and as he crossed the highway to join them, yelled, "You fellows need some help?"

Douglass pushed himself off the fender and said, "Nah. Just a flat and we're getting it fixed. Thanks."

But the driver seemed reluctant to leave. He said, "Name's Glazer, Tom Glazer." He produced a pack of cigarettes, shook one out and put it in his mouth. With a wooden kitchen match, he lit it and then held the pack out to Douglass.

"No, thanks."

"You other fellows?"

Douglass answered for them. "We're fine. We appreciate your stopping and all, but we have the situation under control."

"You boys Army?"

The ambulance was the clue and Douglass could do nothing but acknowledge that. Glazer said, "I was in the Army during the war. Think I must have walked across Europe after we invaded. Got to tell you, that was a time."

Reed walked back, holding out a hand to be shaken. He said, "I flew fighters over most of Europe. I heard that you shouldn't walk when you could ride."

Glazer chuckled and said, "You have that right, friend. Never walked so much in my life."

Reed engaged the man in conversation about their experiences in Europe. Glazer told them that he actually gone across the beaches during the Normandy invasion. He had been a staff sergeant when the war ended, and although he had thought about staying in the service, he decided he would use the GI Bill to go to college. When he finished the degree in a year or two, he might see about being an officer.

"Better than being an enlisted man," he said.

Reed nodded but said, "Lot of responsibility. Top sergeants are worth their weight in gold."

"True, but they still have to take orders from young-ass second lieutenants."

Now Reed laughed. "It's been my experience that good sergeants eat young-ass second lieutenants for breakfast."

"Captain," called Schaffer, "We're ready to roll if you've finished back there."

Reed held out a hand and said, "Thanks for stopping."

The man tossed the cigarette into the middle of the road where it seemed to explode. He shook Reed's hand and said, "Good luck to you, Captain."

As the driver climbed back in his car, Reed said to Douglass, "I'm going to check with Hendricks. You want to drive or you want Campbell to do it."

"Let Campbell."

CHAPTER | 35

July 13, 1947
Over the Rainbow
Nevada

They stopped only once during the night so that they could relieve themselves in the desert. They drove past a number of all-night truck stops and although they were hungry, they kept going because there were too many trucks and too much light. They left New Mexico, entered Arizona, crossed it in quickly, and then turned north into Nevada. Finally they found a small gas station that had just opened for the day. They bought gas, candy and soft drinks. One of the sergeants stood at the rear of the ambulance at all times just in case someone else stopped and got curious. They debated about the small café across the highway, where the lights had just come on, but Reed shook his head.

"We'll be at the base in a couple of hours. We'll just have to gut it out."

Once they had gotten some food, they had visited the latrine, and they had bought extra cups of coffee, they returned to the car and ambulance. Reed watched as Hendricks climbed in the back and shut the door. With that accomplished, Reed got into the passenger's side of the car. Douglass had slipped behind the wheel.

"Drive," said Reed.

"Are we close?" asked Douglass.

"Yeah. We're close. Schaffer has a map." Reed looked at his watch. "Should be there by nine. Ten at the latest."

They drove for two or three hours after sunrise, found a dirt and gravel road, then finally turned down another. They came to a guard shack that seemed to be set out on the open desert with no real sign of a base anywhere around. They slowed and then stopped. Reed got out of the car and walked toward an armed guard who was looking into the driver's side of the ambulance.

"This is a restricted facility, sir," said the guard.

Reed pulled a set of orders from his shirt pocket and handed them to the guard. "You should have been alerted that we were on the way."

"Yes, sir," he said, but he walked into the guard shack. He returned a moment later and said, "You'll need to proceed to Hangar 84. Do you know where that is?"

Reed shook his head and the guard provided the directions, pointing. Reed then walked to the ambulance and looked through the passenger's side window. To the driver, he said, "You'll follow me."

"Yes, sir."

Reed walked back to the driver's side of the car. He motioned Douglass to slide over, got in, and then pulled around the ambulance. He drove onto the base, made the turns and then drove through a gate in the fence that separated the base from the airfield proper. He noticed that the fence, unlike the rest of the facility, looked brand new. When he stopped in front of the hangar, he blew the horn once, and an instant later one of the massive doors began to roll open. They drove through, stopped and shut off the engines.

As Reed climbed out of the car, a half dozen men, three of them armed with rifles, appeared and walked toward them. One of the men, dressed in a white coat, called out, "Doctor Hendricks?"

Reed was surprised that they knew Hendricks was with them. It just showed that the communications between the base and Roswell was operating smoothly. Reed walked forward and said, "I'm Jack Reed. Doctor Hendricks is in the rear of the ambulance with our passenger."

The man looked toward the ambulance and then said, "One of them is really alive?"

"Yes, one of them is really alive. We have been unable to communicate with it yet, but it is alive."

He giggled, sounding like a kid who had just seen the presents under the Christmas tree and knew that Santa Claus wouldn't let him down this year. He took a step and then stopped. "Is there anything that I should know?"

Reed realized that he was playing fast and loose with security here. Reed stepped between the man and the ambulance. He asked, "Who are you?"

"Oh, I'm sorry. I've been awake all night, waiting. We didn't know when you would arrive."

"Yes, sir. You are?"

"Doctor Block." He grinned and chuckled. "I'm a major in the Army Reserve."

Reed pulled another piece of paper from his pocket and scanned the list of names. He found a Doctor James Block on it. Next to Block's name, in parenthesis, was the note about him being a reserve major.

Before he could decide on how to approach the vehicle and alert Hendricks, one of the doors was pushed open. Hendricks jumped out, to the dirty hangar floor.

"What's going on?"

Block turned and said, "I'm Doctor Block, Doctor?"

"Hendricks."

"Is he in there?"

"Yes."

"Anything that I need to know?"

"He doesn't like bright light but does like a warmer environment than we are used to."

"Okay. Let's get him out that ambulance and downstairs."

Reed thought there was something else that he should be doing. He thought that some security should be enforced but he didn't know what it was. After all, he was on a secret base, surrounded by armed men who had, obviously, passed the various background and security checks. Everyone here had been cleared and checked and Reed's job had been to deliver, safely, the alien creature and not concern himself with the base personnel or how highly cleared they were. He had completed his task and security would be turned over to someone else.

Behind him, the hangar door groaned closed so that the building was again sealed. No one outside would be able to see inside, if there had been anyone out there to see in. No one would be able to learn what they were doing.

Reed stood back and watched as Hendricks climbed back into the rear of the ambulance. A moment later, the alien appeared and Hendricks helped it climb down. Several of the guards reacted. One of them turned his weapon, his thumb on the safety, toward the creature almost as if he expected it to attack.

Hendricks and Block, one on each side of the alien, began to cross the dirty floor. A door at the far end of the hangar opened and they headed toward it. Reed began to follow them.

"Sir? What about us?" asked one of the sergeants.

Reed stopped and said, "Wait here. I'll find out."

"We haven't had anything to eat."

"Look," said Reed. "There'll be a latrine up here somewhere. Might be some coffee somewhere. I'll get this transfer settled and then I'll get right back to you. But hell, you guys are sergeants. I shouldn't have to hold your hands."

"Yes, sir."

Reed hurried after the others. He was stopped at the door but an armed guard then found his name on the access list and nodded. Reed asked, "What about the drivers?"

"Hell, sir, I don't know."

"Are there any other facilities on this installation?"

"Everything is right here sir and they won't be on the access list."

Reed nodded and turned. He walked back to the ambulance. "I'm not sure what to tell you. You're through here but there is no place for billeting or a mess hall. You aren't on any of the access lists."

The senior sergeant, Schaffer, grinned. He knew a good thing when he heard it. "If I might suggest, Captain, that you call Roswell and let them know that we're on our way back."

Reed nodded, and grinned his understanding. "And I should let them know that it will take two, maybe three days for you to get back, given the help that I'm going to require here before I can officially release the two of you?"

"Why, yes, sir. We've been up all night and we'll need some sleep and some grub. And there will be no reason for us to drive all night again."

"You have a change of clothes?"

"Oh, yes, sir. We've done a couple of these things and know enough to bring some civilian clothes and a shaving kit. We'll just hop into the ambulance and drive back to that little town we came through. Looked like a nice hotel there."

"Okay, sergeant, you deserve it. Don't take too much advantage of this and I'll alert Roswell that you should be back in a couple of days. If they have any trouble about the delay, they should give me a call here. I'll give them a number if they need it when I talk to them."

"Yes, sir. Thank you, sir."

"We'll keep the other car here."

"That's between you and the motor officer in Roswell," said the sergeant.

Reed watched them climb into the ambulance, heard the engine start, and then turned. He walked back to the door, let the guard open it for him, and walked onto the elevator. He wasn't sure that he liked what was happening.

CHAPTER 36

Major General Curtis LeMay was not a happy man. He stared across his desk at the major sitting in a large leather chair, and said, "How can you be so sure?"

The major, whose name tag read Fawcett, and who was wearing an immaculate uniform complete with all awards, decorations and qualification badges, said, "We've been watching the Soviet attempts to penetrate the area for the last six months. There has been a significant increase in activity since the beginning of June."

That made LeMay feel somewhat better. If the increase was traced to the beginning of June, it meant that the Soviets had not begun the latest espionage operation because of the events outside of Roswell. He asked Fawcett, "What are they looking for?"

"As near as we can tell, General, and this is based on limited data, they are interested in the qualifications, the names and training, and anything else they can learn about the men assigned to the base in Roswell. I'm not sure exactly what they hope to gain by targeting the 509th, but maybe they hope to establish a few assets."

LeMay wondered if the man knew that the 509th had the atomic bomb and then realized that the information was not classified. LeMay had seen newspaper accounts that noted the 509th had dropped the atomic bombs on Japan and that the designation of the unit was sometimes written as "509th Bomb Group (Atomic)," in those newspapers.

"Have they had any success?"

"General," said the major, "I'm not sure how much of this that I'm supposed to discuss with you. Your mission is research and development and not counterintelligence."

"Major," said LeMay calmly, evenly, keeping his temper under control, "do not tell me my mission, or what I might need to know. You will answer my questions fully, or you'll quickly find yourself as a second lieutenant in charge of typewriter maintenance in northern Alaska where your ass would freeze off, except that you would no longer have one. Any notion you might have held about a military career and promotion opportunities will have ended if I find that I am annoyed at your attitude."

Although LeMay had not raised his voice, and had appeared calm, his eyes were hard. The major felt sweat bead on his forehead and then drip. He swallowed with some difficulty and said in a high, tight voice, "I was merely reminding the General about . . ."

"Don't remind me about anything at anytime. Answer my fucking question."

"Yes, sir. We picked up one agent in El Paso and another in Ruidoso. The agent in Ruidoso had photographs of the Roswell airfield, obviously taken from far outside the perimeter. These photographs showed some of the aircraft on the airfield and some of the guarded structures on the base."

LeMay nodded. "Interrogation?"

"They didn't say much of anything. One of them tried to say that he had diplomatic immunity and that it was all a big misunderstanding, but the Soviet Embassy denied all knowledge of the man."

"The espionage is directed at the atomic capabilities of the 509th?" asked LeMay.

"That's what we suspect, General."

"Anything else?"

"No, sir."

LeMay leaned back in his chair and stared out the window. He thought for a moment, wondering how to ask the one question he needed to ask without tipping his hand. Almost anything he asked could be combined with the article that Blanchard had released to the newspapers. If that damned Blanchard hadn't told the world that they had a flying saucer, then LeMay could ask about it without anything being inferred. Now, such a question might raise suspicion and if Fawcett was a clever man, he might guess things that he was not supposed to know. Damn it all anyway.

Finally, LeMay asked, "Have they been trying to get to White Sands?"

"We suspect that, General. We haven't anything specific, but, there is important research being conducted there. It only makes sense for the Soviets to be interested in anything going on at White Sands."

"Thank you," said LeMay, dismissing Fawcett.

Fawcett stood, saluted, and then retreated rapidly, happy to be out with his ass intact. LeMay was famous for ripping the ass off those who offended him and Fawcett had offended him.

As Fawcett closed the door on his way out, LeMay was suddenly frightened. Not by Soviet attempts to get close to White Sands or Roswell for the atomic secrets they held, but because of the alien craft that had fallen in that part of New Mexico. He was afraid they would stumble across the secret and then hundreds of Soviet agents would be crossing into the United States from Mexico.

CHAPTER 37

July 14, 1947
Over the Rainbow
Nevada

Captain Jack Reed sat at one end of the table in the conference room and stared at the only woman present. He liked her short hair, liked her bright eyes, and liked the sound of her voice. He was impressed with her general knowledge and the contribution she was making to the discussion at hand. He was making no contribution, having lost the thread minutes ago as it became more technical and medically oriented. He knew they were talking about the alien creature he had escorted from Roswell, but he didn't understand half the things they were saying about it and almost nothing the woman was saying.

He was in the meeting simply because he had come from Roswell with the alien and he had been there when they had picked up the craft, the bodies, and the survivor. They thought he might be able to tell them something important that hadn't been contained in the various written reports, but after they started the meeting, they had ignored him completely. He had waited patiently, but no one addressed any questions to him that couldn't be answered by others who had more and better information, or more and better training than he did.

So, instead, he found himself studying the one woman in the conference room. It was clear from the reaction of the others that she was respected and her opinion important. Reed thought that strange, not because she was a woman, but because she appeared young and the older men would naturally assume that since they were older, they were automatically smarter. Apparently she had said or done something earlier that had impressed them greatly. When he had seen her briefly in New Mexico, he hadn't had much of a chance to talk to her. She had always been surrounded by others who had controlled the situation or who were taking her from one meeting to another.

Hendricks sat almost directly across from him, looking as if he was about to go to sleep or to be sick. Reed didn't know which, but he knew that Hendricks was in bad shape. He found it difficult to believe that the all night ride in the back of the ambulance would have caused Hendricks to get sick. He just had ridden back there and hadn't even been required to stay awake or to drive. He could have slept in the chair which might not have been the most restful sleep but it was better than staying awake all night, especially if it was going to make him that sick.

At the head of the table, a thin man stood, droning on and on about the honeycombed nature of the skin of the craft, trying to impress those listening by describing, in monotonous detail, the ship's lightness and strength which was far beyond the capabilities of modern science. He was saying that he believed it was a technical development that proved, that was his word, proved, that the alien society was two hundred and fifty years ahead of Earth technology. He based that on the current state of metallurgy and the fact that he knew of no one working on anything like the honeycombed composite material that wasn't really metal but closer to plastic. For some reason, this convinced the man, Reed didn't even know his name, that human metal technology would take about two hundred and fifty years to reach the level of the aliens.

The pronouncement raised a number of questions in Reed's mind. He didn't think it was possible to look at a metal and determine the technological advancement of the society that had created it based on the technological development of another society. If someone on another world looked at bronze, would they then assume a technological state consistent with the first introduction of bronze? Would that mean they would assume that Earth technology was a thousand years or more behind where it actually was? In other words, Reed thought the man was full of shit. But no one seemed willing to challenge his claims.

As he sat down, Hendricks started to rise, almost as if he was going to present the next segment of the discussion. But instead, he said, "I don't feel well at all."

With that, his eyes rolled back into his head and he reached out as if to grab a chair to steady himself. He fell backward, one hand smacking the man who had been sitting next to him. As he hit the floor, with no attempt to break the fall, the woman was on her feet. She moved rapidly to where Hendricks fell, crouched next to him and said, "Get a doctor in here."

Another of the men leaped from his chair and opened the conference room door. He shouted something and then turned his attention back to the Hendricks.

Reed pushed his way around the table and knelt next to Hendricks. The woman said, "Do you know him?"

"Not well. We came in this morning. Traveled all night."

She pushed his eyelids back but only the whites showed. She felt his pulse at his throat and then leaned close to his face, putting her cheek near his mouth to check for respiration.

"Is he going to be all right?" asked Reed.

"I don't know," she snapped. "Let me work."

The door opened again and a man in a white coat with a name tag that said "Whitman" pushed his way in. Whitman joined Reed and Hackett by Hendricks, and pulled out a stethoscope. "What do we have here?"

"He stood up, made a comment, and then collapsed."

Whitman loosened the tie and unbuttoned the shirt. He listened to the heart, checked the eyes, respiration and then the blood pressure. To those standing around, he said, "Let's clear the room. I don't need a bunch of spectators."

As some of the people began to file out, Whitman said, "Anyone know this man well?"

Reed repeated what he had told Hackett and then said, "We brought the creature up from Roswell."

"Jesus," said Whitman. "Any sort of quarantine been in effect?"

"No," said Reed. "Not in Roswell."

"Anybody even think of that?"

Reed shook his head. "When we were on the crash site, someone mentioned radiation but that was all. But this guy wasn't even there."

"Were you?" asked Whitman.

"Yeah. I was one of the first on the scene. I entered the craft before anyone else." He stopped talking and wondered if he had violated security and then decided he hadn't. Everyone in the room had been talking about the ship and the bodies. Everyone knew what was going on. The all knew that the events had to be of extraterrestrial origin.

Whitman looked as if he had just been told that he had been exposed to the plague or cholera without the proper vaccinations. He looked as if he wanted to flee the room but stayed where he was, his attention focused on Hendricks.

"I want to get a stretcher in here. I want a list of names of everyone in here. I want this place sealed off with no one going out or coming in until I figure out what we have here. I want this floor completely sealed. I want to make sure that we have this contained, if we need to contain it."

Without thinking, Reed asked, "Do you have the authority to do something like that?"

"I have the authority, if I need it," said Whitman, icily. "And I don't need a lot of discussion from a soldier."

Reed stood up and backed away from Hendricks. He looked to the right, at the door, and saw several people gathered near it, watching Hendricks just as people gathered around the scene of a traffic accident. The difference was that a traffic accident couldn't infect everyone with some sort of new, and possibly deadly, disease.

Hackett stood up and walked to the door. She pushed a couple of people back and shut it. She stood with her back to it, as if she was now the guard or maybe she was just horrified at what had transpired and the door was as far away from Hendricks as she could get.

"If we have some new virus here, or bacteria," said Whitman, thinking out loud, "we have to contain it here, in this facility, right now."

"That might be too late," said Reed. "The craft has been down for more than a week. It was at the base in Roswell. People from Eighth Air Force in Texas, SAC in Washington, have flown in, looked at the craft and bodies. People have come in from Ohio and some of the material has been flown out to Ohio. The bodies have been removed from New Mexico." For the moment, he didn't mention the two sergeants who were now somewhere between the facility and Roswell. Nor did he mention the unidentified motorist who had stopped to chat who hadn't seen the creature but who had been close enough, nor did he mention the gas station attendant they had talked to that morning.

Whitman looked up. He glanced from face to face, took a deep breath, and said, "Then we better hope that there is no new disease here, or to use an old Army phrase, we are well and truly fucked. There is no way to contain it here."

Two men carrying a stretcher arrived, followed by several of those who had been there when Hendricks collapsed. The men set it on the floor next to Hendricks. Reed looked at those in the room and waved them closer. Then Reed waved several men closer and they, including the stretcher bearers, arranged themselves around Hendricks. Carefully, gently, they lifted him a few inches from the floor, and then set him on the stretcher. Without waiting for orders, the two men who had brought the stretcher each took an end and lifted.

"Take him to the dispensary," ordered Whitman.

"Yes, sir."

They, along with Whitman, exited the conference room. Others stood there for a moment, wondering what should be done. One man dropped into his chair and began to thumb through his files. Another stood, just looking from face to face, as if waiting for orders. Reed sat down, on the edge of one of the chairs, and then reached across the table to pick up the water pitcher. He held it up and asked Hackett, "Do you need something to drink?" He ignored the others still in the room.

She stood there looking at him and then smiled slightly. "I need something stronger than water." She looked at Reed. "We met in New Mexico, didn't we?"

"Yeah. You're Hackett. I'm Reed."

"Of course," she said. "I thought I should know you."

"What exactly do you do here?" asked Reed.

She sat down and pushed one of the glasses at him. When he had filled it, she took a drink. Finally she said, "I'm a biologist. I'm suppose to know something about all of this."

"Me too," said Reed, making conversation because he knew that she would already know that. "I was sent out to look when all we had was a radar track." He took a deep breath and then laughed. It was a forced laugh. "Was it only last week?"

"I know the feeling. I was in Washington minding my own business and now I'm here and I'm not even sure where here is."

"I don't think that it is classified, but I think we're in Nevada. I really don't know exactly where." Reed drained the water in his glass and said, "I don't think I've ever said this, but I could use a real drink. A martini I think."

"Believe it or not," said Hackett, "there is a cantina where you can get a martini." She was quiet for a moment and then asked, "Aren't you worried about disease?"

Reed picked up his water glass and studied it for a moment. He hadn't thought about the possibility of disease. There were others, better educated than he, who were responsible for thinking of those things. It wasn't something that he knew enough about to worry about anyway. The experts, and apparently Hackett was one of them, were supposed to figure all that out. And then he realized that if there was some kind of a disease and it had infected Hendricks, it should also have infected him because he had been the first into the alien ship. He felt his stomach flip over and he was suddenly very cold. He realized that they all were making the best guesses they could about the situation, but the situation was unique. Nobody had any answers.

To Hackett, he said, "I was the first one into the craft. If something was going to happen, or if it was related to what happened to Hendricks, then I would expect I would already be infected."

Almost as if she was thinking out loud, she said, "Not necessarily. There are a number of reasons that Hendricks got sick but you did not."

"Still."

Hackett could read the concern on his face. "We just don't know enough. If this had something to do with the alien, I would expect someone in Roswell to be sick."

"Maybe it hasn't had a chance . . ."

Hackett decided that it was time to be reassuring, even if she didn't have all the information. She said, "Remember we have any number of diseases that are species specific. That means, simply, that some of the diseases that affect reptiles will not infect mammals. Some that are deadly to all other primates, don't even make humans sick. Of course, there are some that cross those lines. We don't know that the alien has any disease that can jump species like this."

Reed relaxed slightly but was feeling slightly dizzy. "Are you sure?"

"Well, let's just say that any bacteria brought from another planet could evolve under the influences of our environment. Their life cycles sometimes are measured in hours so that you have multiple generations each day which allows it to adapt to a new environment very quickly." She held up a hand and added quickly, "But I don't believe that is the case."

Reed felt his head spin and realized suddenly that the danger was more real than he had thought. Without thinking, he said, "That martini is becoming more appealing."

"I'm not sure that the middle of the afternoon is the time to begin drinking."

Reed looked at her carefully and briefly wondered if she was even old enough to drink. He decided that she had to be if only because she had talked of college degrees and that would indicated that she was in her twenties.

"I was awake nearly all night, so I could say it is very late in the day for me." His voice didn't sound right to him and he realized that he was getting scared. It was the first time he had felt the gut-chilling fear since he had been in Europe and enemy fighters were swarming all around him. It was the first time that he had felt the cold sweat begin.

They, meaning Douglass and him, and a dozen others, had climbed all over the alien ship, dropped down into the interior, touched the dead occupants, and not once did anybody think of disease. Maybe it was disease that had killed them, and without thinking, he, and those at Roswell, had released it in the United States.

Hackett said something, but he didn't hear it. Instead he was thinking of the two sergeants who were driving back to Roswell. He was thinking of all the men who had been into and out of Roswell in the last ten days, who had seen the bodies, handled the debris from the ship, interviewed those who had been involved and then returned to their home bases. He thought of all the people who had been in and out of the base, who hadn't been involved in any of this, but who had still been close enough to have been infected. If they were infected, they in turn could infect a hundred others who would go out to infect a hundred others who would in turn. . . . He wondered if they could recall all those who had been in contact with the ship or the bodies, and get them all sent to a single location until they knew more. But he realized that it might be impossible already, given the way things had been handled. Too many people traveling to too many locations.

Hackett came out of her chair, reached for his hand, and felt for his pulse. "Are you all right?" she asked. "You turned so pale."

Reed felt suddenly light-headed, as if he was going to pass out. He reached for the glass of water and spilled it. He wasn't sure exactly what happened, and then he felt a glass at his lips and tasted the cold water.

"All you all right?" Hackett asked again.

Reed took a deep breath and tried to focus his attention. There were questions that he wanted to ask, but couldn't think of a way to frame them. He didn't want to start a panic though he was already in a panic.

"Just felt faint," he said. "I was up all night."

"Did you drive in with the other man?"

"No. Yes. He was in the ambulance. We followed in a car. He was with the alien inside the ambulance." He leaned forward, his head on the table. He closed his eyes and listened to the sounds around him.

"When was the last time you ate?" asked Hackett.

"Yesterday. Lunch. Had some candy this morning. A donut or two."

"Okay," said Hackett. "I'm going to make a snap diagnosis here. If the other man hasn't eaten anything either, then you both might be suffering from low blood sugar. Get some food into you and you'll feel much better."

"What about this disease?" asked Reed.

"I don't think that disease has anything to do with this," said Hackett. "I'm just going to have to teach you people that it is important to eat real food once in a while and not snack on crap."

Reed sat up, feeling somewhat better. At least he was no longer as dizzy. He saw the water glass and this time didn't spill it. "Thanks," he said.

Hackett grinned and said, "Nothing to it." She did not say that she was suddenly worried. Too much was happening and she didn't have any good answers for it.

CHAPTER 38

July 13, 1947
Over the Rainbow
Nevada

David Alexander Whitman, who had responded to the conference emergency, had spent most of his career as a pathologist. He had, at one time, been a top surgeon, but he had lost his enthusiasm for treating the same diseases without making progress toward curing them and preventing them. Pathology, he believed, would allow him to determine the cause of disease, and once he understood that, he would be able to develop a way to prevent it or counteract it that might not involve invasive surgery. Too many patients did not survive the cutting.

When he had been approached by three men in dark suits only three days earlier, and had been asked if he was interested in a highly classified assignment that might teach him something new, Whitman was reluctant to accept. He was reminded that during the war he had held a commission as a Navy doctor and that he had worked, at the very end of the war, at Los Alamos where he had learned many interesting things that he couldn't have learned anywhere else. His security clearance was still current, according to those offering the invitation to the new project, and that made him a valuable asset. When they suggested that they didn't have to ask, because of Whitman's commission, Whitman decided that he would see what it was they wanted.

Now he stood in the dispensary of a base somewhere in Nevada that the locals on that base called Over the Rainbow, far from any town that people could easily identify, looking at an unconscious man who had escorted an alien creature out of New Mexico. He didn't know a thing about the alien creature, the unconscious man in front of him, or the circumstances that had caused the man to faint. That worried him greatly.

Then he thought about it and realized that the man had escorted an alien creature out of New Mexico. The impact of that statement hit fully. He was working in a facility where a creature from another world was housed. He was in on one of the greatest events ever in the history of the planet. It was an impossible, science fiction event, but here he was. The whole thing was unbelievable but it was true.

He almost literally shook himself, to wipe those thoughts from his mind, and then checked the man's pulse, eyes, and respiration again. Whitman carefully unbuttoned the man's shirt and looked at the chest. All he saw was that the man's skin was very white and that worried him even more.

One of the medics said, "I think he might have broken his wrist when he fell."

"Get his shirt off him," said Whitman.

The two medics cut the shirt away, and pulled it clear. Whitman saw a huge bruise on the inside of Hendricks' arm, just above the elbow. It looked as if someone had been attempting to give him a blood transfusion and had missed the vein pumping the blood into the arm under the skin by mistake. The blood spread out, darkening the skin.

Whitman pulled the overhead light down to focus it on the arm. He bent down and studied it very carefully. There were a couple of marks that could have been made by a needle, but he couldn't tell for certain. He examined the whole arm but could see nothing that should have bruised the man that badly.

He waved over one of the medics and asked, "What do you make of this?"

"Injection marks?"

"No," said Whitman. "I don't think so. Looks like a transfusion that went bad. Thicker needle than one used for an injection."

Hendricks opened his eyes momentarily, moaned quietly but didn't respond to questions.

"We need to get his wrist set and make sure that we have no internal bleeding," said Whitman.

"Yes, doctor."

Whitman took a step to the rear, and wiped his hands on a towel. He worried if there was more going on than met the eye. There were tests that he wanted to make. To the medic, he said, "We've got quite a bit of work to do here."

CHAPTER 39

July 14, 1947
The White House
Washington, D.C.

Major General Curtis LeMay stood in the Oval Office, not more than three feet from the massive desk that held the world famous plaque that said, "The Buck Stops Here." Sitting behind it was the President who was reading a report, classified at the highest level of security, explaining what had been happening to the flying disk that had been recovered outside of Roswell, New Mexico. LeMay was looking beyond the President, and out the window into what was known as the Rose Garden. Far beyond it, he could see the tourists standing by the black iron fence that separated the President from the rest of the world.

When the President finished reading he said, "Then we have it contained?"

"Yes, sir," said LeMay. "The press is convinced that the officers at Roswell made a simple mistake. The weather balloon explanation is holding well and no one is questioning it. There have been no follow-up inquiries from the press. They seem to be satisfied."

Truman looked up at LeMay and said, "I don't understand that, General. Why is the press so convinced that these men could make such a mistake?"

LeMay took a moment and then said, "I believe, sir, that it is because that is what they want to believe. They do not want to hear of beings from another world landing on our planet. It is a concept that shakes the very foundation of our core beliefs. Some will view it as a challenge to belief in God.

Others will see it as a challenge to our superiority in the world arena, a position that we obtained at great cost in the war. Some will view it as the end of civilization as we know it. And a few will fear it simply because it is unknown."

"We had the commander at Roswell . . ."

"Colonel Blanchard, sir."

Truman stared at him for a moment, letting him know that he didn't like being interrupted, and then said, "Blanchard, who issued the press release. This was the group who ended the war with the atomic bombs on Japan."

"Yes, sir, but I don't think the press has made the connection. At any rate, when General Ramey said it was a weather balloon, and had one on display in his office, the press believed it was the material found in Roswell. That was what they were told."

"They didn't check?"

"With whom, Mister President? The rancher was at the base and unavailable for comment. The intelligence officer quoted in the release was in Fort Worth with the balloon and General Ramey was pointing to it. The local sheriff, also mentioned, was not talking, telling the press to call the Army. Everywhere they went, it was a dead end."

Truman asked, "How did we get so lucky?"

"Combination of factors. Roswell is isolated. It's about two hundred miles from any other large city such as El Paso or Albuquerque. Limited access to the press, with our boys right here, on top of the situation."

"Then how come we had that press release?"

LeMay shook his head. "I don't know what Colonel Blanchard was thinking at that point. Roger, that is, General Ramey, suggested that it was all part of a larger scheme to divert attention from Roswell to Fort Worth."

"No, General," said the President. "I don't like that. If it was true, it was too big a risk to take without authorization."

"Personally, Mr. President, I believe that Butch made a mistake with his press release. However, the ultimate outcome was that it diverted attention away from Roswell and allowed us to suppress the story in a matter of hours."

"You're suggesting no harm, no foul."

"Exactly. And now we have everything out of Roswell, we have a team in place to examine the craft, autopsy the bodies and try to learn what we can from the survivor."

"Do we know where they originate?"

"Craft is being examined for maps or charts," said LeMay "but at the moment, we haven't found anything like that. There has to be something there but we just haven't been able to locate it. No books, papers, maps, charts, manuals or any other written material of that kind. Some symbols on the interior of the ship that reminded the scientists of the signs we put on doors or files, or the warning signs that we put on the sides of aircraft and the like which suggests there is a written language. We just haven't found it yet."

"I take it that everything, ship, bodies, survivor, has been transferred to Nevada?"

"All the major components are now in Nevada, yes, sir There are some sections, just minor bits of metal and the like that are at Wright Field for analysis. We found some interesting electronic devices that Bell Labs has with no hint as to where, or how, we got them. Other than those exceptions, Mr President, everything is in Nevada."

"Do you need to go there, General?"

"Not at the moment, sir. Everything is being handled by the top people in their fields. My presence would draw the attention of the press which we don't want. But I think in a couple of days it might be beneficial if I made a routine inspection of the Las Vegas facilities. I have some research and development going on there. I think if I go out there now, I'd just be in the way."

Truman laughed. "That's exactly the way I feel most of the time. The government would function without me. I'm just sitting here until the real President can be elected next year. I'm a caretaker."

"Yes, sir."

Truman fell silent for a moment. He shook his head and then said, "We have to keep this buried. We can't take a

:hange that this leaks into the public." He turned his attention
m LeMay. "Damn Blanchard, anyway."

"There has been no adverse consequence, Mr. President."

"I'd like to see him court-martialed for that."

LeMay wasn't sure what his response should be. He hesi-
ated before he said, "That would, of course, draw attention to
New Mexico and what has happened there."

"General, do you remember that Orson Welles drama of
vhat, eight, nine years ago? Welles and his Mercury Theater
innounced that Martians had landed in New Jersey. There
vere people in the streets shooting the hell out of all sorts of
hings. People fled their homes. Panic reigned."

"Yes, sir, but that was the story of an invasion."

"The point, General," said Truman, heatedly, "is that people
vere in a panic over a radio drama. Not a real attack, but a
Irama that was clearly a drama but what they heard was that
Martians were in New Jersey."

"Yes, Mr. President."

"That was fiction and it was announced four times during
he broadcast that it was a play and people still panicked. Even
vhen they learned the truth, they weren't sure what to do. I
»elieve that to be a practical demonstration of what will hap-
»en if we announce what we found."

LeMay sat and said only, "Yes, Mr. President."

"Now you waltz in here with the story of an alien ship,
»odies, survivors, and no clue as to where they originate nor
vhat their motivations are. People are not going to like those
inswers, or lack of them."

"It's not our fault . . ."

Truman waved an angry hand. "I'm not trying to lay blame,
'm stating the facts here. We don't know anything. We have
10 answers. Anyone with half a brain can figure out that these
:reatures, if they are not friendly, have the advantage over us.
They can control the skies . . ."

"We shot them down," said LeMay and then was immedi-
itely sorry that he had said anything.

"Jesus H. Christ. What did you say?"

LeMay sat quietly. He had been ordered by Truman, who

understood history better than any other President, except possibly Teddy Roosevelt, to do what had to be done without having to get specific instructions. He had just violated security, and if he were a second lieutenant, he'd be court martialed.

"General," said Truman, his face white with anger.

"We had to know what we faced, Mr. President," said LeMay, but even to him, that sounded lame. "We had to know their limitations and our capabilities."

Truman sat quietly, letting his anger dissipate. Finally, he said, "General, that underscores the need for secrecy. For God's sake, an intelligent race finds its way to Earth and we open fire killing all but one of the crew. If there was no other reason for secrecy, this would be paramount."

"Yes, sir."

Truman took off his glasses and laid them gently on his desk. He pinched his nose and then focused his attention on LeMay. "Until we have more information . . . until we understand more about the motives of these creatures, I want no more discussion of flying saucers and alien life forms. I want it shut down."

"Mr. President, there is little that I can do about the press."

"General," said Truman sharply. "These stories have got to end because if people keep talking about flying saucers it can lead right back to the crash."

He fell silent and shook his head. No one seemed to understand the big picture. No one seemed to understand what a general knowledge of life on another world meant. They all thought of it in narrow terms such as religious impact or scientific thought, but it challenged the whole of human history. It changed everything, and had the potential to destroy civilization. It didn't even require the invasion. Just the knowledge of a technologically superior race could undermine the very foundation of human civilization. No one understood that.

Human history was filled with examples of superior knowledge wiping out civilizations. Sometimes it took little in the way of knowledge to do it. Truman was afraid that mere mention of the craft found in New Mexico would shake the economic, sociological, historical and religious underpinnings of modern civilization. If a radio show could cause the problems that the *War of the Worlds* broadcast had caused, what would happen if it was announced that a real flying saucer and its crew had been found in New Mexico.

He looked at LeMay and thought that the General might be the only other person in the world who could understand the need for secrecy. LeMay understood that the United States could crash and burn if the truth got out. LeMay, Truman was sure, would protect the secret as fiercely as he could because LeMay believed in the United States. To LeMay nothing else mattered. The United States had to be protected and LeMay proved just how ruthless he could be during the war.

"General, I want this thing buried. I don't want another peep heard about it, and if there is, I want the man who spoke out of turn to find himself in deep shit."

"A court-martial . . ."

"I said nothing about a court-martial," flared Truman. "I want the guy buried on an assignment so far away, so deep in the woods, that he'll have to travel a week to get to a backwater so that he can begin the journey. I want him never heard from again. I want it made clear that talk of flying saucers will end a career. I want it understood that the brass, the men at the top, believe that flying saucers are illusions and to suggest otherwise is to commit professional suicide. I want those who report flying saucers to seem uneducated and unsophisticated. I'm sure that you can think of ways of doing this without resorting to a court martial."

"Yes, sir."

Truman took a deep breath, calmed himself, and asked, "Is there anything else?"

"No sir."

Truman sat quietly for a moment and then said, "This is the last time I want you here to brief me on this. I know what is happening now, but I don't want anyone else to know that I know. I want this played very close to the vest. Do you understand?"

"Yes, Mr. President."

He knew that LeMay wouldn't understand it, but if the President was not in the loop, if there were no top secret briefings in the White House, then there could be no leak. Truman knew that he could look a reporter in the eye and lie to him, but he didn't want the reporter to think to ask the question. If he didn't know all the minor details, and there was no reason that he, as President, should, then there could be no mistake and therefore no leak.

LeMay, who hated the press, and might have hated civilians, would be happy to take the heat. He wasn't a politician who had to worry about reelection. He was a general officer, who, in the worst case, might be forced into retirement with a full pension. LeMay was an American hero who had helped defeat the Japanese. His tunic might get muddy, but he could recover from it.

Truman knew that in less than a year, the campaigning would have to begin if he wanted his own term as President. From a purely personal side, if the opposition, and that meant the Republicans, learned that it was his administration that had shot down the alien craft, then his political career was over as well. That might be a minor consideration, but it was an important one. While the fate of the world might be on his shoulders, the fate of his political life was there as well. Two fine reasons for quietly trying to find out more about the object in New Mexico.

Finally, Truman leaned forward and tapped the sign that said, "The Buck Stops Here," and said, "The buck might stop, but I don't want to have to explain this to anyone. You have not briefed me."

LeMay said simply, "I understand."

CHAPTER | 40

July 14, 1947
Over the Rainbow
Nevada

Captain Jack Reed was surprised by what he thought of as a fully equipped bar in the underground, emergency facility stuck in the middle of the Nevada desert. It couldn't be classified as an Officer's Club if only because there were enlisted men and women using it. Reed was somewhat of a snob who believed that the enlisted troops and the officers should not be caught socializing off duty. He believed that a certain amount of interaction was necessary for each to respect the other. The rigid caste system that had existed prior to the war had been eroded as the former top enlisted grades were promoted into the officer corps to cope with the expansion of the service during the Second World War.

So what surprised him was not that the enlisted men and women were in the club with the scientists and technicians and officers, but that the club existed at all. It had a long bar down one side, booths against one wall, a few tables with small candles glowing on them, subdued lighting, air conditioning and music that came from hidden speakers that seemed to ring the perimeter. It was a classy place with quiet talk, mixed drinks, beer and pretzels, and limited food service.

Reed sat in a booth in the rear and across the table from Danni Hackett. She was leaning forward, her elbows on the table, her hands clasped around her martini, and she stared down, into the liquor. She had taken one huge swallow when it arrived and then eaten the onions but hadn't touched it since.

Reed had nearly chugged his first martini, forgetting about

the dizzy spell, and then had ordered a second. He had taken a single taste of it and then set it down, knowing that if he gulped it his face would begin to tingle, his eyes would unfocus and he would be well on his way to getting drunk. A lack of sleep, solid food, and the experiences of the last several days all contributed to the problem.

In the back of his mind were thoughts of alien disease, which he was working very hard to forget. He looked across the table, at Hackett, who, he decided, was one of the most beautiful women that he had ever seen. If she had tried to find the things that appealed to him most, she couldn't have done a better job. He liked the look of her hair, though it was slightly mussed at the moment. He liked the way she wore her lab coat and the way that she tried to avoid looking directly at him. He felt a tension between them and hoped that he wasn't fooling himself into believing that there could be something between them. Oh, he knew it wouldn't be strong yet because they had just met, but he hoped that she found him at least interesting.

To mask those feelings, and to try to forget about alien disease, he said, "I'm at a loss here. There seem to be questions to ask, but I'm damned if I can think of them."

Hackett glanced up at him and said, "I know the feeling and I've been here for several days."

"What's the purpose?"

"Originally? Of this place?" she asked. "I don't know. I think they built this in the belief that they would need a base in the event of an atomic war."

Reed shook his head. "I mean, what we're doing."

"I would have thought that was obvious. We have a problem and we're attempting to find answers."

"No," said Reed. "I understand that. I mean, I don't understand why we're hidden away in the middle of the desert. We should have our top scientists on this." He was beginning to feel clumsy, as he always did when he found himself alone with an attractive woman. He was trying to impress her and all he did was stick his foot in his mouth.

Hackett grinned and said, "Thank you."

"I am not suggesting that the talent and ability of the scientists here isn't good, I would have thought that we'd want to get those with more experience . . ." He stopped, realizing that he was now trying to cram his other foot in his mouth.

"I know what you're trying to say, even if diplomacy isn't among your strong points." Now she smiled softly to take the sting out of her words. "The answer, I believe, is security. We are the ones who could disappear from society without causing a ripple." She stopped and said, "No, that's not quite right. We could disappear from the academic environment without causing a ripple. If Delev Brock or John von Neumann disappeared, someone would notice. If I disappeared, as I have, it's just one more biologist who sought work in a different arena."

"Okay," said Reed, "that makes sense." He took a sip of his martini and set the glass down carefully, wondering if they should order something to eat.

Jacob Wheeler, holding a bottle of beer in one hand and a bowl of pretzels in the other, suddenly appeared. He slipped into the booth next to Hackett and asked, "Do you mind? Is this private?"

Hackett said, "No. Please."

Reed, momentarily annoyed, saw, to his surprise, that there was no spark between Hackett and Wheeler. They were friends, pals, and if one thought of the other as a potential romantic partner, neither was aware of it.

"We were talking about the purpose," said Reed, hoping that Wheeler wouldn't pick up on anything. He grinned broadly and hurriedly added, "Nice to see you again, Jake."

Wheeler put the pretzels down and set his beer on the table. He fumbled for a moment at a package of cigarettes but decided that he didn't want one. Instead, he picked up a pretzel and said, "So, Jack, you're the officer who escorted the living specimen to us." He took a bite of the pretzel.

Reed was momentarily horrified by the breach of security, but then realized that nearly everyone in the facility would be involved in the research in some fashion. They would know about the craft and bodies and survivor. Finally he said, "Is that how you think of it? The living specimen?"

Wheeler took a pull at the beer to wash down the pretzel, and said, smiling, "I think the problem is that we don't have a good name for him, her, it. And that is the other problem. We have no sexual identity for him, her or it."

"I've been and the people I know have been thinking of it as either an it or as male," said Reed.

Wheeler nodded and said, "But that is our own bias here. We, as a society, send the males out to explore, gather food, and fight the wars. The women stay behind to raise the young, cook the food, and supply the next generation of warriors." He grinned at his own wit.

"However," Wheeler said, "we have had societies in which those roles have not held fast and we have numerous examples from the animal kingdom in which the female is the hunter. Lions spring to mind. The point, however, is that we have no reason to assume that this creature is male, female, or that the distinction is important."

Hackett lifted her glass, sipped, and said, "In today's world, the role of the woman has been expanded."

Wheeler nodded emphatically and said, "Look at what they accomplished in the war. While they weren't on the front lines, women were close, providing essential services. They moved into factories, performing jobs that had been exclusively a male domain prior to the war and they performed those jobs quite well, in some cases better than their male counterparts."

Reed grinned and said, "All I wanted to know was what we're doing here. In Nevada. And why we're not at some huge medical facility with dozens of top pathologists, biologists, and scientists working to learn everything they can."

"Is there some kind of urgency that we don't know about here?" asked Wheeler.

"What if they're hostile?" asked Reed. "We've got to have some answers."

"I doubt they're hostile," said Hackett. "Look what they have accomplished. They have built a craft that can travel through space when we can't even reach our moon. Such a society would not have hostile intentions."

"I can't agree with that," said Reed.

"Of course not," said Wheeler. "You're a military man."

"You were too, at one time. But what I mean is that a technologically advanced society does not automatically equate to a civilized society."

"What he means," said Hackett, understanding the point, "is that the vandals sacked Rome."

"Well, yes," said Reed. "And the Europeans, who were technologically advanced, were not overly hostile upon arrival in the New World but the result was the same."

"So what are you suggesting?" asked Wheeler.

"Only that we don't know if these creatures are hostile. They could be surveying us for the coming invasion."

Wheeler laughed and took a long pull at his beer. "There is no reason to assume that. There is no reason to fear these creatures." He ate another of the pretzels.

Reed wanted to say, "Tell it to the Aztecs," but it just wasn't an argument that he wanted to get into. They didn't have enough data. The enemy, if they aliens were an enemy, could take weeks, or months, determining the targets before launching their invasion. The Army could attempt to prepare, but would that be effective? What did they need to do to stop the invasion from outer space?

He had a thought and said, "Have you wondered why they were in New Mexico?"

Wheeler said, "They have been seen all over the country."

"Yeah, but in greater numbers over New Mexico where we dropped the first bomb and where we were taking the first steps into space. Maybe they were conducting a reconnaissance of our capabilities. They wanted to know if we could retaliate."

"But they crashed," said Wheeler.

"So they did," said Reed. He fell silent.

He wasn't really that interested in trying to second guess the alien motives. He was more concerned with the problem of disease. That seemed to be the bigger threat at the moment, though he didn't want to say anything about it. He was happier not having information suggesting that some sort of new disease had been let loose on the American population. Even with his limited understanding of the situation, he knew that if there was some sort of disease, it was already much to late to contain it. That opportunity had been lost when the teams from Washington had flown into Roswell, and then returned to their various assignments. It had been lost when he, along with the alien, had traveled cross country. If there was any sort of contamination, they had already contaminated a large number of people, some of whom couldn't be identified.

Instead, he asked, "What, exactly, is your function here, Jake?"

Wheeler picked up another pretzel, bit into it and glanced at the ceiling as if searching for celestial guidance. He lowered his voice, as if he was concerned about security, and then said, "I'm working on the ship at the moment. We're trying to learn why the windshield enhanced the light at night but doesn't do that during the day. Think about it. No more headlights on cars. The windshield displays the scene as if it was high noon."

"I can see the benefit to that."

"And, we've got some very thin metal that seems to be strong as hell. Can't dent it or cut it or burn it. Amazing stuff. Couple that to the foil that returns to its original shape and we've got something to make cars stronger and lighter and when they hit a tree you just back up for the repair. The fenders smooth out the dents by themselves."

Hackett said, "Really?"

"But we can't find any records, or books, or charts. They must have had a way of retrieving information, but we can't find it. Nothing in there. I can't believe these creatures could keep everything in their heads."

"Why not?" asked Hackett.

"The problems with interstellar flight suggest you would need to have to store a trainload of information. The navigation problems alone would be tremendous. Here, on Earth, it's a two dimensional problem, but in space it is three dimensional and to locate yourself you'd need six plots instead of two or three."

"Then they have the charts and books," said Reed. "You just haven't recognized them yet."

"Hell, we haven't found the wiring yet. Oh, we've been able to pull the tops of some of the panels and we've found what looks like . . . I was going to say wiring, but it looks more like tracings on glass. We think it functions as wiring but we can't detect any electromagnetic fields around it and see no way to connect it to a power source. Of course, we haven't found the power source either. We don't know anything at all."

Reed finished his martini but didn't signal for another. Instead he asked, "What do we do about dinner?"

Hackett said, "We can order a hamburger here. Or a sandwich which comes with a bag of chips, or we can go to the cafeteria. The menu is a little more varied but it's not all that good."

"Is this an invitation?" asked Reed.

She looked at him strangely and then grinned. "Of course. Have to keep the new guy informed as to the procedures."

Wheeler studied Reed for a moment and then turned his attention to Hackett. He saw something in her eyes and said, somewhat formally, "I have been invited to eat with Doctor Taylor, he of the electrical engineering persuasion. I believe that I will indulge him in the hopes that I might learn more about the circuitry of the ship." He slipped to the right and stood and then drained his beer.

"Nice to see you again, Jake," said Reed.

"The same. I shall see you later."

When he was gone, Reed said, "He's a nice fellow."

"Charming," said Hackett.

There was a hint of ice in her voice that Reed didn't understand. He said, "If you will guide me to the cafeteria, I will pay for your dinner."

"Is this now a date?"

"Nah. For a date we would have to change clothes and it would involve proper etiquette. I would have to call for you at your door. This is just a little food."

"Then I must gratefully accept."

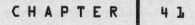

CHAPTER | 41

Jack Reed, having thought about it, realized that he didn't like being stuck in a hole in the middle of the desert, away from civilization, even if that civilization was the distant gambling town of Las Vegas. He wanted to be out in the open where he could see the world outside his window, even if it was hot and uncomfortable. He didn't like being cornered without knowing how to escape the corner. It might be said that his experiences as a fighter pilot worked against him because he was used to operating on a three-dimensional field and now was reduced to one that was buried.

Given his position as an intelligence officer, and given that he was the one who had brought the alien creature to the facility, he was given full access to everything. All assumed that he was cleared at the highest level, so no one questioned his authority. Reed grinned at that, knowing that his access should have been limited by need-to-know, but he wasn't going to tell anyone. So he walked to the base commander's office, which was on the top level, knowing that the plans for the entire facility, if they existed at all, would be filed there. He would have the opportunity to study them.

The outer door was marked with a small sign and Reed believed that it would open into a reception area. He pushed the door and stepped into a large office with a light brown carpet on the floor, light brown walls that were only slightly darker than the carpet, and lights so bright that it was almost overwhelming. Opposite the door was a single, massive desk, with two chairs in front of it, and one behind it. There was a conversation or meeting area off to the right that had another two chairs and a sofa with a coffee table in front of them. The walls contained no pictures, no plaques and no paintings. It almost gave the impression of a new office and that the decorations would be added as soon as they were available to be hung.

Also sitting in the office was the clerk, a short, red-headed woman wearing a jumpsuit with no insignia or badges. She had broad shoulders and a broad but not unpretty face. She looked up when Reed entered, grinned at him and said, "The commander is in a meeting, Captain."

"Then maybe you can help me," he said. "I was wondering if there were any maps of the facility here. Not the base, but this area. I guess what I want are the floor plans."

"I think I know what you want," she said. She turned, and looked into a short, two-shelved book case. She pulled a huge book from the shelf and, for a moment it looked as if it was too heavy for her. She looked as if she was going to fall, but she held on, whirled and tossed the book on her desk. She grinned as it slammed down and said, "I think that everything you want will be there. You can sit down over there, if you would like. If you need anything else, let me know."

Reed walked over and sat down on the couch. He put the big book on the coffee table and opened it to the index. He searched through that, and the table of contents, and then began looking at each of the floor plans, some of which folded out so that they were over two feet long.

The floor plans showed him that above, at ground level, was the hangar, through which he entered. At one end of that hangar, in a small room that had been an office, was what looked like an oversized closet that hid the elevator. There was a single elevator that reached the surface, probably for security. At Level One, there was a bank of elevators that made travel between the levels quicker.

All the levels were virtually the same in overall structure. That meant they were large and circular, with rooms, offices and apartments on the outside of the ring. Some of them had been dug out so that they extended farther than the others. It gave the outer part of the ring a jagged, asymmetrical look that was both disconcerting and somewhat appealing.

The interior held more rooms, most of which were designated as offices, labs, work rooms and meeting rooms. Again some were larger than others, taking up as much as a quarter of the space on the interior of the ring.

Down the center, in what could be called the hub, was a single, thick wall that was probably designed as a load-bearing structure that also served as a security barrier. There were no doors through it so that to move from one side of the circle to the other, a person was required to exit into the hallway and walk around the inner circumference. You couldn't cross directly from one side to the other.

The single exception to this was on the uppermost level where the whole of the center was taken up by a single room labeled Gymnasium.

Reed, after getting the general overview, turned the page which showed Level One in greater detail, with labels on the various rooms. The gymnasium took up about half of the inner circle. It had several doors from the outer hallway. It was almost large enough to have everyone in the facility in the room at one time. It would be good for general meetings, if any were ever necessary.

The rest of the levels were fairly standard with only the functions of the rooms or labs differing. Reed was surprised to find a morgue and autopsy room on the very bottom level.

As he was studying that, he noticed a set of double doors that were on the far side of the circle, opposite the elevator bank. On the chart he had, there was no explanation for them. They were just shown, with a note that suggested they were partially hidden by a retracting wall.

On the next page, he found the answer. The doors hid a large, long tunnel that had been used in the excavation of the facility and to truck in the equipment that couldn't be brought in on the small elevators. As far as he could tell, the tunnel was still there in case something large was needed at a later time, though it was now partially blocked by the wall. He was sure, at the surface, the access would be disguised in some fashion and any doors to it would still be locked.

Reed rocked back on the couch and closed his eyes, trying to understand the facility. It was a circular hole in the ground, filled with rooms, offices, labs and apartments. The exterior wall had been excavated to create more of the same. An elevator shaft was set at one end for access to each of the levels, but there was no stairways connecting them. From Level One there was a stairway to the surface. Each level had its own security in the form of a large bank-vault-type door.

He opened his eyes, glanced at the final page and then closed the big book. He stood up, picked up the book and carried it back to the secretary's desk. To her he said, "I think that does it. You want me to put the book back on the shelf?"

She looked up from her typing and said, "Nah. I'll have one of the guys do it later."

"Thanks," he said.

CHAPTER | 42

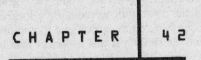

July 14, 1947
Over the Rainbow
Nevada

Staff Sergeant Timothy Routledge had been in the Army since December 8, 1941, joining the day after the bombing of Pearl Harbor. He had seen action, briefly, in North Africa and then, severely wounded, had been returned to the United States. There he learned a new skill and found himself assigned to the G-2, that is, intelligence.

Having seen combat up close, and having survived combat when it got too close, he wasn't interested in a return to a combat unit. Sergeant Routledge had done his part, had proved his courage under fire, and had no desire to return to that environment to again prove his courage.

No one thought of him as a coward since he had been in heavy combat and it was clear from his Silver Star, the third highest award for bravery given by the military, that he was a brave man. If someone thought it necessary to comment on Routledge's military background, it was only to suggest that he had seen the light at a younger age than most men.

But Routledge, because of his intelligence background, had held a top secret security clearance. Because of that, when it became time to assemble, quickly, a staff for the Nevada complex, Routledge's name naturally came up and no one could think of a good reason to remove it from that list. That Routledge was a combat veteran, who knew how to handle weapons, was just one more reason for him to be selected. With hardly much thought, Routledge was put on an airplane, flown to Nevada and eventually found himself working in the underground facility. He didn't mind because it wasn't hard work and the base was air-conditioned, not only by the military, but by mother nature.

Sergeant Routledge was a big man. He weighed about two hundred and fifty pounds and stood about six-four. He had light hair and light skin and bright blue eyes and nearly everyone said that if he had been in the German army he would have been on a recruiting poster. He kept his hair cut short and had once thought about growing a small mustache, but images of Adolf Hitler and his little black patch of a mustache dissuaded him. He was a good looking man, with fine features, though his nose was slightly bent from a school yard fight twenty years earlier.

Routledge now sat at a small desk in the hallway, which happened to be on the floor directly under the club. When the music was turned up loud enough, he could hear the pounding of the drums and the rhythm of the bass. Tonight, the music wasn't very loud. He was virtually alone on the floor, guarding the entrance to the hastily assembled hospital room and quarters that had been assigned to what Routledge thought of as the monster.

He had only seen it when they had brought it in. It was very thin, looking as if the limbs would easily break. It had big eyes that looked through him, a thin, triangular, almost bony face, and pale, pasty skin. To Routledge, who was a fan of horror movies, it had the appearance of one of those creations rather than something that was real and alive. It had scared him even though he knew that it was nearly helpless and that he, Routledge, was armed with a large caliber pistol.

All afternoon, there had been people, doctors, technicians, intelligence officers, and scientists coming and going. Some had stayed for a couple of hours and others had stayed only minutes. Each had been signed in and then logged out under Routledge's watchful eye, and when Routledge was off duty for four hours, under the supervision of a corporal. If anyone ever needed a record of who had been on the inside of the monster's room and for how long, then Routledge's log would provide the precise answer.

But now it was late evening and everyone was one floor up at dinner, at meetings or in their quarters. Few people were on the same level as Routledge and none of them were in sight. All were carrying on their duties, which, given the circumstances were very much like his own. That is, they were guarding some aspect of the facility from those who were not authorized to be at that specific location. Somewhere below him were the bodies of the other monsters and the ship they had crashed into New Mexico.

Routledge felt an itch in the middle of his back, almost as if someone was staring at him. He knew that couldn't be true because his desk was situated so that only he, sitting in the chair, could get between it and the wall. No one was behind him and yet the itch was there.

And he began to think about the monster. It wasn't quite as monstrous as he had originally thought. It did have a human shape which simply meant that it had two arms, two legs and a single head. The face wasn't all that unpleasant and it had all the proper pieces in the proper places. There was no hair on it, but many men Routledge knew were just as bald.

As he thought about it, he realized that he hadn't gotten a very good look at the monster. It had been escorted by a couple of men who took it directly into the room. Routledge had only seen it for ten or twelve seconds and hadn't studied it. Maybe it wasn't as ugly and monstrous as the thought.

The itch in his back was becoming uncomfortable. He tried to reach it, but naturally it was situated at exactly the point where he could not quite reach it no matter how he contorted his body and tried to stretch his fingers. He stood up and stepped to the right where the door frame protruded slightly from the wall. He leaned back and scratched himself.

Now that he was on his feet, he turned and touched the door knob. It twisted in his hand, just as he knew it would. The door couldn't be locked from either inside or outside, which explained why they had put a guard on the door. You don't need a lock when you have an armed man sitting at the door to control access to the room.

Sitting again, Routledge felt himself grow tired. His eyes

were heavy and he wanted to lay down, maybe crawl into the bed. If he could just rest for a few moments he would be fine. His vision was blurry so that it seemed he was looking at the world through a dirty window.

He awakened with a start, looking down the empty corridor. He was sitting in his chair but his back no longer itched. He was still tired, sick to his stomach, and feeling a little faint, as if he had stood up too quickly. For a moment he thought he should call the officer of the guard, or his relief, but then, he began, slowly, to feel somewhat better.

He stood up, just to shake the cobwebs from his mind. He shouldn't have fallen asleep but no one had seen him so it didn't matter. He knew that no one had seem him because, if they had, they would have awakened him and he would have found himself in deep shit. Since he was not standing at attention trying to answer questions, he had not been discovered asleep at his post. The only problem was a dull ache in his arm but he thought nothing of it. As far as he was concerned everything he remembered now was just a part of a frightening dream and that was all it was. Just a horrible dream.

CHAPTER 43

July 14, 1947
Over the Rainbow
Nevada

Hendricks felt better. He had slept for six hours, had been given blood, and then juices, all he could drink. He felt rested, but since it was now after midnight, he thought about asking for a sleeping pill because there was nothing to do and no one to talk to at the moment. There were no books or newspapers and he had seen no commercial radios anywhere in the facility. He wondered if being underground had anything to do with that and then decided that there probably weren't any radio stations close enough that they could receive a signal. The only option left was sleep and, at the moment, he was wide awake. It didn't seem that he would be getting drowsy anytime soon.

He was in what looked to him to be a fairly standard hospital room with a hospital-type bed. The rails were down and the back was raised slightly so that he wasn't lying flat. An IV drip was standing near the bed, but the bag was empty and it was not connected to his arm. There was a single chair for a visitor, or the doctor, a bedside stand with one drawer and one door, and a single lamp that provided little light. Overhead were other lights, and Hendricks supposed they were brighter, but at the moment, they were out.

There were two doors, both closed. He suspected one led into the hallway and the other into a bathroom. Hendricks wasn't sure which was which until there was a tapping one of them. Hendricks assumed that it would be a nurse waking him up to tell him to go to sleep or with some medicine for him to take. When she didn't enter, he called out, "Come on in."

John Douglass, dressed in a rumpled, gray suit, with a white shirt and dark tie, pushed open the door and said, "I hope that I didn't wake you."

"Wasn't asleep. I was thinking that everyone else would be asleep and was wishing that I was among them."

"There are some things that we have to get straight before we can head back to Washington," said Douglass.

"Well, come on in, but I have to tell you, I don't have anything in here to drink."

Douglass reached inside his suit coat and pulled out a small flask. "I might be able to resolve that problem, if alcohol is not going to hurt you."

"I don't know what happened to me," said Hendricks, "but I don't think that it is life threatening and I certainly don't think that alcohol will do me any real harm. I am a medical doctor, after all."

Douglass unscrewed the cap and held up the flask. "You want it neat?"

"No," he said reaching for a glass. "Give me a taste in the water. I'll take it easy for the first drink."

Douglass poured the whiskey into the glass, looked around, and then sat down in the chair. He held up the flask for a toast and said, "Here's to you."

"Same at you." Hendricks took a sip, felt the liquor burn his throat but he suppressed the cough. With his eyes watering, he said, "That's smooth."

Douglass put the cap on the flask and slipped it back into his coat. He stared at Hendricks and said, "What in the hell happened to you?"

"I don't know. I guess I got sick riding in the back of the ambulance. Maybe there was a microscopic leak from the exhaust into the rear. Nothing like that has ever happened to me."

"You've had a physical?"

"I know what the doctor here said. They found nothing. My blood was clear. No evidence of carbon monoxide poisoning and there should have been if it was a leak from the exhaust system. No new diseases either." He thought about that and then amended, "At least none that they could detect."

"Is that something we should be worrying about? New diseases I mean."

Hendricks picked up his glass and took a long sip. "I don't know."

"Some of the scientists have suggested there might be contamination and thought that your illness might have been part of it. Might be telling us something."

"I thought about that, but it seems to be very selective. There were many more people who have come into contact with the alien creatures and their ship, yet none of them have gotten sick. They should have gotten sick long before I did, or, at least, should be sick now."

"Do we know that this is unrelated to the creatures?"

"There are no other cases," said Hendricks, shrugging. "At least none that I know of."

"Are you sure?"

"Unless something has happened at Roswell after we left, then yes, I'm sure. I'm sure that there are people who would be watching, very carefully, for that sort of thing. I just don't see it happening." As he said it, he wondered if he hadn't oversimplified the situation because, now, at that point, there was nothing he, or anyone, could do about it. That cat was out of the bag, and if the cat was diseased, there was no way to stuff it back into the bag to contain the disease.

Douglass touched his coat. "Need a little more?"

"No. I'm fine." He looked at Douglass and asked, "What's your interest in this?"

Douglass sat back, crossed his legs and said, "I'm just gathering information. Thing I've learned is that you never know what might be important down the road, so I ask questions and file away the answers."

Hendricks held up his glass and said, "I have very few answers but I have lots of questions."

"Don't we all?"

"How long are we going to be here?"

Douglass shrugged. "I don't know. I have very little left to do, so I suppose I'll leave in the next few days. I'd think that you could stay a while longer, if you could contribute something to the research. If you want to go home, I suppose that could be arranged as well."

Hendricks rocked to the right and set the glass on the table. He yawned and then said, "Maybe I'll hang around to see if I can't get some of those answers."

Douglass saw that Hendricks was getting tired. He stood up. "Guess I'll get going. Just wanted to see how you were doing in here."

"Thanks for coming."

When Douglass left, Hendricks picked up his glass and finished the drink. He wished he had made it a little stronger because he wasn't as confident about his answers as he had indicated. The incubation period of a disease was not a precise thing. It could affect some people faster than others depending on their own resistance, length of exposure, and half a dozen other unknown factors. What he would have to do, in the morning, was see if he could call Roswell to learn if anyone else had gotten sick. And maybe mention that someone should see if any of the others who had inspected the ship or seen the bodies had gotten sick.

CHAPTER | 44

July 15, 1947
Over the Rainbow
Nevada

They found Sergeant Routledge slumped in his chair, his right arm stained with blood. They sat him up, tried to wake him, and finally had to break an ammonia capsule under his nose. He shook his head, blinked rapidly, and then noticed the others standing around, looking down on him, including both the officer and the sergeant of the guard.

He started to rise, watched his vision narrow until it seemed that he was standing at the bottom of a deep well looking at a pinpoint of light far above him. He dropped back into the chair and leaned forward, his head between his legs.

Finally, the lieutenant of the guard, a young man named Kelly, asked, "What happened?"

Without raising his head, Routledge said, "I don't know. I fell asleep. I don't feel good."

Block, who had responded to the call from the officer of the guard, walked up rapidly, escorted by another officer. He set his black bag on the floor next to Routledge, had taken his pulse, blood pressure, looked into his eyes, he looked at the wound on his arm. He asked, "How did this happen?"

"I don't know." Routledge examined his arm and saw a deep cut that ran from the crook of his elbow upward for about three inches. Blood was still flowing from it and the sight of it made him feel even sicker.

Block pressed a bandage to it and said, "Hold that there. You're going to need a couple of stitches. We'll take you up to the dispensary."

Douglass pushed his way through the crowd and asked, "What the hell happened here?"

Block looked up angrily and said, "I don't know." When the man didn't move, he added, "Let me do my job. Get out of my way."

Routledge said, "I got sick."

"Let's get him to the dispensary," said Block.

Douglass tried to stop him. Using his full authority, he said, "I have to know what happened."

"The sergeant is in no condition to answer your questions, whoever the hell you are. You'll just have to wait until later."

Under Block's supervision, two of the security force put Routledge on a stretcher, lifted him and began carrying him down the corridor. They stopped at the double doors, waited for them to be opened, and stepped through. Douglass watched them go and then turned back to the highest-ranking officer remaining behind. "Captain?"

"Davidson. I command the security company."

"We have to determine what happened here. How did the guard injure himself?"

Davidson studied the man in the rumpled and wrinkled suit. "You are?"

"Douglass. CIC."

"You have credentials, of course."

"Of course," said Douglass grinning. He reached into his pocket and pulled out a scarred and stained leather folder. He flipped it open and held it up so that Davidson could see it. "Satisfactory?"

Davidson couldn't help laughing. "A ridiculous formality. You wouldn't be on this level if you didn't belong here. You wouldn't be in this facility without the proper clearance. But I still have to check."

"No problem."

Davidson sat down behind the desk, pulled open the center drawer, searched it and then looked down at his feet. Blood had spattered the floor but there wasn't much. He examined the rest of the desk but found nothing of interest and nothing that could have inflicted the wound on Routledge's arm.

"What's your plan, now?" asked Douglass.

"I'm going to sit here the rest of the night," said Davidson. "I am going to study this situation very carefully until I figure out what happened here or formulate the questions about it. Then I'm going upstairs, leaving two men on duty here, and question Routledge. By this time tomorrow, I will know what happened."

"Do you think that it had anything to do with the creature in the other room?"

"I don't know what to believe about that. I will find some answers about it, though."

"Do you want some help?"

"I'll take all the help I can get."

CHAPTER 45

July 15, 1947
Over the Rainbow
Nevada

Dr. Christian Smith had again teamed with Lieutenant Colonel Frank Lloyd, and they were now at the head of a small convoy stopped outside the guard shack in the middle of a Nevada desert. Neither man was happy to be in Nevada but the orders had been issued soon after they had met with LeMay in his office. Smith's expensive suit was now dust-covered and Lloyd's uniform was sweat-stained. Behind them were four trucks that contained not only the atomic device as Smith insisted on calling it, but also the trigger that could be controlled by a radio signal, two Naval officers who were the technicians who would do the actual work of installing the weapon, and a dozen men who had been assigned to guard duty but who didn't know what they were guarding or why they were suddenly in the middle of Nevada. Of the men in the convoy, including the drivers, their alternates, the motor pool mechanic, and two privates to assist in repairs, only Smith, Lloyd, and the Naval officers knew what they carried. None of the others had the need to know.

The guard looked at his clipboard, read through his access list which was updated daily and said, "No, sir. You're not here. I can't let you pass."

Lloyd smiled and wondered what a single sentry could do if he ordered his men to bypass the guard shack. The guard couldn't stop them himself.

Smith said, "Might I suggest that you get on your telephone or radio or however the hell you communicate with your superiors and get one of them the hell out here. I wouldn't be here with these Army trucks if I wasn't supposed to be here. I wouldn't even know where here was, if I wasn't supposed to be here."

"Yes, sir," said the guard. He stared at Smith and then said, "Have your men turn off their engines, please."

Smith looked puzzled and said, "Why?"

"My orders are to have unauthorized vehicles halt here and turn off their engines while I make my inquiries."

Lloyd, becoming more annoyed, said sharply, "We outnumber you."

The guard laughed and said, "Do you really believe that this installation has a single guard on the perimeter and that there is no backup for him? Please, do as I ask. We'll get this cleared up in a moment."

Smith said, "Do as he says."

Lloyd stared at the guard for a moment and then realized that he wasn't some young MP just out of school, but a senior man who was used to dealing with all sorts of self-important people. The guard was a highly trained man and that said something about the installation that he guarded. Lloyd was suddenly quite impressed. Without a word, he climbed out of the car and began to walk down the line of vehicles, ordering each of the drives to shut down his engine.

As he returned toward the guard shack, the guard appeared and said, "Dr. Moore will be out to meet you in just a few minutes, sir."

"He didn't say that we were allowed in?"

"No, sir. He said that he would be out to meet you. I don't know what this is all about."

In the distance, back toward the airfield, they could see a cloud of dust rising as if a car was racing down a gravel road. A moment later the black car appeared, came toward them rapidly and then, with a crunching of stone and dirt, slid to a halt next to the guard shack. A civilian emerged, took in the situation quickly, and then walked toward the guard. He said, with authority, "I'll take over, Major."

Lloyd did a double take. Majors did not stand guard duty under any circumstances. That a major, wearing no indications of his rank, was on the guard meant that the installation might be one of the most important in the world. Lloyd wondered what they could be doing on the inside that would create the situation where a major would be a guard.

"Doctor Smith," asked the civilian.

"Yes."

"I'm Doctor Moore. I'm chief of this facility. I have just received the information that you will be coming and that you are authorized access to certain areas of this facility. You have documentation?"

Smith walked back to the lead car and opened the rear door. He leaned in, set his briefcase on the seat and opened it. He shuffled around some of the papers and then extracted a single sheet. He handed a letter to Moore who grinned when he saw it. The letter, on White House stationery, was an almost exact duplicate of the one that he himself carried.

"This will be satisfactory," said Moore. "May I ask the nature of your mission?"

Lloyd was going to speak up, but Smith, waving a hand to indicate the open ground all around them said, "It is, of course, classified."

"Yes."

Smith had some questions of his own, but he didn't want to ask them outside, though he doubted that anyone could be listening in. The desolation worked both ways. Instead of asking his questions, he said, "I need somewhere to park my trucks, I need billeting for my men, and access to your facility plans."

"Let's get you on the base and we'll take care of all that." Moore turned and said, "Major, these people are cleared on my authority."

"Yes, sir."

With that Moore headed back to his car and Smith climbed back into his. He started his engine and then held his arm outside the car and rotated his hand, telling the rest of the drivers to start their engines. He waited until Moore got his car turned around and then dropped into line behind him. The only question that Smith had was how much to tell Moore about his mission.

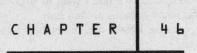

CHAPTER 46

July 15, 1947
Over the Rainbow
Nevada

Although he hadn't gotten the rest that he needed, Hendricks awoke at six in the morning. Neither the doctors nor the nurses were happy about having him awake, and then wandering around so early in the morning. There wasn't much they could do because Hendricks was a doctor who claimed to understand his own health better than anyone else.

Finally, almost as a bribe to get him back into bed, he was given two large glasses of orange juice that amounted to his breakfast. Hendricks, feeling better than he had since he had arrived at the facility, got out of bed again. In a small closet he found his uniform, his boots, and what he thought of as hospital scrubs, meaning a white, loose shirt, loose trousers with a string tie waistband and white shoes and socks.

Dressed, he left his room and walked to the elevator. No one challenged him, though one of the guards did glance at the badge affixed to his uniform. He descended to the next level and when the elevator door opened, he exited. He walked to the small desk where the chief of security, Captain Davidson, and CIC agent John Douglass sat.

Hendricks stopped at the desk and said, "I'm going to take a look at the patient."

Douglass shook his head. "Not now. Two or three are already in there. They'll be at it for a while."

"Maybe I should join them," suggested Hendricks.

"Well, Doctor," said Douglass, "there is a security consideration here and that will not be minimized. There is also a psychological consideration which I would have thought that you would recognize. We don't want to overwhelm the creature with too many humans around him."

"But the creature knows me, remember. I traveled with it from Roswell."

"Of course," said Douglass. He nodded and then said, "Just sign the log."

Hendricks signed as requested, opened the door and took a step inside. Inside the room were Wheeler and Hackett. They were standing on either side of the being, looking down at it, but neither seemed inclined to touch it or talk to it.

As he entered, he asked, "What's that odor?"

"There's some fluid on the floor, too," said Wheeler.

"What in the hell is going on in here?" asked Hendricks. "Is he still alive?"

Wheeler reached out to touch the creature and then stopped. He looked back at Hendricks as if waiting for his permission to make any move.

Hackett bent at the waist so that she was staring down at the creature. The eyes were closed but the mouth hung open so that the teeth, looking more like ten-penny nails made of ivory than teeth, were showing. There was no tongue visible but blood had pooled in the bottom of the mouth.

Surprised and alarmed, she jerked the blanket and sheet away, flinging them over the end of the bed, exposing the whole body. The creature was shrunken, as if all the fluids had been drained from it. There were pock marks, not unlike the craters of the moon on the chest and abdomen. Fluid had collected in the bottom of each of them. At the crook of his arm was a huge bruise looking just like the injury that had been seen on Hendricks.

"Is it still alive?" asked Wheeler.

"I don't know," said Hackett.

Hendricks, still near the door, found the light switch, and flipped it. He blinked in the sudden brightness and moved to the bed. He looked down at the creature, studied it for a moment, and then said, "I believe that it is dead."

"How do you know?"

"It's not moving and not breathing. We have observed it breathing in the past. We know a little about the physiology of them now."

Hackett lifted one of the arms and felt no resistance. She then probed around the wounds on the chest with a gloved finger. "These are not gunshot wounds. I don't know what would have made them."

"They look like the wounds made by small pox," said Wheeler, "except they're larger."

"Disease?" said Hackett, thinking of the discussion she'd had with Reed earlier.

"Possibly," said Hendricks. "It doesn't seem likely, but it is possible."

"Maybe we had better seal this room and this level," said Hackett. "That is, until we figure out what we have here."

Hendricks retreated from the bed and reached the door. He waved at Douglass, who moved closer. Speaking quietly, he said, "We have to seal this floor. No one on or off it."

"What happened?"

"We don't know. We think the creature is dead."

"Jesus."

"I think we're okay," said Hendricks, thinking out loud. "I don't think we have to worry about disease. This is more of a precaution than anything else."

Douglass took an unconscious step to the rear, as if he suddenly suspected that Hendricks was infected. He glanced toward the elevator as if it was an escape hatch, but he didn't move toward it.

Davidson, who had been sitting behind the desk, stood suddenly and asked, "Are we to go to quarantine?"

"I think that might be a good idea," said Hendricks. He sounded distracted, as if he was thinking about something else.

Davidson bent, opened a drawer and extracted a red telephone. He touched a button on it, and put the handset to his ear. He then said, "Seal the base. I say again. Seal the base."

An instant later a klaxon sounded, fell silent, and sounded again. Red lights mounted on the wall began to rotate. People stepped into the corridor looking confused.

"I can seal off movement between the levels," said Davidson.

"Restrict it so that we can get up to level three. No one else comes down," said Douglass. He lifted an eyebrow in question.

Hendricks said, "I think that would be right. If we have had much movement between levels three and two, we'll have to shut them down. I think we're going to have to meet with the rest of the team on three to work out some of the problems."

"Yes, sir."

Hendricks returned the room. Wheeler had lowered the upper third of the bed so that it was completely flat. He said, "We have to do an autopsy."

Hackett said, "I can get that arranged."

"We need to figure out what is going on here," said Wheeler. "And we need to do it quickly."

CHAPTER 47

July 15, 1947
Over the Rainbow
Nevada

The first time that Reed realized that he was sealed in the underground facility was when he tried to access an outside telephone line to advise his general of the current circumstances. He thought that it was just a failure of the telephone line, but when he tried again, ten minutes later, he was told that all outside calls had been suspended for the time being. That surprised him because it would have been less traumatic to simply suggest there was a technical problem in the telephone, rather than announce that someone had made a decision to stop the outgoing telephone calls. It was then that he heard the distant sound of the klaxon and realized that the situation was more serious than he thought.

He sat in his small room with its single chair, a chest, a cot and a nightstand with a single lamp on it. There was a rod mounted under a shelf where Reed had hung his clean uniforms the night before. There was an overhead light that was so bright that it belonged in an operating theater and not in an officer's personal quarters even if those quarters were transient. There were no books, no radio, and no refrigerator. At least the floor was carpeted, though it looked to be a cheap rug. The quarters were spartan, nearly barren, compared to some that he had been assigned in the past.

Unable to call the base in Roswell, he changed into a fatigue uniform and boots that had been polished to a mirror-like surface one boring afternoon, and went in search of something to eat, hoping to find Hackett again. He should have asked her to breakfast, but she hadn't been dressed, it was still fairly early, and he hadn't been hungry then.

He walked out into the brightly lighted corridor and found it to be deserted just as it had been a couple of hours earlier. He didn't know if that was normal or if something unusual was going on. In the distance was a flashing red light that told him the morning was not normal.

Wondering about the trouble that had developed, he opened what he hoped was an office, just to look inside. Like the corridor, it was bright and it seemed to be deserted. Then, as he was closing the door, he spotted, lying on the floor, with only her feet visible from behind her desk, a body. Reed rushed in, crouched over the unconscious woman and put his fingers on her throat. There was a thin, thready pulse.

The woman was dressed in an Army Class A uniform with the long, tailored skirt hiked above her stocking tops. She was a thin woman, with thick blonde hair piled on the top of her head. Her face was pasty white, making her look sick.

Reed examined her quickly, looking for a wound or a sign of disease, but found nothing threatening. He noticed one of her stockings was badly ripped, the shreds of it around her right ankle. There was blood staining the nylon with a huge bruise from about mid-thigh down to her calf.

Reed pulled at one of her eyelids and saw the pupil contract as the light hit it. That meant that she might be unconscious, but she wasn't dying, at least at the moment, or so he believed. He stood, grabbed the telephone and touched the button for the local operator.

"I'm sorry," said the operator, "but we are unable to call out."

"This is Captain Reed. I'm on the third level, in one of the offices, and there is an unconscious woman here." He glanced at her blouse, saw the black plastic name tag pinned there. "Woodson. Corporal Woodson."

"Yes, sir. Thank you, sir. I'll have some from the dispensary come to you."

Without another word Reed hung up and then knelt near the woman again. He picked up her wrist, felt her pulse, and then counted the heartbeats for fifteen seconds. Although still weak, her heart was beating regularly and it seemed to be gaining strength.

The door flew open seconds later and three people entered. "What's going on here?" shouted one of them, looking agitated.

Reed waved them over and said, "She's been injured."

One of the medics pushed Reed roughly out of the way and then bent over the injured woman. He produced a stethoscope and began listening to her chest. Another of them asked, "Is this how you found her?"

"Yes. I didn't move her or touch her, other than to check for a pulse."

Hackett appeared at the door. She glanced at the woman on the floor and then at Reed. She raised an eyebrow in question, but said nothing to him. Instead, she walked to the woman, crouched and examined the wound on the woman's leg.

"This shouldn't be life threatening. There can't be much blood loss. She shouldn't be unconscious."

Two men with a stretcher pushed through the door and set it near the woman. One of the first medics into the room nodded. Without a word those around her lifted her onto the stretcher. One of the men pulled the skirt down and another put a blanket over her.

"You taking her to the dispensary?" asked Hackett.

"Yes."

"Have them draw three vials of blood for me. Refrigerate two. I'll be by in about thirty minutes to look at them."

"Do you have the authorization to make that request?" asked one of the men.

"I'm Doctor Hackett. You check with your chief administrator. He'll tell you about authorization."

"Yes, ma'am."

He, along with the other man, lifted the stretcher and worked their way to the door. Once they were through, the three who had responded to Reed's telephone call followed. Everyone except Reed and Hackett then walked out.

"Well, well," said Reed.

"You found her?" asked Hackett.

"Yep. Just lying there. Called for assistance after I checked her pulse."

"Then you touched her?"

"Yes."

"Okay. I don't think that is a problem, but come with me. We'll wash your hands."

"I am fully capable of washing my own hands," said Reed.

"Certainly, but I want to use something a little stronger than soap." She looked into his eyes, saw that he was confused and said, "This is the third case like this I've seen, all of them here. Now it doesn't look like a disease I've seen before, but it is an amazing coincidence. Therefore, I think we should take a few precautions."

"You think that we've picked up something from those creatures?"

Hackett shook her head. "I think that is highly unlikely since all of this looks more like an injury than any sort of disease. However, something is going on here and I don't think I'm being an alarmist by instituting a few safeguards."

"One of which is washing my hands."

She laughed. "Well, I'm not going to do it. I'm going to give you an antibacterial and a strong soap and let you do it."

"I wasn't objecting," said Reed. He hesitated and then said, seriously, "Are you sure there is no disease?"

That stopped Hackett near the door. She turned and looked at him and then shook her head. "I'm of the same opinion now that I had this morning."

Reed wasn't ready to let it drop. He said, "First Hendricks gets sick on the trip here. Now others seem to be getting sick.

Hackett closed the office door and sat back against a desk. She clasped her hands in front of herself and stared at the floor. After a moment, she asked, "Just how long ago did you first come into contact with all of this?"

"About July first," he said, and then realized that wasn't what she wanted to know. "Early on the morning of July fifth."

"That was what, ten, eleven days ago."

"Yeah."

"You feel sick? Dizzy? Anything like that?"

"No."

Hackett rubbed her jaw in a fashion that looked masculine. She closed her eyes for a moment. When she opened them, she said, "It's like I said this morning. I doubt we could catch anything from the aliens and all this," she waved a hand, "doesn't remind me of disease."

Reed nodded and said, "So you're telling me that you don't think I should be worried."

"That is exactly what I'm saying."

"So I don't need to recall the sergeants."

Hackett shook her head. "If it is a disease, then that would be of no use. Not now. I think we should look elsewhere for the cause of the trauma here."

"Rape?" asked Reed.

"No. I didn't notice the proper sorts of wounds. I would have expected more tearing of the clothing. There would have been some other, more obvious signs."

"Her skirt was pulled up when I found her," said Reed.

"Probably happened when she fell." Hackett was lost in thought for several seconds and then said, "No. I don't think this is a case of rape. That answer your questions?"

Reed moved toward the door and put his hand on the knob. "Yeah." But it didn't actually rule out disease, at least in his mind. Hackett said she didn't think it was disease, but she wasn't sure.

Reed tugged open the door and together they left the room. As they walked down the corridor, he realized that the red lights still flashed. Obviously, some sort of heightened state of alert had gone into effect, but he didn't know what it was, or the significance of it. Apparently that alert didn't concern those around him.

They reached a door and Hackett took a key from her pocket. She unlocked the door and then stood back so that Reed could enter it first. When he had done so, she followed and then closed and locked the door behind them.

"No interruptions that way," she said. She moved to the

sink, turned on the water and then handed him a bottle. "Antibacterial."

He asked, "Just what are you concerned about here?"

"I want to be safe. I told you that. We'll take care of you and then I'm going to collect my blood samples."

"Just what are you looking for?"

"Nothing in particular," she said. "I want to make sure that we haven't overlooked something."

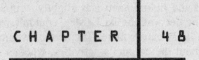

CHAPTER 48

July 15, 1947
The Pentagon
Arlington, Virginia

The meeting was held in the small conference room that adjoined Major General Curtis LeMay's office. It was a secure room where he could discuss classified matters with his colleagues and subordinates and not have to worry about unwanted listeners or foreign spies. And, although it was small, the furnishings were first class. The small table that held room for six was of the finest mahogany, the carpeting was a thick, rich blue, and the walls freshly painted in a lighter, contrasting blue.

LeMay, of course, wearing a class A uniform complete with all his awards and decorations, sat at the head of the table, a leather notepad and a heavy crystal ashtray in front of him. He had laid his pen beside the pad. He had no classified material with him and there was none in the leather notepad. The classified material had been brought by the others.

Seated to his right was Doctor Theodore Johnson, who had attended the original meeting at the Pentagon chaired by Moore who was now in Nevada. LeMay had wondered at the time who Johnson was, and now knew that he was a scientist who worked for John von Neumann. Johnson had been von Neumann's representative at the meeting, though no one had known that at the time.

Next to Johnson was a military officer, a lieutenant colonel, who had been acting as a courier from the Nevada site. He had a thick file folder in front of him that held the latest of the message traffic from Nevada, as well as the special report that had been prepared for LeMay the day before. The colonel looked tired and his uniform was slightly wrinkled and held no awards or decorations so LeMay couldn't read anything about his military career there. The awards would provide information about the colonel's activities, whether he had been a combat officer or a paper-pusher. LeMay didn't know his first name, but saw from his nametag that his last name was Greaber.

Across from Greaber was LeMay's aide who was sitting in so that he could take unofficial notes of the meeting, or so that he could retrieve anything that LeMay felt he would need as the meeting progressed. After the meeting ended, depending on the nature of it, LeMay might quiz him about his impressions, have him prepare a short "after action" report, or have him write out a more comprehensive analysis of what had transpired. It depended on a number of factors.

LeMay waved impatiently at Johnson and said, "You thought we should meet?"

"Yes, General, given what is happening in Nevada."

"And that is?" asked LeMay, exasperated by Johnson.

Greaber opened one of the files and produced a teletype message. He started to hand it to LeMay, but the General waved it aside and said, "Tell me."

"Yes, sir. We are seeing some sort of . . . I'm not sure of the word to use here. A problem, in Nevada. Some sort of . . . medical problem has developed . . . It's a sort of . . ."

"Shit, Colonel, spit it out. We'll sort through the words later. What in the hell is going on?"

"Yes, sir. Several people have been injured, or developed some serious wounds or lesions on their bodies. These wounds seem to bleed heavily, causing additional symptoms related to blood loss. A half-dozen people are down with it. We have one death in Roswell, but we're not sure how it relates to what is happening in Nevada and we wonder if it might relate to the creature or the ship."

"You've just come from there, right?"

"Yes, General," said Greaber.

"What is the impression on the scene about this?" LeMay

spoke calmly, but there was a hard edge to his voice.

"Given that these people were injured after the creature was brought into the facility, most people believe that there is a connection."

"Why did you say, 'injury'?"

Greaber looked uncomfortable and turned toward Johnson for inspiration. There was none there. He said, "Remembering that I have no medical expertise, I believe that the wounds or lesions, look as if they are injuries rather than the result of disease. I haven't seen them myself and even if I had, I couldn't tell you if they were injuries or disease."

LeMay turned his attention to Johnson. "Do you have any information that might be of use here?"

"Only that as the research continues, they are becoming convinced that the creature is responsible for the injuries."

"What? It's sneaking out at night? Isn't it under twenty-four hour observation?"

Now Johnson looked uncomfortable. He smiled and said, "Not observation, but certainly guard. Had it left its room, then the guard would have noticed."

LeMay smiled and said, "Provides an interesting image. What's the guard going to do, shoot it?"

"The protocols require it to be escorted back into the room and then for a number of the staff to be notified. To this point, the creature has been passive. It has gone where it has been directed and has not resisted anything that we have attempted to do."

"Does that strike you as strange, Doctor?" asked LeMay.

Johnson took a deep breath and then shook his head. "I'm not sure that we can speculate about its reactions because it is, well, alien."

"I think I would be trying to escape," said LeMay.

"And go where? Do what? You can't get home."

"How do you know?" asked LeMay. "Hell, we took its ship into Nevada. Maybe it knows the ship is there. Escape from the room and grab the ship."

"It's on the bottom level," said Greaber.

LeMay shot him an annoyed glance but said, "And it has

traveled through space. From what you fellows have said, that's no easy task. What makes you think it couldn't manage to blast its way out of our facility?"

LeMay turned his attention back to Greaber. "Now, you were saying that it is the belief of those in Nevada that these injuries are not related to the creature."

"General, they really don't know. It hasn't left the room in which it was treated. When it died, they removed it to the morgue, but there is a twenty-four hour watch there."

"Then disease seems to be the answer," said LeMay.

"Or coincidence," said Johnson. "I will point out, General, that no one other than those in Nevada have reported these symptoms. No one at Roswell, other than the one possible death, and no one at any of the other bases where our people have gone, have been infected or reported anything that matches the problem in Nevada. Basically, it is just those at the Nevada facility."

"I thought everything and everybody was now in Nevada," said LeMay.

Greaber said, "One body was taken to Lowry, in Denver, where the mortuary service could examine it to determine the best method of preservation. Some small metallic structures have been sent on to Wright Field for analysis, and several small devices have been given to corporate entities for examination. In none of those locations, or here in Washington, where General Thomas and his crew have returned, do we find any of the same symptoms as those displayed in Nevada."

"Then the problem, if it exists, is confined to New Mexico and Nevada?"

"Yes, General," said Johnson. "Nearly everything is in Nevada from the living creature to the whole of the craft."

Greaber interrupted again. "Excuse me, Doctor, but the living creature seems to have died."

LeMay laughed. "I seem to remember that they drew that conclusion once before."

"Yes, sir. They're fairly certain this time."

Johnson started to speak, but LeMay held up his hand. He

said, "If I understand this then, we may have some sort of a medical problem that is related to the alien creatures or craft, but it is contained, to the best of our knowledge, to New Mexico and Nevada. There have been no outbreaks of a similar problem anywhere else."

"Yes, General," said Johnson.

"Then we must seal the Nevada facility and we have the problem contained."

"So it would seem," said Johnson.

"I would also think that our next course of action is to return the one body at Lowry to Nevada, get the debris or other samples at Wright Field sent to Nevada, and get anyone who has had extended exposure to Nevada."

"That might not be necessary," said Johnson.

"Forgive me, Doctor," said LeMay nastily, "but you people have already screwed the pooch, as we say. You took no precautions, shipped bits and pieces around the country, and now you suggest that it might not be necessary. You have one dead in Roswell and others sick in Nevada."

"We don't know that it is related."

"Christ," snapped LeMay, his voice rising. "You don't know a thing about this. Maybe, if there is a medical problem, we have a chance to contain, but you'd rather sit on your hands."

"General, quick action on limited data . . ."

"Is the only way to prevent a disaster. I want those people sent to Nevada, I want everything collected in Nevada, and I want that facility sealed."

"General," said Greaber, "I believe that Doctor Moore has already taken that precaution."

"Then we're wasting our time here. Gentlemen, if you'll excuse me," said LeMay. He stood up.

The others followed suit and LeMay's aide escorted them to the hallway. He returned to collect anything left behind, but found LeMay sitting again at the head of the table. The aide asked, "Do you have anything for me?"

"Get Colonel Cavanaugh on the line and tell him that the

base has been sealed. His job is to now make sure that nothing leaves it until I give permission."

"Yes, General." The aide hesitated.

LeMay grinned and took a puff of his cigar. "Yes, I have that authority."

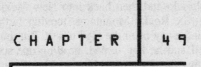

Major Thomas P. Ellis had only limited success as a fighter pilot during the Second World War. He had gotten into the battle over Europe late, and although a very good pilot, luck had not been with him. When he was escorting the bombers into Germany, the Luftwaffe had not come up to attack. When he was not with the bombers, the Luftwaffe attacked with vigor. Somehow the luck of the draw always went against him so that when the war ended, Ellis had engaged in aerial combat rarely and had shot down but two enemy aircraft.

That didn't mean he wasn't a good fighter pilot, just an unlucky one, if victories over the enemy counted as luck. But when the war ended and his fellows were counting points so that they could return to civilian life, Ellis was trying to figure out how to avoid the reduction in force. He liked the military, he liked flying, and he didn't want to drive multi-engine airplanes for an airline. To Ellis, that wasn't flying, especially when the airlines dictated slow climbs and descents and abhorred violent, stomach churning aerobatic maneuvers that were the lifeblood of a fighter pilot.

Now he was at fifteen thousand feet in a clear blue sky that seemed to go on forever. Above him was the darkening violet hue that marked the beginning of space and below him was the patchwork of brown and green that showed where agriculture was successful. The polished plexiglass of the fighter's canopy gleamed and was nearly invisible it was so clean.

The search had taken him from northern New Mexico into

southern Colorado and then back into New Mexico. He had been skirting the Rocky Mountains, moving farther into the high plains and away from the high desert. But the search had not gone well and he had turned, heading due south at high speed, watching the sky around him, looking for anything that didn't belong.

A flash of bright silver that could have been fifty miles away caught his attention as he rolled out of the turn. When he looked for it, he could see nothing, but he knew what the reflection had meant. An aircraft had turned and the sunlight had caught the silver of the wings reflecting from it with the same brightness as that of a mirror. Those sorts of reflections were the way fighter pilots found their enemies at great distances when they were too far to see any other way.

Ellis turned toward the flash and pushed on the throttle, picking up the last fifty miles an hour available to the plane. He raced across New Mexico, climbing slightly, hoping to get above the target, whatever it might be, for the advantage that gave him. He wanted to dive out of the sun at it.

As he crossed above Portales, New Mexico, heading toward Roswell, some ninety miles to the southwest, he caught sight of another flash from the corner of his eye. He banked sharply, rolled out, and saw, thirty miles away, a streak of silver moving toward the south. Ellis turned again, giving him an angle that should allow him to intercept the object, unless it turned to the west and began running directly away from him.

As he closed on it, he began to see a shape. Not the disk shape he had expected based on what he had read in the newspapers, but not the conventional shape of an airplane either. The fuselage was flatter and wider and the wings were larger and molded into the sides of the aircraft rather than looking as if they had been attached. It was a smooth, streamlined whole that give the impression of a disk, though one end was more pointed than the other.

The object turned, banking, giving Ellis a good look at the bottom. Now he could see that it was more triangular shaped with the edges blunted and rounded. The nose, though rounded, had a sharper angle. The object looked like nothing he had ever seen and he didn't understand how it flew given its shape.

Then, as if its crew had spotted him, the object turned again, slowed almost to a stop and then rapidly accelerated. One moment it was in sight and the next it was nothing more than a streak of silver disappearing in the distance. Finally, in two seconds, it was out of sight.

Ellis turned to follow but knew it was useless. Even if he could catch it, which would mean that it slowed to allow him closer, it could run away from him at any moment. The craft was so far superior to his frontline fighter that it seemed to be running on magic. Ellis thought that in five hundred years people of Earth might be able to build something like that, as science and technology improved. In five hundred years, he would be flying the magic craft, but now, today, he was stuck with a fighter that was as primitive to that alien ship as a Wright Flyer would be to his Mustang. He was outclassed, outpowered, and outrun.

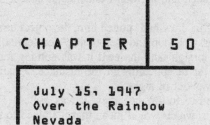

CHAPTER 50

July 15, 1947
Over the Rainbow
Nevada

The communications center was on the second floor and on the inner side of the ring. The antennae were strung so that they were protected from damage, but could be easily repaired. And, given the nature of the facility, Reed knew that they would have the capability for secure communications. He would be able to talk with the general without having to worry about eavesdropping or wire taps.

He explained his need to the communications NCO, a man who looked to be in his mid-fifties, who had gray hair and a huge belly that hung over his belt. His uniform, however, was well pressed, the insignia placed on it correctly, and all the pockets buttoned. He looked as if his body had let him down while he tried to maintain a proper military appearance.

The sergeant led Reed into a small room that was filled with radios, telephones, recorders, clocks, charts, weather instruments, and even a few typewriters. He said, "This would be the command post if everything went to shit, pardon my French. We can talk to anyone here who has a radio or a telephone. This is as secure as it can get."

"I can call out?"

"You got authorization and you got a telephone number, then it's no fucking problem, pardon my French."

Reed grinned and said, "Doctor Moore authorized it. I need a secure telephone and a little privacy."

"Phone's right there, Cap'n. Shouldn't be any trouble. You got to dial nine, then one, one, two, and you got yourself into the secure net. Phone at the other end hooked into the net, and you can make the connection."

"I think I've got it," said Reed.

The sergeant grinned broadly showing surprisingly perfect teeth. He pulled a chair away from one of the desks and said, "Then have a seat and have at it, sir."

Reed dropped into the chair and said, "Thank you."

"I'll be outside, on the other side of the closed door, if you need me."

"Thanks, again."

Without another word, the sergeant slipped through the door and closed it. Reed spun the chair around, leaned an elbow on the desk, and pulled the telephone close. He dialed the nine, listened, and then dialed one, one, two. There was a momentary silence, a series of clicks, and then a voice that said, "You are on a secured system."

There was another click and it sounded as if the line had gone dead. Reed concentrated on the number he needed for a moment, and then dialed. Again there was a series of clicks, a pop and a burst of static.

"This is the general."

Momentarily, Reed was taken aback. He had expected someone else to answer. He said, "This is Reed. The line is secure."

"What can I do for you, Captain?"

"I have a question, General."

"Let's have it."

"Disease, sir. We have taken no precautions against the possibility of alien disease."

The line was silent, almost dead. Reed wasn't sure if they had lost the connection or if the general was thinking. Finally, he said, "There a reason that this comes up now?"

Reed leaned back and looked at the blank wall, wondering why everything was painted light green. Finally he said, "Well, we have some people who seem to be ill and nobody knows what their problem is."

"Aren't we being a little premature, Captain?"

"General, this is already getting out of hand. We've had

people into Roswell from around the country. We've shipped the craft and the bodies off for examination. We brought the living being across country and could have contaminated who knows how many."

"I have been in consultation with various authorities and even given what has transpired in the last few days, there is a consensus that disease is not a problem. They have taken steps and have suggested an upgrade in the protocols used around the alien creatures and their ship. At the moment they seem to believe that we do not have to worry about disease and that if disease becomes a problem, we can contain it."

Reed wasn't sure that he was satisfied, but there was nowhere else to go and no one else to question. Everyone seemed to believe that disease was not a problem.

"Is that all, Captain?"

"Well, I've had a couple of other random thoughts, General."

"Let's have them all."

"Why has there been no rescue mission?" asked Reed. "Why haven't they tried to find their lost friends?"

There was silence at the other end for a moment and then the General said, "We should avoid speculating about the motivations of an alien race. We don't know anything about them."

"Still, you would think they would want to find their fellows and recover the craft, if for no other reason than to keep it out of our hands. Once we have a chance to examine their craft, we can build one like it."

"Not necessarily," said the General. "From the reports I've seen, it's going to take us a few years just to figure out how to make the metal. So far we know nothing about it and that is after subjecting it to every test that we know. Our technology isn't sufficiently advanced that we can understand their technology."

"I've been thinking about this for some time," said Reed. "I have questions."

"We all have questions. Lots of questions."

Reed shrugged even though the General couldn't see him.

He leaned back in the chair and spun to the right. "Shouldn't we be worried about a search party?"

"We are on the lookout," said the General. "Aircraft are in the sky."

"Anything seen?"

"There have been a couple of interesting sightings, but there has been nothing that I would describe as a concentrated search effort."

"We'd be out in force," said Reed.

"If we knew the craft was down, if we knew where, if we knew there had been survivors. But, if it was a lone scout, out of touch, maybe it hasn't missed a reporting time. We just don't know. All we can do is plan."

"Yes, sir."

"We have people, in other locations, working on these aspects of the problem. They aren't necessarily fully aware of the situation, but we are watching the situation. Is there anything else?"

"No, sir. That's it."

"You'll be there for how much longer?"

Reed had to grin at that. He had thought the general was directly responsible for him being there. He said, "I'll hang around until they begin doing the real science and then, after I have been debriefed, and after I have all the information I need, I'll go back to Roswell."

"Why don't you just stay there until you hear from me? There might be a few additional questions."

"Yes, sir. No problem."

"Thanks."

The line seemed to go dead, but Reed wasn't sure. Before he could say anything, a voice announced, "Connection has been terminated."

CHAPTER | 51

July 16, 1947
Over the Rainbow
Nevada

The body of the alien creature had been moved from the room it had occupied to the morgue for cold storage, and then on to the autopsy/dissection room for further work. To get to the room, it was necessary to walk through the morgue, which provided an added measure of security. It had white walls, a white floor and a light fixture centered on the ceiling that could be manipulated so that the four bright lights, backed by curved mirrors, shone on the area where the doctor worked. A microphone hung down from the ceiling, near the lights, and off to one side, out of the way, yet handy, was a scale.

Centered, almost under the lights, was an operating table that stood just over three feet high. It allowed the doctors to work comfortably without having to bend over. It was about seven feet long and four feet wide and made of stainless steel. Around the perimeter was a shallow trough designed to drain away fluids. There were a couple of drains in the table as well. Bottles could be attached to all the drains to collect the fluids for later analysis.

Standing near the table was an instrument tray that held scalpels, knives, saws, a chest cutter, probes, and a small, steel hammer. They had been set up by the attendants in the morgue and waited for the doctors.

On the table, covered with a white sheet, was the body. It was so slight that it was barely noticeable under the sheet. It was covered from head to foot. In most cases, one foot with

toe-tag would be exposed, but the body was completely cov-
red.

Hackett, along with Hendricks, was preparing for the au-
opsy of the alien creature. Although not normally done, she
ad scrubbed her hands, up to her elbows, to remove any
ource of contamination. She had pulled her hair back, pinned
t up, and then tucked it into a surgical cap. She didn't want
tray hair falling into the middle of her work.

Hackett entered the room wearing a surgical gown, covers
n her shoes, and with a mask tied around her neck, but not
ulled up to cover her mouth and nose. The gloves she wore
overed her hands to her wrists, and the ends of her sleeves
vere tucked into the tops of the gloves and then taped in place.
t was to prevent contamination in either direction. She pulled
he towel from the instrument tray, making sure that it held
utopsy instruments and not those needed for surgery. Satis-
ied, she looked up at the clock and then at the two motion-
icture cameras that had been mounted so that one or the other
vould be in a position to record the finer points of the autopsy.
3oth were fixed and held color film. There was a technician,
lressed in white that included a cap and surgical mask that
vas already in place so that she could only see his brown eyes.
lis job was to reload each of the cameras as it ran out of film.

A man wearing a white coat, but no cap or mask, and carry-
ng a camera bag entered. He looked up at the motion-picture
ameras and then down into his bag. He extracted a 35mm
.eica, changed the lens on it, and then stepped back, setting
iis bag in a corner of the room, out of the way.

"You going to do the cutting?" he asked Hackett.

Hackett nodded. "Or, at the very least, I'll be assisting."

"I'm Sergeant Hayes. I get in your way here, you just let
ne know."

"I'm sure that someone will mention it, Sergeant."

The still photographer looked at the movie cameras and then
it the technician. He joined that man, standing off in the cor-
ier, out of the way.

A third man, dressed like Hackett, entered, looked at the
utopsy table. He looked as if he should be a football player

wide broad shoulders a thick neck and a bullet-shaped head. His hands, in stark contrast, were small with thin fingers which made the delicate work easier for him. He stood for a moment, surveyed the room, the technicians, and then asked, "Everybody here?"

"Yes," said Hackett unnecessarily.

The man pointed at Hendricks. "Who're you?"

"Hendricks."

"The medical doctor? You here to cut or observe?"

"Observe."

The man turned to stare at Hackett. "Then who are you?"

"Doctor Hackett."

"Ah, Doctor, you're the biologist?" He held out a hand. "I'm David Brown. University of Iowa School of Medicine. I'm sorry. I expected the specimen to be prepared and ready."

Hackett said, "That's not a problem." She pulled her mask up and tied the strings behind her head. She then reached out, grabbed the top of the sheet and whipped it aside, almost like a matador swirling the cape.

The creature was fully exposed. Hackett had never seen it except in the rooms where it had been clothed. Now she could see just how fragile it was. The arms and legs were all stick-thin with no noticeable muscle tone or shape. There were no external sex organs, which, to her, meant nothing at the moment. Sexual identification, if even a relevant question, might be revealed in the internal structure.

"First thing," said Brown, "is a complete set of photographs." He looked at the photographer. "We'll stay our of your way."

"Okay, Doc. You need anything specific, you let me know what it is and I'll get it for you."

"Thank you, Sergeant," said Hackett.

Hayes moved around the body taking photographs, starting with the head and working his way down the right side. He had set a scale near the head as a reference, and as he took the pictures, he moved the scale. He took close ups of the face, the shoulder, the arms, hands, trunk, legs and feet. Then, just to be thorough, he worked his way up the left side, photographing it all. From the head, looking down, he shot the whole body, and then from the foot, did the same thing.

Hackett asked, "You been briefed on what is going on here?"

"I know a little, but they said that they wanted to keep my insights fresh. They told me we would be doing in an autopsy and that another had been completed. I asked for information but they said they'd rather not."

Hackett laughed. "Typical. So afraid that someone will learn something to sell to the Russians. I don't know why they want to keep us in the dark."

"Maybe there is something to this fresh insight stuff," said Brown. "If I haven't been contaminated," he looked at Hackett and added, "or if you haven't been contaminated by the theories and thoughts of others, then we might be inspired in some way the others weren't."

"Or we could be making the same mistakes they made."

"I would think," said Hendricks, "if there were other mistakes, those would have been mentioned."

"Well, whatever their reasoning," said Brown, "I would prefer going into this will a little more information."

"I doubt there is much more in the way of information," said Hackett.

Hayes finished photographing the alien's front side and Hackett and Hendricks then turned the body over so that it was face down. The back was as plain as the front. The musculature did not match that of a human, but seemed more directed at the hips and pelvic girdle. There was a gluteal bunch that worked for locomotion and there was a large muscle down the back of the thigh, attached at the knee. The calf didn't bulge as it would on a human, and the heel was wider and more rounded as if built for stability rather than speed.

When the second series of photographs was finished, Hackett and Brown turned the body over again. She bent forward, looking at the pock marks on the trunk. There were three on each side, in an equilateral formation with a seventh over the sternum.

As she set the ruler near one of the them, Hackett said, "Let's get a couple of close-ups of these."

Once the pictures had been taken, Hackett leaned close and examined one of them. It was only a inch across and about half an inch deep. It looked as if a ball of tissue had been pulled from the skin, leaving a shallow crater. It didn't seem to be bleeding and no fluids were collecting in it.

She picked up one of the small scalpels and a glass slide. She scraped some of the tissue from one of the injuries, placed it on a slide, marked it, and then repeated the process two more times so that she had a number of slides with samples of the tissue on them. As the last step, she recorded exactly where each sample had been collected so that, when they did the finer lab work, she would be able to identify the source of the sample.

They then carefully measured the body, the arms, legs, feet, hands and fingers. They measured the circumference of the skull, the distance between the eyes, and even the size of the eyes. Brown and Hackett did the work and Hendricks made the notes.

Finally satisfied, Brown said, "Let's get the motion-picture cameras rolling and get started."

The technician started the cameras, and then stepped back, out of the way.

Brown stood at the head of the table and picked up the head, one hand on each side. He manipulated right and left and then forward and back. He set it back, and probed at the eye, looking down into the deep black orb. He then opened the mouth and probed there. He found no real teeth, just a strip of flesh that was hard and a couple of small, sharp points where the canines would be in a human.

As Hackett and Hendricks watched, Brown worked his way down the body, examining the joints and manipulating the arms, the wrists and fingers and then the knees, ankles and toes. Brown noticed that the toes were almost prehensile.

Finished with that, he asked, "We get a length and weight on this thing yet?"

Hendricks said, "They did that when it was taken to the morgue this morning."

"Okay." Brown took a large knife from the instrument tray and said, "I think we'll use the standard y-shaped incision."

Hackett nodded and stood back.

Brown carefully made the incision, cutting carefully so that it did not penetrate any of the organs in the chest or abdomen. Finished, he set the knife on the instrument tray and picked up a retractor and inserted it, opening up the chest.

"Don't see anything that looks human in here. Got a large organ, purplish, that has a blunted upper surface. If I had to guess, this is a single, large lung. Surface is smooth with no sign of striation. I see no connecting tissue and no evidence of blood vessels."

Hackett picked up a clear sheet of plastic that held a black grid of inch squares. She laid it across the alien's chest and then stepped back. Haynes moved in, focused and shot a picture. He moved around the table, shot another and then a third.

This photographic record could be thought of as a schematic. They wanted to know exactly how everything fit together because Hackett wasn't sure if she would ever get to see another alien and they needed a complete record.

She pulled the grid out of the way and then reached up and adjusted the light. She probed with her fingers, feeling along the side of the mass of tissue, pushing it slightly out of the way so that she could see deeper into the chest.

"I don't see any major vessels here."

Brown leaned forward and said, "If I lift here, what can you see?"

"Nothing."

"Okay," said Brown. He looked at the lower end of the incision near what would have been the pubic bone in a human. "I don't see anything resembling the stomach, large or small intestines, liver or any other normal structure." He sounded frustrated.

Hackett looked at the bones. There was a rib cage, but it was all connected higher so that the sternum was closer to the throat. If the organ they saw near the surface was a heart of some kind, there was no protection for it as there was in a human. These bones were light and flexible.

Hackett, using a large-gauge needle with a sealed tube, tried to draw some fluid from the large center organ. She couldn't get very much. It was a dark, brown, pulpy fluid. Holding it up to the light, she could see nothing familiar about it.

Brown reached in and worked his fingers under the structure and began to lift. There was resistance and Hackett moved forward with a scalpel. She cut away some muscle and two small vessels at the base of the organ. Brown lifted it free and turned, placing it in the scale to be weighed.

"Grossly," he said, "it resembles a heart and lung if it was a single organ, but it seems to have no real circulatory or respiratory function. I would expect to see something that would indicate a function."

He looked back into the chest cavity and saw the rib cage with the bones spaced three or four inches apart. It appeared that the ribs were designed to hold the organ in place, but offered little in the way of protection for it.

"I see a lack of circulatory structure here. There are no veins or arteries, or any analogous structures. There is nothing to carry blood to the brain, or through the lungs, if that's what we have here."

He leaned his head to the right to wipe the perspiration from his forehead onto the shoulder of his scrubs. "Maybe the arteries are protected inside the organ. But then, we should see something in the way of connective tissue."

"There isn't the diversity of organs that we would see in a human," said Hackett. "We have removed the one structure and that has left the upper chest open. I see no evidence of an esophagus or trachea." She probed gently and said, "I don't see any purpose for the mouth."

Hendricks finally said, "This seems too simple, as if someone had taken a human body and redesigned it for simplicity. Combine the function of the organs to reduce the need for ancillary structure."

Brown turned his attention back to the body. He said, "There is another large organ placed about where the liver would be in a human. There seem to be no blood vessels attached here other than a single vein that attached to the first organ. It's about an inch thick." Brown touched it and then added, "It seems to be semi-rigid with little flexibility."

Hackett, moved around and reached forward. "There isn't good musculature here. The connecting tissues are thin and porous. I don't see any peritoneum." She looked over at Hendricks. "Maybe that is what killed the others. The shock of impact jarred the internal structures loose and there was internal bleeding."

"Except I don't seem much in the way of blood," said Brown.

"You know, given this internal structure, I would have suspected that the entire chest would have been filled with some sort of fluid. That certainly would reduce the damage if there was a high speed impact," said Hackett.

"Hyperstatic shock," offered Hendricks.

Hackett shrugged. "Given what we see here, I would expect the danger from hyperstatic shock would be less than to have the organs breaking free."

Hayes continued to move around, taking photographs as they worked. He made sure that he recorded everything that happened, while the technician reloaded one movie camera or the other to make a continuous film record.

"I don't see anything that would pass for a digestive system," said Brown. "I see no structures that would allow for elimination of waste."

Hackett shook her head. "I don't understand this. No method for the intake of nourishment and no elimination system."

"I think we have just defined alien," said Hendricks.

"I would like to take a closer look at the lower abdomen," said Brown. "I see nothing analogous to the spleen, stomach, intestines, the colon, cecum or rectum."

Hackett moved closer. She probed and prodded and then shook her head. "I really don't understand this," she repeated.

Brown stepped back from the body and the table. "This is more complicated than I thought it would be. I thought we would open him up and find an internal structure that, while not the same, would, at the very least, be recognizable. This is just a mess."

Hackett asked, "Why would you assume a similar structure?"

"Because the outside is similar. We've got a humanoid that even has two eyes, a nose, such as it is, and a mouth. That suggested that the internal structure would be similar."

"Okay," said Hackett. "This is going to take some time here. I think we need to devise a new strategy for this. We're going to have to take each section of the body and dissect it. I confess that I have been thinking of this as an autopsy, but it's not. It is a dissection. We're looking at new structures here. We have to document everything to establish a baseline for future work."

Brown said, "This could take a couple of weeks to do, if we do it right."

"We have the facilities for tissue preservation. We can keep the body on ice," said Hackett. "I see no need to rush forward with this. It's not as if we have a sick alien and need to understand its internal make-up to save the life."

Brown looked at the clock. "We've been at this for three hours. Maybe we should take a break now and come back after we eat."

"I'd like to prepare some more slides," said Hackett. "And I want to look at the musculature in the chest and maybe draw some more fluids before we quit."

Hayes spoke up. "If it matters, I've burned through a lot of film here. I didn't expect this to be as detailed as its been." He held up a hand and added, "Not that I'm complaining. I don't pay for the film. I just need to replenish my supply."

"Well," said Brown. "Okay. Let's take a break and then plan for a long afternoon. I'm thinking this is going to take several days."

Hendricks said, "I'll get the body back into the freezer and make sure that we have things cleaned up in here."

"Okay," said Brown. "Back here in an hour?"

Hackett was going to protest that Brown had just assumed that he was in charge and they weren't under his supervision, but decided it didn't matter now. If it became a problem, she would speak with him later.

CHAPTER | 52

July 16, 1947
On the surface
Over the Rainbow

Lieutenant Colonel Cavanaugh stood holding the message form in his hand, surprised and confused. The wording was plain, but the mission surprised him. Ever since he had landed in Nevada with nearly four hundred highly trained soldiers, and ever since they had completed their tent city set in the mountains northwest of Las Vegas, he had been waiting for some kind of instruction. Now that he had it, he wished that he didn't because it was confusing. Well, not really confusing because the orders were quite clear. It was . . . weird.

Cavanaugh scratched at the back of his neck, sure that some desert insect had bitten him there, and called, "Get the first sergeant up here now."

A corporal called, "Yes, sir," and trotted off.

Cavanaugh dropped into a folding chair, his back to the tent that served as both his quarters and his office. One side held his office that included a field desk which was a box-like object with drawers and slots for the papers, documents, pens, pencils, and other office supplies. The other side had a cot and a sleeping bag. Much of his equipment wasn't unpacked, and had this been a combat assignment, he wouldn't have been sitting outside, looking up into the barren mountains around him, wishing for a cool breeze, a warm breeze, or anything else to stir the air. It was hot and miserable and Cavanaugh was sorry that he had told LeMay that he would take the assignment.

The first sergeant, a tall, heavyset man with only a fringe

of hair near his ears, and wearing a fatigue uniform that had been tailored to his body, stopped close and lifted a hand in salute. Cavanaugh returned it.

"You wanted to see me, sir?"

"Sit down Chambers so that I don't have to look up at you."

"Yes, sir."

When Chambers was comfortable, Cavanaugh said, "I suppose you realized that our assignment was something more complicated than to just train for some ill-defined desert mission some time in the near future."

"Yes, sir. Rumor control said something about a military base around here that would need protecting."

Cavanaugh was amazed, as he usually was because rumor control often had many of the mission elements correct. It was very good at the gross details and less so at the refinements. Cavanaugh asked, "You know where this base is?"

"Ten, twelve miles to the northwest. Old abandoned Air Force training base, as I understand it."

Cavanaugh nodded. He held up the piece of paper and waved it. "These are our orders."

"Yes, sir."

"Okay," said Cavanaugh. "For your consumption, but not for general distribution, the base is active, or rather a portion of it is. There is an underground facility, and I don't know any more about it than that, and there are a couple of hundred people, if that, assigned there." Cavanaugh stopped talking to wait for questions, but Chambers said nothing. He continued. "Okay. I don't know what they're doing, but we have been ordered to seal the place off. No one in and no one out. We close it up tight and sit on it until we get further orders."

"How far do we go to keep the people in or out?"

"Deadly force has been authorized," said Cavanaugh. Before Chambers could speak, he added, "And, according to my instructions here, they would rather that we shot first and then asked questions. It is that important."

"Christ," said Chambers.

"Okay, we have to be ready to move out in about an hour. I want two companies on the scene immediately and we'll secure the area. The remainder of the troops can bring up the rest of the equipment, and then we'll see what facilities on the base we can use. I'm told that we want the base to still look deserted, so I'm thinking that we'll have to use the buildings and hangars for billeting and forgo the tents."

Chambers laughed. "I would think that a barracks set up inside a hangar would be preferable to a tent."

Cavanaugh nodded and said, "We don't have a lot of time to get into place. Each man should be issued a basic load. But, I want every bullet accounted for. I don't want them firing the weapons unless necessary."

"Yes, sir. I'll have the ammunition passed out but make sure the armorers account for it."

"Same with the artillery, though, what we need there is willey peat."

"That'll set the dry grass on fire."

"If we need to use the artillery, I don't thing a few grass fires are going to be the major concern. I don't think anyone is going to care if we set some of those buildings on fire with the artillery."

Chambers stood up. "Anything else, sir?"

"I think that is quite enough."

CHAPTER | 53

July 15, 1947
Over the Rainbow
Nevada

Corporal Wendelle James had little to do other than sit in the avionics lab and wonder why he had been assigned to the facility. They had no aircraft and therefore, no avionics for him to maintain. They did have radios, and the spare parts for them, as well as spare radios, which were housed in the avionics lab but a regular radioman, trained in the repair of radios, could do the job just as well. James wasn't needed here as an avionics repairman, so he was used as a radio repairman, a job he could do, but not the one for which he had been specifically trained nor one that he actually wanted.

He spent most of his on-duty time sitting behind the waist-high, wooden counter reading the magazines and books that he could find. There wasn't much floor space in front of the counter. Just enough for a couple of people, two chairs, and a small table that held a couple of old magazines. The important parts of the lab were behind the counter. Here there were five rows of floor to ceiling shelves that held the spare radios, the spare parts and the tools that he would need to repair radios. Back at the rear of the middle three shelves were the work benches, one that was a heavy-duty table and the other standing about four feet high.

Rarely did anyone come in to talk to him, rarely did anyone have a radio for him to fix, and rarely did he venture out from behind his counter. In the Army, if they didn't know where you were, they couldn't assign you to a cleaning detail. If they thought you were doing your job, they gave you a good evaluation and eventually you were promoted. He could just sit in his shop, read and not bother anyone, waiting for his promotion.

From that point of view, James had the perfect job. Nothing to really do, no details to perform, and no one to find something for him to do because he was just sitting around. He showed up at eight, though no one told him to, and he stayed until sixteen-thirty, though no one had told him to. It was an easy, quiet job with no real drawbacks.

So, when he heard something in the rear of the room, back among the stacked and cataloged spare parts, his first thought was of an animal. A rat, actually. He had seen no evidence of rodents, and he thought the place was carefully constructed so that rodents wouldn't be able to invade it. But the noise came again and James knew that he would have to go to investigate. A rodent could gnaw its way through the wiring and circuits of a radio in a matter of minutes, making it impossible to repair because damage was so widespread.

He picked up a large screwdriver, though what he wanted was a baseball bat or an entrenching tool, something with a little weight to it, and a little length to it so that if he found the rat, he could club it from a couple of feet away. He walked into the rear where the light wasn't quite as good and swore that he could see the shadows moving. He jumped back, his heart pounding and his palms sweating.

"It's a fucking rat," he said out loud to comfort himself. "What are you scared of? You can take a little fucking rat."

He moved back along one of the shelves until he reached the rear wall. From there he could use the light from the front to silhouette the rat and spot it. One good swing with the handle end of the big screwdriver, and he would have ended the confrontation permanently.

The noise came again, but this time from one aisle over. James had to walk all the way to his counter because this shelf was pushed up against the rear wall so there was no way to move from where he was. It had been designed that way so that someone in the back couldn't sneak around and steal the spare parts, as if there would be any reason to do it.

He thought he saw movement low, along the bottom shelf, among the boxes that contained a specific series of tubes. He wished that he had a flashlight, but continued walking, his eyes fixed on the shelf. If the rat was there, he would get it.

Quietly, to himself, he said, "I see you, you little bastard." His voice betrayed him because he sounded scared. Maybe not scared, but agitated. He didn't want to find a rat. He would rather that it ran from him, into another office or lab where the people there could take care of it.

When he was close, he crouched and stared into the gloom. There was movement but not the panicked jump that he had expected. James thought he finally had the rat cornered and hoped that the handle of the screwdriver was heavy enough to stun it if it attacked him. Carefully, slowly, he reached out to push a box back, out of the way. He could feel his skin crawl and there was a cold lump in the base of his stomach.

"Son of a bitch," he said. "This is getting ridiculous."

Something dropped on his back and he screamed involuntarily. He stood and whirled and saw something fly back toward the front of the room. It scurried away, to hide in the shadows and boxes on the shelves. James was sure that he had seen the rat and started to advance on it slowly. He then heard something move behind him and wondered if somehow he had missed the nest of them. There might be more than one.

"Damn. Okay. Let's just calm down here. Nothing to be afraid of. You can handle a couple of rats. You're bigger than they are. Just kill them and be done with it."

Something scurried behind him and then something was at his ankle. He felt a sudden, sharp pain there but it was behind him and when he turned he could see nothing on the floor. The fire remained in his ankle and there was a warm fluid that he was sure was his blood.

James knew that he had to catch the rat now because he didn't want to undergo the shots for rabies. If he didn't catch it, then he would have to take the shots as a precaution.

His plan was to lock his door so that the rats would be trapped and he would systematically hunt them down and kill them. He would find every one of them and make sure that they didn't have the rabies.

As he took a step toward the door, there was pain in his knee. He swiped at it with the screw driver, felt it connect and heard a noise that didn't sound as if it had come from a rat. The thing that dropped to the floor and slipped into the shadows certainly didn't resemble a rat. It didn't resemble anything living, but then, he hadn't gotten a very good look at it. If he'd had to guess, he would say that it was a large, thick dust bunny with short stubby legs and a charcoal head.

James got down on his hands and knees, sure that he was about to make his first kill. He pushed a box out of the way and reached in with his bare hand. Something fastened on it. The pain burned up his arm and into his shoulder, making him sick. He dropped back into a sitting position and saw, for the first time, what he had been chasing. It wasn't a rat. It didn't look at all like a rat. It was larger, gray, hairless and had teeth that looked an inch long. These had penetrated his hand so that the blood was pouring from the wound onto the floor.

"Shit."

Something moved on the shelf above him. He looked up and saw another one sitting there, ready to pounce on him. He raised a hand to block it, felt pain along his hip and cried out. With his uninjured hand, he swatted at the thing at his hip. And then his blood was flowing too fast and he felt himself getting light-headed. A curtain of black began to descend and he slipped to his side as he lost consciousness.

CHAPTER | 5 4

July 15, 1947
Over the Rainbow
Nevada

The sound of the klaxon, with the spinning lights, startled Smith as he sat outside the small maintenance room at the bottom of the underground facility smoking one cigarette after another. Inside the room, the two Naval officers were attempting to arm the atomic bomb, set the explosive trigger, and then ig the radio controlled detonation system. They had been at work since before dawn which was wholly irrelevant in an underground facility, being careful that their mission and their equipment was not compromised, meaning that no one saw them as they attempted to install the device. Smith wanted the device installed before Moore or any of the military people realized what was happening and could object to a higher headquarters. Such a fight could turn nasty in a hurry.

The atomic device was little more than an atomic bomb. It as more sophisticated that the tape, baling wire, jury-rigged device that had been detonated in New Mexico just two years arlier. This one resembled fat man, one of the two bombs at had been used on Japan at the end of the war. They had moved the stabilization fins so that it looked more like a age gray distorted tear-drop than a bomb of any sort.

Before they had arrived, they removed the barometric trigger that had been designed to detonate the sphere of explosive at would create the compression that would cause critical ass. An air burst, about a third of mile above the surface, d been judged to be most destructive. Here, in the facility, e rapid change of barometric pressure, as the bomb dropped,

wouldn't be possible. Instead, an electronic pulse would detonate the trigger to create the atomic explosion.

The door opened and the taller of the two officers, Commander Harold Owens, looked out. Since he wasn't in uniform, he looked more like the janitor. He was wearing
wrinkled and stained khaki pants and an unironed blue shirt.
There was stubble on his face and his thinning hair needed
combing. He looked as if he hadn't slept since they had
sneaked the bomb in through the access tunnel used for the
large-scale resupply. He asked, "What's happening?"

Smith threw his cigarette on the floor and crushed it with
his toe. "I don't have a clue. Some kind of alert, I think. How
soon until you're done?"

"Maybe an hour," said Owens. "I don't want to hurry. It's
not overly complicated, it's just that there are so many little
wires to connect."

"That hour include installation of the radio-controlled trigger?"

"Yes, sir," said Owens. He looked down at the floor, to
avoid Smith's eyes. "I know that my job is to install the equipment with the requirements that you have provided, but I'm
not comfortable with this radio-controlled trigger."

"You let me worry about the other aspects," said Smith
sharply. "That's my job."

"Certainly," said Owens. "It's just that a spurious radio signal could detonate the bomb. I don't know what the electromagnetic signature of this facility is, I don't know what radio
equipment they have, and I don't know if new equipment will
be brought in. These things worry me."

"Please don't," said Smith. "The radio signal needed is in
a range that is not currently used commercially or by the military. It requires a very specific sequence before there is an
initiation of the detonation sequencing. Spurious signals are
not a problem. There will be no accident."

"The more complex the firing sequence," said Owens, "the
bigger the chance that'll we'll get some complication if you
decide to detonate."

"Christ," snapped Smith. "What worries you the most?

spurious radio signal or that the firing sequence will be too complicated?"

"I'm just trying to make you aware of the various problems that we face here. One does not preclude the other."

"And your job," said Smith nastily, "is to basically do what I tell you to do." He stared at Owens until Owens looked away.

Finally, Owens took a deep breath, as if preparing for a long run. He nodded and said, "I better get at it again."

CHAPTER 55

On the Surface
Near Over the Rainbow
Nevada

From his position on the hillside, Cavanaugh could look down at the base. At the perimeter, on the outside of the fence, he could see his rangers beginning to deploy. They were moving quickly, quietly, using the terrain and the vegetation to hide their progress.

He watched as two of his men, moving from opposite directions, slipped up on the guard shack that blocked entry into the base. The single soldier there started to raise his weapon and then noticed that both the rangers had their rifles aimed at him. He carefully set his rifle on the ground, straightened and raised his hands.

It looked as if a firefight would break out as two hidden guards moved to protect the man at the gate. But other rangers had already spotted them, and as they moved, the rangers disarmed them without a fight. The guards had been rounded up their weapons taken, and now they were being moved to holding area, until Cavanaugh learned what was happening on the inside.

The first sergeant, Chambers, approached and said, "We control the perimeter and all access into and out of the base. We've taken fifteen prisoners." He grinned broadly. "Some of them aren't too happy with us."

"It did look easy," said Cavanaugh.

"And no one got hurt. Now what?"

That was the question that had Cavanaugh bothered. He held the perimeter so that no one could get out. He could sto anyone from getting in, as well. He just didn't know why he was supposed to do it.

"Do we move onto the base, Colonel?"

"We have been given orders to hold everyone on the base. We have to find the motor pool and either disable the vehicles or set up a guard on them."

"Disable?"

"Remove the distributor caps or flatten the tires, but do no real damage."

"Yes, sir."

"I think most of the civilian vehicles are parked in one of the hangars. Same thing there. I don't want any working POVs on the base."

"Yes, sir. Telephonic communication?"

Cavanaugh sat for a moment and then said, "I have no orders on that. I see no reason to shut down the communications. Put a couple of our people in the switching house and locate the antenna for the radios. If we get orders to shut it down, let's be ready."

"Yes, sir."

Cavanaugh raised his binoculars to his eyes again, and watched as his men surrounded the base. He felt like the chief of an attacking tribe, watching his warriors as they went about their work. He was safe, on top of the hill, outside the range of enemy bullets and weapons. Of course, no shots had been fired.

"That all, Colonel?" asked Chambers.

"Yeah," said Cavanaugh. "That should do it."

CHAPTER | 56

July 15, 1947
Over the Rainbow
Nevada

The man at the head of the table wore a starched fatigue uniform that looked as fresh as it did when it came from the laundry. There was the silver oak leaf of a lieutenant colonel on the right side of the collar and there were the golden crossed rifles of the infantry on the other. He stood there, leaning forward on his hands, staring into the faces of the others in the room with him.

Without much in the way of preamble, he said, "Each of you is here because he has seen combat in some environment. You have faced the enemy in a deadly situation and have survived to talk about it. There are no scientists, technicians, or medical personnel here for that very reason. The situation has changed and the skills of those, ah, civilians, are not going to be of value here."

Jack Reed sat about halfway down the highly polished table and looked at the others in there with him. There were two other officers at the table, both of them captains. One of them wore a name tag that identified him as Euless. He was a fairly young man, maybe twenty-eight, maybe younger. He had short, dark hair, brown eyes and was deeply tanned as if he spent a great deal of his duty day in the field, which given the facility here might be true. Somebody had to be responsible for the guards outside, for the perimeter, and for security.

The other was a captain named Davidson, who was older. He was in his mid-to-late thirties, had light hair that concealed the beginnings of the gray, a solid, heavy face that gave him a somewhat simian look. He had very large hands but a slender body. The hands looked out of place.

The last was a master sergeant who looked as if he had been in the Army since it had been formed for the Revolutionary War. He might have been fifty or older but his uniform was perfect, his hair cut short and he was clean shaven. If there was a flaw, it was his nose, covered with a network of broken vessels that suggested the sergeant liked to drink. That he was still in the Army meant little, but that he was sitting in this conference room, at this facility meant the drinking was not a problem.

Reed turned his attention back to the man at the head of the table and shook his head again. He just couldn't believe that Douglass would be in uniform because CIC agents were rarely seen in uniform, and that Douglass would be wearing the silver oak leaves of a lieutenant colonel. Reed knew Douglass was an Army officer, as were many in the CIC. He just hadn't realized that Douglass was a lieutenant colonel and didn't know that he had an infantry training to go with the counter-intelligence training.

Douglass said, "We will form the core of the search teams. We will hunt down this creature and kill it."

Euless looked confused. He said, "Creature? Kill it?

Douglass shot him a cold glance but then said, "I think I may have gotten ahead of myself here. Some of you are not familiar with all the events of the morning. Captain Davidson will brief us all on the situation as it now stands." Douglass dropped into the chair nearest him.

Reed stared at him, trying to get his attention, but Douglass ignored him, as if extremely interested in what Davidson had to say. Or, he glanced down at the file folder on the table in front of him, keeping his eyes focused there.

Davidson, was shorter than he looked when he was sitting. He stood and said, "This morning the body of the communications technician was found in the avionics lab. He died from massive blood loss from a large number of small but very deep wounds inflicted on various points on his body. He had been dead for no more than an hour when the body was found. The blood loss was not evident when the body was found, meaning that he didn't bleed out in the lab."

Davidson let that sink in. He then said, "In consultation with the medical staff and the resident biologist, it was determined that the wounds were not part of a new disease pathology, but the result of a physical attack. The wounds were similar to those found on others in this facility and it is our belief they were inflicted in some fashion by the alien creature, or an alien creature, brought here a couple of days ago. We say that because we have seen, or they have seen, nothing like these wounds before. That tells them they are dealing with something new and the only new thing here is, are, the creatures."

Without thinking about it, Reed interrupted to ask, "Then why didn't Hendricks remember being attacked?"

Davidson turned to face him, stared for a moment, angry at the interruption, but didn't bother to answer the question. Instead, he said, "Although it was reported by the scientific staff that the creature had died, we now believe that it had entered into a state similar to that of hibernation."

Reed couldn't let that pass unchallenged. "What do you mean hibernation? For God's sake, they cut it open and removed its organs. If that didn't kill it, if it was still alive, there isn't much that we can do to it now."

Douglass stood up, taking over from Davidson, and said, "We are not here to debate the questions of alien life. A policy has already been decided at a higher headquarters." Douglass finally looked right at Reed. "Our orders have been issued. We are here to carry out our orders which is to find and kill this beast."

"Kill what? Are you saying that the body is not in the morgue? Did it escape? Just what in the hell are you talking about here."

Douglass snapped, "Who in the hell appointed you a spokesman?"

Euless said, "I think the questions have some merit. Just what in the hell is going on?"

Douglass, exasperated, said, "I would have thought that

fairly obvious. We have something loose inside the facility and we're going hunting for it."

"Surely not one of the creatures," said Reed. "They're all dead."

"We think they're dead," said Douglass.

"Haven't they all been autopsied?"

Douglass looked at Reed as if he had just committed a major security breach. Instead, he said, "We are going on the assumption that we simply do not know everything about them. We don't know what kills them or if they have some kind of deep hibernation that mimics death."

"I would think when you begin to remove the internal organs," said Reed, tired of being treated like a backward child, "that you can pretty well say they're dead."

"Maybe you should be on the scientific teams," said Douglass, raising his voice.

Euless said, "Gentleman, let's not fight in front of the children." He pointed at the old master sergeant.

"Don't mind me, sir, I've heard it all before."

Reed took a deep breath and then said, "If we could communicate with it, there is so much that it could tell us."

"And if we have its ship and the information on it, which we do, then the creature itself is of no real importance to us," said Douglass. "The problem is the potential threat that it poses, or one of its fellows poses here and now, and the simplest, most effective mean to neutralize that threat is to eliminate it as quickly as possible."

Reed rocked back in his chair and felt nothing but an icy calm. He knew that he should be outraged by the decision which didn't seem to take in the larger picture, but he wasn't. What he had felt most often, from the moment he had stood on the cliff and looked down at the ship impacted in the side of the cliff, was fear. He was frightened about what the discovery had meant for the human race and the civilization it had built on Earth. The appearance of the creatures and their ship had changed everything that he knew or believed. He hadn't understood it fully until that moment. The military course, or whoever orchestrated the latest plan, was right.

Douglass said, "Gentleman, this is not a debate. For our protection and survival we are going to kill this thing and let those in Washington figure out what to do next."

Euless said, "Aren't we declaring war on these creatures by hunting them down?"

"They invaded our territory. They have injured and killed our citizens. That is sufficient justification for our reaction here."

"Sir, with all due respect, but even foreign agents are given a trial."

Douglass whirled and faced the man. He screamed at him. "We are not a police force. We do not arrest criminals. We attack and kill the enemy. If you have a problem with that, you are in the wrong business. Go join the fucking police force."

"Yes, sir," said Euless, his eyes suddenly on the table.

Reed looked at Douglass, surprised by the venom of Douglass' response. He said, "Has anyone thought about their reaction to this? This is an act of war."

"How do you figure?" asked Douglass.

"We are going to hunt it down and kill it," said Reed.

"Look," said Douglass, "No one invited them to land . . ." He held up a hand to stop the protests. "Yes, I know they crashed, but the point is, no one invited them. We have attempted to provide aid to the injured and have worried about the psychological reaction of it. Now, in this facility, we have something killing our people. That sounds like an act of war to me."

Reed nodded. "Has anyone in Washington thought about this?"

"Do you think I just grabbed the authority to do this? Do you think I'm in uniform because I need to be? Yes, I have the authority and I want to begin this search."

Davidson, who had been quiet for a while said, "You know, we're all assuming that the problem here is alien in nature. Maybe these injuries and deaths have nothing to do with the creatures brought in here. Maybe it is all just a coincidence."

Douglass looked at each of the men around the table. "That

doesn't matter now. We are going hunting for something and
when we find it, we're going to kill it, unless there is some
other objection. Is there still anyone else who thinks we should
arrest this creature?"

The master sergeant, who was afraid of no one, especially
lieutenant colonels in fatigues, asked, "If we have the chance
to capture it?"

"I'll make this perfectly clear for everyone in this fucking
room. We are not going to capture this creature. We are going
to kill it. Is that clear?"

Someone said, "Yes, sir."

CHAPTER | 57

Dr. Danni Hackett, along with Dr. David Brown, stood over the body of Corporal Wendelle James in the morgue and carefully, using a large magnifying glass, studied the wounds on his ankles and calves. They were small but deep cuts around large areas of bruising that looked exactly like the wound she had seen on Hendricks when he first arrived at the facility and on the others here and which she had once thought might have been the symptoms of a disease.

These were wounds inflicted from a thin, sharp instrument that could best be described as very thin ice pick. She didn't believe it to be an ice pick because of the bruising. If an ice pick was the instrument, there would have been some bruising around the wound but not the large, extensive dark area that she was looking at on the body. Something else was responsible, something smaller and sharper.

Most of the wounds were low on the body, around the feet, ankles, calves and the knees. It would be difficult to inflict a fatal wound there, unless there was excessive bleeding or the blood was somehow drawn from the wound. When there was sufficient blood loss, no matter how the body lost the blood, the body would respond in various ways including the shutting down of the brain functions and then ultimately, death.

There was a single wound higher on the back that looked just like the others, but again it wasn't in a position to be fatal. It wasn't deep enough to be fatal. Even if the knife, or ice pick, or whatever, had been pushed completely through the body at that point, it would have hit no vital organs. It might inhibit the natural function of the shoulder, it might make it difficult for James to move his arm, but it wouldn't have been fatal. It was obvious that blood loss was the cause of death.

She straightened up and set the magnifying glass on the table near her. She made a couple of notes and then covered the body so that the neither the face nor the sexual organs were visible. She stepped back and pulled the rubber gloves from her hands.

"What do you think, Doctor?" asked Brown.

"Blood loss. I see no sign of disease here though I'll want to examine both tissues and what blood remains. There is always the possibility that we're seeing something new here, but I doubt it now. These are injuries that were inflicted and have nothing to do with the pathology of disease."

"I would concur," said Brown, sounding unnaturally formal.

"Since I have never seen wounds of this nature before, and because we have an alien creature on the base, I would guess that the two events are somehow related," she said.

"You don't think such a conclusion is a bit premature?" asked Brown.

Hackett shot him a glance, wondering what he was thinking and then said, "From a strictly scientific point of view, it is quite premature. But, I think we can safely assume some sort of relationship here. Once the creature has been recaptured, we'll be able to learn the truth."

"What's your the next step?"

Hackett leaned back, against a table and said, "My next step is to do the blood work, I suppose, just to make sure that there is no new microscopic organism to account for these deaths."

"Will you need some help?"

"Need it? No. Appreciate it however."

"The let's get to work."

CHAPTER 58

July 15, 1947
Over the Rainbow
Nevada

The search teams were assembled at the entrance to the facility on level one. There were three teams of fifteen men each. All were armed with the Colt 1911A1 ACP pistol and the M-1 Garand rifle with the exception of Douglass who had a Thompson submachine gun because he thought it gave him the look of authority and a look of combat experience, though he had never fired the weapon.

The plan was simple enough. One team of fifteen men would start down the right side of the corridor, checking the rooms, offices, and other areas as completely and carefully as they could. A second team would start down the left side doing the same thing. The third team would stay near the elevators and the doors, guarding both corridors and the exit, acting as a blocking force. It was assumed that the creature would be forced from hiding, would flee, and run into one or the other of the corridor teams. If it managed to evade both of them in some fashion, the backup team would catch it before it could reach the elevators and make its escape to the outside world.

They would start on the top level and work their way down, assuming that they were driving the creature lower if it was somehow evading them. In the worst-case scenario, they would find it at the bottom level. They would keep searching as long as it took or until they reached the bottom level and killed the beast. If, for some reason, they failed to find it, they would begin again, and they would keep searching until the alien was found and killed.

Douglass stood with his back at the elevator door and said, "Once we have cleared a level, we will descend to the next in relays. The elevator will not be allowed to rise to the surface, or to a level above us until the search has been completed. All other means of egress should have been closed and locked. Are there any questions?"

The old master sergeant, William Levinson, said, "We go firing these rifles down here and we're going to start cutting down our friends."

"I would have thought, sergeant, no one is going to fire until we find the creature and it isn't armed. There shouldn't be a lot of shooting. A little fire discipline should solve the problem."

"Yes, sir."

"Let me stress this," said Douglass. "We are not going to be doing a recon by fire here. We are not going to be tossing grenades into the rooms to clear them. We are going to search, carefully, every room and office and vent and closet and anywhere else you think this thing can hide and all those places you think that it can't hide.

"Captain Reed, you take the right corridor. Captain Euless, you take the left. I will remain here with the back up team. We will rotate assignments so that everyone has a chance to search. Good luck, gentlemen, and remember, the sooner you get it, the sooner we can get the hell out of here."

Reed checked the safety on the Garand, and then put his thumb on it so that he could flip it off if he needed to fire it. Without a word, he stepped into the right side corridor and began to move along one of the walls. He glanced over his shoulder, saw one man near the opposite wall and the others strung out behind him almost as a blocking force. They were moving slowly, carefully, like men on a patrol through thick jungle, in enemy-held territory. They were waiting for the surprise they all knew would come and kill them.

They reached the first door. Reed stopped, rubbed his chin with his left hand, as if thinking about his next move. He had not been involved in anything like this since basic training before he went to flight school.

Trying to remember that training, he pointed to the wall on the other side of the door and waited until one of the men had taken the position. He snapped his fingers for the attention of the others and realized that there was no reason for them not to talk. They were not in enemy territory and he would be giving away no secrets.

"I want two of you watching the door and the rest of you watching our backs. I don't want something sneaking up on us while we're all looking at the door."

Once everyone was in place, Reed crouched down and reached out to the door knob. He twisted it slowly, and quietly, and then shoved hard. The door flew open and hit the wall behind it. Reed dived into the room, rolled and waited. There was no movement, just a startled clerk who had stood up and screamed.

Quickly Reed got to his feet and held up a hand. "I'm sorry."

The young woman, a sergeant and dressed in a khaki uniform, asked, "What in the hell do you think you were doing?"

To Reed, that was a very good question. He wasn't at all sure what the hell he was doing. For some reason, he had assumed that the rooms and offices would all be vacant. He had assumed that the staff had been collected and taken to a waiting area while the teams moved from room to room. Obviously that hadn't happened. Apparently the klaxon did not signal a general evacuation. Someone hadn't thought his way through the whole plan.

One of the men entered, looked around at the standard military desks, the four chairs pushed against one wall and the bookcase with looseleaf binders against the opposite, and asked, simply, "How long have you been in here?"

"Since they ended the alert this morning. I came to work when released from my quarters."

Reed picked up the ball. "And no one has come in or gone out since?"

"I've been here all along and haven't seen a soul."

"We're going to take a look around," he said. To his team, he said, "You people check this out and then wait here. I'm going to talk to the colonel."

"Yes, sir."

Reed walked back down the corridor and found Douglass sitting in a chair, his back to the elevators. The reserve team was spread out in a semi-circle, watching both corridors and seeming to protect Douglass. They were arranged so that no one could sneak up on them from any direction at all.

"Colonel, I have a question."

Douglass set his coffee cup down. He stared up at Reed, a strange smile on his lips. It was almost as if he was challenging Reed to say anything about his taking command. He hesitated and then asked, "What is it?"

"What do I do with the people?"

"What people?"

"Seems that the alert has been cancelled and that the people have been released to go back to work."

For a moment, Douglass stared as if he couldn't understand what Reed had said. "You mean there are people in some of the offices?"

"Yeah." Reed wasn't intimidated by Douglass' rank. He had worked with him for too long as an equal to think of him as a superior.

"Send them back here once the room or office is cleared. We'll take them to into the central meeting room and keep everyone together."

"Okay."

Reed moved close to Douglass and said, "Mind if we have a word, Colonel?"

Douglass said, "Sure, Jack."

When they were out of earshot of the other soldiers, Reed gestured at the uniform. "Lieutenant colonel?"

"Sometimes we have to improvise," said Douglass. "I am authorized, by higher headquarters, to conduct this operation. I was advised to take whatever steps were necessary, to assume whatever rank was appropriate, and to organize the search for the alien creature."

Reed shook his head. "When did you get those orders?"

"Passed along to me this morning, when it was decided that things were getting out of hand here."

"They're not out of hand."

"The living creature has died. People are sick, or injured, and some are dying. No one really understands what is happening to those people and if it is related to association with the creature. To contain the problem, they have elected to take a radical approach."

Reed wiped a hand over his face and then rubbed the sweat on the front of his fatigue shirt. "You and me were the first to make real contact. We both got into the ship. We've touched the dead creatures, and the living one. If anyone was to get sick, it should be us. It should be us by now."

Douglass shrugged. "What can I tell you? There is something going on here and it must be related to the creature. Now it's loose, or something is loose, and we've got several dead."

"Then shouldn't Roswell be quarantined? Shouldn't we be trying to assemble those who have been exposed?"

"My job is to worry about this facility and not anywhere else. Those decisions are made at a higher level. I can only worry about what I'm supposed to be doing here. I have no idea what is happening in Roswell."

"That seems to be shortsighted," said Reed.

"Why? I can't affect those other locations. All I can do is make sure that I have contained the problem here. Someone else with a lot more rank than I will have to decide about the overall picture. What would you do if it was your decision to make?"

Reed thought for a moment and then said, "Not worry about those other locations."

"And, remember it has not communicated with us. There is nothing to learn from it and the situation is now out of hand. This way, we solve the problem once and for all. Look, we don't know what we have here. It would seem that the creature is dead. It has been cut up, to some extent. The others never showed any sign of life. So, we search out whatever we have, we kill it now and we don't have to worry about the creature getting loose in society. We end the danger here. We end it now."

"We don't know that it has killed anyone on purpose. All we know is that a few people seem to be sick."

"Sick and dead," said Douglass. He was growing tired of the conversation. "Don't you have a job to do?"

"Yeah. I have a job."

"Then maybe you ought to get to it."

Before Reed could say more, Davidson and his team appeared. The men dropped to the carpeted floor, stripping their helmets and setting their weapons aside. Davidson walked over, stopped, and then said, "We didn't see anything or anybody."

"Good," said Douglass. He glanced at Reed and then said, "We through?"

"I guess we are."

"Then you had better finish your end of the search."

"If you say so, sir." The sarcasm was unmistakable in his voice.

CHAPTER 59

July 15, 1947
Over the Rainbow
Nevada

Dr. Danni Hackett stood in front of the autopsy table and carefully sectioned a part of the wound on the ankle of Corporal Wendelle James. She wanted to see how deep it was, if she could determine what had made it, if any sort of toxin had been injected, and more importantly, if there had been an anticoagulant to make it bleed freely. If she found traces of an anticoagulant, that would, in her mind, rule out all possibility of disease as the cause of death. Yes, she would check the major organs, she would look at the abdomen, chest and brain, but the nature of the wounds and the anticoagulant provided the clues that she needed.

She had arranged for the autopsy of James to fit into the narrow window of opportunity she had between the sessions of the dissection of the alien being. She wanted to be able to work uninterrupted on this project. The dissection would continue in about two hours, when she had finished her work on James, so she was not pleased when she heard the crackle and pop of the intercom system that seemed to announce something new every ten or fifteen minutes.

"Attention all personnel. Attention all personnel. This is an immediate evacuation order. This is an immediate evacuation order. All personnel will report to the nearest elevator for immediate transport to Level One. I say again. All personnel will report to the nearest elevator for immediate transport to Level One. There will be no exceptions."

Hackett looked up at the speaker but said nothing. She

turned her attention back to the body in front of her and began to prepare a slide. When the door opened, she didn't look up, but stayed focused on her task. She wasn't worried about contamination of either the person entering or the body because she was almost certain she knew the cause of death.

"Doctor, we've been ordered out of here." The soldier, a very young man, about the age of the corporal on the table, carried a rifle at port arms, and wore a helmet, fatigues and boots. He took a single step into the room. He looked around, as if suspecting an ambush. He seemed to be frightened. His face was pale and his voice shook when he spoke. Satisfied that nothing was going to attack him, he turned his attention to Hackett.

"I heard," she said after a moment.

"We have to go."

"I will be along shortly. I have very important work to finish here."

"Doctor, I can't let you stay. The orders are quite clear. We have to get out now."

At that moment there was a loud hum and the lights dimmed for a few seconds before flashing back brightly. The hum faded slightly and Hackett wasn't sure if she could hear it or feel it because it was pitched so low. Unconsciously, she reached up to her left ear as if to plug it. "What's that?"

"I don't know, Doctor. All I know is that we have to get out of here."

Hackett felt dizzy and slightly sick to her stomach. She stepped back, away from the body, afraid that she was going to throw up.

The door opened again and Wheeler appeared. He smiled broadly and said, "I knew that you wouldn't leave."

"I have work to do."

"Not here and not anymore. We're all getting out."

"Why?"

Wheeler shrugged. "I don't know. The word has been passed for us all to get out."

"You hear that?"

"What?"

"That hum. A low pitched hum."

"I don't hear anything, Danni."

She pulled the mask from her face and then stripped off the rubber gloves, dropping them to the floor. She reached out and grabbed the sheet, covering the face of her subject.

"Okay. I'll go, but I was doing something important here. I could have found some answers."

With Wheeler, she left the autopsy room and walked along the corridor. They were joined by others who were leaving their offices or their labs. Some closed and locked the doors, others didn't bother.

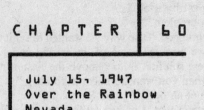

CHAPTER | 60

July 15, 1947
Over the Rainbow
Nevada

Smith had been glad when the racket of the klaxon had stopped. He stood outside the tiny room that was in the maintenance area basically under the fifth level. Inside the room, the two Naval officers still worked to arm the atomic device. He stood leaning back, against the smooth, cool wall, smoking cigarette after cigarette, wishing that he could enter the room to supervise the operation. Oh, he knew that he would just be in the way because the officers were the experts in what they were doing. They didn't need his help and probably didn't want his supervision, but Smith liked to know what was happening. He wanted to see things completed so that when he reported to LeMay that the device was ready, he would be sure that the device was ready.

He finished the cigarette and dropped it to the floor, crushing it under the toe of his shoe. It joined the other nine already there in a small pile of litter. Smith smiled as he realized that the smokers used the world as their ashtray and rarely gave it thought.

Owens emerged from the room, sweat dripping down the side of his face. He rubbed a hand through his hair. "I think we've got it. Another five minutes or so."

"Good," said Smith. "Taking a long time."

"Well, we don't want to fuck up," said Owens. "And you wanted this electronic trigger. We have to move carefully and make sure the shielding around the fission material is thick enough to prevent decay in the circuitry. You don't want this thing going off by itself."

"Is that a problem?"

Owens, shrugged. "The way we wanted to set it up wouldn't work, but we rerouted some of the wiring and I think we'll be okay. Best solution is to remove the fission material and replace it when you want to make it go bang."

"That is not an option," said Smith.

"I understand that. I'm just telling you what the optimum solution would be."

"Okay," said Smith.

"You find out what all the noise was about?" asked Owens.

"Yeah, they want us all up on the top level. I don't know why, but there was some kind of an announcement."

Owens took a deep breath and said, "I'm not thrilled with being in here now. Once we get done here, anybody outside, with the proper code, can set this thing off."

"Not without the right codes and only I have the codes here. LeMay could do it, but he's in Washington. You have nothing to worry about."

Owens grinned and said, "I'm tap dancing on an atomic bomb and you tell me I've got nothing to worry about."

The door opened and other Navy men appeared. His face was pale and his uniform was sweat-drenched. He looked badly frightened. "We're done in here. This is the craziest thing that I have ever had to do."

"No, Commander," said Smith. "You weren't even here so this couldn't be the craziest thing you've done."

CHAPTER 61

July 15, 1947
Over the Rainbow
Nevada

According to their count, there were still twenty-two people somewhere in the bowels of the facility who should have been evacuated from the lower floors long ago. No one had reported seeing them and no one knew where they were, other than they were somewhere below the third level. Everyone else had been accounted for and were already in the gymnasium area on the top level awaiting further orders.

Then there was the annoying hum that rumbled through the floor and the walls, that almost demanded attention. It was at the threshold of hearing, and like those whispering in the distance, they could hear the noise but they just couldn't make anything of it.

Reed, along with the other search teams, had been recalled from what they had been doing and were now gathered on the third level, near the elevator, watching the two corridors. Douglass and two other officers, Euless and Davidson, were at the desk with a map of the facility spread out in front of them. Douglass looked up, spotted Reed and waved him over.

Douglass looked at his officers and said, "The plan is simple. Just like before, we'll have one team down one corridor, a second down the second, and the remainder of the men remaining here to be deployed as either a blocking force or reinforcements. I've now put one squad in the gymnasium, and one squad on each of the other levels so we're now spread pretty thin."

Douglass stopped talking for a moment and then added,

"When you find someone, just send them back here. We'll take care of guarding them. This sweep is to find the missing and then we'll start over, looking for the creature."

"We have a list of those who are missing?" asked Euless.

"They're trying to get that together upstairs. Dr. Moore and a couple of his people are making a list."

"What happens if we find it?" asked Davidson.

"You kill it."

"What in the hell is that noise?" asked Reed.

"Nothing that belongs in the facility," said Douglass. "Moore told me that he knows of nothing that would create that hum."

Reed turned his attention from the map. "So what is it?"

"I don't know any more about this than you do," snapped Douglass. "There is something going on here that we don't understand. It has to be related to the alien creatures. This is not a coincidence."

"They were all dead," said Reed.

"So you said before. But how do you know?" said Douglass. "Just how in the hell do you know?"

"Because they cut them all up," said Reed. "They're in pieces. That's how I know."

"Then how do you explain that noise? How do you explain those deaths and injuries?"

"I don't have any explanation."

"Well, when you have one, you let me know," said Douglass. "Until then, keep your damned opinions to yourself."

Reed looked as if he was going to protest further, but then said nothing.

"We must assume," said Douglass, "that some sort of machine has been constructed down here. Something that gives off that humming sound. If you find that, see if you can stop it functioning without completely wrecking it. I think we have to stop it working. That has to be the first priority. If you can't stop it, then destroy it. Understood?" Douglass looked directly at Reed and raised an eyebrow in question.

"Yes," said Reed.

"Okay, we move down in the elevator as quickly as possible. We stay out of the corridors until everyone is in position and then we move at once."

As Douglass gathered up his maps, Reed turned to his platoon. They were standing near the elevator, grim-faced. He had seen the look before, on pilots who were about to fly into danger, knowing that the German Air Force was going to meet them. It was a look of determination tinged with a little fear. Each man believed he would survive, but all knew that some might not.

They were all dressed in olive drab fatigues, brown boots, and steel helmets. They looked like combat soldiers set to cross the beach at Normandy except that they weren't wearing web gear or knapsacks. They were wearing pistol belts that held a small first aid kit and pouches containing extra ammunition for their rifles. One or two had canteens, though inside the facility, few thought a canteen necessary and a few others had brought their flashlights with them. One man carried a large radio strapped to his back so that they could maintain communications with Douglass, the other team, and even with those up on the first level, inside the gymnasium.

Without a word, he moved to the elevator bank and pushed the call button. The door opened and he stepped across the threshold, his back against the slot for the door. He said, "This is going to be a little dicey. We've got to find the missing people and get them off the level. We've got to see if we can find the creature or whatever is down there, but our first concern is the people. Once we have everyone off the level, then we return to the search. Questions?"

"We still kill it when we find it?"

"Yeah. We kill it. I want all weapons on safe, but I think we should have a round chambered. I don't want to have to worry about flipping off the safety and chambering a round before you can shoot. If we have to shoot, I think we're going to have to shoot fast. Okay, let's go."

Reed let the men enter the elevator and then stepped out of the way. The door closed and they made the quick descent to the next level. When the door opened, three men jumped through, spreading out to provide cover, but the corridor outside the vault door was empty.

When the other teams reached the level, all of them gathered outside the vault door, Douglass walked forward. He used the combination lock, opened the door and then stepped back, out of the way.

"Okay, let's get going. And be careful."

Reed stepped forward, almost as if taking the point. His team, and that of Euless, began to infiltrate the corridors. Reed walked along the wall, moving slowly, his rifle pointed in the direction of march, his eyes shifting from side to side as if he expected something to be concealed in the carpeting or near the wall.

They quickly checked the various rooms and offices, leaving one man on guard every thirty feet or so. With the curvature of the corridors, it meant that each man could see the next in the line, but not the one beyond. They were maintaining visual contact with the entrance to the corridor in that fashion even though Reed and the majority of his team couldn't see it.

As they continued along the corridor, the hum became louder. The vibration could be felt in the floor under their feet. No one was sure he could actually hear the hum. The vibrations that it gave off might have been the only way they could detect it.

They came to a point where the corridor began to darken, which made no sense. Reed held up a hand and dropped to one knee. He then reached out and touched the wall which seemed to be vibrating with a low frequency. His teeth began to hurt.

One of the sergeants, a young man named Clifford, approached and crouched next to him. "What now, Captain?"

"I think that we move with a little more caution now. We'll have to check each of the rooms carefully to make sure that nothing is in them. I don't want to get caught from behind."

"That'll slow us up some. Other team will get in first."

"This is not a race, sergeant. I want us all to get out of here alive."

"Yes, sir."

There was a sudden increase in the hum and the lights dimmed further. The hallway was now gloomy, looking as if the sun had set and no one had turned on the interior lights. Something seemed to be sucking the light and the energy out of the air. Reed noticed that he was getting tired. He didn't know if it was the long day, or if there was something in the corridor that made him believe he was tired.

The dimming lights worried him. Those behind them, farther down the corridor, closer to the main entrance, were burning bright. The lights near him were at about three-quarters power and farther ahead, they seemed to be darker, dimmer.

They stopped then. Reed slipped to one knee and reached out, as if trying to feel the air in front of him. He shook his head and then waved Clifford forward. "Let's take a more aggressive posture. I don't want any of our people hurt."

"I understand, Captain." Clifford stood and turned. He pointed at one of the doors, made a kicking motion and ordered, "Check that room."

One of the men kicked at the door and it crashed opened. Two men entered. There was a crash on the inside and then one of the men reappeared. "It's clear."

"Go," Clifford ordered the next two men.

They followed that procedure, first kicking in the door and then diving in. The men moved along carefully, slowly, clearing each of the rooms as they did, looking not for signs of the alien, but for the people who were missing. They were not worried about breaking equipment, furniture, or anything else they found now. This was a quick search.

As they moved along, the noise from in front of them became louder, and the corridor darkened further. Reed found it difficult to see. Only he and a few of the men had brought flashlights. Reed's batteries were dead, and the other lights didn't work well. If something was drawing energy out of the air, it was also drawing down the energy in the batteries in the flashlights and the radio.

Clifford slipped up close to Reed and asked, "Are the weapons going to fire?"

At first Reed was going to snap at the stupid question because there was no reason for the rifles not to fire, but as he opened his mouth, he realized that he just didn't know. True, the rifle required first a mechanical action and then a chemical reaction to fire and didn't rely on electricity, but if something could draw the electricity from the air as seemed to be happening, if it could suck the power of a battery, couldn't it also halt a chemical reaction as a rifle cartridge fired?

He stopped where he was, and leaned back against the wall. "I don't know, Sergeant. I assume they will."

"Couple of the guys have bayonets, sir."

Reed understood that but he didn't want to create a panic by issuing an order to fix bayonets. Too many soldiers thought of the order as a last, desperation move. He shook his head and said, "Not yet. Let's see what happens first."

"Captain," called one of the men.

Reed said, "Yeah?"

"We got a problem here."

Reed walked forward and saw what looked like a wall across the corridor. It was a charcoal barrier that he couldn't see beyond yet it didn't look to be solid.

"What is it?" he asked.

"Don't know, Captain. We just stopped right here."

Reed snapped his fingers and the man with the radio came forward. Reed held out his hand, and then put the handset against his ear. There was no carrier wave.

The RTO checked and said, "Battery's dead."

Reed said nothing about that. He was sure that the same force that had killed the flashlights had killed the radio.

"You run back to the colonel and alert him to what we've seen here. Tell him that we are holding in place for a few minutes while we try to figure this out."

"Yes, sir."

Clifford said, quietly, "Rooms to this point are all clear, Captain."

"Then we advance very slowly. I don't want to take any chances now," said Reed.

CHAPTER 62

July 15, 1947
Over the Rainbow
Nevada

Under new orders from Douglass, received by runner, Reed and his men pushed forward, into the gloom that had infected the hallway. It was almost like penetrating a physical barrier of some lightweight fabric. There was a momentary resistance and then they were through it, into the darkened corridor. They all felt slightly dizzy, slightly sick, and slightly off balance.

Reed halted them, consulted the floor plan and realized that they reached the top of the loop on that level, on the opposite of the facility from the vault-like door and elevators. They were near a huge room that had been designated as a conference area. There were large double doors that could be locked from the inside for security. There were two other rooms that branched off it, both set up as small offices where private meetings could take place while the larger conference went on. There was a third, small room that was behind a reverse screen, where the projectionist, the audio recorder, and all special equipment could be kept while waiting for the meeting to begin.

Using hand gestures, Reed pointed right and left so that his team split, taking positions on either side of the door. He waited as they snapped off the safeties on their rifles, and then, their backs to the wall, slipped down to a knee, so that they could spring in any direction.

The light had been reduced to the point where it was dusk in the corridor, difficult to see more than five or six feet. The low pitched hum was now throbbing through the area with enough force to cause the walls to pulsate.

With his men placed, Reed reached over from his position next to the wall, and grabbed the knob on the right door. He turned it slowly until it stopped. Now he hesitated, took a single deep breath, and then, fearing a trap of some kind, shoved the door inward.

There was no reaction from inside. Reed peeked around the corner, and then jumped back. He closed his eyes to replay the scene in his mind. It was chaos. Furniture was overturned. Files, paper, books, and other small items such as the serving set that would have been on the center of the table, were thrown on the floor. There was a twinkling of broken glass, and the pieces of a smashed chair. Light from one of the side rooms blazed out, illuminating the scene.

Now the hum was even louder. Reed knew that they had found the source, and that told him that something had built a machine in one part of the conference room. He knew nothing about its purpose, but only that it was either in a side room, or very near the door to one of those rooms. It was the source of the light he had seen and probably of the hum they felt.

Crouched there, one knee on the floor, Reed pointed at two men, and then pointed at the wall directly across the corridor from the conference room. The men, staying low, moved until they were centered on the door.

Reed then motioned the rest of the men forward, until they were next to the open door, or lined up along the wall next to him. He held up one hand with his fist closed and then extended his fingers, quietly counting down. When he reached one, he dived into the room, rolled and came up in a firing position, facing the bright light and open door of the side room.

Two men followed him, to provide cover, and then, slowly, the rest infiltrated the room, taking up positions behind the furniture, focusing their attention on the side room where the throbbing hum was centered, and where the lights were all brightly glowing.

Under Reed's quiet orders, the men spread out, focusing

their attention on the side room. They used the furniture for cover and pointed their weapons at the open door and its bright light.

Kneeling behind a chair, his rifle aimed, Reed suddenly understood the situation. There was an alien loose. He didn't know where it had come from. Those in the ship had been dead and autopsied, and the one that had survived was now also dead and dissected. But somehow, from somewhere, an alien had appeared and it was going attack his men. He knew it because there was no other answer and there was nothing else it could do. They had it trapped in that side room, where it built some kind of machine that sent out that maddening hum, and produced that bright, blinding white light. It would remain right there until it decided it wanted to leave and then it would come into the main room where he and his men waited for it.

Reed thought about attacking first, but he couldn't think of a way to do it without taking too many casualties. He didn't know the distribution of the enemy, though he couldn't believe there was more than one. He didn't know where it might be hiding and he would have liked to capture it, though his orders prevented it. He wanted to stop the alien, wanted to destroy the equipment it had built, but he didn't want to sacrifice any of his men to do it.

Something moved behind the light and two of the men opened fire. The rounds tore into the wall near the doorway, ripping several chunks of wood from it. There was a shattering noise like a window breaking. And there was a shriek that might have been pain that came from inside the room.

"Hold your fire," Reed yelled. "Hold your fire."

He glanced over the top of the chair, and then dropped back so that he was sitting on the floor, his back against the wood. Now Reed felt a terror deep in his belly. In that brief instant of movement, Reed had seen two small creatures. Or maybe three.

"Captain," said Clifford.

Before he could say more, the wall on the other side of the side door began to glow. A moment later it exploded outward but without a sound or a shock wave. The material that had been part of the wall shot across the floor. Debris was scattered in a floating cloud of dust.

Reed whirled and lifted his rifle. Before he could fire, a ruby-colored light touched the barrel, melting it. Reed dropped the now useless weapon to the floor and clawed at his holster. He jerked the pistol clear as small alien creatures swarmed into the room.

The aliens that Reed had seen originally in New Mexico were larger, maybe twice as big. The skin of these was darker, almost as if developed as a type of camouflage. They ran with a strange gait, their shoulders moving back and forth and their arms swinging. Only a few held weapons that looked like tubes with batteries attached to the end.

Reed fired as rapidly as he could, his pistol kicking upward. The slide locked back and he touched a button on the side. The magazine dropped and he pulled another from the pouch on his belt. He slammed it home, and opened fire again. He saw the bullets strike a little creature, knocking it down, but it then leaped up again, almost as if uninjured. It staggered forward.

Around him, his men were firing their weapons. The noise in the room, the chattering of the weapons, the shouting of the men, became overwhelming. It all blended into one loud, long roar that destroyed all other sound as a choking smoke from the firing began to obscure everything.

To his right, one of his men was touched by a red light, screamed and collapsed. On the left, two more fell, one tumbling over a chair to sprawl on the floor, half his head burned away. The other just screamed and screamed.

Reed's men kept firing, the smoke from the gunpowder combining with the haze drifting from the side area to make it nearly impossible to see anything other than flickers of movement and the ruby lights that flashed through the air, touching men, equipment and broken furniture. Flames erupted and the room filled with sudden heat.

The aliens tried to create a corridor, from the hole in the wall to the corridor door, that was impenetrable. They were somehow protecting some of their fellows and opening a pathway for escape. Reed fired at one of the aliens near the door, trying to aim for the same spot on the creature's chest as if he could punch a hole through it if he could hit it enough times in the right place quickly. It staggered back under the impact, and then toppled over.

An alien creature screamed with a sound like rubber tires on dry concrete. It toppled over, blood erupting from its chest. It was dragged out of the way by its fellows.

A second creature, smaller than the first, came from the door. Reed fired and saw the head explode. This creature was a foot tall, and seemed ill defined. Its legs and arms were fat and looked almost useless, as if stuck on the body as an afterthought. Later Reed would think of a dust bunny.

And then from the side room came a deep rumbling sound as if the machine, or whatever that had been causing the low frequency hum, had sped up. There was a detonation heard clearly over the sounds of the firing. The bright light went out and it was difficult, nearly impossible, to see inside the conference room where Reed and his men fought.

Now a larger creature, nearly full size, came from the room. Trailing it were five or six smaller replicas of itself. They moved in the jerky motion of an old-fashioned movie, the strobing of muzzle flashes giving little light. Reed aimed carefully, and fired three rapid shots. He hit one of the creatures in the shoulder. It spun and fell, its head outside the protective field. Reed fired again, and the creature snapped back, and flopped to its back. The others ignored it. They ran to door that led to the outside corridor, and disappeared through it. In seconds the last of them was out of the room.

Without an order, the men ceased firing. One man leaped forward, to the door, and then fired two last shots at the fleeing aliens.

The other soldiers lowered their weapons and surveyed the damage around them. Reed sat back, and then leaned back against the wall. He studied the destruction, giving himself a moment to think. They room was still filled with smoke, but the noise had stopped. It was suddenly quiet as a tomb.

Broken bits of furniture, chunks of the wall, and pieces of the doors were scattered on the floor. Several men lay sprawled, not moving. One of the smaller alien creatures was still where it had fallen earlier, either overlooked by its fellows or ignored because it was dead.

Ventilators began to suck the smoke from the room and lights that had been dimmed slowly brightened. The atmosphere inside was beginning to return to normal. One of the men who had been hit in the fight rolled over and sat up slowly. He now seemed to be uninjured.

Reed took a deep breath. The air smelled of cordite. It was a sulphur stink that he knew well from the firing line. He stood up, unsure of what to do. Military training told him he should pursue the aliens, but rational thought told him that was useless. They had the power to overwhelm any human force sent after them and they were only interested in getting out.

"Captain?" said Clifford.

"Check on the men. Get a casuality count. And get a couple men on the door."

"Yes, sir."

Reed turned and walked to the door so that he could look out into the hallway. Two men were sprawled there, but it was clear that they were very much alive. Only one seemed injured and the other still under partial effects of the alien technology.

Reed turned and shouted over his shoulder, "Need some medical assistance here." He walked to the injured man, saw a smoking hole in his uniform and then a bad burn on the point of his shoulder and along his neck.

He looked up and tried to grin. "I'm not hurt bad, Captain."

"You just take it easy."

The other man had moved around so that he was sitting on the floor, his back to the wall. His head hung down, almost as if he was drunk, or about to be sick. Finally he lifted his head and said, "Now what?"

To Reed that was a very good question. He knew that the alien had reproduced, though he didn't know how. There was no other answer because all the creatures had been accounted for in the morgue and lab. Five on the craft and five bodies.

But here there had been more, ranging from a nearly full sized replica to small, juvenile-like creatures.

He knew that he need to tell all this to Douglass. Had to let him know that there were more creatures in the facility. He didn't have to explain it. That would be the job of the scientists. All he had to do was report the new information.

He got to his feet and walked into the conference. He spotted Clifford kneeling near the body of one man. Reed said, "I need a runner to alert Douglass."

Before Clifford could move, one of the man came forward. "I'll go, Captain."

"Okay. Tell him what happened in here. Tell him that the aliens have reproduced in some fashion, and tell him that they got away from us. They headed down the right hallway, but we didn't give chase. Tell him what you saw here."

"Yes, sir."

"And I don't suppose that I have to tell you to take the other corridor?"

"No, sir."

"When you get there, tell him we need medical assistance, and that we'll be coming in. You stay with them."

"Yes, sir."

Reed then walked over to inspect the side room. Sitting in the center of it was something about the size of a fifty-five gallon drum but that looked more like a canister vacuum cleaner. There were wires hooked to the top that led to another device, this one square, about a foot high, that sat on the floor. It was plugged into the wall, which meant the aliens had been drawing their power from the facility. Although there was no indication that the device, whatever it was, was still working, Reed crossed the floor and pulled the plug. Nothing happened.

Clifford looked in. "Captain, we're set out here."

Reed nodded and looked at Clifford. "You know what we have to do now?"

"Yes, sir, I know."

"How about the men? They know?"

"Yes, sir."

"Okay, we see if we can pick up a trail from those creatures.

We know a little about them. The bigger ones won't be able to hide easily. The smaller ones will probably be around the first. We'll go after them and we shoot to kill."

"Yes, sir."

Reed thought about leaving a guard, but for what reason. The whole floor was sealed and he didn't want to expose any of his men to danger of remaining behind. If Douglass wanted a guard here, let him make that decision. Let him tell the scientists about this.

He walked to the door and looked down the corridor. It didn't look as if there was anything amiss in it. The only damage done by the combat was right in front of him. Farther down, there wasn't even trash on the floor.

"Okay. Let's get going and let's be careful."

Clifford grinned. "Yes, sir."

CHAPTER 63

July 15, 1947
Over the Rainbow
Nevada

Moore wasn't sure who had an overall roster, or how he could get one at that time. All the records were stored in his administrative assistant's safe on Level Two. There he had a list of everyone who was assigned to the facility, a list of who was on temporary assignment, and who had signed in, or out, in the last seventy-two hours. But that was in his office and did him no good now.

So, Moore, standing at the front of the gymnasium slash auditorium, didn't know exactly how many people were assigned to the facility, and more importantly, he didn't know how many people were inside it when he was ordered to move everyone up to Level One. He knew the majority of them were there, in the gymnasium, with the exception of the soldiers who were conducting the search and some of the scientists, including the woman, Danni Hackett, who was, the last he heard, on the lowest level. He didn't know how he was supposed to account for everyone without his records and with people circulating at their whim.

Moore looked around and spotted his assistant, an older woman who was quite good at her job. She took all aspects of it seriously, believing in national security. Her husband of fifteen years had been killed trying to get off the beach at Tarawa. They had no children, so her life had shifted from caring for her husband to caring for Moore's office.

She was standing with a small group of women, all near a couple of cots that had been set up by the soldiers who were

now creating an emergency shelter. The soldiers were she-
parding the people toward one end of the gym so that they
could work in the other. The cots were separated by small
tables, a few of which had lamps on them.

Another group of soldiers were bringing blankets, sheets
and pillows into the gym. They were placing them on the bare
mattresses of the cots. Moore knew that somewhere there were
Army cooks preparing a meal, probably just sandwiches for
noon but they would come up with something better for the
evening.

Moore walked across the hardwood floor and raised a hand
as he shouted "Mrs. Harvey?" As he called her name the word
matronly popped into his mind. She was matronly. Attractive,
but somewhat stocky. She wore he hair pulled back in a bun
that looked almost stained with white. Moore had never seen
her hair down loose, or in any other style.

She separated herself from a knot of younger women and
walked over quickly. "Yes, Doctor Moore. How might I be of
service?" she asked.

"Can you get me some sort of figures on how many people
have not responded to our evacuation order. The soldiers are
engaged in their hunt or working up here so I'm not concerned
about them. I want to know about our civilians. Get with the
various supervisors and see if we can identify who might be
missing."

"Certainly, Doctor. Though such a count might not be very
accurate."

"Yes, yes, I know. It's just that I would like some kind of
idea about who is still on the lower levels and who is up here
with us."

She turned to go and then stopped, looking frightened.
"What are we going to do?"

Moore glanced at her, surprised by the question. She rarely
asked them, unless there was something that she didn't understand. She carried out her instructions as best she could,
delegating the responsibility throughout the organization to
complete all the assignments. She never seemed to be bothered
by a request and she never allowed her personal opinions or

feelings to infect her once given an assignment.

"I think that we are going to get out of here," said Moore, quietly. "I think the military here, or the Pentagon, is going to want us to evacuate until they can figure out what they are going to do. They're going to want us out because they're not going to want civilian critique of their actions. I want to be ready to carry out that assignment, when it comes, and to do it, I need to know who is where."

"Yes, Doctor."

Moore watched her begin to work her way through the crowd, talking to the area supervisors, who then began to search for their subordinates. He walked back, toward the platform that was used as a stage during official presentations.

He heard something near the entrance and turned. The doors were thrown open and four men, three in uniform and one in a wrinkled gray suit, entered. One of the military men turned to talk with a guard. The others seemed to search the gymnasium.

Moore turned toward them and hurried across the floor. As he approached, he said, "Doctor Smith?"

"What in the hell is happening in here, Doctor," asked Smith sharply.

Moore looked at the man whose instructions had been so secret that Moore was unable to learn what they were, even though he had been cleared at the highest level. He looked at the man who was now demanding answers and resented the attitude. He was tempted to tell him it was none of his business, but said, instead, "We are engaged in an exercise here."

"Exercise?" repeated Smith. "What sort of exercise?"

"Doctor Smith, I'm sure that you understand the security regulations that are in effect here." Moore was proud of himself for that. It gave Smith a taste of his own medicine.

"This is not idle curiosity," said Smith. "I have a valid reason for asking."

"I'm sure that you do," said Moore. "However, at this point in time, I believe that our security outweighs whatever reason you have for asking."

Smith glared at Moore, but Moore stared right back. It was

clear that Moore was not going to be intimidated. "If something happens, I need to know," said Smith.

Moore nodded and then turned his attention to another ten or twelve people walked through the far double doors. He moved as if he was going to greet them. He said nothing else to Smith. He thought that he had won that confrontation.

CHAPTER 64

Reed and his team had reached the area of the elevators without seeing a sign of the alien creatures. They had probed into offices, apartments, closets, storage areas, labs and break rooms. They had opened cabinets, looked under sinks, and behind file cabinets, bookcases, workbenches and desks. They had found nothing to suggest that the aliens had been around, or how they had gotten off that level.

There, they had seen Douglass and Reed had told him that they would continue down, into the bowels of the facility, searching for Hackett and others. Douglass had not objected and Reed had broken his team down into a smaller unit that included Clifford and several others including Don Hammon, Anthony Franzone, David Johnson, Tim Dupont and Dean Simpson.

When he had gathered his men, he pulled his pistol and dropped the partially filled magazine to the floor. He had held out a hand and said, "Let me have some ammo."

Douglass had taken two magazines from his ammo pouch and handed them over. Reed slammed one home in the butt of his pistol and let the slide chamber a round. Carefully, he lowered the hammer.

"You men get as much ammo as you can here. I don't know how much we'll need, or if we'll need it at all, but it is better to have it."

Clifford said, "Yes, sir. You heard the Captain. Let's get ready to go."

As Douglass had gathered his men to move up toward the surface, Reed moved to the elevator and pushed the call button. The incongruity of the act was not lost on him. He was about to move into another possible combat environment and he was going to take the elevator into a fight. Not only that, he was waiting for an elevator like a couple about to head for the honeymoon suite, or a businessman about to ride down to the restaurant.

The light over the door came on, and the doors slid open. Reed, as he had done before, stepped in so that he could block the door and waved his men in. Once everyone was inside, Reed pushed the button to take them down.

When they reached the bottom, Reed held the door closed, and set the men where he wanted them so that they would all have some protection and all fields of fire would be covered when the door opened. As they leveled their weapons, Reed allowed the door to slide open. The corridor in front of them, though brightly lighted, was empty.

"Captain," said Clifford, his voice seeming unnaturally loud.

"Yes?"

"Might I suggest that one man stay here to hold the elevator?"

Reed grinned because he had told Douglass that he would send it back up. But there were other elevators that could take them to the top level and no reason for Reed to cut off his only line of retreat.

"Yes, sergeant," said Reed. "You may suggest that. Dupont, you wait here and hold the door open. If, somehow, they recall the elevator, you bring it back down as quickly as you can."

"Yes, sir."

Reed stepped out into the corridor, his pistol in his hand. He walked slowly to the vault door, which stood open, a result of the general evacuation order. The guard area, behind the thick, bulletproof glass, though empty, was still lighted. One chair was tipped over, but everything else looked as it should. There was even the sign-in and -out sheet on the clipboard sitting on the guard's desk.

Walking along the wall, his left shoulder nearly touching it, Reed moved forward, to the vault door. He looked down the corridor and again saw nothing and no one. When the others had joined him, and fanned out, he stepped though and began walking along the wall, his weapon pointed out in front of him, his eyes moving from one side of the corridor to the other.

He stopped at the first closed door. He believed that all the alien creatures were on the upper levels, but he didn't know that for sure. He could think of no reason they would try to reach the lowest level, unless it was to get at the ship. Reed knew that it had been brought in, but he didn't know exactly where it was. Maybe the aliens were trying to get to the ship, but then they would have to try to launch it through the facility and he didn't believe that to be possible.

He stopped for a moment to think about the tactics. It was a simple recon and rescue. Grab the people and retreat to the elevators. Get out and let Douglass and his superiors decide what to do. All he had to do was make sure that his line of retreat was preserved.

"Captain?"

Reed waved a hand at Clifford to silence him. The aliens hadn't sortied from their location. They hadn't attacked until Reed and his men had trapped them in one small room. Then they had fought their way out and run. If the aliens maintained that attitude, then Reed should be able to get to Hackett and the morgue without any trouble.

All this meant that Reed could take a calculated risk and push forward toward the morgue without dividing his small force, and without searching for the enemy. Infantry tactics demanded that he understand the size and distribution of the enemy forces before he formed any sort of a battle plan. But this situation was different. It was a rescue of sorts that demanded he avoid the enemy and to retreat at the first hint of trouble.

Reed nodded once to himself, and then waved a hand. He passed the closed door, sure that he was making a tactical error but he kept pushing forward, until he reached the double, brushed aluminum doors that marked the morgue. There he hesitated, not sure of what he would find beyond them.

Without words, he deployed the men as he had at the conference room. The sergeant on one side of the door, his weapon ready, the two soldiers with him. One of them leaned forward, knelt, and put a hand on the door knob. When Reed nodded, the man twisted the knob and threw the door open.

Reed leaned through the opening, hit the floor and rolled once, coming up on a knee, his weapon at the ready. He was up against a cabinet, aware of the knobs behind him, pressing into him.

The room was empty. There was a desk to the right and there were the refrigerated storage units to the left. There were stainless steel sinks near them, and a preparation table. The floor was clean, the walls painted white and a number of long flourescent lights overhead.

Across from there was another set of doors. These led into the autopsy room. Reed moved toward them, ready to dive right or left or to open fire. He wasn't sure what to expect when he reached those doors, afraid that Hackett might be dead beyond them. He was sure he would find her. She had to be there.

He reached those doors, moved along them carefully, and then pushed them open. Centered in the room was a table the looked more like a pedestal. There was a huge, bright light over it, shining down. Two motion picture cameras, on tripods, were pointed down at the naked body on the table. Two people stood over it, one male and one female. Both wore cloth face masks, gloves, and surgical scrubs.

"What in the hell are you doing here?" asked Hackett, her voice unmistakable and filled with anger.

Slowly Reed stood up as he lowered his weapon. He took a single step forward and then froze, unsure of what he should do. After all, there was a body on the table.

"Captain," said Clifford, who stood just inside the door, his weapon held at the ready.

Reed shot him a glance and then looked back at Hackett. "We've got to get out of here."

"I have work to do."

"Not anymore. The situation has gotten out of hand. We have been ordered to evacuate."

Hackett put her scalpel back on the instrument tray that was next to her. She started to pull at her gloves, but stopped. "I can't leave now."

Reed said, "The orders have been given. We are all to evacuate now." Then he added, "Danni, things are beginning to break down. We have got to get out."

She looked at the body, knowing that it wouldn't go anywhere but that it would continue to decay and that it would be contaminated, if by nothing else than the air around them. Anything that she had hoped to learn from it would be lost if she didn't complete her work, or get it back into one of the refrigerated lockers. She made a snap decision. "Help me," she said.

One of the other soldiers, Simpson, set his rifle down, leaning it against the wall. He jumped forward, standing ready.

The man with Hackett, who was standing to the side watching, looking bemused, removed his mask and grinned. "So, Jack. You don't say anything to your friends."

Reed laughed. "Didn't expect to see you down here."

"Someone had to protect Danni while you were off playing soldier. I volunteered."

"We need to get out of here," said Reed.

There was a distant, dull, explosion of some kind.

"What was that?" asked Hackett.

"Sounded like artillery," said Reed. "Distant artillery. We need to get moving."

Wheeler rolled a gurney into position near the autopsy table. Carefully they lifted the body from the table to the gurney, and then rolled it over to the storage area. They opened one of the refrigerated containers, loaded in the body and then closed the door.

Simpson hurried back and grabbed his weapon. Hackett stripped off the rubber gloves and mask and dropped them on the floor. When she and Wheeler were ready, Reed turned and walked to the door.

They began to hurry down the corridor. From somewhere above came a deep rumble and then a loud crash. As they reached the vault door area, smoke and dust boiled through the doors, blocking vision and choking them. Reed turned his back, closed his eyes and held his breath.

When the dust settled, Reed moved forward cautiously. He could see the elevator door was partially opened and beyond it was a rock strewn rubble that held dark black cable and a few bits of painted wood.

Clifford said, "That's it. We're fucked."

Reed wasn't thinking of that. He was thinking of the man who had been left behind to cover the access to the elevator to make sure that the wasn't called to a higher floor. He had been inside the elevator. Reed crouched and looked through the opening in the door. There was a spreading red stain that was blood. It had pooled in one spot and was beginning to run. Reed knew that it meant the man was dead. There was too much blood and too much debris in the elevator.

"How are we going to get out?" asked Hackett.

Reed fell back so that he was sitting on the floor, his eyes on the blood. He wiped a hand over his face and said, "Maybe we can climb out through the shaft. Should be a maintenance ladder in there."

Clifford moved forward, pushed on one of the doors, forcing it to open about a foot wider. He stuck his head in, and then backed away. "There's tons of debris in here. We're not going to be able to clear it."

"Then we're trapped," said Hackett.

But Reed knew that wasn't quite right. Something tickled the back of his head and then he remembered. "There is an access tunnel. Big tunnel that they built when they created this place. They wanted access in case they needed to bring in something larger than the elevator would allow."

"So what?" asked Clifford.

"Leads to the surface. We can use it to get out."

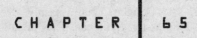

CHAPTER 65

Once Reed had taken his men down to the bottom level, Douglass began to evacuate the third level, sending his men up to the top. Douglass followed them up and when the doors opened, he stepped out, into the main corridor. He followed his men to the double doors that lead inward, to the gymnasium, was stopped by the guard who added his name to a list, and then walked out, onto the floor, looking for Dr. Moore.

Douglass found him, surrounded by a small group of men and women. Moore was saying that he thought the military might have overreacted when they suggested that everyone move to the top level. He was sure that the danger wasn't as bad as the military had said it was.

Douglass just shook his head and interrupted. He said, "Doctor Moore, if I might have a moment of your time."

Moore grinned broadly and said, "We were just talking about you."

"Yes, I heard," said Douglass, his voice hard. "But never mind that now. We need, or rather I need, to make a secure telephone call."

"The communications room is on the second level, Colonel."

"I know where it is," snapped Douglass. "I was telling you about the need to use it as a courtesy. One that I am not required to extend."

"What do you plan on telling them?"

"That, Doctor, is none of your business."

Moore waved a hand and said, "I can't keep everyone bottled up in here for very long."

"Actually," said Douglass, rather nastily, "you can keep them here as long as I say you can. They are all government employees or military men. They'll do as ordered."

Moore was surprised by the tone and by the attitude. He said, "Of course."

Douglass said, "I'm trying to get some instructions here. I'll let you know what I learn."

"Thank you."

Douglass headed for the door. He snapped his fingers, got Euless' attention and yelled, "I want half a dozen men with me."

Euless pointed to several of his men and waved them forward. They hurried to the door and then followed Douglass through it. They ran down the corridor, through the vault door, and to the elevators. Douglass entered one, waited for the soldiers to join him, and then pushed the button for the second level.

The only difference between the top level and the second was that the second was deserted. Nothing was out of place. The vault door was closed, the guard's room brightly lighted but empty, and the reception area vacant. Douglass walked to the vault door, dialed in a combination, and then, with the help of two enlisted men, opened it.

With the door opened, Douglass hurried down the corridor and found the communications center. The door was locked, but he pointed an M-1 rifle at the knob and lock and fired twice. The first round dented the metal plate and the second one destroyed it. The door knob fell free and the door swung partially open.

"You're going to catch hell for that, Colonel," said Euless.

"I doubt anyone is ever going to know what I have done," responded Douglass.

He pushed open the door. Beyond it was a waist-high desk and beyond that were a number of radio and telephone stations. There were teletype machines in the corner to receive and transmit message traffic, radio set to the various military nets, which would receive or transmit unclassified material, and several telephones linked into the secure net. Encryption devices, code machines, classified typewriters, and classified documents were housed in the small vault off in a side room.

Douglass walked to the counter, lifted a segment of it and then opened the half-door. He walked to where the telephones were set and sat down. He picked up the handset and then looked back at Euless and the men with him. "Okay. Someone guard the door, someone watch the main entrance to this level. I'll be through here in a few minutes."

When that was set, Douglass turned around and dialed a four digit number which connected him to the net. He waited and when he heard the operator's voice said, "I need scramble communications with Jolly Roger." That was LeMay's code name for the month.

"Wait one."

There was a series of snaps, clicks and beeps and then someone answered at the far end. Douglass could barely hear the voice. All he understood was that LeMay was out of the office and that it would be a moment before a secure line could be established.

After several minutes, Douglass heard, "LeMay."

"General. John Douglass here."

There was a moment's hesitation and then, "Okay, Douglass."

"This is a secure line."

"Go ahead." Even with the jury-rigged hookup, LeMay's irritation came through.

"We have a situation here."

"I'm aware of some of that problem. I have been in communication with Doctor Moore."

"Yes, sir, but he is not cognizant of all the facts."

"Stop beating around the bush and tell me your problems."

"Yes, sir." Douglass filled LeMay in on everything that had happened, including the firefight that had taken place.

"He let them get away?" asked LeMay. "I'll have his ass for that."

"It might not have been his fault," said Douglass. "We don't understand a lot of what has been happening."

"Cut the shit, Douglass."

"Yes, sir."

"Here is what you do, now. You get the people out of there. You move them off the base. You'll find that rangers now control the perimeter. I'll have their orders amended within the quarter hour. I want everyone thirty miles away in an hour. Do you understand that?"

Douglass understood the orders but he didn't know the reason. He was about to ask when he realized that LeMay would not tell him. LeMay would just say that he had his orders and he was to obey them.

"Yes, sir."

"There is one other thing," said LeMay. "You must ensure that the creatures stay below ground. I want each level sealed. I want no one moving lower. You get the people out, but you make sure that no one goes below. You destroy the elevators and you seal the stairs. You got that?"

"Yes, sir."

"I don't care how you do it, but you make sure that those lower levels are sealed. I don't want these things escaping into the desert."

"Yes, sir."

"You do this right and they won't be able to get to their ship. They'll remain right there, stuck in that hole."

"I understand, General."

"If you have nothing else," said LeMay, but then broke the connection.

Douglass cradled the headset and then rocked back in his chair. He took a deep breath as he thought about what he had been told. He was to seal off the upper level from those below it and the best way to do that was with explosives. He would need to destroy the elevator shafts and the stairways. He would have to bury them under rock and dirt and debris. Those below would have to take their chances because Douglass understood that LeMay feared the aliens would somehow grab their ship and get it out of the facility. If he plugged the exit routes, the aliens would not be able to survive and they would not get out into the desert and they would not get their ship out. Later, LeMay could send in another team who would excavate the elevator shafts or the stairways, and he would again have access to the ship.

Douglass stood up and walked to the door. To Euless he said, "We've got an assignment."

"Yes, sir."

"I need to talk to Moore and then we'll get busy."

CHAPTER | 66

July 15, 1947
Over the Rainbow
Nevada

Douglass stood back, near the vault door, as Sergeant Thomas Oyler worked to set the explosive charge that would close the elevator shaft. Oyler was that rare man: an explosives expert who still had all his fingers, his hearing, and had no scars from a premature detonation. Although in his mid-thirties, his hair was jet black. He had even, somewhat thin features and a chin that was larger than normal. There was a twinkle in his eyes that told all he enjoyed blowing things up because he was very good at it. Douglass was glad that Oyler was on the team.

Oyler, who had been crouched near the open door of one of the elevators, stood up and backed away. He looked at Douglass and said, "What I have done is set this up to drop the cars themselves into the shaft, or, to drop the equipment and then some support into the shaft. Should get some good cratering on the sides which will dump rock and dirt and plug the hole."

"I'm not sure what that means."

"It means, sir, that I have set the charges in such a way that rather than expending all their force outward, they will create craters in the walls and dump that material into the elevator shafts, plugging them. It sort of digs a hole on the wall of the shaft and that material falls down, into it, blocking it."

"How easy will it be to clean it out?"

Oyler shrugged. "Depends on the equipment you bring in. Shouldn't be all that difficult, but the better plan would be to fill these shafts with concrete and dig new ones."

"When can you detonate?"

"Just as soon as you give the word." Oyler grinned. "We can use the vault doors for protection. Use an electric detonator, and we can drop it at any time."

"Okay," said Douglass. "Give me five minutes and then we'll go."

"Yes, sir. That's up to you. I've got the charges set and tamped down."

Douglass hurried back up corridor to the gymnasium. He saw that there was a double line of people at the far end, exiting into the emergency stairway. He walked across the floor and found Moore standing near the doors with a clipboard in his hand.

Douglass said, "We're ready to drop the elevators."

"No, no, no," said Moore. "I don't have everyone accounted for. You have to wait."

"I don't think you understand, Doctor, I have my orders and I'm ready."

Moore looked horrified. "But we still have people inside the facility. They'll be trapped on the lower floors."

"Yes, that might be, but there are other considerations."

"Other considerations? How in the hell can you think like that? These are people whose lives you are about to take."

"On the contrary," said Douglass, "I'm not taking anyone's life. I am sealing the lower levels of this facility so that we can be assured that the . . ." he looked at the crowd moving forward and lowered his voice. "So that certain events, escapes, don't take place. We'll be able to enter later."

"My God, man, I don't understand you at all."

"Doctor, just get your people to the surface. We'll be closing off this exit next and if you are not clear, then you won't get clear."

"But . . ."

"Doctor, we'll give everyone a fair chance. They all know about the evacuation order. If they are not here, we must assume that they have exited through some other means."

"Other than the elevators, this is it," said Moore.

Douglass tired of the argument. "I have my orders and I intend to carry them out. You need to hurry." He spun then and walked back across the hard wood floor.

Outside, he found two of his men and said, "I want you to wait right here. Make sure that no one exits. We'll be back in five or ten minutes and then we'll all get out."

"Yes, sir."

Douglass, the adrenalin pumping now, ran back down the corridor to the vault door. Oyler was sitting in the guard's room, behind the desk, his feet up. Had he not been wearing fatigues, and had he been smoking a cigar, he would have looked like an executive waiting for his next appointment.

"You ready?" asked Douglass.

Oyler dropped his feet to the floor and stood up. "I'm set, sir. All I have to do is attach the leads to the detonator and we can go."

"Then let's do it."

Oyler walked to the door and bent over. He picked up the small detonator. It was green, had two connections for the wires, and a black L-shaped handle on top. He would twist it rapidly to the left, generate an electric current that was strong enough to fire the blasting caps, and the explosives would detonate.

He walked into the corridor and picked up the wire that came through a small crack between the vault door and the wall. He looked at Douglass and said, "I don't think the shock wave out here will be strong enough to push the door shut, sir, but even if it does, it won't matter. It'll cut the wire but we'll have already detonated the explosives."

Douglass wanted to tell Oyler to shut up because he had no interest in the mechanics of blocking the elevator shafts, but Oyler was obviously enjoying his work. Douglass didn't want to dampen that enthusiasm. He said again, "Let's do it."

Oyler dropped to one knee, attached the wires, fitted the black handle into the top of the detonator and then grinned broadly. He yelled, "Fire in the hole! Fire in the hole!" He waited two, three seconds, and twisted the handle.

Douglass was about to say the explosives had failed to det

onate, when there was a flat bang that threw dust out of the elevator shaft and into the hall. There was a tremble in the floor and then a rumble as rock, dirt and debris fell into the elevator shaft.

Oyler fell back, against the wall, grinning. "I think that's got it."

Douglass pushed open the vault door and walked to the elevator shaft. One of the stainless steel doors was buckled outward. Douglass looked through the opening into the semi-darkness. Dust hung in the air. Cables, cut by the explosion, swung like a pendulum, and the access ladder was twisted out of shape, hanging by a single support. Douglass wished that he had a flashlight so that he could inspect the shaft.

Almost as if reading his mind, Oyler handed him one, saying, "I think you'll need this."

The blockage began about four feet down the shaft. Douglass didn't know if the rubble filled the shaft or if these was just the one blockage, but he didn't care. His job had been done. The elevators would provide no escape for the aliens.

To Oyler, he said, "That's got it. Let's get out of here."

Oyler was disappointed. "That's it? That explosion was a thing of beauty. I filled that shaft with rocks and dirt and all you can say is 'That's got it.' " Then he remembered that Douglass was an officer and appended, "Sir."

"Take a commendation medal out of petty cash," said Douglass. "Let's get out of here. You have another explosion to arrange."

"Glad to do it." After a moment, he remembered to append, "Sir."

CHAPTER 67

```
July 15, 1947
Over the Rainbow
Nevada
```

The sounds of explosions, though very distant, and almost impossible to hear, rumbled up through the floor. Moore knew that Douglass was destroying the elevators but was surprised, not by a single detonation or two, but several, in rapid succession. Moore looked around, but there were no high-ranking military people in the gymnasium. They were all out somewhere, either moving people up, into the hangar, or with Douglass.

Mrs. Harvey, who had finally been able to get him a count of how many were missing, came toward him, her face pale. She said, "What is happening?"

Moore said, "Nothing to worry about."

"What are we going to do?"

"I think it's time for you and me to move to the surface."

The relief on her face was unmistakable. She almost smiled. "Now?"

"Now. Anyone left here who is unable to use the stairs?"

"I don't think so."

"Okay. Let's get everyone moved back toward the side doors. Get McMann over here. He should have the keys to unlock any of the doors up top and to pop the emergency exit."

"I think I saw him sitting over by the engineers."

"I'll need him and the supervisors so that we can get organized. Did we get the names of those who aren't here?"

Harvey said, "Most of them but I figure that we will b

back in our office in a few hours and then we can learn exactly who missed the evacuation order."

Moore rubbed a hand over his face, and then used a knuckle on his eye. He was thinking rapidly. The only thing that he could think of was that they needed to get to the surface and he was no longer all that interested in those who remain trapped on the lower levels.

CHAPTER 68

July 15, 1947
Over the Rainbow
Nevada

Cavanaugh's soldiers moved onto the base carefully, spreading out along the runways of the old airfield and beginning to infiltrate the buildings and hangars. They found the car park, looking like an overstocked auto dealership, the supply depot that held enough dry goods and canned food to last a battalion for the better part of a year, and the military motor pool that held everything from jeeps and small trucks to a single tank that looked as if it had last been serviced the day before. Everything was parked inside the hangars, or stored in the larger buildings so that nothing was visible from the air. Soviet surveillance, if that had been a threat, would have been defeated by the careful placement of the equipment and supplies.

Cavanaugh knew that there were several hundred people on the base, though he had seen no sign of them. At night there were lights on the perimeter, lights along the streets, and lights on the exterior of the buildings, but nothing showing at the windows and no indication of any movement through the dark. Given his observations, he would have guessed that no one was assigned to the base other than a few caretakers, and that the lights were set on some sort of timing device, or the few guards that they had seen were required to turn on the lights at some kind of central power station.

Through the binoculars, he could pick out the individual soldiers as they opened doors, peeked in windows, and searched through buildings, looking for the people of the base. They moved slowly, toward the center, to one hangar set near the main, east-west runway. Cavanaugh, based on his observations, believed that some of the people were on the inside of the hangar.

A company of soldiers surrounded the area, standing in a large circle, facing the building while extra men covered the various exits including the huge doors that could accommodate transport aircraft. They seemed to hesitate, as if waiting for orders, but Cavanaugh knew that they were letting the rest of the battalion finish sweeping the area so that they could be used as a reserve, if such was needed.

Then, as if warning that the base perimeter had been penetrated, a klaxon sounded. The soldiers didn't react to it, their mission to guard the hangar area. One of the huge doors began to open automatically. Cavanaugh could see into the interior, but it seemed to be deserted.

A squad moved forward, cautiously, and two men broke off, running for the side of the door. The others spread out to protect one another as they walked forward, into the hangar. At the far end, a door flew open and people began to pour out. At first, surprised that there were soldiers in the hangar, they hesitated, and then swarmed forward.

The squad leader, afraid they would be overrun, held up a hand and ordered, "Halt where you are. Stop right there."

One of the older men, wearing a business suit smeared with dirt, hurried forward. He was followed by three other men, one in a suit and two in Navy officer's uniforms. As Moore approached, he said, "I'm Doctor Moore and am in charge of this facility. Who are you?"

"U.S. Army with orders to contain the perimeter."

Moore laughed and then nodded. "Right. Well, you can let us out of here now."

"No sir. You will remain here."

Moore came forward. "You don't understand. We have got to get off this facility."

"No sir. You don't understand. You will be held here until I hear different."

Moore looked at the man, the contempt on his face. He said, "You're making a career decision here, sergeant. I am ordering vou to retreat and allow us to get to our cars."

The sergeant took a step back and said, "My orders are quite clear and very simple."

Moore shouted. "You will get the hell out of the way right now."

The sergeant reached down and flipped off the safety on his rifle. He raised his eyebrows in question, but didn't say a word to Moore.

"Okay, Sergeant. Point taken. Let me suggest that you communicate with your commanding officer and suggest that we ᵇe allowed to leave this facility."

"Let's get everyone rounded up, sir, and then I'll alert the Colonel for additional instructions. I'm sure that we can get this worked out."

Major General Curtis LeMay sat in a padded seat that had plenty of leg room, a reclining back, and a wide seat. It was as comfortable as any office chair he had ever had, and it was locked to the floor in the back of a transport aircraft on what was known as the "comfort pallet." It was used by the Army Air Forces when general officers, members of congress, or other important people were required to use a military transport. It just wouldn't be right for those important people to be relegated to the troop seats that amounted to little more than canvas stretched between two hollow metal poles.

LeMay was wearing a class A uniform complete with his various awards and decorations stacked above the left breast pocket and topped by a shiny pair of command pilot's wings. He looked as if he was about to be called into the White House, rather than on an aircraft heading for Nevada. He was sitting quietly, his briefcase open by the side of his seat, and a file folder open on his lap. He was ignoring the open file folder, but had a hand on the briefcase as if afraid that one of the crew might try to steal it.

He had carried with him all the information he thought he needed concerning the operation in Nevada, including the speculations by some of the medical staff that some sort of new infection had broken out there. LeMay was no physician, but he was enough of a scientist to realize that they were just flat wrong on that point. An infection, if brought by the alien creatures, would have appeared in other locations first. Too many people who traveled too far and wide had been exposed for the infection to be limited to just the Nevada facility. Clearly the problem was something else and LeMay suspected that it was related to the living creature. The problems had all occurred within close proximity of it.

LeMay had been reading the latest of the reports, transmitted by secure telephone line from Nevada to the communications center in the Pentagon where it had been decoded and typed for him. Almost no one knew what it said, or what the half dozen other reports had told him. On the subject of the alien creatures, he was the best-informed man on the planet, which explained why he was not concerned with a deadly disease. He had some answers that others didn't have.

Some of the reports were amusing. The speculation by scientists who have little in the way of information was wild. The alien creatures, because of their light weight and brittle bone structures were the products of a planet smaller than Earth, or rather an environment that had a lower gravitational pull. Gravity much heavier than Earth's would crush the little creatures and break their bones. To some of the scientists, this suggested Mars as the likely home world, though most believe the beings were from a planet outside the Solar System.

The eyes, according to some, suggested the alien home world was dim. That they might be farther from their sun than Earth was from its sun. LeMay realized it might also mean that the aliens developed as nocturnal hunters which would put an evolutionary premium on sight in a dark environment.

LeMay grinned. Nocturnal hunters. Predators. He was assuming that evolution favored the predator with intelligence. Pack hunting and solo pursuit demanded that the predator be smarter than the prey. All the prey had to do was run, the faster the better, but the predator had to figure out the best way to capture the prey. Those predators that couldn't, starved to death. For LeMay, intelligence developed in the predator, and to him, it meant the alien creatures had developed from predators. It made them deadly, skillful, intelligent and untrustworthy.

LeMay had seen information on the alien industrial base,

but he believed it to be more fantasy than rational, intelligent extrapolation. All they knew was that the aliens had created a ship that could travel interstellar distances. LeMay and his scientists knew nothing about the investment needed to do that. Flying Lindbergh across the Atlantic was an expensive proposition, but now it didn't require the same sort of financial investment. That might hold true for interstellar flight. Once they figured out how to do it, the cost per flight fell off sharply.

LeMay had looked at the biologist reports on the dissections but those were incomplete. Study of the organs and their relation to the body had not been conducted yet. The function of many were not understood, though there seemed to be a consensus that the large organ in the chest was a combination of lung and heart creating a central pumping station. To LeMay, trained in redundancy, the single organ would make the aliens easily vulnerable. Compared to humans, the aliens seemed overly fragile.

What LeMay knew from reading the reports was that very little was known. Had their craft contained any books, any written records, and photographic records, additional information could have been derived. But they had found nothing like that. LeMay knew it had to be there, they just didn't recognize it for what it was. When they found it, then they would make some progress at understanding the aliens. Until then, about all they could say was that the aliens were technologically advanced because they had built a spaceship, they were social creatures because there had been a flight crew, and that they were biologically fragile creatures. And that was about it.

One of the flight engineers, a young sergeant who had been in a bomber crew in the South Pacific during the war, approached cautiously. He knelt with one knee on the hard metal plating of the aircraft's deck and waited for LeMay to acknowledge him.

LeMay closed the file folder and then looked down at the sergeant. "Yes?"

"Communication for you, General. On the flight deck."

LeMay stuffed the file back into his briefcase, unbuckled his seatbelt, and then stood up, swaying slightly in the gentle rocking of the aircraft as it droned on. He walked toward the cockpit, nearly fell as the plane dipped suddenly, but steadied himself against the bulkhead.

The pilot looked up and grinned. "Have someone on the radio for you, General. Scrambled communication." The pilot stripped the earphones from his head and offered them to LeMay.

"Thank you," said LeMay. He put on the earphones and heard the carrier wave, letting him know that the radio was working. He took the microphone and said, "This is LeMay." As he did, he thought about the war. No one would have used his own name over the radio in a combat environment because the enemy might hear it and then use that information against the United States. Call signs were important to keep everyone guessing and to keep the enemy from finding a man's family and using that information against him.

"General, I'm on the primary location."

LeMay grinned, translating that in his mind. It was simply code that told him there was a problem in Nevada.

"Understood."

"The word is, 'Platinum.' "

LeMay heard the word, understood what in meant in this context, but couldn't believe it. He wished that there was some place for him to sit. He wished that he was in his office, where he had access to a hundred files, or codes, or people, that could help him. Now, somewhere over western Tennessee, he couldn't get to any of that.

"General. The word is 'Platinum.' "

"Understood," said LeMay automatically.

"Is there a response?"

LeMay knew what the response had to be. Platinum was the code word to use the bomb. It meant that the situation was such that the detonation of the bomb was the only way to rectify it. He wished that he had more information, that he was on the scene to evaluate it himself. He didn't like relying on others who often let emotions color their thinking.

Over the radio, he said, "Wait one." He was buying time, knowing that the situation wouldn't turn critical in a matter of seconds. It was already critical, otherwise the word wouldn't have been transmitted. It meant that a situation that Douglass had described to him had deteriorated. He didn't believe that Smith would be on the radio using that code if the situation didn't warrant it. Smith wouldn't want to use the bomb just to see the mushroom cloud.

LeMay knew there could be but one response.

LeMay closed his eyes and then said, "Casino. I say again. Casino."

CHAPTER | 70

July 15, 1947
On the Surface
Over the Rainbow,
Nevada

Smith spotted Moore standing at the far end of the hangar, near a dark green car that might have been a Cadillac, though he wasn't sure. Moore was talking to an older woman who held a clipboard in one hand and a pencil in the other. Smith started across the hangar floor, ignoring the dozens of other people who were standing around among the cars and trucks that were lined up on the inside.

"Doctor Moore?"

Moore turned, saw Smith, and some of the life drained from his face. Cordially, he said, "Yes, Doctor Smith?"

"Might I suggest that we get everyone off the base now?"

"Why would I want to do that?"

Smith smiled and said, "Well, for one thing, we've been chased out of the facility and I don't think we'll be going back into it very soon."

"How would you know that?"

"Let's just say that I know. I think that we need to get out of here and into town as quickly as we can."

Moore shook his head. "I do not have a full accounting of my people yet." He then pointed at the soldiers standing around the perimeter. "And these gentlemen have suggested that we remain right where we are."

"I don't think you understand," said Smith. "You don't have time right now to play these silly games. We need to get off this base."

"I don't believe you have the authority to order us out of here." He gestured to the soldiers again.

Smith wiped the sweat from his face with his hand. He wiped it off on his trousers. He looked beyond Moore, at some of the people and at the cars. Light was filtering in through the windows that ringed the hangar fifteen or twenty feet off the ground. It was a strange looking building, from Smith's point of view.

He turned his attention back to Moore and said, "We have an hour. A little less and we had better be thirty miles away."

Moore started to respond and then the blood drained from his face. He suddenly understood. "You can't be serious."

"I'm as serious as a heart attack."

"We just can't evacuate this base," said Moore. "There are security considerations."

"I'm not at all that concerned with the security at the moment," said Smith. "Might I suggest you try to get into Las Vegas and the air field there, or head for Fallon. That's Navy, but it is a military installation. Security has now been trumped. You have fifty-nine minutes."

"Well, there are some Army people who don't want us to leave."

Smith shook his head. "I'll take care of the Army people. You just get organized."

Moore called, "Mrs. Harvey?" He saw her separate herself from a small group and hurry toward him. When she was close, he said, "We need to get everyone into a truck or car and get out of here."

She looked at him and then at the cars and trucks lined up inside the hangar. "That'll take several hours."

Smith interrupted. "At the moment, you don't need to worry about getting someone into his car. Load them up in the order they're parked in here and have everyone meet at the guard shack. That'll take care of the problem in the quickest time. Just move it."

Moore looked at Mrs. Harvey. He said, "Find out who owns the cars over there, get them to their cars and have them get ready to move out."

He turned, saw a row of military trucks as the other end of the hangar, near the other set of doors. He walked over to one of the officers and said, "We need to get those trucks ready to move."

"Not my job. I'm communications."

"Doesn't mean you're not an officer," snapped Moore.

"But it does mean that I have nothing to do with this." He surveyed the crowd and then pointed. "Over there. Captain Nathan. He's the motor officer. He'll get things organized for you."

Moore nodded and then turned. He walked over to Nathan and repeated his request. Nathan looked at the line of trucks, then saw a group of his soldiers and said, "This'll be no problem. I can have those ready to roll in ten minutes. Then it's just a question of getting the people loaded."

"We'll need to open the doors," said Moore.

"I got guys to do that," said Nathan.

"Assemble at the guard shack. I'll be along as quickly as I can."

"Yes, sir." Nathan turned and trotted across the hangar floor, shouting orders. Men broke out of their groups and headed for the doors. They began to muscle them out of the way.

A sergeant ran across the hangar, climbed into the cab of one of the trucks and then leaned to the right. He sat up a moment later and there was a grinding until the truck's engine coughed, spit black smoke and then smoothed out.

Nathan yelled, but then the hangar doors at both ends of the building began to open rapidly. A breeze blew through and dragged the smoke out with it.

Moore talked to a number of military officers and then they began to spread out. Three or four men ran to the rear, and opened doors of the cars. Other people were herded toward the military trucks. Moore was doing what he said, now that he understood the problem.

Smith, seeing that the evacuation would be accomplished without too much trouble, turned to Lloyd and said, "We'll want either a staff car or a jeep. Once they get out of here and out of the blast radius, we'll find a protected place and detonate the device."

Lloyd said, "I think I would be happier if I was going with these people and would be forty or fifty miles away."

"This will be an underground explosion, not an air blast. Damage, and radiation, should be severely limited. We get behind a ridge line and detonate from there, we'll be okay."

"And there were no Indians on the Little Big Horn."

"What's that supposed to mean."

"That comes under the category of Famous Last Words," said Lloyd.

Smith had to grin. "Don't be so pessimistic. We'll be okay."

As he said that, the first of the Army trucks pulled out of the hangar and onto the tarmac. He sat there belching smoke, idling, waiting for the others to join it.

CHAPTER | 71

July 15, 1947
Over the Rainbow
Nevada

With the elevator blocked, and with no stairway access to the level above, it seemed that Reed, along with the people with him, including Hackett, Wheeler, and Clifford, were trapped where they were. Reed sat at the guard's desk inside the fish-bowl room and tried to think of something. The telephone system seemed to be out of service, and they had found no radios for communication with the levels above them.

Everyone seemed to believe that Reed had the answer, and for some reason, he agreed. He knew that there was a way out and suddenly he remembered it. The access tunnels. He had seen no indication that they had been filled in, and, in fact, were probably still opened. It allowed them to bring in large equipment or anything that might be needed with a certain secrecy. The alien ship, which wouldn't have fit into the elevators, could have been brought in through the access tunnels. The ship was here, so the tunnel was here.

Reed walked out of the guard's room, looked at the men sitting on the floor, waiting for his bit of wisdom. He glanced at Hackett, smiled and said, "Who's up for a little hike?"

"What do you plan to do?" asked Wheeler. "Walk around and around?"

"Had you ever looked at the facility plan," said Reed, "you would have known that there is an access tunnel that leads directly to the surface. It was used as the facility was constructed and it was left in place."

"That'd tear up security," said Wheeler.

"I'm not so sure," said Reed, "But right now, I don't care. I know that the tunnel is there and I know that it leads to the surface. And, I even know where to look for the doors."

Using standard squad tactics, which meant the civilians, Hackett and Wheeler, were in the middle, that there was one man separated from the squad to the front and two in the rear, they worked their way along the corridor. Although Reed didn't think the aliens would attack them now, he wasn't going to walk into an ambush.

According to what he had seen on the floor plan, he believed he knew about where the access doors had to be. It took only fifteen minutes for Reed to find the recessed and hidden double doorway that was nearly opposite the elevators at the far end of the Level Five loop. It was on what would have been the outside wall of the corridor had they not been nearly a hundred feet below the surface. It had been concealed behind wooden paneling that gave the impression of a solid wall. Had Reed not been running his fingertips over the surface and felt the slight indentation, they might never have found it. The camouflage had been expertly applied.

Reed finally found the latch, pulled it, and the paneling popped outward. When that was pulled out of the way, he found another, thicker door. Reed had expected to find some sort of combination lock, or another bank vault type door that controlled access to each level, but instead, it looked more like a large hangar door and opened like a garage door.

Reed reached down for the handle, twisted it and pulled. To his surprise, the door shifted slightly but was heavy. Using both hands, and then with an assist from two of the soldiers, they lifted it and pushed, until it was fully opened. Beyond it Reed could see a long tunnel. The floor looked flat and made of concrete. The walls were flat as well, giving the tunnel the look of a long, wide, dark room. There seemed to be a slight rise in the floor as he looked down the tunnel, but that could have been an illusion because he knew the tunnel led to the surface, based on the floor plans that he had reviewed.

"We'll need some light," said Hackett.

Clifford pulled the flashlight from his web gear and flipped the switch. "That'll do it."

Reed nodded and watched as several of the others did the same. He stood there for a moment, trying to see something in the tunnel, but it looked empty, abandoned, yet somehow as if it had been maintained. He wasn't sure what frightened him about it, but he knew that he didn't want to enter it. There was, of course, no other choice.

Clifford hesitated, looked to Reed for an instruction, and then stepped into the tunnel. He flashed his light from side to side, showing the signs of use that were concealed in the gloom. The road bed was cracked in places and there were several small potholes but in keeping with military tradition, the roadway, or floor, had been heavily waxed.

Reed waved the men forward and said, "I'll bring up the rear." He waited until they all had passed him, taking their positions without orders, staggering their routes so that they were walking along either side of the tunnel, their lights bobbing up and down as they looked at the walls near them or the road bed under their feet.

When they all had passed him, Reed turned and thought about lowering the door but decided against it. He turned and followed after the others. The point man was about fifty yards out in front, sweeping his light from right to left. The floor had a white line painted down the center, looking as if it was part of a highway tunnel. Along the walls, every hundred yards or so, were large, glowing numbers, decreasing in value. These were some kind of waypoints, but Reed didn't know if they referred to distances to the surface, some kind of code for the level, or if they were similar to addresses. He just didn't have enough information.

As they walked forward, leaning forward into the slight slope of the floor, Hackett asked, "What happens when we get to the surface?"

"What do you mean?" asked Reed.

"I mean that the door there will certainly be locked."

"Of course. But I would think that it will be easier to open it from the inside rather than if we were coming from the outside. We'll deal with that when we get there."

From the surface came the rumbling again. There was only the slightest vibration and there was no odor of dirt, or cordite, in the air.

"What in the hell is happening?" asked Hackett.

Reed shifted his weapon to his right hand. "I don't know."

"Captain?" said Clifford.

Reed moved forward quickly. He found the man standing near another door, not unlike the one they had used to enter the tunnel. There was a large number painted on it.

"The floor above where we entered. We might be able to access one of the other elevators. Easier than walking."

"No," said Reed. "I don't know what has gone on in there and it puts us back into the facility. Let's just continue here until we reach the surface. A little exercise won't hurt any of us."

Clifford checked his watch. "I make it another twenty minutes or so, if we don't slow down or stop to rest."

"Let's just get the hell out of here."

"Yes, sir. If I might be so bold. We're kind of leaving our rear hanging out."

"Don't know what you expect me to do about it. I'll hang back and fire a shot if something happens."

"Yes, sir. Just thinking about what went on in there. Don't know where those monsters are."

"They're behind us and I don't really care. Once we're outside, we can worry about them."

The scream seemed to echo down the tunnel, bouncing off the walls and growing louder as if it had somehow been amplified. There was the sound of two or three men running and then a shout that was unintelligible.

"What in the hell?" asked Hackett, her voice high and strained.

Reed felt a shiver up his spine and flipped off the safety of his rifle. He couldn't tell Hackett to wait there because there was no protection in that. All he knew was that something had happened in front of him.

Clifford's head kept swiveling back and forth as if he was

watching a high speed tennis match. Finally he just stared into the darkness ahead and said, "Captain?"

There was a shot, a scream, and then a burst of fire. Reed could see the muzzle flashes in the distance, and heard a round or two ricochet off the walls and floor.

Again Clifford said, "Captain."

"Forward, slowly. We don't know what is happening."

There were two more shots. Reed saw the muzzle flashes plainly. He knew that the cavalry's battle cry was "Ride to the sound of the guns." He also knew that it was the attitude that had killed Custer at the Little Bighorn. He rushed in without understanding exactly what he had faced and the Indians had overrun half his command in less than an hour.

Reed pushed Hackett behind him and then slipped toward the wall, feeling the harsh coolness at his back. He kept moving forward, toward the flashlight that lay on the floor, the beam pointed up the tunnel.

He saw a shadowy figured that was clearly human holding a rifle, pointed down at the floor. Reed stopped, crouched, and then called, "What you got?"

"Hammond's down."

Reed wasn't sure about the wisdom of shouting the information all over the tunnel, but then wondered who could benefit from it. There wasn't a human enemy anywhere around.

"What happened?"

"Something came out of the dark and attacked his knees. When he fell, it went after his throat. Blood all over the place."

Reed rubbed a hand over his dry lips and wished that he had a drink. He looked back at Hackett, raised an eyebrow in question, and realized that she probably couldn't see his face all that well in the dark. To her, he said, "Thoughts?"

"We saw some wounds on the ankles and lower legs. Great way to bring down a larger animal."

"Captain," said Clifford. "Sounds like they're in the tunnel with us."

"How in the hell did they get into the tunnel?" asked Wheeler.

"I don't know," said Clifford. "I just know that I think they're in here with us."

"Probably got in here the same way they have been moving through the facility," said Reed. "We saw them blow a hole in a wall and run through it."

"But we saw no damage to the wall or the door," said Wheeler.

"Damage could be up higher," said Reed. "We're just going to have to be very careful now."

"Yes, sir," said Clifford.

Reed sat down, his back against the tunnel wall. He sat quietly for a minute, trying to figure out a way to get out of the tunnel. The best plan seemed to be to continue to the surface, keeping everyone clumped together using their flashlights to create a roving band of light. They could provide mutual protection with their rifles, making it impossible for anything to get close enough to them to do any real harm.

Finally, Reed climbed to his feet, wondering when it was all going to end. First the crash, then the trip to this facility, and now the assault, if it could be termed that, by the alien beast. He didn't pretend to understand what was happening, other to understand they had to get out of the dark.

Cautiously, with the others now grouped around him in a circular formation, flashlights playing over all the surface area of the tunnel including the ceiling, they moved forward. Reed had his eyes fixed on the fallen flashlight that still burned near the downed man. As they approached, they slowed and then stopped.

Reed walked forward, toward the body. Blood had pooled around the head, almost like the halo that was seen in some of the older religious paintings. There was blood on the ankles, and the leather of the boots was shredded.

Johnson, the other soldier, was crouched near the wall, watching the tunnel, his eyes shifting right and left quickly. He saw Reed looking at him and said, in a high strained voice, "I didn't see all that much, sir. Something came running at us and hit Franzone low, in the knee, ankles. He fired a shot or two and fell. They went for his throat. I shot at them, but they ran back up the tunnel."

Reed studied the tunnel for a moment, wondering how anything could hide in it. The walls were flat, the floor was flat and the ceiling was flat. It was a long square cut through the rock and earth of the Nevada desert.

"You said, 'They.' "

"Yes, sir. Three or four of them. About the size of a large cat or small dog, running on two legs. Came out of the dark and then retreated."

Reed reached out and touched Franzone's throat knowing full well that the man was dead. There was too much blood on the floor, and Johnson would have said something if Franzone had still been alive.

"Okay," said Reed standing. "We've got to get moving. We'll send someone back to retrieve the body later."

"Yes, sir." Johnson hesitated and then said, "Those things are up ahead of us."

Reed shot a glance at Johnson. "I know that. But our only choice is to continue to march. We'll just change our tactics."

When Reed had briefed the others, which mainly meant he told them to be careful, they continued to climb upward. Reed noticed that it was getting warmer, and then wondered if the exertion of climbing was making him think it was warmer. He wiped his free hand over his face and wiped the sweat on his fatigue shirt.

They passed the Level Three access door. Reed thought about trying to penetrate the facility there, possibly above the damage done to the elevators, but decided against it. They couldn't have much further to go and if the elevators were down, they'd either have to find a way to climb up the interior of the shaft or return to the tunnel. The emergency stairs only existed on the top level.

They stopped for a moment, near the door that had a gigantic numeral three painted on it in a yellow reflective paint. Reed knelt on a single knee, the rifle clutched in his right hand. He wished that he could remember how long the tunnel was so that he could figure out how much farther they would have to walk. They were about halfway to the surface, if the distance between each of the levels was equal and there was an extra long distance between Level One and the surface.

"Let's extinguish half the lights to conserve the batteries," he said. "Take a little water. I figure no more than an hour to the surface."

"You know what's happening up there, Captain?"

Reed grinned at that. These men had been with him the whole time and had just as much information as he did. They all figured that some way he had received more and better information because he was an officer, or that he knew something that they didn't. He would be able to keep them fully informed, if he chose to do so. What he didn't understand is why they thought he knew more about the situation than they did.

Speculating, and based on what he had heard, he said, "Evacuation. I would guess that everyone is getting off the base and into town."

Hackett leaned in close and asked, "Is that a good idea?"

"Is what a good idea?"

"Sending these people into town."

Reed shrugged and said, "Hell, I don't know if anyone's going into town. They probably will just congregate on the surface and move them to a different base until they can get everything organized."

"Then why . . ."

Reed cut her off. "Because soldiers always want to go into town."

They all fell silent, sitting in the small pools of light created by their flashlights. Reed might have heard it first, though it was Clifford who reacted first. It was a hard scrabbling of claws on concrete. Reed merely looked in the direction, but the Clifford turned on his flashlight and shined it in the direction of the noise.

"Rats," said Johnson.

Reed didn't think so. He stood up, and flipped off the safety on his rifle. He stared into the darkness up-tunnel, searching for some sign of movement. He stepped forward and let the men fill in behind him, creating a formation ready to receive an attack.

From the rear, Hackett asked, "What is it?"

"I don't know," said Reed, his eyes still searching the gloom.

"Maybe we should move forward," said Clifford.

Reed shot him a glance but before he could answer, there was a swarming motion near the floor. Reacting, Reed fired once, the round striking the concrete with a slight spark before whining off into the distance.

Around him, the others began to fire, Clifford using his Thompson sub-machine gun. The hammering echoed and reverberated throughout the tunnel making it sound as if a thousand weapons were being fired at once. The strobing of the muzzle flashes illuminated the scene as the creatures, some over eighteen inches tall, came running at them. Some were hit, spinning. One seemed to explode into red blood, green fluid and shiny white bone. It hit the floor and skidded toward Reed.

One of the men, maybe Johnson, maybe Simpson, on the right flank of the makeshift formation, screamed, dropped his rifle and fell to the rear. A gray ball was wrapped around his lower leg. Once he was on the floor, others ran toward him, attacking his hands, elbow and finally his throat. He thrashed, tried to throw the little beasts away from him, but they scrambled over him, not giving anyone a chance to help him. They couldn't shoot for fear of hitting him.

And others, a half dozen, maybe more, were running around on the floor. They no longer ran straight for the human line, but danced around it, almost as if they were Sioux attempting to count coup. They moved quickly, jumping and rolling. Shots ricocheted off the floor and walls, bouncing up the tunnel.

As quickly as it started, it ended. One instant there were creatures in the dark with them, and the next, the aliens were fleeing back up the tunnel.

"Anyone hurt?" asked Reed.

"Simpson is down."

"I know."

One of the men crouched near Simpson, examining him with a flashlight. His uniform was ripped and bloody and it was apparent from the wounds that he was dead.

Hackett walked over and knelt. She looked at the man's wounds and the blood loss and said, "I think I know what we're facing here. These wounds look like those we've found on the others. They were attacked."

"Then we have an even more important reason for getting out of here," said Reed. "We can end some of the speculation."

CHAPTER 72

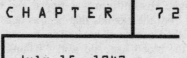

July 15, 1947
Over the Rainbow
Nevada

There was no way, given the circumstances, that Reed and his small team could carry the bodies with them. He knew where they were, and once they had reached the surface, Reed, with a larger force, could return. He also thought that he should find a few flame throwers. Those bizarre little creatures would have no chance against a man with a flamethrower. It was an answer that was perfect for the situation.

They were now spread out in a oval-shaped formation so that each man could cover the men on his right or left. If the little creatures attacked again, everyone could easily cover everyone else. They shouldn't be able to reach another living target.

As they climbed higher in the tunnel, they heard nothing to suggest the beings were coming again. Everything was quiet, except for the scraping of boot leather on concrete, and the labored breathing of the men as they climbed through the tunnel. There was no talking, no rattling of loose equipment, and no other extra noise. Each was listening carefully for sounds that the enemy, the aliens, were coming after them again. Their flashlights illuminated little of the tunnel, though Reed noticed it was now somewhat wider, as if they planned to bring the bigger trucks in only so far.

Then, suddenly, they were near the surface. They passed the large glowing numeral "One," painted on the wall. Now, however, there was no hangar-like door. The concrete floor and walls gave way to rock. The floor was fairly smooth, but it was no longer a flat surface. There were bumps and dips and potholes. The walls looked as if they had been chiseled from solid stone. Now the tunnel looked as if it had originally been a cave, enlarged to accommodate trucks and jeeps and other military equipment.

Reed understood some of the camouflage that had gone on. Someone had selected a cave, followed it until it played out, and then dug the rest of the way down, into the facility. The natural opening of the cave would provide a disguise for the tunnel. He wondered how they discouraged the curious from entering the cave, and then remembered that they were literally a hundred miles from anywhere. The curious would be discouraged by the vast distance that had to be traveled across desert just to find the cave.

The team stopped and Reed caught up to the point man. He was sitting on a rock that had fallen away from the wall, though it didn't actually block the access to the cave.

"We're close to the surface."

Reed knelt and nodded.

"I think we're about a hundred yards or so from the entrance," said Clifford.

"Why?"

"Well, sir, there is a hint of fresh air in here."

Reed said, "Let's push on."

Reluctantly, the sergeant pushed himself off his rock. He swept the flashlight from side to side and then moved forward. An instant later he stopped and turned. "We're here."

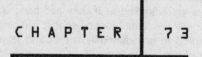

CHAPTER | 7 3

```
July 15, 1947
Over the Rainbow
Nevada
```

Reed stood next to the door. It was heavy metal and cool to the touch. There was a wheel in the center of it, looking like the locking mechanism of a ship's hatch. It was padlocked shut, and explained one of the ways they planned to discourage the idle curious.

To the right was another door, this one smaller, looking as if it was guarding an access shaft or a storeroom. Reed walked to it and used his flashlight to examine it. There was a padlock on it which struck him as odd. He would have expected that on the other side. He reached out, grabbed it and jerked on it, surprised when the wood gave way.

He opened the door and shined his light inside. Steps led up and Reed entered. He climbed the steps and found another door, this one locked. He jerked on the knob but it didn't open. He knelt and examined the lock and then grinned to himself. He was thinking of every locked door that had ever barred someone's way in the movies. They just opened fire with their pistol or rifle and the door opened as if by magic.

Hackett, who had quietly followed him, said, "Now what?"

Reed jerked around and then put a hand on his heart. "Don't do that."

"I thought you knew I was here."

Reed didn't tell her that as an officer on patrol, he should have been aware of her. He had been concentrating on what he was seeing in front of him, and on getting out of the tunnel. He hadn't expected anyone behind him.

To Hackett, he said, "I could try to break the lock with a bullet or two.

"Okay."

"Step back." He stood for a moment, studying the lock and the surrounding wood. The last thing he wanted was a ricochet. Aiming from the hip, he pulled the trigger of his pistol. The detonation was astonishingly loud in the confined space and the flash from the muzzle nearly blinding.

The bullet hit the center of the lock, punched through, and exited on the other side. The door looked as if it was still locked, so Reed fired again, this time at the knob. The metal exploded and the knob fell away. There was a huge hole where the knob and the lock had been. Splintered wood and bits of metal were scattered on the floor. Reed reached over, careful to avoid the jagged edges, and pulled. When the door didn't move, he kicked it once, near where the lock had been. The door swung open and slammed into the wall.

"Let's go."

On the other side of the door was a narrow tunnel with a set of wooden stairs leading to it. They came to a second door, but this one was bolted on the inside, where Reed could get at it. He threw the bolts and pulled on the door. It swung inward.

On the other side was another cavern, narrow, with a low ceiling. In the dirt, on the cavern floor, were footprints. Slowly, carefully, Reed moved along the wall. There was warm air blowing in from somewhere, though he could see no light, suggesting that the entrance was still some distance away.

Reed waited for the others to join him, and then, again, moved forward. The tunnel narrowed and the ceiling lowered, so that it was difficult to pass but not impossible. Reed was sure that this was just another attempt to keep the curious from finding the door and entering into the tunnel complex.

Then, suddenly, he could see light. He stopped, turned off his flashlight, and let the others catch him. He pointed and said, "We're out."

"Good," said Clifford, grinning broadly. "About time."

Reed walked into the sunlight. He stood, blinking, letting his eyes adjust. Below him, on the valley floor, he had expected to see the base, but it wasn't there. He turned and looked back, at the summit, only a few yards from where he stood. There was a path that led to the top.

When he was joined by Hackett, he said, "I'm going to make a quick trip to the top to see what's happening."

"I'm going with you."

He shrugged, unsure why he believed that she should remain behind. He waited for Clifford and the others to emerge, pointed to positions where he wanted them, and then, with Hackett, began to climb to the top. As he approached, he ducked slightly, and finally got down on his hands and knees. Using the low crawl, he moved forward, watching for sharp rocks, stinging insects, scorpions, rattlesnakes and barbed plants. He moved forward slowly, keeping low, as he had been taught in basic training so long ago.

Hackett followed him, staying low herself. She waited until he had reached the top and had taken a position behind a large rock, peeking around the base of it. She then crawled up to him and looked around the other side.

The base was spread out on a flat desert plain that extended into the distance as far as he could see. About a mile away and a couple of hundred feet lower, it looked almost like a model built on an HO scale railroad table, the roads narrow ribbons of black, the vehicles now thumb-sized, and a huge open area crisscrossed with concrete that made up the airfield and taxiways. The hangars, looking like oversized boxes with curved roofs and lots of windows, stood in a long row on the northern side of the runways and in the middle of that row was a slightly larger building with a flat roof and the control tower rising from it.

The rest of the base was made of neat rows of buildings all constructed using the same basic plan, all painted a dust brown to blend in with the landscape and all no more than two stories tall. Some structures, such as the churches and the movie theater, were identifiable because of their function. Finally, on the far side, was the family housing area made small houses, all basically the same except for a single row of houses that were larger and partially shaded by transplanted trees. At the far end of one street was the biggest of the houses that had once been occupied by the facility commander.

There was dust or smoke rising from one part of the airfield, but every base Reed had ever seen had dust or smoke rising from part of it.

Then, he became aware of the low pitched hum that he had heard in the lower levels of the facility. Now it was louder and vibrating throughout the ground around him. He didn't know what it meant, but he didn't like it.

"What is going on down there?" asked Hackett, her voice quiet, subdued.

"I don't know," said Reed.

But the hum increased in volume and a vortex, swirling the smoke, appeared near one of the hangars. Light seemed to flash. Bright blue lights that were streaked with red, orange and green and some flashing a brilliant white. The winds picked up, sucking up the smoke and dust and blowing it away, giving Reed an unobstructed view.

The hangar, large enough to accommodate the biggest bombers in the Air Force inventory, began to shake, the windows break, and pieces began to fall away from the roof. One end of it fell, erupting into a cloud of dust and debris. Slowly, the other walls collapsed and the roof fell. For a moment everything held still with only the hum getting louder. Then the center of the debris seemed to bulge upward, like the lava dome of a volcano ready to explode.

"Shit," said Reed.

Now the lights brightened as the hum increased into a high-pitched scream. His ears hurt with the sound and his eyes burned with the light. The alien creatures were doing something down there, but Reed didn't know what.

Suddenly the concrete dome exploded, throwing huge chunks of material hundreds of feet into the air. They crashed back, demolishing cars, flattening small buildings, and digging their own craters of five or six feet.

The glow burst from the hole, now a red so bright that even

in the sunlight of the afternoon it was impossible to watch. The top of the craft, the machine that Reed had entered only days earlier, appeared as if pushing its way out of the ground. There was something surrounding it, protecting it from the rain of destruction that was falling and burning.

Then came another, deeper rumbling. The ground seemed to leap up and dust rose. Everything around the facility bulged and smoked and ruptured. From the center of the hangar, almost directly under the alien machine, came a visible shock wave, flashing out mimicking the ripples of a stone thrown into a smooth and tranquil pond.

The shock wave hit the mountain and Reed felt the ground vibrate. There was a moment of heat, like a puff of air from a blast furnace but it was gone in an instant. He closed his eyes momentarily and when he looked down, the ground had fallen back into a crater that had to be five or six hundred yards across. Smoke was rising from the center of it, where the hangar and the facility had been, and where nothing moved.

The craft that had been rising was gone. Reed didn't know if it had escaped the blast or been consumed by it. But the hum and the light show had vanished.

"Did you see it?" asked Reed.

Hackett lifted her head and said, "I didn't see anything. What happened?"

"I suspect an atomic explosion, underground."

"Did the craft survive?"

Reed glanced into the bright blue sky overhead. Fighters were circling like birds of prey, or maybe vultures, waiting for something to die. If the craft had gotten clear, the fighters would have given chase. At least that it is what he would have done. With them overhead, it suggested that the alien ship had not escaped, unless it had been so fast the pilots hadn't seen it.

"I don't know," said Reed. "I don't think so, but I just don't know."

Hackett sat up, her back to the rock. "Now what?"

"I guess we collect the others, and see who survived down there."

CHAPTER | 74

Captain Jack Reed sat in the darkened room of the communications center at Muroc Army Air Field near Los Angeles, California. There was a single desk in the room, a single lamp on the desk, a single chair, a wastebasket and one black telephone with four buttons across the bottom. This was a secure facility designed so that high ranking officers at Muroc would be able to confer with other high ranking officers, often at the other military bases, sometimes at the Pentagon, and periodically with the White House.

Reed sat at the desk, the handset of the telephone to his ear, and listened to the pops and buzzes as the operator attempted to arrange the connection with General LeMay. Reed had been debriefed after the desert explosion, had told, for the most part, what he knew about the destruction of the facility in Nevada. Now, he was going to make his final report to the general.

There was a tinkling on the line, like ice cubes in a glass of bourbon, and the general said, "Reed?"

"Here, sir."

"Tell me what happened."

"We blew it up. The ship. The facility. Killed them all."

"I'm not clear on that. I thought there were five aliens. Four killed in the crash and the last dying some days later."

Reed scratched the back of his neck. "I'm not sure anyone understands this. Might be some sort of reproductive imperative. Might have been some sort of colonization plan."

"Maybe you should explain that."

Reed nodded knowing full well the General wouldn't be able to see the gesture over the telephone. "As I understand it, as it was explained to me, these alien creatures put their ship down purposefully in a remote area of New Mexico. The damage was incidental and had nothing to do with the landing of the ship. These creatures then go dormant, or die, and their bodies are used to nourish the next generation."

"This is confirmed?"

"No, sir, this is speculation based on what we observed in Nevada. This allows them to adapt to the environment in which they find themselves. The creatures seemed to generate copies of themselves, using the bodies of the dead. They regenerated quickly. They can spread over an area in a few days. Sort of like rats."

"That would seem to limit their abilities to create a civilization, if their life span is so short," said the General.

"Well, I'm not going to pretend to understand the biology here. Doctor Hackett has more specific details. It boils down to this. They go through a couple of phases, starting with a small, larva stage, then change into a juvenile and finally into an adult. Some of the stages might have been accelerated based on their introduction into our environment. Once established, then the normal development cycle would return. I guess, from what Hackett said, this sort of thing does happen on Earth when there has been a serious decline in a population. Some species generate more offspring, their gestation cycles change, and I think there is a frog in Africa that can change gender if there are too few males or females."

"This is beyond me," said the General. "I'm more concerned with the military aspects."

"Yes, sir. We didn't get an opportunity to examine any of the equipment they built . . ."

"Yeah," said the General, "That was what I wanted to know. How did they know what to build and how to build it?"

"Hackett had an answer. She suggested that some behavior is passed down genetically . . ."

The General interrupted. "If I remember my high school biology, I thought only the more primitive forms passed on information that way. Hunting, for example, and not technical information."

"Hackett said that she thought they could somehow program the information so that it could be passed through the genes in much the same way that we can transmit information using morse code. They manipulate themselves on a genetic level and that would allow them to tell future generations information that is not contained in books or other written documents."

"Which might explain the lack of written material," said the General.

"I don't know, sir. I'm thinking that you'd need some written language for day to day use. It's hard to navigate in space if you have to keep everything in your brain."

"Did they salvage anything from the ship?"

"Bits of metal that were given to industry in an attempt to analyze it. Some small equipment that we didn't understand. We tried to tell them that these were things we had stolen from the Russians so that security wouldn't be compromised."

"Speaking of security, it seems that there were too many people in on this."

"Well," said Reed, leaning back, "I think the numbers are smaller than you might think. Of those in the facility, very few knew everything that was happening. Some knew only of the ship. Some knew only of the aliens. Some knew only that we were investigating something that we had recovered and again, there was thought that it might be Russian. I think that mistake was encouraged."

"This is something that we don't need to get out," said the General, changing the subject again. "We make contact with an alien race and we then blow up their ship with an atomic bomb. Not only that, we seem to kill their children. That'd play well in the press. Army kills alien children."

"Yes, sir."

"So, what happens now?" It was more of a rhetorical question.

Reed said, "We did salvage some of this. The metal will help us develop lightweight composites. Their electronics will help us refine our electronics. There are samples of alien tissue at some laboratories, there are the documents that were obtained during the first of the autopsies. There is a great deal of information that needs to be studied. There is a great deal of work that needs to be done."

"The question that everyone is going to ask is if they are going to be coming back."

Reed had thought about this long and hard. To the general, he said, "The best analogy I can think of is the idea that Vikings landed here about one thousand years ago. It was another five hundred years or so before the next real attempt at exploration was made. Then, of course, with better ships, better navigation, and a little more in the way of a technological civilization, the Europeans began the real assault on the New World."

He stopped for a moment and then said, "The technical problem, of traveling over the ocean, was refined between the time of the Vikings and the time of Columbus. It was still a Herculean task, but it was easier than it had been about a thousand years ago. The only thing I don't know is how difficult it is to travel interstellar distances. If it was difficult then the odds of a second ship in the near future are remote. If not, then they should have been back already, General."

"We're still getting these flying disk reports," said the general.

"Yes, sir and I have looked at them carefully. They are not as rich with detail as those in late June. They're little more than lights in the night sky now with a dose of mass hysteria thrown in."

"Then you don't think we have to worry about an invasion?"

"No, General, I don't. I think the invasion already came and we stopped it."

EPILOGUE

Two decades later, as Colonel Jack Reed, brigadier general designee, waited for his retirement party at Fort Meade officer's club to begin, he thought about the path that had brought him here. He believed, at the beginning of his career, as he had learned to fly and then had deployed to Europe as a fighter pilot, that he would be in aviation the whole time. He hadn't anticipated the detour into intelligence that would indelibly stain him from the moment the alien spaceship fell outside of Roswell, New Mexico, in 1947.

Now, the public knew about flying saucers, but they debated the reality of them, listened to people who claimed to have ridden in them at the invitation of the alien creatures, and accused the Air Force of hiding the truth. Reed smiled at that, because the public had no real clue about the truth. They, meaning the military, had brought down an alien craft, had fought the alien crew in an underground facility, turned back what might have been the invasion, and then had buried everything including the truth in the Nevada desert.

True, the direction of some modern research had been guided by what they had found in the short weeks before the atomic bomb had destroyed the ship and killed the alien creatures. There had been theories about the composite skin of the ship, the electronic components that had led to the idea of the printed circuit board, light enhancers that led to night vision equipment, and the use of the shape as a lifting body and to help hide aircraft from radar. A great deal had been discov-

ered, invented, designed and conceived because of that alien
ship, even though that ship had been lost in the explosion.

There had been enough information left over, after the
atomic blast that destroyed the base, that some scientific progress had been made. The scientists who had been working at
the facility were offered jobs in government labs, or allowed
to move into the private sector. Those who knew the truth
were warned about spreading wild tales, told that their em-
ployers would learn unflattering things, and would find their
credentials challenged if they talked about what they had seen
in Nevada in 1947. In other words, be quiet and prosper, or
talk out of turn and find your life in ruins.

Reed knew that most of those at the facility had known
almost nothing about the real nature of the research. But even
those people had been drawn from a pool of those who held
security clearances. They understood the nature of security and
were honorable enough to follow their orders. They didn't
really know anything, had no proof to corroborate their speculations, and they found themselves rewarded for their discre-
tion.

Reed thought it funny that in all the years, the only time
anyone had come close to the truth about the crashed flying
saucer, the story was effectively suppressed. The men who told
it found themselves in jail and the public believed that flying
saucers might be real but they didn't crash.

The campaign to suppress the information had been done
quietly and effectively. The real point was that those who
knew the absolute truth just didn't talk about it to anyone.
They keep their mouths shut.

Reed drained his drink and wondered about the wisdom of
retiring so early. He could stay on another five or ten years
and maybe earn another star or two. But then he shook himself. No, he'd devoted enough of his life to the Army, and he
was about to be rewarded with a general's star as a retirement
present. There was no need to press his luck.

Jacob Wheeler, looking old, and more than a little over-
weight, walked into the club, stood with hands on his hips,
surveying the crowd as if they were prizes in a contest. He

spotted Reed, lifted a hand and then walked over.

"Where's Danni?" he asked.

"She's with the children," said Reed. "She said she'd be here on time."

Wheeler pointed at the bar. "Buy me a drink."

"You can afford your own drinks. I'm just a humble soldier while you're a fat cat corporate weenie."

"Okay," said Wheeler. "I'll buy my own booze. And, given the circumstances, I'll even buy one for you."

They ordered the next round and then Wheeler got serious. "You sure you want to retire?"

"It's time. Danni's career has been inhibited by mine for too long. Let her do some of the research that she wants to do. Let her take the university job she was offered."

"What are you going to do?" asked Wheeler.

"Well, I'd write my memoirs, but the really good stuff has to be left out. Consulting, maybe. Security or aviation. Or, I might just sit around and count the money from the big, fat retirement checks."

"You deserve it."

Reed grinned. He'd given Wheeler an opening, but Wheeler didn't want to talk about New Mexico. He'd just as soon forget it ever happened. Maybe that was the best thing. Until the aliens returned, if they returned, maybe the best thing was to forget it happened while the government quietly developed weapons and space travel as a way of preventing the next invasion, if one were to come.

Kennedy had wanted to put a man on the moon and Reed knew why. Kennedy wanted to take the high ground. Give the human race a chance if the aliens came back with a larger force with evil in their hearts . . . if they had hearts. Not that he expected them to return. If they were coming back, they would have been here long ago, or so he believed.

He saw Wheeler glance toward the door and then saw his wife enter. She still turned heads, but now she also had a quiet dignity that intrigued nearly everyone who met her. Reed stood up, waved, and said, "Glad you could make it, Danni."

She kissed his cheek and asked, "Is it too early to call you General?"

"By about two weeks," he said, putting the thoughts of New Mexico and alien invaders out of his head.

"The kids will not be home until tomorrow.".

Reed laughed. "Damn. I have this party I have to go to."

"Yeah, well, don't get too drunk."

"Never," he said, thinking only momentarily of the secrets that had been buried so long ago.